SAGEBRUSH & LACE

SUGAR LEE RYDER

&

J.D. CUTLER

SAGEBRUSH & LACE

Copyright © 2012 by Sugar Lee Ryder and J.D. Cutler

All rights reserved, including the right of reproduction, in whole or in part in any form. Trademarked names appear throughout this book. Rather than use a trademark symbol with every occurrence of a trademarked name, names are used in an editorial fashion, with no intention of infringement of the respective owner's trademark. This is a work of fiction. Names, characters, places, and incidents either are the product of the author's imagination or are used fictitiously, and any resemblance to actual persons, living or dead, business establishments, events or locales is entirely coincidental.

ISBN-13: 978-1475260182
ISBN-10: 1475260180

Paperback Edition printed in the United States and published by Banty Hen Publishing, May 2012.

For more about Banty Hen Publishing, please visit our website at:
www.bantyhenpublishing.com

Other Books from Banty Hen Publishing

By Sugar Lee Ryder

Cowgirl Up

Sugar Lee Ryder brings us into the modern world of the western with a hot romance!

Young, independent ranch woman Honey Durbin meets her match in this novella about bulls, rodeo cowboys and the difference between sex and love making.

See the full listing of
Sugar Lee Ryder's works at:

http://tinyurl.com/SugarLeeRyder

By Michael Angel

Centaur of the Crime

Dayna Chrissie, the leading Crime Scene Analyst for the LAPD, finds herself transported to the magical kingdom of Andeluvia. She's given three days to solve the king's murder, before war breaks out between Andeluvia and the Centaur Kingdoms. The price of failure? A war that will kill millions.

Hope she works best under pressure.

Dedication

To Sugar Lee Ryder, for showing me how the greatest tales can grow from the most unlikely of stories.

~ J.D. Cutler

To Dean Wesley Smith, who believed in my talent, gave me encouragement, and set my compass in the right direction.

Thank you for teaching me that when all else fails, come in with guns blazing!

~ Sugar Lee Ryder

CHAPTER ONE

Samantha burst through the kitchen door, running like the devil himself pursued her, claws grasping at the tail of her shirt. She rounded the corner of the marble counter, almost knocking over the cook. As it was, Samantha startled the woman into splashing hot chestnut soup onto her apron from the large copper pot in her hands.

"Mercy sakes alive, child!" the cook exclaimed.

Not stopping for apologies, Samantha bounded up the servant's staircase to her room. The delicate glass mantle of the house's gas lamp at the top of the steep passage rattled as she took the steps two at a time.

Samantha opened the door to her room. Caked mud dribbled from her riding boots and onto the polished wooden floor. She slid to a halt.

Her father, McKinley Williams, stood before her.

His arms, sheathed in the fine woolen sleeves of a burgundy frock coat, were firmly crossed. His wide, jowly face held a scowl as dark and ominous as a thundercloud. One foot, clad in an elegant Italian leather shoe draped in a white cloth spat, tapped out an impatient beat.

"Young lady," he growled, "you have gone against my wishes for the last time."

"Father," Samantha replied, "Let me explain—"

"Unfortunately, there is no time right now to discuss suitable punishment for you," McKinley continued. If he heard his daughter speak, he gave no sign. "Percy Hanover is waiting downstairs for you. You will immediately wash the stink of the stable off yourself and put on something suitable to receive your guest."

Samantha's father shoved past her brusquely. He jutted his chin out, gripped his coat lapels in his hands, and puffed his chest out like a purple-tinted strutting rooster. His time-honored way of signifying that he'd rendered a final judgment on a matter. He made one last comment to her in passing.

"Do try not to embarrass me or our family."

It took all of Samantha's self-control to gently close the door after he left. When every fiber of her being screamed to slam it shut. She hurried over to the side of her four-poster canopy bed. She hopped on one leg, then the other, as she tugged off her dirty riding boots and kicked them out-of-sight, out-of-mind under the bed.

Samantha followed this up by stripping off her shirt, pants, and undergarments. Barefoot, she approached the porcelain washbasin opposite the bed and snatched up the rough washcloth that hung from a brass rail at the side. Thankfully, the water remained lukewarm from when the maid had poured it earlier. Between the wet cloth and a few squeezes of lavender scent from her atomizer, she washed away the scents of leather, steed, and straw.

She squinted at her face in the mirror for a moment, making sure she'd removed all trace of dust and mud. Delicately painted bluebells danced around the carved wooden frame of the mirror, framing her long dark hair and making her expression look more cheery than she felt.

It took her a minute to select a pair of shoes that matched a sunny-day organza frock. She slipped it over her head and reached around to lace it up the back. Stopping just long enough to run a brush through her hair and loosely pin it up, she hurried out to the top of the landing.

She forced herself to take a deep breath before going to meet her suitor, a man hand-picked by her father. A man the same age as her father. Someone who came with the impeccable quality of 'old money'. Percy Hanover had come to look her over. To see if she would be a suitable wife.

Samantha gritted her teeth.

I'm to be paraded in front of him. Just like a prize brood mare! I'll be damned if I'm going to marry Percy Hanover. Or any man, for that matter.

But for now she had to go downstairs and pretend to be an obedient and proper young woman.

For now.

Samantha descended the staircase and entered the parlor, careful to present herself as a virtuous young woman. The demure tilt of her head and the loose gathers of her raven-colored locks softened her features.

Her father stood imposingly by the mantel, a pear-shaped snifter of brandy held firmly in one grasping hand. But her gaze came to rest on the man who sat in the wingback chair nearby. His fine, tailored clothes and impeccably trimmed vest couldn't disguise the roll of fat that bulged above his belt line. Samantha noted that his pale complexion held the damp sheen of fresh wallpaper paste, stippled with comma-shaped pock marks.

Percy Hanover, the man of her father's dreams, simply stared. His eyes were the lifeless color of weak tea. But they drank in the vision of loveliness before him.

"Percy, this is my daughter," McKinley said grandly, his outstretched hand beckoning her to come closer. He gestured with the other hand. "Samantha, this is Percy Hanover, from the Lake Forest branch of the Hanovers."

Percy stood, joints creaking, and extended a pudgy pink palm.

"Eminently pleased to meet you, my dear Samantha, eminently pleased."

Samantha took his hand in hers, repressing a shudder at the clammy feel of the man's skin. He bent forward to bestow a moist kiss on her knuckles, one that reeked of burnt tobacco and alcohol.

She noticed her father's grim look out of the corner of her eye, and then remembered to enhance her greeting with a little curtsy. At the last second, she added an eyelash-fluttered glance at the floor. With any luck, that gesture would appease her father.

"The pleasure is all mine, Mister Hanover."

"Oh my dear," he gushed, "do call me Percy."

Before Samantha could tackle the task of speaking her suitor's name, the maid stepped into the parlor and announced that dinner had been set out. For the next hour, Samantha could only pick at the slabs of roast lamb, ovoid mountains of boiled red potatoes, and what chestnut soup that had been saved by the cook.

Percy and her McKinley jawboned endlessly about the sorry state of the stock market. How President Ulysses S. Grant was ruining the nation. How the newfangled game of 'baseball' would soon prove to be a silly, forgotten fad of a sport.

And all the while, Samantha could feel Percy's eyes crawl over her, like a pair of mud-colored spiders.

By the time the cook brought out silver platters of scones and snifters of warmed brandy, Samantha's patience had reached its limit. She stood, her cheeks feeling flushed and warm, and then spoke her mind.

CHAPTER TWO

"Father," Samantha said apologetically, "I'm afraid that I can't stay here. All of this…excitement…has gone to my head. I simply must leave."

"Certainly, girl, certainly," he said grandly, with a dismissive wave. "Percy's seen enough of the quality of your company, I take it?"

"Oh, I dare say," Percy Hanover agreed immediately, answering Samantha's question for her. "You go rest, my sweet darling. Your father and I have plenty of men's matters to discuss."

She said her polite goodbye to Percy, thinking that maybe her *father* should marry him. After all, they got along like a house on fire. She suppressed a giggle at the notion of the two men in the marriage bed together.

The thought threatened to send her into hysterics, so she hurried up to her room as fast as she could. Once there, she leaned against the door, busting out in laughter at the vision of the two fat old men rutting at each other.

Sometimes, the dislike that Samantha felt for her father made her chest twinge with stabs of guilt. Her mother, gone these long years, would have chided her, encouraged her to think better of the man. But she couldn't get past his insatiable hunger for status in Chicago's Social Register.

McKinley's churning textile mills, founded on the city's south side, had made her father incredibly wealthy. But all of those mills couldn't make him respectable. Free of the taint of 'new money'.

Only Samantha's status as a wife to the right man could do that.

She sat down at her desk, pulled out ink, pen and paper from the drawer, and set to writing.

My Dearest Charlotte,

The time is now. We must leave as soon as you are able to make arrangements. I can be ready in two days. I need you to come to the house to visit me tomorrow so we can make our plans.

Father has caught me riding again and I fear that I may be unable to leave save for the last and final time. Then, my love, we will be together and no one can keep us apart.

Yours forever,
Samantha

Heart pounding, Samantha folded up her note, slipped it into an envelope, and pressed it closed with a hot glob of fragrant sealing wax. She rang for the maid, and then took her by the arm as she handed over the envelope.

"Daisy," Samantha said, "I need you to take this over to the Harte's house."

The young girl blinked. "Right now, Miss Samantha? I haven't touched the silver yet, and it's in frightful need of polish."

"Yes, right now. And Daisy, you are to give it to no one except Charlotte. No one else is to see this note, do you understand?"

"Yes ma'am, I'll set to it right now."

With that, as soon as Daisy left, Samantha almost jumped on the bed with the joy she felt. Soon she and her beloved Charlotte would be on their way. After four long years of planning, dreaming, it was finally going to happen.

No longer prisoner to her father's will. Samantha felt absolutely giddy as she lay back on the bed. She grabbed a pillow, hugged it close, and then closed her eyes. Dreaming that it was Charlotte in her arms.

She woke with a start as she heard a knock. She sat up, saw that the failing light of the evening had been replaced by the rising sun.

"Miss Samantha," Daisy called, "Are you ready to change for breakfast?"

"I am," she replied, as she rubbed sleep sand from her eyes. "Daisy, come in. I must've fallen asleep after you left."

Daisy entered, her kind face lit up with a brilliant smile. Samantha couldn't contain her excitement at the maid's expression.

"Did you give my note to Miss Harte?"

"Yes, ma'am, I did. She read it and said she'll be visiting this very morning."

"Wonderful! Now I've got something good to focus on while you help me change."

Giddy with the good news, Samantha slipped out of the dress she had hastily donned earlier the evening before.

"Oh!" Daisy giggled, "Miss Samantha, you ain't got no underthings on. Do you want me to get your corset?"

"No thank you! I'll never wear one of those things again, if I have my way about it."

Daisy let out a helpless sigh.

She proceeded to help dress her mistress as fashionably as she could, even without the corset to enhance her feminine charms. Once properly attired, Samantha descended to the dining room once again.

Percy had vanished from the scene, but the gleeful look on her father's face chilled her in a way that his anger could not. Good fortune for McKinley Williams more often than not meant bad fortune for his daughter.

Samantha took her seat, nerves jangling as her father took a trio of hearty puffs at his first cigar of the morning.

"You're tardy," he pronounced, with bluff good cheer. "And when I have such excellent news for you, too!"

"And what good news might that be?"

"It's about Percy Hanover," he said, with a smile full of shark's teeth. "He has asked for your hand in marriage."

CHAPTER THREE

Samantha's eyes burned into her father's face like a pair of hot coals.

"He asked you for my hand in marriage," she repeated slowly. "And you of course refused?"

"Don't be impertinent! He is a good catch, and you know it." Almost as an afterthought, he added, "The wedding will be in two weeks."

She tamped down the urge to scream bloody murder. He sat there, so smug and secure. Auctioning her off like she was a prize heifer.

"Why was I not consulted in the matter of my own marriage?"

McKinley shrugged. "I hardly need to consult you to make a decision concerning your welfare."

Thoughts ran wild in her head, like telegraph lines spitting out streams of Morse code.

I won't be here anyway, so it doesn't matter. Pay no mind.

But act normal! Don't be too complacent. He'll think something is amiss.

"You mean *your* welfare, don't you?" she said, in an icy tone. "Percy's your age. Why on earth would I want to marry him?"

"The decision has been made, girl! I'll be making the arrangements tomorrow, so you had better get used to the idea."

"So I have no choice in the matter?"

"No, you don't. And there is one more thing," he said, shaking a finger at his daughter, "I don't want to catch you riding again, not before your wedding! After that, I don't care. You and your unseemly ways will be Percy's problem."

Daisy approached the table, tentatively whenever in the presence of Samantha's father. More than once, she'd fainted dead away from a blast of McKinley's gruff temper.

"Mister Williams, it's Miss Harte, here to see Miss Samantha."

"Father," Samantha said, hiding her eagerness, "May I go tell her the news?"

"By all means, go ahead." He dismissed her with an out of hand gesture and picked up his fork and knife as the cook set out a runny mound of fried eggs and a slab of steak before him. "I'm sure that you girls will have all sorts of things that need doing."

"You are so right," Samantha said, with a cold smile. "We girls *do* have lots of plans to make."

Charlotte Harte looked every inch the properly dressed debutante as she stood at the parlor window, watching hummingbirds sip nectar from a patch of foxglove. Dressed in mint green chiffon, with a straw bonnet festooned with ribbons and silk flowers set upon her russet curls, she looked as fresh and verdant as a spring day.

Samantha caught her breath as she came into the parlor and saw the young woman standing there, aglow in a shaft of warm spring sunlight.

"Oh, Char," she said, "I'm so glad you're here."

Charlotte took Samantha's hands in hers and led her to the window seat. They sat down and embraced, careful, always careful not to show too much affection in public. But Samantha knew better. Behind closed doors, Charlotte would nuzzle and rub up against her like a tigress in heat!

"Samantha," Charlotte breathed. The southern belle's delicate voice trilled with a drawl that sent warm shivers down Samantha's spine. "I got your note, but I want to know – what in the world's gotten your dander up so?"

"We have to leave as soon as possible. My father gave me to Percy Hanover for marriage."

"What?" Charlotte said, amazed. "That fat old man? Why, he's your daddy's age, and stinks of cee-gars. What's your father thinkin'? Oh, it makes me ill. I am ever so sorry for you!"

"Yes. That fat old man. So you see, we *have* to leave. It's not like we can wait anymore."

"Well, I see, but..."

"It's not like we haven't been planning on this before! Everything's already laid out, all we have to do is put it into action."

Charlotte pulled back, her dark doe eyes wide and filled with surprise.

"But Samantha...that was only play actin'. Weren't it? We were just pretending...weren't we?"

Disbelief crept onto Samantha face.

"No, it wasn't, and we weren't! I meant everything I said. And now is the time. The wedding date's been set. Two weeks from now."

Charlotte wrung her hands. She turned toward the garden. Away from Samantha's pleading look.

"I...I don't know..."

Samantha fought to control her emotions once more. She brought her voice down to a whisper full of reproach.

"I thought you loved me."

"I do love you! It's just..."

"Just what?"

"I need some time to think on it. My momma would be plumb devastated if I just up an' lit out with you. And my daddy? Why, my daddy would disown me, sure as the sun comes up tomorrow."

Samantha stared in disbelief. She stood up and her voice trembled as she spoke. "I will leave day after tomorrow at daybreak. With or without you."

"Samantha, please—"

"No," Samantha shook her head. "You need to make up your mind, Charlotte Harte. And you need to make it up before tomorrow night."

Charlotte sat as if rooted to the spot. Her eyes never left Samantha's face.

"If you decide that you want to be with me," Samantha continued, "I'll meet you just outside of town. By the bridge at Parker's Slough."

Charlotte's voice trembled. "Do you know what you're askin' me to do?"

"Yes." She reached down and caressed Charlotte's cheek. "But I'll hope that you find enough courage in your heart. Enough love in there. Enough to leave all this behind and come with me."

Beyond caring if anyone saw, Samantha drew Charlotte's face up towards hers. She tenderly touched her lips to Charlotte's, as tears began to fall from her eyes.

Charlotte's eyes closed. She shivered with the intensity of the kiss that passed between the two women.

But she didn't say another word.

With a choked sob, Samantha turned and ran from the room.

CHAPTER FOUR

Samantha spent much of the morning packing everything she could possibly think she'd need in a pair of saddlebags. It turned out to be easier than she'd anticipated. No need to leave room for delicate frippery or taffeta dresses anymore.

She needed heavy trousers, work shirts, clothes that could withstand travel and heavy wear from saddle leather and the elements. She fished out her muddy riding boots and cleaned them lovingly. She stashed the boots and the full-to-bursting saddlebags under her bed. Just in case her father – or, God forbid, Percy Hanover – were to make an appearance.

Through Daisy, she smuggled a small assortment of pans and cutlery up to her room. And she was able to send orders to have her horse, Jubilee, to be put in the stall and given an extra ration of oats for the night.

Dinnertime came and went. Samantha knew that she should eat, but her stomach played host to a whole flock of butterflies. Once done with the chore of packing, her mind ran riot, thinking about Charlotte's answer.

The months of planning for this day…were they truly just a game to her? Surely Charlotte knew how Samantha felt! Until that morning, she'd been so sure that Charlotte had felt the same way. The two of them, against the entire world.

Could it be that tomorrow, she was fated to be totally on her own? Forever? Samantha rubbed her eyes with the heels of her hands and sank back on her bed as the darkness of the night finally fell. With those evil thoughts rumbling through her brain, she fell into an uneasy sleep.

She woke to the glow of a candle and a whisper at the side of her bed.

"Miss Samantha?"

"Daisy!" she whispered in return. "What is it?"

"If you're set on leaving, dawn's an hour away," Daisy said quietly. "And I made sure that your father got his full bottle of brandy last night. He's three sheets to the wind and not going to be stirring, 'less you drop an anvil on his pate."

Samantha threw her arms around her maid, stifling a cry of joy and a sob. Tousling the girl's hair, she spoke with true affection in her voice.

"Thank you, Daisy. I'll never forget you."

"You've always been kind to me, Miss Samantha. I'll miss you something awful too."

And with that, Samantha slipped out of her feminine house wear and into her riding gear. She grasped the saddlebags in one hand, the cooking gear in the other. Though the pots clanged and rattled as she went down the stairs, the sound had nothing on the seismic rumble of her father's alcohol-induced snoring.

The morning air hung heavy with a damp chill as Samantha hurried to the stables. Smell of horse manure, tingle of wood fires burning in distant hearths. And yet, under these scents lay something exhilarating. Subtle, like morning dew, like fresh-bloomed honeysuckle, like new-mown hay.

Samantha knew what it was, as soon as she tacked up Jubilee and swung herself into the saddle.

Freedom.

Calling her. Drawing her like a moth to a lantern's flame. Dawn peeked over her left shoulder as Jubilee trotted down Chicago's cobblestoned street, heading for the outskirts of town.

Mist continued to collect in goose-pimpling droplets against Samantha's eyelashes and forearms as she rode on. The early morning sun, rather than burning off the fog, simply turned it pinker, harder to see through. Around her, the houses gradually diminished in size. Open lots and fields began to appear. And up ahead, the road reared up over a marshy stream into a small stone arch.

Someone mounted atop a small brown-and-white paint horse waited by the old bridge. The figure wore a man's denim jacket, a riding cap, and trousers. The animal's white spots reflected the morning light and gave a mottled, camouflaged look to whomever sat in the saddle.

A whisper echoed in the fog bank as the figure leaned forward, as if squinting.

"Sam? Is that you?"

Samantha's heart gave a lurch and for a moment she held her breath. Almost afraid to believe that Charlotte waited for her.

"Char?"

"'Course it is! Who else would be fool enough to go riding on a godforsaken mornin' like this?"

Samantha's horse ambled over and came nose to nose with Charlotte's little paint steed, Patches. The two young women dismounted, then and came together and embraced.

But Charlotte pulled away from Samantha. Her breaths came out rapid and harsh. On the edge of panic.

"We better get a move-on. I'm sure that we'll be missed soon, and I…well, I might lose my nerve."

"Yes, we had better get going," Samantha agreed, as they remounted. She indicated the heavier, masculine clothing they both wore. "Though I don't think anyone would recognize us in this get up."

"I thought as much," Charlotte admitted, as they nudged their horses into a trot. "It's stiff, this outfit. Got it as a parting gift from our old Aussie stable hand."

"You got yours from Quincy?" Samantha shook her head in amazement. "I bought mine, but only when he had time to go to the shop with me, show me what I needed, how to use it."

"Sounds like what he taught us might well come in handy," Charlotte said, "Never thought I'd use any of his teachings this way…but I'm not findin' that I mind it especially much."

A burst of warmth settled in Samantha's heart as the two emerged from the fog and headed west. They kept a steady pace, anxious to put distance between them and the town's outermost limits.

The sun finally decided to burn away the fog. But what they gained in visibility, they paid for in heat and glare. A few hours into their ride, and Charlotte reeled in her saddle. Samantha spurred Jubilee up to Patches' side and steadied her with a hand to the shoulder.

"Sam," Charlotte said wearily, "Can we stop a moment? I am plum tuckered out, and my stomach thinks my throat's been cut."

Samantha saw the stress and strain on her companion's face. Charlotte simply wasn't accustomed to long hours of riding. Especially not astride like a man. She nodded towards a wooded glen, just off the road.

"Sure, let's head over there."

Sunlight through birch and elm branches dappled the two as they stopped their horses and dismounted. Charlotte's legs almost gave way as she dismounted, and her thighs fairly burned with soreness from the ride, and the rough cloth that made up the men's trousers.

"I don't know how on earth you stand this," Charlotte waddled in a stiff, bowlegged gait over to a rock sitting on the edge of the pool.

Samantha laughed. "Trust me, you'll get used to it."

She unsaddled the horses and put hobbles on them so that they could graze without wandering too far. Samantha untied a rucksack that hung from her saddle, pulled out hunks of bread and cheese, and then handed them to Charlotte. In a rather unladylike fashion, Charlotte took a big bite of one, then the other, stuffing her mouth till her cheeks bulged.

Samantha laughed merrily and pulled out a second helping for herself. She shared out a canteen of water with Charlotte. Though fresh, the liquid had already taken on a metallic flavor. Charlotte grimaced at the taste.

"Sorry," Samantha said. "Until we get out to the wilderness proper, we're not bound to find water fresh enough to drink right from a stream."

Charlotte shook her head in amazement. "I don't rightly know which I'd find more troublesome right now – wading into an ice-cold stream for water, or gettin' atop Patches. My legs haven't decided that they can come back together."

"Yeah, I know. But we need to put a few more miles on before it gets dark. I'll bet our fathers will be keen to put someone on our trail in no time."

"You're right." Charlotte said ruefully, as she creakily got up and took her hat off for the first time that morning. Samantha started as she saw that Charlotte had cut her russet-colored tresses all off, leaving a short fringe of curls about her face. "Got any ideas as to where we're headed, in the end?"

"We're following the sun. We'll know when we get there."

Charlotte stared at her for a moment. "I like poetry, but it don't sit well with me right now. Samantha honey, are y'all sure about this?"

Samantha looked back with serious determination in her eyes.

"I won't go back. Not to that life. Not *ever!*"

Charlotte said nothing in reply. But Samantha couldn't help but feel a chill steal over her heart as her lover's cherubic face took on a sullen, crestfallen look.

CHAPTER FIVE

McKinley Williams flung his morning's coffee as hard as he could across the room. The cup shattered against the wall in an explosion of sweet-smelling steam. Richly scented drops of Arabia's best dripped down the imported wallpaper, staining it as if the house itself had come down with the measles.

His voice boomed out in irritation. "What do you mean, 'she's vanished'?"

"It just that, Mister McKinley!" Daisy shrunk away from him. "I looked for Miss Samantha in her room, in the stable. Jubilee, her horse, he's gone too."

"Get out," he rumbled, and then raised his voice to a shout. "*Get out!*"

Daisy dashed out of the room as if expecting another volley of crockery and coffee to follow.

McKinley slumped in his chair just as the butler entered and timidly faced his employer.

"Sir, Nathaniel and Mary Harte are here to see you. On a most urgent matter."

"What in blue blazes do they want, Tom?"

"I would suggest that you speak with them yourself, sir."

"Don't be impertinent!"

The door to the parlor swung open with a *bang*. Tom adroitly stepped aside as Charlotte's parents, both as pale skinned and russet-haired as a matched pair of porcelain dolls, burst into the room. Charlotte's mother shook as if in a high fever. Tears streamed from her red, puffy eyes. Her father's voice, tinged with the same hint of Dixie as his daughter's, rung in McKinley's ears.

"She's gone!" he shouted, "My dear baby Charlotte, she's gone!"

Charlotte's mother let out a wail in counterpoint. McKinley Williams stared at the couple for a moment, his earlier outburst forgotten. He knew Mary Harte from the woman's penchant for throwing elaborate garden parties. And he was familiar with Nathaniel Harte from meetings at the Chamber of Commerce and the odd gentlemanly game of whist at the club.

Neither had struck him as prone to hysterics.

"What are you looking at me for, Nathaniel? Why don't you go to the police?"

"Because I'm certain that your family's got somethin' to do with this." Nathaniel Harte drew himself up, tugged at the ends of his jacket, and jabbed a gloved finger in McKinley's face. "It was your daughter, McKinley! Your daughter who kept dragging ours to those damned equestrian events, kept her out late nights, and got her into who-knows-what mischief."

McKinley Williams stared at the man. A deep suspicion began to grow in the back of his mind, but he kept it tamped down for now.

"My daughter's gone missing too," McKinley grated. Charlotte's mother stopped in mid-sniffle to listen as Samantha's father called over to the butler. "Tom, get me the Pinkerton Detective Agency, right away. Have them send me their best man."

Two hours crawled by. Hours made all the longer by Mary Harte's near-constant crying. Her caterwauling stopped as a solid-sounding *tap* came from the entryway's brass knocker. All eyes followed the butler as he went to the door.

McKinley fought to control his fidgeting as he heard the muffled sounds of talking and steps inside the front hall. Last night, he'd thought his fortune had been made. When Percy Hanover all but drooled over Samantha. Then asked for her hand in marriage. At last his goal had become within reach. The prestige he so justly deserved!

And now this.

Well, he wouldn't stand for it. No, he would get her back, at any cost. She would not upset his plans.

Tom returned to the parlor, announcing solemnly, "Sir, Mister Matthew Slade of the Pinkerton Agency is here to see you."

Mary Harte remained seated while Nathaniel and McKinley rose to greet the new arrival. The Pinkerton man stood a full head taller than either of them. A smart tweed suit outlined his tall, lean frame, and his strong hand held a dapper bowler hat by a worn brim. His waxed handlebar mustache, smelling pleasantly of barbershop cologne, preceded his strong handshake as he greeted everyone in turn.

"Well, Mister Williams," Slade said grandly, in a voice one part Western drawl, one part smooth Tennessee whiskey. "What can Pinkerton do for you this time?"

"Hopefully, a great deal," McKinley stated. In a matter-of-fact tone, he added, "Our daughters have been kidnapped."

At his statement, Mary Harte let out a blubbering sob and fainted dead away in her chair. Nathaniel went to her side as McKinley looked on with annoyance.

"Tom," he called, "Bring us some smelling salts. Any more of this nonsense and I might go into feminine hysterics myself."

Matthew Slade pinched one end of his mustache in his fingers as he looked on in calculation and amusement. However, his tone dropped a shade as he grew deadly serious.

"Mister Williams, what makes you think that your daughter Samantha has been kidnapped?"

"Why else would she just disappear with her wedding so close?"

"Oh?" One eyebrow rose. "She's gettin' married?"

"As a matter of fact, she is. To Percy Hanover, of the Lake Forest—"

"I'm aware of them. Quite a rich family. Percy's been born with an entire drawer of silver spoons in his mouth. All the more strange."

McKinley gave him a puzzled look. "How do you mean?"

"A kidnapper should've waited by-the-by. Taking the brand-new wife of a man like Percy Hanover would've reaped a much tidier sum. Was there a ransom note?"

"Well, ah, no. No note was found."

The butler arrived, with Daisy and her vial of smelling salts in tow. She attended to Mary Harte as Nathaniel turned his attention to focus on Slade.

"I understand that the Harte girl has gone missing also? Is that correct?"

Harte nodded. "Yes, that's quite right. Charlotte's gone."

"Any ransom note?" Harte shook his head in the negative, which brought out a frown on Slade's face for the first time. "Does it not seem a bit odd that both of your daughters have gone missing at the same time? And that no ransom note was left for either one?"

"Hellfire, man!" McKinley burst out. "What else do you need to know? They're missing. We want them back, and you're wasting time!"

Slade gave the man a non-plussed look.

"Mister McKinley, I've been the lead investigator for some sixty cases for Pinkerton. In that time, I've never failed to close one. That's because I knew exactly what I was getting into from the start, each time."

Matthew Slade looked each man in the eye as he spoke. He drew himself to his full height and made his next statement in a tone that brooked no disagreement.

"So, gentlemen. How about each of you tellin' me what's *really* going on here?"

CHAPTER SIX

McKinley Williams clamped his jaw as tight as a steel trap. When no answer was forthcoming, Slade let out a tired sigh and spoke again.

"Mister Williams," Slade said, "How did your daughter feel about getting hitched to Percy Hanover?"

As if against his will, McKinley said, "Elated, of course. The man's from one of the oldest and wealthiest families in Chicago."

"He's also a man of your age. And your daughter is...what? Nineteen or twenty? Sir, it's very important that you be honest with me. I am askin' you again. Did Samantha want this marriage?"

McKinley Williams grabbed his jacket lapels in both hands. "What does that matter? I'm her father, and she'll do as I say. It's no business of yours, anyway. If you can't find her and bring her to me, then I'll hire someone who will."

Slade ignored the last of McKinley's statements. Instead, he turned to Nathaniel. "Mister Harte, Charlotte's horse is missing, I expect?"

"You're correct," Harte said, surprised. "How did you know that?"

"Because I passed the stable on the way in." Slade held up a hand to forestall McKinley's reaction. "One whole side's laid out for a female rider, from the type of tack on the shelves to the height they're laid out at. And though there's no sign of struggle, the stall hasn't been mucked out yet."

"What're you implying, Slade?"

"I'm not much for 'implying', Mister Harte." Slade shrugged. "I'm a simple man who just calls it as he sees it. Like I said, no sign of a struggle. And muckin' a stall is a morning task. It all adds up to one thing: Samantha Williams took her horse out on her own, before anyone was awake. No one kidnapped your daughters. They left on their own."

"But why would Charlotte leave?" Harte threw Williams a dark look. "We've tried to encourage her to see some boys. She hasn't been excited about that...but she wasn't about to be pressured into no marriage."

McKinley's uneasy look attracted Slade's eye. "Is there something that you want to tell me, Mister Williams?"

"There may be a reason for that. Samantha is good friends with Charlotte. And Samantha has...un-natural tendencies."

"What do you mean? Un-natural tendencies?"

"She prefers the company of women rather than men."

This time it was Mary Harte who jumped to her feet, pushing away the maid and butler's ministrations.

"Not my Charlotte," she said. "She's a chaste and proper young woman!"

"Oh, please!" McKinley snapped. "She's as much a Sapphist as Samantha. I've seen them returning late at night, trading kisses that were anything but sisterly."

"Why didn't you tell us?"

"Because they just need a good man, Mary. Marriage and children will take care of that nonsense!" McKinley turned to glare at Slade. "So now you know. These two may not want to be found. I don't care. I will not have my plans for my daughter thwarted by some silly nonsense."

Slade ran a finger along one side of his mustache in thought. Nodding to himself, he fixed his steely gray eyes on the two men.

"I'll take this case," he pronounced. "Mister Williams, your daughter is a very resourceful young lady. That said, I don't think they're going to blaze a trail into the Great White North or out west into Indian country."

Mary Harte let out a gasp at that, but Nathaniel steadied her, while adding, "Charlotte's got a bunch of relations down south. Georgia, mostly."

"And the branches of my family are in Pennsylvania and Boston," McKinley said. "It's possible that they hopped a train back to Philadelphia."

Slade nodded. "I'll have a telegraph sent to all Pinkerton branches within a day's train ride from Chicago to watch the rail stations. Myself, I'll get to trailing them as soon as I get my gear together."

Nathaniel Harte looked up at Slade with a haggard expression. "I just want to know what's happened to my daughter. If she's gone off on her own, I want to know, and I want to know why. Please Mister Slade, please find her."

"Count on it," Slade said firmly. "There's a reason I was picked to run the Chicago branch of Pinkerton's. I've never failed to bring in my man."

Slade excused himself and left the room. He stopped by the front door and carefully placed his bowler hat back on his head. The butler graciously opened the door with a slight bow.

"Tell me something, Tom." Slade tilted his head, indicating the parlor. "Is Mister Williams always this pleasant?"

"Sir, one never speaks ill of their employer. To do so would lead to short term employment."

"Thank you, Tom. You just told me what I wanted to know."

"Quite right, sir."

Matthew Slade stepped out into the bright, cool morning. The air echoed with the busy *clack-clack* of horses' hooves and drawn carriage wheels on cobblestone streets. He looked back up at the Williams' house. The sound of muffled, heated conversation came from the leaded glass of the parlor window.

Slade grimaced, and then raised the brim of his hat to look further up the side of the house. His gaze roved over the dark red of the clinker-brick siding, a spray of ivy, and rested on the black metal weather vane that perched atop the roof. The vane's arrow swung uneasily in the slight breeze, indicating no certain direction.

He shook his head. *How very fitting.*

The sun had sunk low on the horizon when Samantha turned to see Charlotte trailing behind her. Her companion looked as tired and bedraggled as her horse.

"Char," she called, "How about we find a place to camp for the night?"

For the first time in hours, Charlotte's eyes lit up and a smile crept across her face.

"You mean it? My fanny seems to've *growed* to this saddle."

Samantha made sure not to laugh at Charlotte's discomfort. She'd had more than a few days like that when she first started riding.

"Of course I mean it." Samantha pointed to a tall bluff up ahead, one with a slight overhang. As best as she could see, the place would give them a little extra shelter. The tall trees stood dense and close enough for a tether line for the horses.

"Well, so long as I can just get down offen' this horse."

Samantha dismounted, then helped Charlotte all but slide down the side of the saddle. Her companion hunched over stiffly, as if she'd aged thirty years in the last eight hours.

"God in heaven, I won't be able to put my legs back together ever again."

Samantha picked up Patches' reins and nodded towards the base of the bluff. "You go on over there and sit a spell. I'll take care of the horses."

Charlotte limped over to sit on a fallen log. She almost collapsed onto the ground with a howl as the rough fabric of her trousers rubbed against her chaffed legs. Samantha did her best to pay no mind to the noise as she removed their mounts' bridles and replaced them with halters and lead lines, tying them next to each other.

After removing the saddles, she gave the horses a rub down with the saddle blankets. Next, she put the feed bags over their heads with the ration of grain she'd thought to bring along. Having taken care of the horses, Samantha brought the saddlebags over to where Charlotte sat, rubbing her thighs and groaning.

"It's getting dark," Samantha said. "I'd better get us a fire going."

No comment from Charlotte.

Samantha gathered some rocks and put them in a circle. She gathered dry twigs and pieces of bracken piling it up into a heap in the middle, thankful that she had brought a lot of matches with her, as the fire took six tries before catching.

She jumped as the sky opened with a peal of thunder. The smell of rain hung heavy in the air for a moment. The first drops started to fall, causing the fire to sputter and pop.

The *plinks* of water on the fire matched the first tears from Charlotte's eyes. Before Samantha could think of anything to say, to ask what was wrong, more tears streamed down Charlotte's cheeks.

Charlotte buried her head in her hands and sobbed.

CHAPTER SEVEN

Samantha rushed to Charlotte's side.

"What's the matter, Char?"

"What do you think's the matter?" Charlotte flared at her. "I'm tired. Hungry. I hurt all over. I've been dropped down smack in the middle of God-knows-where and now it's *raining!*"

Not knowing what else to do, Samantha pulled a heavy woolen blanket from the bedroll pack and wrapped it around the two of them. Samantha held Charlotte close, using her body heat to warm her as she stroked the soft curls of hair and rocked her gently.

"I know you're tired and all." A pause, as Samantha held her tighter. "But it'll get better, I promise."

Samantha drew back her head and raised her hands to take Charlotte's face in them, leaned forward and kissed the tear stained cheeks. Charlotte looked back at her. Doubt simmered in her eyes.

"Right now, I want you to just sit here while I get us some supper. I got us some fine canned beans here that'll fix you right up. Thank goodness this cliff hangs out enough to protect the fire from the rain."

On cue, the fire sputtered as a burst of lightening and a loud thunderclap exploded over their heads.

Somehow, the fire kept going and a grateful Samantha opened a can of beans and heated them in the same can. She held a spoon toward Charlotte and coaxed her to eat them.

Samantha then broke out a saucepan, heated water in it to a boil, and added coffee to the bubbling liquid. To Samantha, the rising fumes smelled heavenly. But even so, between the bland food, the bitter taste of the coffee, and the sandy grit of the grounds, Charlotte couldn't do more than finish half of what Samantha put out for her.

The rain slackened off, but a chilling wind kicked up. Charlotte just stared dully into the distance, until she finally broke her silence.

"I want to go home."

Samantha looked down at her hands. "You know I can't ever do that. You know what waits for me there."

"I know. But I do ever so want to go home. To be home again…" Charlotte's voice wound down, and she went quiet again. Samantha could feel the silence weighing down on them like a sodden tarp.

She left her companion to make sure the horses were alright and secure for the night. When she came back Charlotte had fallen asleep, huddled up like a little girl. The rain finally stopped. Samantha fed a long brand into the fire as it burned, and then sat down and stretched her hands out to warm them. She realized for the first time since they had arrived at the campsite how tired she really felt.

From where she sat she could see the black sky, like a piece of fine velvet studded and spangled with diamonds. It reminded her of a dress her mother had worn at one of the parties given to impress her father's so-called friends.

The thought made her shudder.

No, I'll never go back.

Unable to sleep, not knowing what the next day would bring. Not knowing if it had been wise to ask Charlotte to go with her. Wondering if her love for Charlotte would be enough of a bond.

Knowing in her heart that she would go through hell's fire rather than going back to her father's tyranny. Before she'd be forced into a man's bed. And as sleep finally stole upon her, Samantha realized that she just might have to face the devil himself.

Alone.

McKinley Williams watched with gimlet eyes as the Pinkerton detective patted the sturdy blue roan mustang. The man then slipped his Winchester into the scabbard on his mount's rig. Matthew Slade was almost unrecognizable in the leather britches, the silver concho'd vest and the low slung Colt. A gunfighter's rig, except for the tie downs left loose for riding.

"Slade, I demand to know why you're heading out on horseback," McKinley said loftily, "You should be looking for clues to where my daughter has gone, down at the train station!"

Slade tamped down the response that first came to mind before he spoke. "Mister Williams, rule number one when you hire my firm: don't tell a Pinkerton man how to run his case."

He paused, letting McKinley stew before he went on.

"My men are covering train stations and the telegraph posts in a two-hundred mile radius from Chicago. I'll be in touch with them, they'll be giving me reports. I'll be passing on what I hear to you as I see fit."

"Second, it don't take a genius to see that, unless they're desperate, those two ain't going to be taking the trains. Samantha at least knows that you'd be hiring someone like me. They'll stick to horseback. And so will I."

"Well, they can't have gone far," McKinley declared. "At least, not so that nobody would notice."

"That's the first thing you've been right about, so far," Slade said.

McKinley blinked, unsure whether to be insulted or not.

"It is?"

"Yup. On horseback, the roads are good down south to Saint Louie, or back east to Toledo. Good, and busy. I should be able to find out in a couple of days if anyone's seen them."

"That should be the end of it, then."

"That's not what my gut says," Slade remarked, as he put his foot up into the stirrup and swung his lanky frame up and into the saddle. "Going south or east, that's the right thing to do, if they're seeking help from a relative. But…what if they're not doing that? Where would they go, if they decided that they'd be puttin' it all on one throw?"

McKinley bristled. "I'm not in the habit of visiting gambling halls, so I don't understand your 'colorful' way of speaking.

These are just two girls, Slade. What could they possibly do that's unexpected?"

"What indeed?" Slade replied quietly. He tipped his hat to McKinley Williams, and then nudged the mustang into a trot. The horse's hooves threw up dirt clods that sprayed the man's trousers, causing him to jump back and curse.

Slade chuckled to himself. He didn't like McKinley, or any man like him. It got to him, being on a case he didn't like. Samantha had no choice but to run from her father and a repulsive arranged marriage. He wasn't sure about Charlotte, but anyone willing to cut loose the way she did…it could only mean one thing.

Love.

Slade couldn't blame either of them. A lot at stake. A shame he had to get this job. The two young women didn't stand a chance.

"Git up." Slade nudged the mustang to a fast lope as they headed out of Chicago and into the vast open spaces of the West.

CHAPTER EIGHT

Samantha woke to the sound of meadowlarks and the dying glow of embers from last night's campfire. She breathed in deep, smelled damp earth mixed with rain and charred wood.

Stiff from lying on the ground, she sat up and stretched. A little *pop* in her back as something snapped into its proper place. She covered her mouth to stifle a yawn, and then looked over to where Charlotte lay still sleeping. She wondered what the day would bring between them. Part of her didn't want to know.

Samantha decided to let Charlotte sleep.

After poking the fire back to life and answering the call of nature, Samantha busied herself with coffee and frying a slab of fatback bacon for breakfast. The greasy, smoky odor mixed with the campfire smoke smelled marvelous to her.

She heard a yawn, and then turned to see a groggy but awake young woman sitting cross legged next to the fire.

"Good morning. Feel any better?"

Charlotte looked up at her dully. Then down toward her hands, where they clasped the blanket in a pair of tight fists.

"I'm powerful sorry. I wasn't pleasant last night. Not. At. All."

"You were just tired. How are your legs this morning?"

"I reckon that I can walk," Charlotte threw aside her blanket, and then winced as she got to her feet. She did a few slow, painful knee bends, and sat to rub her legs. She watched, eyes wide, as Samantha worked on fixing breakfast. Her lips trembled as she spoke again. "Sam, I've been right terrible. Felt right terrible. It's just that…I ain't never even been campin' before. Let alone being away from home like this."

Samantha listened without comment. She handed Charlotte a plate with a piece of fatty, sizzling bacon, a chunk of flat bread, and a cup of tar-black coffee. Charlotte hesitated. But after a single taste of the bacon strip, she gobbled it down then used the remnants of the bread to mop up any grease left on the plate. She sipped at the coffee, shuddered, and set it down.

"You don't have to be sorry for anything," Samantha said, as she dug into her own plate, "I know it's going to be hard for you. Hell, it's hard for me. Just remember all the stuff that Quincy told us, and we'll be fine. How are your legs?"

Between more sips and shudders, Charlotte replied, "They feel a mite raw, to be sure."

Samantha got up and rummaged in her saddle bags. She came up with a box of talcum powder. "This'll help."

"Good. 'Cause nature's callin' me with a will." Charlotte took the box and headed toward the bushes in a half-walk, half waddle. By the time she returned, the camp had been cleared and the horses saddled.

"Aw, *more* riding?"

"Sorry, Char. I've got a feeling in my bones that we need to get moving today. You keep the talcum. We've got a long way to go."

Charlotte let out a curse that would have made her mother blanch.

✶ ✶ ✶

The first week on horseback gave each woman a new understanding to the term *saddle sore*. Both were well used to riding. But neither one had realized that it was different to ride twenty to thirty miles a day.

Their thighs adapted to the spread and the working of the muscles in about three days. However, it took the full week to get used to the roughness of the heavy wool pants. It had been worse for Charlotte, because she hadn't worn men's pants before. But finally her skin quit burning.

Her mood improved, though in fits and jerks. An evening by the campfire could easily find the two cuddled close and affectionately. It was equally likely to find them staring hatefully at each other across the flames.

But they finally got familiar with the meager comfort of the saddle, and their sunburned faces were getting tan. If pressed, Samantha would have had to admit that the freckling across Charlotte's nose enhanced her prairie prettiness. Her short cropped hair had settled into ringlets that framed her face. Whenever she looked out from underneath the wide brimmed hat, Samantha's heart gave a little *thrum*.

On the second week out, their trail took them to the crest of a windswept hill. A bustling little town lay below. The weather had been good, though rain threatened again. And Samantha hadn't seen hide nor hair of anyone tracking them.

"What d'you think?" This from Charlotte.

"What do I think?" Samantha rubbed her chin with a grimy hand. "We're going to need provisions, that's for sure."

"And I'd like a good night's sleep on something other than the ground. A bath, too. And some meat that we didn't have to kill, clean and cook ourselves."

Samantha considered. "How much money do you have?"

"About twenty dollars. Why?"

"Well with my twenty, that makes forty. That'll be enough for all the stuff we need to buy, that's for sure."

"Right now I don't really care! I'd be ever so grateful for a bath, and it don't even have to be in a tub!"

"And how would my Char like to get some right fine vittles with that bath?"

Charlotte's face lit up with a smile that Samantha hadn't seen since Chicago. It calmed Samantha's fears. Fears that the only reason her love hadn't turned back was because Charlotte didn't know the way.

They headed down the hill, excited, and yet jumpy at the same time. Many nights around the campfire had passed with the two speculating about what had taken place after they left. Charlotte's mother would have fainted. Her father would be worried over her mother.

Samantha's father would swing back and forth, first damning her hide and wanting to call out the Militia to get his marker for society back. Ever since her mother had died that was the way it was with him and her. Love or hate, without much in between. And lately, long on the hate.

But none of the townspeople gave the two so much as a second glance. They rode down the dusty main street. Though it was small to their eyes, after the suburbs of Chicago, the town had an air of genial prosperity. On the main street alone they spotted well-turned out livery, a pair of upscale saloon-hotels, and a brace of attorney's offices. Anchoring the main intersection at the heart of the town was a freshly painted general store, a good-sized bank, and a clock tower with a barrel-sized bell. It gloomily chimed ten o'clock as they passed by.

But their ride came rudely to a halt at the sight of a man in a ranch hand's getup struggling with a well-dressed young woman on the boardwalk at the end of the street. Charlotte saw Samantha's face crease into a dangerous frown.

"This don't concern us," Charlotte warned. Her companion nodded, and they prepared to ride by.

Then the woman screamed as the man hit her. She fell to one knee and let out a wail.

Samantha didn't wait a moment. She spurred Jubilee and the horse all but leapt to where the man was obviously forcing his attention on the young woman. Samantha swung down off her horse and stepped forward as Charlotte came up behind.

"Take your hands off her!" Samantha demanded.

Caught off guard, the man's grip loosened on the woman's wrist. She twisted free, but froze at the sight of her assailant confronting the newcomer.

"Well, lookee what we got here," the man said. A leer crossed his face and he swaggered forward a step.

Samantha moved without conscious thought. With reflexes that she didn't know she had, her gun appeared in her hand. The weapon made a deadly, metallic sound as she cocked it.

"Back off, mister."

She got a leer in return. "Aw, is the little woman gonna shoot me?"

"Only if I have to."

"I don't think you got the sinew to do that," the man said. "Girls from around these parts ain't made of stern enough stuff."

He took another step forward.

A *bang!* and dust exploded from the splintered board next to the toe of the man's boot. He stopped dead in his tracks.

Her voice came out a shade above a growl.

"Didn't say I was *from* around these parts, did I?"

The man's face paled as Samantha cocked the trigger a second time and leveled the barrel at his chest.

CHAPTER NINE

For a single, timeless moment, no one moved. A bead of sweat ran down the side of the man's face. His fingers twitched. But his hands didn't move a millimeter towards the gun at his belt.

A short man with a pot belly and a face covered in a mass of beard stubble came stomping down the wooden boardwalk at a limping half-run. Charlotte breathed a sigh of relief as she saw the bright silver star pinned to the man's vest.

He came up short at the sight of the drawn gun. Snorted. Then he looked over at the woman who Samantha had rescued from the manhandling.

"Cindy," he said, "What in tarnation is goin' on here?"

"Thank heavens that you're here!" Cindy replied. "Sheriff Moody, this fella was getting rough with me and this woman here stopped him dead in his tracks."

Moody chewed it over for a moment. Slowly, he approached the ranch hand, making sure not to block Samantha's shot. He reached over and removed the gun from the man's holster.

"You can put your shootin' iron away now ma'am," he said, addressing Samantha. "This cur must be new 'round here. Otherwise he would've recognized one of Miz Pleasance's girls."

Samantha nodded, and then put her gun away. Charlotte let out a long-held gasp of air.

Moody cuffed the man on his ear. "Well, what have you got to say for yourself?"

"I was only funnin'," the man protested. "'Sides, she ain't nothing cept' a whore, anyways."

"Couple days in jail will teach you a lesson. Cindy, you tell Miz Pleasance I said 'hello'."

"I sure will, Sheriff." And with that exchange, the sheriff gave the man a shove, moving him off towards the town jail.

"I owe you for that one," Cindy said, not taking her eye off her assailant until Sheriff Moody had taken him out of sight.

"Nothing's owed," Samantha said, abashed. "I just did what was right."

"Well, you did what no one else'd do, at the right time," The young woman smiled broadly. "I'm Cindy Mae O'Reilly, and as the Sheriff said, I'm one of the town's Pleasance girls. Say, where you two from? Don't reckon I've seen either of you before."

Samantha traded a glance with Charlotte before answering.

"This is Charlotte, and I'm Samantha. We're...not from around here."

"Well, I can tell *that* from the way you look. I reckon that cowpoke didn't know you two were women, leastwise when he first laid eyes on you."

Charlotte spoke up. "I suppose we do look a mite unkempt. But maybe you know where we can get a bath? And some hot food?"

"That much, I do know. Come with me."

They followed Cindy down the main street. At the end lay a large Victorian mansion trimmed in blue and white, one that Samantha had figured for the town hall from a distance. An immaculately tended garden lay behind a whitewashed iron fence. A carriage path decorated with crushed pink gravel wound up to the door from the entry gate. At the apex of the gate hung a sign: *Mrs. Pleasance's Hotel & Social Club*.

"Well, don't that take the biscuit!" Charlotte said, amazed. "Who'd have thought that we would find a place like this out here?"

"A lot of people are surprised," Cindy said. "But this is home."

A boy came out as they walked up the gravel path. Cindy instructed him to look after the horses. Samantha and Charlotte each removed a saddlebag with a spare change of clothes, and then allowed the boy to walk their mounts off to where they could be watered.

Sunlight glinted off panels of leaded crystal set into the house's double doors as the three women started up porch steps.

Suddenly, the doors burst open and the trio was met by a buxom woman wearing a green satin morning gown and sporting a tousled mass of hair the color of ripe tangerines. She beckoned them to approach with an open, friendly smile on her well-made up face.

The edges of her smile drooped as she saw the rent in Cindy's dress. "What on earth happened to you, girl?"

"Some grub-liner tried to get somethin' for free, and he wouldn't take no for an answer. I'd have been hurt bad and to the quick, if these two ladies hadn't come along and changed his mind. Sheriff Moody's got the ruffian stewin' in the hoosegow now."

The woman appraised them anew. She nodded, as if approving of what she saw.

"Welcome, welcome. I am Mrs. Pleasance. Thank you for helping Cindy out. Now, who are you ladies? And more importantly, what can I do for you?"

Samantha introduced herself and Charlotte in the same way that they'd done with Cindy. She added, "We've been on the trail for a while. Our bodies and souls could use some nurturing. Perhaps we could purchase a hot bath, something to eat, and a room?"

"Oh, I'm afraid we couldn't allow that," Mrs. Pleasance said seriously. Then, as a disappointed look crossed Charlotte's face, she added, "For rescuin' our Cindy Mae, I insist that you stay with us tonight, *gratis*. Meals, bath, and two rooms for the night, on the house."

Samantha smiled at Mrs. Pleasance. "We don't need separate rooms, actually. We'll be staying with each other."

Mrs. Pleasance looked from one woman's face to the other, reading their expressions without passing judgment. "Well, then. Cindy, why don't you show our guests up to the Rosewater suite. These ladies need the trail dust off before they join us for lunch."

"I...well, thank you," Samantha stammered, and Charlotte nodded vigorously in agreement.

"It's my pleasure, Samantha. We'll look forward to your company in a couple hours."

Cindy showed the way inside. Flocked velvet wallpaper the color of strawberries and masses of ornately carved wooden furniture made up the decor. The rooms were empty of people, save for a couple small groups of well-made up young women, busy fanning themselves, chatting quietly, or playing cards. They looked up curiously as Samantha and Charlotte went by.

"It's always slow this time of day," Cindy explained, "But at least it'll be quiet till evening, which I think you two will appreciate."

And with that, she led them up a staircase and into a spacious bedroom with a large poster bed, a chaise lounge and dressing table. As was appropriate for the name of the suite, the scent of rose water tickled their noses. Charlotte let out a tiny 'ooh' as she spotted a smaller room off to the side that held a magnificent brass and white porcelain claw-foot tub.

Above it was a tank with a spigot that held water with a gas burner under it to heat it. Cindy knelt and lit the burner. She indicated the pile of bath robes and towels on the bed.

"You should have everything you need now. I'll leave you two be, but I'll be back at noon. Mrs. Pleasance's formal dining room stays closed until the evening, but lunch is on before that. It's wonderful, having meal-time for just us girls."

With that, she made a little curtsey and took her leave. Abruptly, the two young women found themselves alone in the midst of luxury that was as unexpected as it was tempting.

"Oh my," Charlotte said, laughing, "I believe that we've landed in the lap of...well, as my daddy would say, a 'nest of soiled doves'."

"That may be," Samantha said, scratching her chin, "But right now I don't mind. That tub looks so good, I'm ready to dive into it, clothes on!"

"Samantha Williams, don't you dare!" Charlotte said, in mock warning.

Laughing, Samantha opened the faucet on the tub and warm, steaming water gushed out. Charlotte opened a nearby tin of salts labeled with a picture of flowers, and shook a handful into the porcelain tub.

Inhaling the soothing smell of lavender that filled the bathroom, the two quickly shucked off their clothes, down to their travel-stained undergarments.

And stopped.

The air, perfumed with lavender and caressed by tendrils of hot steam, turned still.

Charged.

Almost imperceptibly, Charlotte brought her legs together, knees pressed tight. Samantha saw the movement. Charlotte saw that she saw, and a hot flare of red blossomed on her cheeks.

"Sam…" she husked, in her soft Southern drawl, "What we've done before…the kissin'…the fondlin'…it was only play actin'. Weren't it? We were just pretending…weren't we?"

"It wasn't for me," Samantha said, with a shake of her head. "And I know it wasn't for you, either. Not when you were so very wet…down under."

Charlotte trembled. "And I'm that way now…"

"What about before? Back home?"

"I got that way every time you walked in the room, seems like."

Samantha came to her, took a hand in hers. "Then what's the problem?"

"It's just…I don't know what to do! I mean, beyond touching you, holding you!"

"It's a good start." Samantha drew the smaller woman in. Kissed her, held her close. "You just got to let nature take its course."

"What we got…*is* it natural? It's not what the preachers say, not a'tall."

"I don't care what the preachers say, Char. The love I feel for you…it comes from inside. It feels natural enough." She nodded towards the tub. "Come on now. I'll make sure we *both* fit."

CHAPTER TEN

Samantha began first. She stripped off the last of her clothing and stood before Charlotte for the first time in the nude. She could feel Charlotte's curious gaze rove over her almost palpably, like a set of warm hands.

She laughed ruefully and ran a hand through the sweaty, dusty tangles of her hair. "Sorry, you had to see me like this at first. I'm a mess, a damned mess."

"You look...gosh darned pretty, Sam." She slipped out of her own underclothes, examining her darkly tanned hands against the milky-white of the rest of her body. "Me, I just plum look silly. Like a darned two-toned puppy."

"You stop that, Char. Come on, before the water gets cold."

Samantha slipped into the tub first with an *ahhh*. She scooted over, spotted a dish holding a bar of goat's milk soap and grabbed it. Charlotte tucked one foot into the warm water, followed suit with the other, and then slowly lowered herself in. The outside of the lovers' legs rested against one another, and with a sigh, they each reclined against the warm slope of porcelain at their backs.

After a good, long soak, Samantha lathered up the soap. Gingerly, not wanting to rush or spoil the moment, they took turns soaping up a small facecloth and using it to wash each other. Their hands caressed each other's breasts and thighs, allowing each woman to luxuriate in the softness of their skin, the slickness of the water. They each took turns washing their hair, then reluctantly only got out as the water finally cooled.

As they dried off and each brushed out the tangles in their hair, Samantha eyed herself in the least fogged portion of the bathroom's mirror. She felt clean, truly cleansed, for the first time since she'd ridden out of Chicago with Charlotte at her side.

Impulsively, she grabbed the last bath towel from when it hung on the brass bathroom rails and wrapped it around Charlotte. She was rewarded with a pleased, but startled *squeak*.

"Shhh...there's nothing to be afraid of," Samantha said, as she pulled Charlotte in tight up against her. Her mouth found Charlotte's. Their tongues did a hot, wet dance and they rubbed against one another, creating a heat that needed to be quenched before it consumed them both.

Samantha took Charlotte's hand and led her into the bedroom. With a soft sound, the towels dropped to the floor, forgotten. Samantha bore Charlotte back to the bed, sat her on the edge, and then pressed her lips to the side of her lover's neck, gently nibbling.

Charlotte moaned; Samantha's pulse raced, but she forced herself with an iron will to continue, slow and teasing, nibbling and sucking her way down from neck to nipple, nipple to navel, and navel south to Charlotte's dark pelt of hair between her legs.

The two women halted for a moment. The sound of harsh breaths, almost panting, escaped their lips. Charlotte's cheeks flushed with a fresh charge of blood, not from embarrassment, but anticipation. Of knowing that the next touch would change her world forever. Forever, and for the better.

Samantha spread Charlotte's knees. Spread her dark curliness gentle with both hands. Saw the unripe-berry pinkness of the butterfly beneath, quivering.

She touched her set of lips to another. Earned a gasp with a kiss.

Followed it up with a more insistent kiss.

Followed it up with a swipe of a tongue.

"Sam...please..." Charlotte gasped, "Don't wait...I can't wait...no more..."

Using her fingers, Samantha gentle probed into the soft hot, wetness as she brought her tongue back into play. The butterfly under her fingers turned from pink berry to cherry-red. Samantha pulled her fingers back, buried her face into that wetness.

Charlotte's throat exploded with a teakettle-hiss, a *snarl* of ecstasy that delighted and surprised Samantha. Charlotte's thighs convulsed, her trim buttocks raised off the bed, and she cried out in delight. No words, just animal sounds of pleasure.

Samantha sat back on her heels, keeping her hands on each of Charlotte's inner thighs. Electric quivers ran up and down the young woman's legs.

"Oh my stars," Charlotte murmured, as Samantha came up to lie on the bed next to her, "I never thought it could be so...so..."

But whatever her mind might have come up with, it was lost as she saw Samantha's shining face. Charlotte turned on her side. Kissed and licked the salty trace of her own scent from Samantha's lips and chin.

"I'm just glad you liked it," Samantha said, honestly.

"And I'm glad that you went so slow."

"Well, I didn't want to fright you, Char—"

Charlotte quirked a grin at her. "Not exactly what I was aimin' at there."

"Oh?"

"I liked you going slow, all the way...so I could figure out what you did. So's I could try it out myself on *you*."

Charlotte rolled over, putting her weight on the taller woman. Breasts pressed together, nipple to nipple, touching, becoming almost painfully swollen and erect. Charlotte brought her lips to nuzzle the cleft in Samantha's collarbone, at the base of the throat. Then she slowly, ever so slowly, began to move down in a warm, wet swirl of movement.

Samantha's mind formed one last thought as it gave in to the non-verbal, animalistic pleasure that bloomed between her legs.

If we're going to make supper with Mrs. Pleasance and her girls, darned if we ain't going to need another bath.

CHAPTER ELEVEN

With one more round of gas-heated water and a sprinkle of lavender bathing salt, Samantha and Charlotte were able to get ready in the nick of time. Cindy brought them downstairs to an antique solarium that had been converted into a dining room. Glass walls and a veritable hedge of potted plants that surrounded the table gave the room an open, sunny feel.

Ten young women sat around a long dining table, all dressed in pastel dressing gowns that bore hues ranging from peach to periwinkle. They chatted amiably amongst themselves until Mrs. Pleasance, who presided at the head of the table like a monarch, tapped the edge of her glass with a silver-tined fork. At the sound of the tinny chime, the girls quieted down.

"Well, you both look a lot better than when you first came in," Mrs. Pleasance observed. She noticed the two eyeing the gleaming, empty plates and the immaculate silverware that perched atop the table's cloth napkins. "I take it that you're both hungry?"

"Oh, yes," Samantha agreed, as she took in the aroma of roasting meat and vegetables.

"Take a seat then," she said, and the two did just that. "The food'll be out shortly. You know Cindy Mae already, but no one else. Girls, be so kind as to introduce yourselves." She indicated a stunning young blonde on her right. "Trudy, would you start us off."

"Hi, I'm Trudy." And around the table it went: "My name's Amy." "Susie." "Mimi." "Judith." "Ruth." "Esther." "Dora." "Velma." "Florence, Flo for short."

"Hello everyone, I'm Samantha, and this is Charlotte," Samantha said in return.

"It's good to have you for company," Mrs. Pleasance said, as she turned her eye on Charlotte. "I hope you both enjoy your time here. Your friend Charlotte here hasn't said one way or the other."

"Oh, I'm right well enjoyin' myself," Charlotte said quickly, and it gave her a jolt as she thought of Samantha's lovemaking. "I'm not as...forthright as Sam is, sometimes."

"Might be a pity, that. You have a fine Southern cant to your voice. It would be a shame not to hear it more often."

With the tinkling of a bell, the servants emerged from the kitchen bearing platters of sliced roast beef, green beans slathered in butter, scalloped potatoes, freshly baked rolls, and a selection of candied fruit. Conversation came to a screeching halt as the food was served and carafes of lemonade made with nose-tickling soda water were passed around the table. For the two women, it was a special kind of torture to have to eat slowly, delicately, to match their hosts' pace. Inside, their stomachs clamored for them to greedily stuff their faces.

Around the time that everyone had finished their second helping, or were finishing up the meal with a tart piece of candied fruit, a *ping* came from a bell out in the parlor area. Mrs. Pleasance looked slightly surprised, but not alarmed.

"My, now that's an early customer," she remarked.

"Oh, that should be the town alderman," Trudy said. "He, ah, mentioned that he might be dropping by for an early visit. To see me, I mean."

"I see," Mrs. Pleasance said dryly. "Well, I suppose that you can handle this yourself?"

"At once, ma'am," Trudy said, curtseying as she left the table. A bevy of smiles and some whispered giggles ran through the assembly of young women.

"That's the second time he's been back for her," Mrs. Pleasance sighed. "I do believe that Trudy's gotten some rich buck smitten. And if I know her, she'll seal the deal. Pity. I'd been hoping she'd stay longer. She's one of the few who really had a head for the books."

"Do you mean ledgers and the like?" Charlotte asked. "They're not that hard, keeping them straight. My daddy made his fortune in dry goods, he taught me how the double-entry and depreciation tables work."

"Really," Mrs. Pleasance said, speculatively eyeing the Southern brunette.

"Yeah, really," Samantha echoed. "I had no idea you knew book keeping."

"There's lots you don't rightly know about me, Sam," Charlotte said. "Not yet, anyway."

Samantha let out a gentle laugh and took Charlotte's hand in hers. "Well, now. How was I supposed to know all that beauty came with an extra helping of smarts?"

"And a useful helping, at that," Mrs. Pleasance put in. "I don't know where you two are from, and what you're doing here, but is there any chance I could persuade you two to stay on and work with me?"

Charlotte traded the briefest of glances with Samantha before answering.

"Pardon me for asking..." Charlotte carefully watched Mrs. Pleasance and the girls for their reaction, "But y'all are...'soiled doves', ain't you?"

The women around the table broke out laughing, but in a good natured manner. Mrs. Pleasance let the laughter rise and fall, and then raised her hand until the chatter ceased. "That is what some might say, my dear. I run my social club here because this town is tolerably close to 'civilization' for comfortable living. But near enough to the frontier so that folks – lawmen and the clergy, specifically – know better than to poke their nose where it doesn't belong."

"Well...thank you, but I'd have to say 'no'. Ours is a special case."

"Special, is it? Oh, this we must hear."

"Char," Samantha said, "Do you really think we should–"

"Yes," Charlotte replied coolly. "'Way I figure it, we got to trust *somebody*. I think Missus Pleasance and her crew here will be downright sympathetic."

Surprised at Charlotte's new firmness, Samantha nodded. With that, the girls pulled up their chairs and gathered around for the story. Samantha began by explaining about her and Charlotte's lives in Chicago. Their burgeoning love, which surprised and shocked a couple of the girls, but none enough to interrupt the narrative. She then moved to their early morning escape from the city and subsequent flight west, and finished with the events of the morning.

Mrs. Pleasance steepled her fingers and remarked, "Well, it is obvious that neither of you are going to want a man in your bed. Not for love, and not for purposes of trade."

The two young women nodded vigorously at that.

"But it's also clear that you're going to need a way to make a living as you head west. You can't depend on the Lord's kindness in steering you, not alone." Her eyes swiveled to rest on Samantha's face. "You need to rely on other talents. So you need to tell me something about the run-in you had with that ruffian, Miss Williams."

"Okay," Samantha said, perplexed.

"When you put that bullet into the boardwalk, an inch from his big toe, how much of that was by *chance*, and how much of it was by *choice?*"

CHAPTER TWELVE

"I chose to put that bullet where it went," Samantha said plainly.

"As I thought." Mrs. Pleasance leaned forward in her chair and took one of Samantha's hands in her own. She manipulated the younger woman's digits, felt her palm before releasing it. "Miss Harte's hands look soft, save for marks where she's been gripping reins for the past week. Yours are different, Miss Williams. They're hard from work. Your fingers are hard from squeezing a trigger. Yet I don't get the sense that you like pulling iron on people."

"I don't. But I know how. Practiced a lot, too." Samantha hesitated, but continued as Mrs. Pleasance made a 'go on' gesture. "Before Charlotte and I went on our way, we learned an awful lot from an Aussie stable hand, old friend of the Harte family."

"He went by the name of 'Quincy'," Charlotte put in. "At least, that was his 'carnival' name. Never did find out his family name, if he had one. He only stayed with us a couple years, but he'd tell us stories fit to raise the hair on your head!"

"And he said that any daughter of a rich family had to know how to protect herself. So he taught me shooting," Samantha said proudly. "Trick shooting. Trick riding, too."

Mrs. Pleasance looked out the window for a moment, seemingly lost in thought. She nodded to herself, as if she'd made a decision.

"There's an open area around the back of the house," she said. "And no neighbors for a half-mile. Would either of you mind giving me and my girls a 'demonstration' of the skills that Mister Quincy taught you?"

Samantha shook her head. Charlotte hesitated for a moment, and then followed suit.

✳ ✳ ✳

A pair of magnificent black walnut trees provided shade for Mrs. Pleasance and the girls as they watched Samantha ride in, astride her horse. A row of playing cards, each clipped to the tops of the nearby picket fence, made a *hum* as the breeze blew past.

The women gasped in amazement as Samantha leaped out of her saddle, bounced her feet on the ground, and vaulted up and over her horse. She came back the other way, this time hanging off the side. One hand on the saddle horn, the other waving in mid-air. Her left knee stayed bent up under the stirrup fender and the other leg out straight alongside her mount.

On her next pass, she stood in the saddle with her rifle. While at a gallop, she fired at the cards along the fence. Neat holes appeared in each of the card faces.

When she'd finished, she dropped down in the saddle and rode her horse over to where the women were seated. The horse bowed down and she hopped off. Mrs. Pleasance jumped to her feet, applauding, as the girls cried out in amazement.

"Astounding!"

"You're a crack shot!"

"I ain't' never seen the like, not ever!"

"All right," Mrs. Pleasance said, quieting the little assembly. "I'd like to see what Miss Harte is planning to show us."

"Well, I don't got something as...well, as showy as Samantha." Charlotte reached into her saddlebag, which she'd brought down from the room, and pulled out a pair of thick leather coils. She let an end drop from each palm. The coils unrolled into lethal-looking bullwhips.

"Before signing on with the carnival, Quincy was a master drover," she explained, as she hoisted the whips. "He taught me what I know about these."

Charlotte went to stand out in the middle of the yard. She did a few warm ups by cracking first one whip, then the other. Alternating her wind milling action, she finishing by cracking the leather tips over her head at the same time. The girls winced at the sound at first, and then leaned forward in their wicker chairs as if hypnotized. Samantha followed suit, though her gaze conveyed more than a little dream-struck amazement.

"Sam," Charlotte called, "Pick up that rolled up piece of paper I left out on the table."

Samantha did so, stepped out fifteen feet from Charlotte's swirling whips, and gingerly held the paper by her fingers.

With a *crack*, Charlotte deftly cut a strip from the top, about an inch wide. She repeated the trick several more times, until there was only a piece about two inches long left. Samantha turned sideways and held it out from her. Charlotte cut it away with a *snap*.

"Would someone kindly give Samantha an unlit match?" Charlotte asked.

Cindy Mae did so. Samantha held the match between her index finger and thumb. Charlotte dropped one whip, then swung the other in a perfect arc from one side and across to the other.

Crack.

The match sprang to life in a puff of sulfur and a blaze of flame.

The girls let out a cheer that made the house's windows rattle, and then burst into a series of questions and exclamations.

"Oh, my stars! Have you ever seen the like?"

"Do you think you could teach me a little, Charlotte?"

Mrs. Pleasance stood up. "Ladies, please. Inside, and make yourself ready for our evening's guests." The girls did so as Samantha and Charlotte stowed away their gear, and the servant boy returned Samantha's mount to the stable.

"We're glad you liked our little performance," Samantha said.

"More than 'liked', Miss Williams. I dare say that I have a solution for your money needs. And I may have a business proposition for you. Come with me, if you please."

And with that, the two followed Mrs. Pleasance through the house and into a lushly appointed office. The furnishings had a distinct, masculine feel with dark wood, and floor to ceiling shelves stuffed to bursting with books. Tan leather chairs and rich wooden tables adorned with Tiffany lamps lightened the room. Mrs. Pleasance moved to sit behind an ornately carved mahogany desk, and then indicated to Samantha and Charlotte to sit across from her.

"All journeys, whether planned at leisure or executed in haste, have one thing in common: they must *end* somewhere. Have you given any thought to this at all?"

"Well, I've thought about San Francisco, in California. As far as a body can get from Chicago, and it's civilized enough to make us feel better than hardscrabble."

"Good, good. Then we can do business. I'm willing to put up a stake for you two, under certain conditions." She paused to pull out poster from her desk drawer. "And this is what I want you to start doing, from the moment you head out west."

CHAPTER THIRTEEN

The poster lay worn and tattered on Mrs. Pleasance's desk. But the colors were bright, and the faintest trace of freshly buttered popcorn emanated from the paper. The two young women paused to study the brightly colored images of circus tents and sparkle-spangled performers standing precariously atop white horses. A swirl of black and red ink proclaimed the title across the top: *Exhibition Extraordinary!*

Charlotte sat back, dumbstruck. "Y'all want us to be...carnies?"

"Not quite," Mrs. Pleasance pointed out. "Carnies go in large groups, and to support a large group, they'll avoid the areas you two will be travelling. You'd go as travelling performers."

"I don't mean to be rude," Samantha said, jabbing a finger towards the figures on the poster, "But I don't see how in the world Char and I can keep out of sight if we're going to be doing things like this!"

Mrs. Pleasance let out a *tsk*. "Someone's education has left out Poe's *The Purloined Letter*. The best place to hide..."

"...is in plain sight," Samantha finished. "I did read that, come to think of it. I've kept up to date with the latest books, after all. I just didn't think that such advice would come in handy."

"Then consider it for a moment. Your parents – specifically, your father – will have people looking for two young American women, each riding a specifically described horse, travelling the off roads and trying to stay out of sight. They won't be looking for two foreign-born performers driving a couple wagon carts and playing to audiences in all sorts of towns along the way."

"Sam and I...we know a little French, but that's just a smidge," Charlotte said, though it was a weak protest. Her eyes gleamed with interest.

"Really?" Mrs. Pleasance laughed heartily. "And who do you think you'll be playing to out in the Territories, the Parisian consulate? I'll provide you with some continental *couture*. Trust me: when you head west of the Mississippi, just stay quiet, mysterious. All you need to do is drop a couple words of *la belle Française* from time to time. No one will know the difference."

"You're a step away from convincing me," Samantha said, trying vainly to damp down her hopes. "But what are these 'wagon carts' you're talking about? We don't have the funds—"

"I know you don't. That's why I plan to extend a loan to you. But only if you want to go into business with me."

"We're listening, Missus Pleasance."

"The reason I'm so well off isn't because I run a high-class social club here in town," she explained. "It's because I run *three*." She raised a hand to forestall their questions. "If I meet a woman of extraordinary character and skill, I agree to back them to found their own social club, saloon, or house of ill-repute. They in turn send me back a percentage of their profits. Everyone wins. Even our hard-up customers."

A glance to Charlotte; a quick nod. "We're *still* listening."

"You girls are a special pair, and I don't mean your choice of bed partners. You've got pluck and dash aplenty. You've got the skills to get out west and run a house like this. And you've proven that you're willing to stand up and defend yourself as well as others."

Mrs. Pleasance paused. Made sure she had their attention before she continued.

"I've traveled the territories before myself. I can promise you one thing: the trip won't be easy. In fact it'll be damned hard, even if you have the proper equipment. So. How bad do you want to go to California?"

Samantha looked Mrs. Pleasance straight in the eyes and replied, "Char and I have dreamt about being together for four years."

"Fair enough. I'll draw up a contract that gives me one-third interest in the profits of your travelling show, and the social club you start in San Francisco. For my part of the investment, once you arrive at your destination, I'll introduce you to my contacts in the city, get you the capital you'll need. And at the outset, I'll outfit you with the equipment to get you from here to California."

"The wagon carts, you mean?" Charlotte asked.

"For a start." Mrs. Pleasance said, and her voice took on a deadly serious tone. "But there's some mighty untamed country between here and California. A pair of fillies like you, traveling across country alone are bound to be an invitation to trouble. I'll be sending an assistant along with you. For starters, he'll help you with setting up and tear down of the shows equipment."

"He? Look, we don't need another–" Samantha began. She quieted at Mrs. Pleasant's glare.

"I said for *starters*. I'm sending this man with you to protect my investment. He's a trusted hand with animals and firearms. He's also a trusted friend of the family. And he's part of the deal, take it or leave it." Mrs. Pleasance sat back in her plush chair and surveyed the two women. "So. What do you say?"

A moment of silence passed between the two young women.

"Charlotte," Samantha said, softly, "You were right, you know...we did need to trust someone. And now we have this opportunity."

"You don't need to convince me," Charlotte said. "I'm in if you're in."

Samantha nodded. She stood and extended her hand to Mrs. Pleasance. "The answer's yes. Wholeheartedly yes!"

"Then it's settled," Mrs. Pleasance also stood, and shook Samantha's hand firmly. Her eyes twinkled. "When I was growin' up, we used to seal deals with a 'spit and a handshake'. But instead of the spit, how about we pour ourselves a sip of bourbon? We're short on ice, but I'm sure you girls can handle it straight-up neat."

"We're game," Samantha said, and Mrs. Pleasance pulled a bottle from a shelf behind her desk and set out three small glasses.

"Here's a thought," she said, as she poured, "You'll need to come up with some stage names. Make it tough for your families to track you down."

"They'll have to be good names," Samantha said. "Not based on our real names, or middle names. Otherwise it'll be obvious."

"Good names..." Charlotte mused, and the title of the poster caught her eye. "Extraordinary names, I'd venture."

"You have an idea, Char?"

"Not about our stage names. But for the act...I rather fancy *'Exhibition Extraordinary'*. Let's say we adapt it for us women, make it more 'continental'. *La Femme Exhibition Extraordinaire*, as the French would say."

"I like the sound of that," Mrs. Pleasance said, as she passed around the glasses. Holding the amber-colored liquid in her glass to the light, she proclaimed: "A toast to the success of *La Femme Exhibition Extraordinaire!*"

The sips of bourbon went down the hatch with a blaze of creamy-tasting molasses smoke. Mrs. Pleasance sighed, savoring the flavor. Samantha and Charlotte each let out a cough as the strong alcohol overwhelmed their taste buds.

"It's an acquired taste, my dears," she reassured them. "Much like my clientele. So unless you want to be pulled into the festivities tonight, stay up in your suite and work on the details of your show's acts. Breakfast tomorrow – and then, all three of us have a lot of work ahead."

CHAPTER FOURTEEN

The pounding of hooves coming down the road at a gallop made the telegraph clerk sit up straight. He glanced at the beat-up clock on the wall; surely, no one could be out this late at night. Not when there were no trains due into Springfield until the morning. Curious, he leaned out the window of his little railway office. A man rode up and brought his horse to a stop, just within the bright glow of the station lanterns.

The man dismounted stiffly, with great weariness. He brought his mud-spattered mustang over to the horse trough and hurriedly untacked his mount while the animal drank deeply from the cool water. The clerk's gimlet-eyed stare inventoried the newcomer's gear: a Winchester stuck out from the man's saddle and a Colt rested in a quick draw rig on his hip.

Whoever it was, he meant business. The clerk watched as the man trudged up the station house steps, pausing only to brush off the worst of the road dust. His silver concho'd vest glinted in the dim light as he pushed his way through the office door.

"Howdy, stranger," the clerk said. "Y'all are out in some strange hours."

"Don't I know it," the man replied. "I'm here to pick up a bundle of messages. Should be addressed to Matthew Slade."

"Slade, Slade..." The clerk turned to pull a small bundle of folded paper from a shelf. "Yup, it's right here. How d'you plan on paying for the Western Union's service?"

In answer, Slade pulled back his vest and laid his Pinkerton badge on the clerk's desk with a *thump*. The clerk swallowed and handed over the bundle without another word. Slade picked up his badge, and then spread the messages out on a nearby table. The papers glistened like buttery wax in the yellow light of the lanterns outside.

From Saint Louis, Missouri: "CARRIAGE POSTS WATCHED FROM CHESTERFIELD TO CARLYLE -(STOP)- NO SIGHTINGS REPORTED"

From Madison, Wisconsin: "ALL HORSE TRAFFIC PUSHED INTO NORTHERN LAKE CORRIDOR DUE TO FLOODING -(STOP)- EVERY RIDER AND CONVEYANCE WATCHED WITH NO SIGHTINGS"

From Toledo, Ohio: "REPORTS OF GIRL RIDERS INVESTIGATED -(STOP)- NOT OUR TARGETS -(STOP)- CONTINUING TO MONITOR"

From Indianapolis, Indiana: "WATCHING ALL ROADS -(STOP)- NO ENTRIES ALONG ROADS REPORTED THAT MATCH REQUEST"

Slade's heel scraped on the wooden floor as he turned to face the adjoining wall. A map of the entire region, dotted with passing travelers' notes, hung precariously by a single nail. Murmuring to himself, Slade traced out routes and cities with one grimy finger.

"So you two ain't been goin' north, south, or east." Slade's palm swept in an arc along Illinois' sparsely populated western border. "I should've listened to my instincts."

The clerk watched Matthew Slade warily as the man got more agitated. The Pinkerton detective tapped his fingers along a wide, ragged blue line to the west of Springfield. With a gleam in his eye, Slade turned and spoke.

"I need to get across that river." he declared. "What's the fastest place for me to cross?"

"Hmm," the clerk said, joining Slade at the map. "Beardstown's closest as the crow flies."

"What if the crow's riding a tired horse at this time of night?"

"In that case, you're gonna have to ride north to Peoria."

Slade cursed. "That'll take me an extra two days! The party I'm chasing down has gotten a four, five day head start on me as it is!"

"Well, then I'd try Beardstown. But the bridge there is washed out," the clerk said carefully, his Midwestern accent cutting 'washed' into *warshed*. "I hear that there's a ferry service too, but it only runs twice a day."

"I'll chance it," came the terse reply. He turned over one of the telegrams and scribbled a message on the blank side.

"NOTIFY CLIENTS SW&CH NOT FOUND IN REPORTS FROM PINKERTON OFFICES NORTH-SOUTH-EAST -(STOP)- HEADING WEST OF ILLINOIS RIVER AND INTO MISSOURI IF NECESSARY -(STOP)- NEXT POST AS SOON AS TRAIL PICKED UP"

"Address this to the Pinkerton office in Cook County, Chicago," Slade instructed, as he slid the paper into the telegraph clerk's waiting hands.

The clerk took out his spectacles and scrutinized the message. "Right away, Mister–"

But the Pinkerton man had already strode out of the room, leaving behind only a cloud of dust.

※ ※ ※

Morning sun streamed in through the Rosewood room's leaded glass windows as Samantha and Charlotte repacked their last change of clothes. The garments had been freshly washed and line-dried, courtesy of Mrs. Pleasance's staff. Samantha pulled the last saddlebag shut and buckled it with an air of finality as a knock came at the door.

"Missus Pleasance!" Charlotte said happily, as the older woman stood in the open doorway, appraising the couple, now nattily re-attired in their riding gear. "We were expectin' to see you at breakfast."

"Indeed, breakfast is waiting for us," Mrs. Pleasance replied, "But I wanted to see how you two were getting along. Did you sleep at all?"

Charlotte blushed a little as Samantha answered. "Well enough, after a little while. One of your girls got busy entertaining a gentleman in the next room. She must've done one heck of a job, between the moaning and the banging of the bed against the wall."

"My apologies for keeping you up. Business is business, after all."

"Oh, no worries. Matter of fact, the sounds got us both a little bothered, and we had to..."

"Find our own sources of entertainment," Charlotte finished, blushing more deeply.

Mrs. Pleasance struggled to contain herself, but in the end, she gave up and laughed. "Well then, come on down and let me show you how you'll be travelling in style from here on."

The two girls followed her down the stairs, where the aromas of fresh coffee, fried eggs, and the salty scent of bacon greeted them. But instead of entering the dining room, Mrs. Pleasance led the girls down a side hallway and out into the back courtyard.

Charlotte gasped at the sight of a large red wagon. Samantha just stared.

"Well? What do you think?"

"What do I think?" Samantha's voice came out in a near squeak. "I think...it's beautiful!"

The pair of matched sorrel draft horses attached to the wagon snorted disdainfully as the two girls explored the strange-looking conveyance. The wagon's sides had been painted in a bright apple red and decorated in elaborate gilt trim. A window dotted each side and the rear section sloped out into a 'porch' with Dutch-style doors each with a second set of windows, protected by bright blue shutters.

Charlotte threw open the doors and folded down a set of well-worn wooden steps. The scent of tea and peppermint greeted the two girls as they gazed inside. A cozy double-sleeping berth framed with white curtains took up one side; on the other, a tiny stove fitted with a tin chimney that stuck up through the roof. Samantha gave a low whistle as she looked over the stuffed pantry, a filled-to-the-brim water crock, and the packed shelves – which had each been outfitted with raised lips like those of a ship's kitchen.

"It's called a *vardo*," Mrs. Pleasance said. "It's designed for living in, especially for show folks that have to travel a long ways."

"Where did you ever find something like this?" Samantha asked.

"I didn't. My assistant, the one who'll be accompanying you, did." She turned to a tall, lanky figure that emerged from the doorway like a dusky shadow. "Ain't that right, Jude?"

"Indeed, I did find it. It still makes me think of it as mine, in a way."

At the newcomer's tone, the girls quickly stepped down from the wagon, as if they'd been caught trespassing.

Jude's hair was the gray of puddled steel, cropped close to a perfectly round skull. An equally gray beard had been trimmed within an inch, Army-style, across his chin. Wrinkles lined his eyes and neck, the sign of age and hard outdoor living. But masses of ropy muscle bulged under his denim leggings and rough-hewn shirt.

The color of the man's skin matched the ebony credenza in the private dining room. Save for the weathered look of his hands and the light coffee-brown of his eyes. Those same eyes swept over them, judging them with a practiced gaze.

"So you're the two who thought you could gallivant across the country on your own," Jude said, in a cultured baritone voice. He turned to Mrs. Pleasance. "Why, in all of God's wisdom, must he make those in love so blind to danger around them?"

CHAPTER FIFTEEN

"Jude Davis," Mrs. Pleasance said sternly, "Don't be so hard on them. They were brought up city girls, and they're still learnin' their way."

The man made a snort not unlike the one from the draft horses in reply. Samantha stepped forward. She looked up at the tall man, direct but as friendly as she could make her expression.

"Mister Davis," she said, "We're honored to be given the use of this wagon. And Missus Pleasance is right, at least in part. We're city girls. But we're *from* the city, not *of* it, if you see what I mean. With your help, we can take care of ourselves. Please don't judge us until you've ridden with us."

Jude gave them a look-over once more. Charlotte added her beaming smile to Samantha's. The man's stern expression wavered. He rubbed the back of his neck with one weathered hand before he spoke.

"I've been on the trail too long, ladies. It can make a man unduly harsh. I hope you can excuse me. I know what it's like to be judged at first sight, sure enough." He sighed, adding, "But we're going to pass through some tough parts, that much is true. I want you to promise that you will heed me when I need you to!"

"We will!" the girls replied.

With that settled, Mrs. Pleasance took Jude by the arm and led them all inside to the dining room. In a flash, plates were laid out with heaping portions of eggs, bacon, and summer sausage. Between bites, the conversation went on.

"Aside from being your trail guide," Mrs. Pleasance said, "Jude's going along to take care of my interests. He carries letters from me introducing you to my contacts where you will be performing along the way. With him along, you'll be in safe hands. I trust him with my life."

"And you have," Jude said, between fragrant sips of coffee.

Mrs. Pleasance nodded. "It's true. He's got an experienced hand with horses and with firearms."

"If you don't mind, Mister Davis, I'm curious to know where–" Charlotte started to say, before the man shook his head.

"Just call me by my first name," he said. "I've not been 'Mister Davis' for over a decade. Back when I played second-fiddle to a Lieutenant who was too big for his britches."

"Well, I was just curious..." Charlotte began again, "Jude, where did you learn where to ride, where to shoot? The Union Army? During our country's...late unpleasantness?"

Jude gave her a look. "Miss Charlotte, in my experience, only our Southern neighbors call our Civil War by its more pleasant alternatives."

"I'm Southern by birth. But my Daddy lit out for Chicago once the guns fired on Fort Sumter. He supported the Union, and my family...well, at least I know that my folks...they ain't never owned nobody. They didn't believe in treating people as property, and neither do I."

He nodded at that. "Thank you for putting my mind at ease, then. I was born free, in Philadelphia, and fortunate enough to have been home schooled. I learned how to shoot when I joined up with the Union Army, and got sergeant's bars sewn to my shoulder when someone found out that I knew how to read and write."

"And the ridin'?"

"After the war, I was still pig-headed about wanting to serve. So they put me in the 10th Cavalry, out here on the frontier."

"Put the fear of God into a lot of the Indians," Mrs. Pleasance added.

"Yes, ma'am, we did. They called us the Buffalo Soldiers, for our pains. I left the service a while back, bummed around as a cowpoke until Missus Pleasance hired me on. But if I've learned one thing out here, it's this: it doesn't matter if a man's red, black, or white. They can be angels, or they can be devils biding their time, waiting to stick a knife in your back."

Charlotte repressed a shudder. "Is that...what happened to whoever owned the vardo? Before you found it, I mean."

"No, thank the Lord. That vardo belonged to an honest-to-goodness real gypsy. He pulled into Beardstown, just east of here across the river, a few years ago, dying of consumption. I got him to the hospital, but he didn't make it. At the last, he willed his wagon over to me."

"And when Jude came to work for my social club, I purchased it," Mrs. Pleasance finished. "I've kept it in good repair, thinking I might use it someday to head back East in style, see some more of the country. But I think you two can put it to better use."

"I figure we can," Samantha said, "But what of our own horses?"

"They'll be coming along, no worries. But they don't have the build to handle long-distance hauling. You can keep them tied behind the vardo, or the freight wagon."

Samantha blinked at that. Mrs. Pleasance let out a laugh and Jude slapped his knee as he laughed alongside of her.

"Yes, we'll need a freight wagon, one big enough to need a four-mule team. We've got to have some way of carrying enough equipment, water and grain for all our stock. And a place for me to sleep." Jude's face crinkled into a grin. "Even if you gals weren't into the fairer of the two genders, it's a mite too cozy in that vardo for three."

"I don't know if I could handle a set of draft horses, let alone mules," Charlotte said. "I ain't never done anything like that before. Straight up ridin' is all I know, and not much of that."

"I know riding well enough," Samantha put in. "But I'll admit, driving a team? That's a new one for me, too."

"Well, then," Jude said. He put down his coffee cup with a *clink*. "There's no time like the present to get some experience."

"What, you mean, right...now?"

"I had your bags and saddles taken from your mounts and stowed in the vardo," Mrs. Pleasance explained. Her voice caught in her throat as she added, "I didn't think you'd mind. And although I enjoy your girls' company, we're starting to burn precious daylight with all our talkin'."

Tearfully, Charlotte and Samantha hugged Mrs. Pleasance and promised to send a telegram from their first performance, as soon as they crossed into Missouri. And just when the two thought that they had to leave, each and every one of Mrs. Pleasance's girls gathered in the parlor to wish them tearful farewells.

Jude had to silence any more conversation with a silent, dark glare. He led the two young women outside, where they climbed into the vardo's seat while he mounted the freight wagon. With a whistle and a crack of the reins, Jude got his wagon, its sturdy side piled high with the party's stores, rolling along. Samantha followed suit as she got the vardo's heavy draft horses moving.

Mrs. Pleasance watched as the two teams shrank slowly in the distance. Her heart lay heavy, though she knew that she'd outfitted them the best that she could. The shiny tip of the vardo's chimney glinted one last time as they crested a hill to the west, and then they were gone.

Suddenly, she heard a series of distant *bangs* and the whinnies of frightened horses. She turned and squinted down towards the opposite end of Main Street. Her hand flew to her mouth as she saw the unmistakable flash of gunfire.

CHAPTER SIXTEEN

Matthew Slade pulled his mustang up short as he rode past a newly painted street sign labeled *Welcome to Pleasance, Illinois – Pop. 3016 & Growing*. His horse blew hard, tired from the hours of fast riding. Slade dismounted and looped his reins hurriedly over the hitching rail at a nearby trough. The Pinkerton man stepped into the shadow of the nearest of the town's buildings and pulled his Colt.

He'd heard the muffled sound of a gunshot, from inside one of the buildings ahead. He stepped forward along the makeshift sidewalk. The fresh boards squeaked under his boots. He hadn't gone more than a dozen steps when heard a gruff voice.

"That's far enough, stranger."

Slade froze, and then slowly lifted his hands. The bearded, pot-bellied man who approached, gun in hand, bore a silver star on his vest. The man scowled, though not unkindly.

"You got a look about you that says 'law'," the man said. "Put your iron away, slow-like, and show me if I'm right."

"You're right," Slade replied. He carefully holstered his Colt and then pulled out his own badge. "I'm Matthew Slade, Pinkerton Detective Agency."

"I'm Elias Moody, sheriff for this town." The two shook hands as Moody added, "Pinkerton, eh? Damn fine luck you're here. Townsfolk say that there's a holdup goin' on in the bank. I just sent my deputies on over. From the description, it sounds like the James brothers."

Slade's eyes blazed with a terrible eagerness. "You're on target again, old-timer. Damn fine luck. Damn fine."

The two men approached the bank warily, keeping to the doorways and shadows. Across the street, two deputies, each armed with a rifle, also kept under cover as the sounds of shouts echoed from inside the bank's main office.

Slade frowned. The James-Younger gang had been at the top of Pinkerton list for a long time – not in the least for killing three veteran agents in as many years. But the gang supposedly operated in Missouri and Arkansas. What had drawn them here?

His musing cut short as six men burst through the bank doors. Black bandannas hid the lower half of their faces. Their garb ranged from mud-spattered black to ragged, patchwork gray dusters. Two carried bulging cloth sacks. But the remaining four came out with guns blazing.

The deputies opened up. None of their shots hit, but it kept the bank robbers from mounting up. The robbers returned fire with deadly accuracy. One of the deputies dropped where he stood. A quiver, and the man went still.

"Damn it!" Moody raged.

The sheriff fired wildly in the bank's general direction. His shots shattered windows and wounded one of the robbers' horses. Panicked, the animal reared and galloped madly down the street.

Slade carefully took aim and dropped the first man who swung into his saddle. He squinted at the man's face as he rolled to the ground, his chest marked with a ragged red hole. Recognized him as one of Jesse's henchmen. One of the men who'd slaughtered three of Pinkerton's finest. Slade's face went red with anger.

Moody's gun clicked empty. The sheriff dropped back behind a water barrel for cover as he reloaded. Two of the taller men, the James brothers for sure, put up a murderous fire. Slade rolled, got to his feet, and emptied his gun as quickly as he could.

His first shot ruffled the edge of one of the James' black jackets. The last knocked a second man from his horse with an agonized scream. The man grabbed his leg, while the bag of money he'd been carrying spilled out on the muddy ground.

Slade moved to one side, seeking cover to reload. He felt a terrific *CRACK* along the side of his head. His vision went red and shimmery. He staggered, then collapsed as all went black.

It stayed dark as Slade swam in and out of consciousness for a while. He felt himself being bandaged, being moved. The tang of rubbing alcohol and the taste of some horrible elixir.

More darkness. More jostling. Then his nose picked up the scent of bourbon. Flowers. Fine French perfume. The sound of young women laughing. The tinkle of a piano.

A thought ran through his mind: *Damn strange hospital this is.*

He opened his eyes with a groan.

"Well, looks like you decided to join the living after all, Detective," came the jocular voice of Sheriff Moody.

Slade blinked. His eyes focused on Moody's rotund figure. Next to him sat a buxom, orange-haired woman done up in fine Continental fashion. He blinked. Instead of the plain walls of a country sawbones house, he saw fine wallpaper and carved wooden cabinets. Instead of a hospital bed, he reclined comfortably in a four-poster bed. Save for the massive bandage around his head, he felt reasonably whole.

"What the...where am I?"

"You're the guest at my Social Club," said the woman. "I'm Mrs. Pleasance, and this is the least I could do for someone who took down two of the James gang."

"Two?"

"We identified the one you killed as part of the James gang," Moody said. "The other's a local boy that was dumb enough to sign on with them. Thanks to you, they're on the run now, and with less than half of what they were tryin' to steal from the bank. We looked through your papers and figured that we better notify the Pinkerton office in Chicago."

"You went through my..." Slade scowled. "How long have I been out?"

"A whole day," Mrs. Pleasance informed him. "Your office said that you're in for a nice bonus, once you're able to get to your feet again."

"I feel fine," Slade insisted. He sat up in bed. Felt the entire room sway sickeningly. He flopped back down, head aching.

"That's the nature of a concussion, Mister Slade. Especially one given by a glancing bullet. On your back, you think you can conquer the world. Sitting up is goin' to take a little longer."

"Aw, damn it all..." Slade said. He put his forearm across his eyes, felt the dull throb of pain in his temples. "I'm on a job. Looking for two young women..."

Sheriff Moody and Mrs. Pleasance traded the quickest of glances. He opened his mouth to speak. She shook her head quickly: *No.*

"You need your rest," Mrs. Pleasance said firmly. She tapped some more powder into the water by his bedside and brought it to his mouth. "Drink up. This will help you sleep."

Slade did so gratefully. In a moment, he let out a snore.

Moody gave her a sharp glance. "Are you sure you know what you're doing?"

"As sure as I know that the sun'll come up in the east, and set in the west. When Slade heals up, you can tell him all you want. But until then, he's my responsibility." She smiled wickedly. "And I know that my girls can keep him 'convalescing' quite happily for some time yet."

CHAPTER SEVENTEEN

Samantha hadn't felt so happy, so alive, since she'd made the decision to head west with Charlotte. The sun finally broke through the clouds, turning the day warm and muggy, but she hardly noticed. The rolling hills and open country smelled like a spirit-lifting mix of freshly cut hay and fragrant wildflowers.

Lost in her thoughts, she almost missed it when Jude Davis, who led the way with the freight wagon, called out 'Whoa!' and slowly brought his team to a halt.

She gave the reins of her wagon team a strong pull back. A bit too strong. The draft horses stopped with a jerk and pair of annoyed snorts. Charlotte, who had been drowsing on the seat next to her, startled awake.

"What is it?"

"Easy, Char," Samantha replied. "Sorry. I'm still getting used to driving the big girls here."

Charlotte looked around. "Why'd we stop? Jude, is it lunchtime already?"

"Yes, but we're not set for an early supper, not yet." Jude said, as he set his wagon's brake, stepped down, and strode over to the side of their vardo. He stretched his arms wide and indicated the areas off to the sides of the road. The stretch of road bisected a large clearing. A small creek burbled off to one edge, but the rest of the ground was flat and dry. "We're in a perfect spot for you two to practice driving your teams."

Samantha set her own brake and handed the reins of the vardo over to Charlotte. She got down and then took Jude's now-empty seat on the freight wagon. Charlotte listened intently as Jude explained how the small front wheels on the vardo were used for steering, while the larger back wheels allowed it to navigate rougher terrain.

He then explained to Samantha how to gently handle the pairs of mules; her biggest challenge would be turning the heavy freight wagon in a reasonable time. With that, he unhitched the two riding horses from the back of the vardo and stood back. Charlotte and Samantha drove their teams in wide circles or back-and-forth serpentine patterns on either side of the clearing.

Jude stayed where he was, calling out instructions or advice as needed; but to his surprise, they never got stuck, never asked for help. By the time an hour had gone by, both young women had worked up a sweat. Their hands ached from tugging the reins. Their voices had started to get raspy from the constant calls (and a few curses) they directed at their teams.

"Very good!" Jude called. "Now, *switch teams!*"

With a groan, they did so.

Another hour went by, though it seemed to fly. When Jude called a halt, he pronounced their 'basic road manners' acceptable. After the wagons had been driven back to the side of the road, he reached into the back of the freight wagon. He came up with a jug of fresh water, a picnic blanket, and a wicker basket.

"Courtesies of Missus Pleasance," he said, as he handed the items to Samantha. "The basket's full of stuff that won't keep past a day, so be sure and get it eaten."

"Oh, that we can do. Should we save some for dinner as well?"

Jude shook his head. "Not planning on spending this night on the road. By dusk, we should be at the ferry crossing into Hannibal."

"Crossing the Mississippi River," Charlotte breathed. Samantha looked at her curiously. "Sam, this is a mighty big thing for me. I always saw it on the map as...well, the final boundary between the settled part of the country..."

"...And the unsettled one. I know how you feel." Samantha agreed. "I figured that Missus Pleasance had a route in mind for us."

"She did indeed," Jude agreed. "And she figured that the first, best place for you to test out your 'Exhibition Extra-Ordinary' would be just outside Hannibal. The place is big enough to give you a decent sized audience. We'll soon find out if you two can earn enough coin to keep our trip going."

With that, Jude climbed into the freight wagon and began rummaging around. Charlotte looked up from where she'd spread out the red-and-white checkered picnic blanket under a nearby tree. "Aren't you going to join us?"

"In due time. You both have been running our stock pretty hard, with the exception of the riding horses. I need to tend to our draft mares and mules first." Jude began whistling as he brought the teams down to the creek in turns for watering, and then made sure that the animals all got fed.

When he returned to join Charlotte and Samantha for the remainder of the basket's contents, they were laughing merrily. He sat, and with a trace of his old scowl, he asked, "What's gotten into you two?"

"The French, that's what's gotten into us!" Samantha said, chuckling.

"*Les Français*, you mean" Charlotte corrected her. "We still had to pick our stage names, our travelling names for our show: *La Femme Exhibition Extraordinaire! Bonjour Monsieur Davis, je suis...Dominique!*"

"*Et moi...*oh, hell...*je suis 'Veronica'.*" Samantha quirked a grin at Jude. "*C'est un bon nom, n'est pas?*"

"Now you're speaking all fancy on me." Jude took a swig out of the water jug as he shook his head. "Ironic, that's what it is. Just as your speech is going to get more refined, mine's got to get a lot worse."

"What do you mean?"

"You'll hear it soon enough. Remember, I'm your hired servant, so you're letting me do the talking. And keep in mind, we're heading into *Missouri*. One of the states that the Confederacy claimed as their own. And trust me, they don't let people like me forget it for one second."

CHAPTER EIGHTEEN

Samantha watched the swift, coffee-colored water slip by under the ferry's bow from the upper deck. The sun hung low on the horizon before her, a dull red ember buried in banks of iron-gray clouds. The country ahead looked the same as the landscape behind her – low, lush, and dark green. But it held promise.

The West.

So far, the ferry ride over the Mississippi had been uneventful, save for the stares they'd drawn upon boarding. The heavy freight wagon pulled by the team of stout mules didn't attract attention. The two young French women, and their bright red gypsy wagon got more than a few strange looks.

And yet, Mrs. Pleasance's idea to 'hide in plain sight' was working. Despite the looks, no one challenged them or even so much as spoke to them. Once the onlookers spotted the brightly colored vardo, their interest abruptly waned. As if their minds finally figured out where to classify them: *Show People.*

Samantha heard a footstep behind her, just as her nose was tickled – no, assaulted – by the scent of flowers mixed with fresh cedar shavings.

"*Bon soir,* Mademoiselle Dominique," she said, half turning to where Charlotte came up to lean against the railing with her.

"Well, I'll be," said Charlotte, "How did you know I was comin' up?"

Samantha glanced about, saw that they were alone on the upper deck. She relaxed. "That scent you're wearing. I bet half the ferry would guess you're around."

Charlotte laughed. "It's powerful stuff, give it that. But I find it a mite helpful in keepin' with our 'continental' role."

"Speaking of which, who's down with the vardo? Jude?"

"He's off makin' talk with some of the other drivers. Says he wants to know the lay of the land ahead of us. But he said it'd be okay if I wanted to come up here to be with you."

Shyly, Charlotte placed her hand on Samantha's, intertwining their fingers. Together, they watched as the far shore drew close. Soon, they were able to pick out the individual buildings that lined Hannibal's streets. Rows of whitewashed buildings. A handful of church steeples. And a set of long piers that jutted out like welcoming arms towards the approaching ferry.

Samantha watched the first scattering of lights brighten the town's windows as dusk settled. She was about to comment on it when she heard a lecherous wolf-whistle from behind them. Charlotte let out a gasp as a pair of men sauntered out from the shadows.

"Well, lookee here," said the first, a man with a scraggly beard and the build of a swollen rain barrel. "Din' I tell you, Ezra? Follow the smell of a gen-wine French cat house to find our two birds."

The second man, who was as whippet-lean as his companion was fat, nodded along with an idiotic, snaggle-toothed grin on his face.

"That's what y'all said, Zeke. And here are our birds," Ezra replied. He pursed his lips and made a second whistle, this one mimicking the warbling of a bird. "Real chicks made for pluckin'! Ain't that right, ladies? Or is it 'Maddy-mah-zells'?"

Charlotte froze. She couldn't make out the two men's features well in the failing light, but she saw the evil glint in their eyes. Samantha shook free of Charlotte's grasp. The last thing she wanted was to attract attention – but in her fear, her hand went right to her gun.

And then, to her relief, she heard Jude's voice calling for them.

"Missus Veronica! Missus Dominique!" Jude passed to one side of the two men and shuffled his way in front of them. His eyes caught Samantha's, nodded towards her grip on her gun. He shook his head *no* as he continued his patter. "My, am I shore glad I found you! We got to get shovin' if we're gitten off!"

Now it was Samantha's turn to freeze. Her brain tripped on whatever French phrases she'd practiced before. But this time, Charlotte stepped in to save them.

"*Qu'est que vous...*" She stomped her foot, playing as if she were annoyed, then continued on, erasing her Southern accent with a comic French one. "Who says zat we must be 'shoving'?"

"The captain o' dis here boat, he's tole me dat he bin watchin' y'all." Jude pointed up at the wheelhouse window, high above the deck. "He said we best git goin'!"

Ezra and Zeke glanced up towards the wheelhouse. Without another word, they faded back into the shadows. Samantha released her hold on her weapon, but tensed one final time. As they slunk away, she thought she spotted a third figure. Whoever it was waited a moment longer, and then followed the two men as they withdrew.

Jude's voice sounded terse in her ear. "Been talkin' to the other drivers. Word has it that there's some folks on this boat that don't take too kindly to 'darkies'. Or women who're uppity enough to step outside without a chaperone."

"Damned bad luck," Samantha groused.

"Real bad. You two remember what I said about heeding me when I said to?"

The two women nodded.

"Now's one of them times. Time for us to get back to the wagons. Keep your gun handy. As soon as this ferry docks, just follow me. Figure that if they follow us, we can lose 'em on the dark roads outside of town."

Charlotte grimaced. "Guess it was too much to hope for, gettin' another night in a nice soft bed. And the way y'all have to talk..."

Jude laughed mirthlessly. "Well, now iffen I don't, folks out here might take to hang me, while I is a carryin' on with two high born white gals."

Back on the lower deck, Charlotte swallowed hard, but picked up the reins to the vardo as Samantha sat next to her, tense but alert. Samantha's eyes scanned the deck restlessly, fully expecting Ezra and Zeke to make a return appearance.

But no one gave them so much as a second glance as the ferry bumped to a stop and tied up next to the dock. With a clatter, they disembarked and rode along dusty streets lit by smoky, will o' the wisp lantern light. Jude took them completely through town and out into the fields to the west.

By then, night had truly fallen. In place of the lanterns, the moon rose full and bright, illuminating the way. Another hour, and Jude called a halt. They hastily set up camp. Given their tired state, Samantha and Charlotte really started to appreciate the vardo. The set-up was absurdly simple. A chock for the wheels, and it was ready for the night. They began to gather firewood, but Jude waved them off.

"No fire tonight," Jude called over from the seat of his wagon. "Might attract attention. Stick with one of the lanterns inside your vardo. You two get yourself some sleep. I'm staying up tonight, keep an eye on things."

"Are you sure you don't need me to–" Samantha began.

Jude hefted the rifle he'd kept next to him. "There's nothing out here that Mister Winchester and I can't handle."

With that, the two women opened up the rear of the vardo and went inside. Between the dim light of the lantern and the unfamiliar confines of the cabin, they bumped shins and elbows as they shed their clothes.

"I've been wound as tight as a watch-spring since those two men approached us," Charlotte said, plaintively. "I could...I mean, I could really use some comfort tonight."

"Come here," Samantha replied, and Charlotte buried herself in Samantha's arms, shivering. The two lay down in the vardo's bed, snug as two peas in a pod.

Samantha nuzzled the lush crown of hair on Charlotte's head, breathing in her scent. She listened to the chirp of crickets outside. She continued to caress Charlotte until the shudders slowly ceased. She smiled. It wasn't lovemaking, not exactly, but it was something else.

Charlotte's voice floated up from somewhere below in the darkness.

"Sam?"

"Hm?"

"I don't think I've ever felt what I did today, on that boat. I mean, I've been scared before, bad like." Charlotte shifted to her side and turned her head so that she could look at the woman who held her close. "But today...in those men's eyes...we didn't mean *nothin'*. Like we were just somethin' for them to use. Then throw away. Or kill, if it were more convenient."

"Yeah...men like that exist." Samantha shuddered. "I know."

Charlotte threw her a startled look. "What do you mean?"

Samantha looked away for a moment. "I thought I'd be ready for this," she murmured. "To tell you."

A moment of silence stretched awkwardly between them.

"Tell me. Please."

Samantha took a deep breath, as if ready to plunge into icy waters, and began to speak.

CHAPTER NINETEEN

"You know that my father wanted me marrying so that our family could move up in the world," Samantha began. "But he never knew that his little...social marker...was actually damaged goods."

Charlotte gave her an uneasy look. "What do you mean?"

"I mean that I lost my virginity when I was fifteen. Back when we still lived in Boston. It was one of my father's old cronies. Father was on a business trip the first time he raped me. It hurt, Char. A lot."

Charlotte squeezed her tighter. Samantha bit back her tears.

"I thought it was the worst thing he could've done. But when he was...done...he told me something worse."

"What was that?" Charlotte whispered.

"The truth. That my father wouldn't have believed me even if I had told him."

"My God...do you really think that?"

"Even if he did, all he'd want would be some kind of payment for the use of his daughter."

"I'm...sorry to hear that, Sam."

"Hush, now." Samantha reached up, turned down the flame on the lantern so that it guttered out. "I think that sometimes, things happen – even bad things – for some kind of purpose."

Charlotte shuddered. "What kind of purpose would there have been, for some man to take you...against your will like that?"

"We never really know. But I think that's when I knew what my future would be. That I'd have to leave someday. And if that's what was going to happen, I had to figure out how to get tougher. To do the things to survive out here. To do the things..."

"Yes?"

"To do the things that would bring me here. With you."

Charlotte thought about it for a while in the darkness. She raised up for a moment and pressed her warm lips to her lover's. She sensed more than saw the sleepy smile that resulted.

Samantha sighed contentedly and pulled Charlotte on top of her like a blanket as she dozed off.

※ ※ ※

Charlotte woke to the sounds of chopping wood and nearby conversation. She pulled the rough cloth of the bed around her and sat up, coming within an inch of knocking her forehead on the vardo's roof. Samantha was nowhere to be seen. Sunlight gleamed through the cracks of the vardo's shutters and she cautiously peeked outside.

She caught a glimpse of Jude ambling by. A couple of red-headed teenagers with axes slung over their shoulders followed him. Charlotte let out a squeak as the vardo's rear door swung open and Samantha poked her head inside.

"Well, it's about time you're up, Miss Sleeping Beauty."

"Oh, my...how long was I out?"

"Long enough so that you missed it when a bunch of local boys showed up," Samantha grinned. She disappeared for a moment, then came back and handed Charlotte a plate of scrambled eggs and charred toast. "I think they smelled Jude's cooking fire."

Charlotte's stomach let out a growl. Quickly, she broke off a corner of the toast and used it to scoop up a mouthful of the eggs. "Did you, ah, remember to practice your French on them?"

"Only *un peu*," Samantha said, pinching her fingers together. "Jude worked out a deal for them to set us up a show area, and even to put up some flyers in town."

Charlotte sat up at that. "I'd have thought...well, Jude said that the people here aren't too fond of...well, you know..."

"Darkies?" Samantha made an unladylike snort. "Yeah, but their attitude sure improves when you offer them some dollar coins."

"Well, then...I guess you have everything under control?"

"We do. But come on, get dressed and out here before the coffee's all gone. And grab our show gear; we need to work on our act with the horses. Jude made sure that they got fed and watered. But we need them limbered up for tonight's performance."

Charlotte dressed quickly, excitedly. Though her outfit didn't show any undue skin, she got more than a few once-overs from the boys as they worked alongside Jude. She repressed a shiver as she joined Samantha with a hearty *bonjour*.

Together, the women left the men to their work as they saddled up Jubilee and Patches. Charlotte and Samantha spent the remainder of the morning and much of the afternoon at a remote clearing further up the trail. They discussed their routines, using a stick and an open patch of dirt to work out their ideas. The horses got a workout as Samantha rode one, then the other, while Charlotte practiced cracking her whips for maximum effect and precision.

By the time they returned to camp, sweaty and tired, an amazing sight greeted their eyes. Under Jude's direction, the farmhands had set up a large circular perimeter made up of tall canvas bunting to provide a temporary corral, with both an entrance and an exit in the opposite side. The former Buffalo soldier had hitched two of the mules up to a heavy log and they pulled it around inside of the arena interior to flatten and smooth the ground. The last team of farmhands was busy setting up split-log bleachers along the sloped far side.

Jude walked up to them, looking happier than he had since they'd left Mrs. Pleasance's house. "Ladies," he said, with an air of tired satisfaction, "It appears that I still know how to lead a team of young bucks in basic carpentry. And, to my surprise, carnie setup."

"It looks just dashing!" Charlotte gushed. "Do you reckon we'll get anyone to show up to our little show tonight?"

"Based on what the boys have been saying, we should. Two pretty French girls starring in a show about 'ridin' and shootin'? That's the most interesting happenings in these parts in a while. Probably get the local press to show up and everything."

Charlotte's grin went from ear to ear. "Wouldn't that just take the biscuit, Sam?"

"That it would," Samantha said. "Who knows? It looks like we just might have a career in show business."

CHAPTER TWENTY

The crowd, which all but spilled off the edge of the bleachers, stood and cheered as Samantha made her horse rear up theatrically. Another chorus of whoops and hollers followed as her form was silhouetted against the sunset-reddened sky. With a wave, she galloped off-stage.

Jude signaled to one of the two farm boys he'd kept on for the evening show. The boy nodded, and then walked around the edges of the fencing and lit a series of torches, throwing a smoky yellow light into the stage area. Charlotte, clad in a French-styled riding outfit from Mrs. Pleasance's stores, walked out into the arena with something close to a swagger. All eyes remained on her as she stood in the middle and held up a long leather bullwhip in each hand.

She cracked them over her head a few times. First one, then the other. She whirled the whips faster and faster, soon becoming a blur of leather and sound, a constant *whip-CRACK!* like a string of Chinese firecrackers.

Suddenly, she brought the whips down together, hard. The simultaneous cracks echoed against the surrounding hills like a rifle shot. A moment of stunned silence, and then a round of applause. Charlotte made a sweeping bow.

Samantha returned to the arena, a small table and cloth bundle in her arms and a lever action Winchester slung over her shoulder. As the audience's attention shifted to her, she placed the table on the ground. Next, she swung the Winchester down and balanced it atop the smooth wooden table top.

She undid the bundle and pulled out a packet of paper. With a sigh, she opened a handful of sheets and used it to fan herself as if the evening's work had grown too hot for her. A laugh from the crowd came in response. She strutted to Charlotte's side, allowing their outfits to complement one another, Charlotte's blue and white against Samantha's scarlet and gold.

"*Mesdames et messieurs*," she proclaimed, using the pseudo-French phrases that she had memorized that afternoon, "We *presente* to you...the *acte de l'exécution de papier!*"

An excited murmur from the crowd. They weren't sure what to expect, but they definitely had heard the word 'execution'.

Samantha rolled a piece of paper into a three inch long cigarillo. She clenched it between her lips. A gasp from the ladies in the crowd as Charlotte slashed her whip through the air and cut it in two.

Next Samantha took one long piece of paper, carefully folded it, and then counted off a half dozen long strides away from Charlotte. Giving a supremely unconcerned look towards the audience, she held it up.

Another gasp as Charlotte's whip cut the air, deftly slicing the corner of the paper. Samantha repositioned the same piece of paper and again, Charlotte sliced a piece out of it with a *crack*. They did this two more times. Samantha then unfolded the paper and there for all to see was a string of paper dolls.

This time, an explosion of applause.

As Samantha and Charlotte began their bows, Jude signaled to the pair of farm boys again. Hurriedly, they stuck playing cards into the top of several of the corral posts, interspersed with green glass bottles, each with a lit candle stuck in the top.

"*Et maintenant*," Charlotte trilled, with her southern-tinged accent Française, "*La grande finale!*"

The two women stood shoulder to shoulder in the center of the arena. Samantha smoothly drew her pistols from their holsters. She systematically shot out the candle flames on each of the bottles, from right to left. In the twinkling of an eye, she swung back the other direction, this time shattering bottles with every bullet.

She holstered her guns, grabbed the Winchester, and dashed off the stage. Before the crowd could catch its breath, Charlotte stepped forward, swinging her whips and began snapping each of the playing cards, this time from left to right. Jude's impromptu stage hands propped up a metal sheet on a wooden pole that had been fashioned into a swinging target. With one last crack of her whips, Charlotte gave the sheet a push so that it would swing like a pendulum, and then moved off to one side of the arena.

Samantha burst out onto the stage one more time, this time riding Roman style on their two draft horses. The two big horses seemed to like the variety to their jobs as they kept perfectly in step so that Samantha's feet on each of the horses back would not slip. Their rocking horse cadence and wide backs were perfect for this standing form that was used in the Roman circuses of old.

Just as the crowd 'oohed' and 'aahed' over her riding, Samantha raised the rifle and proceeded to empty its magazine into the swinging metal plate. The sheet pinged and twanged as the bullets struck it, louder and louder, making a perfect crescendo of sound as Samantha brought the horses to a halt at the edge of the arena.

Charlotte came to her side, the two linked arms, and they gave one final bow. The crowd roared with appreciation. Samantha laughed, her face red with exertion and joy. Charlotte followed suit, bowing again into the wild applause.

"It looked like the girls enjoyed themselves," Charlotte observed, meaning the draft horses.

"They did just fine. And we did too!"

"Damn *straight* we did! Why, I reckon this'll get us all the way to California."

Samantha blinked. The first time Charlotte had spoken about their journey with firm, unwavering determination. It took all of her effort to avoid planting a kiss on Charlotte's lips right then and there. Samantha, her eyes brimming with tears, managed to restrain herself. With effort, she turned and bowed into the cheers and applause one more time.

CHAPTER TWENTY-ONE

"I must say," Jude chortled, as he hefted a sack of coins with a jingle, "You two keep performing like that, and we'll be heading out west in *style*."

Charlotte let out a weary sigh as she cast an eye over the empty bleachers, the scuffed, well-trodden turf that surrounded the arena, and the guttering light from the torches. Samantha placed the last of her gear on the table and stretched. A couple vertebrae in her neck popped. Crickets chorused around the campsite as night finally fell.

"I don't know about you," Charlotte said, "But no matter how late it is, I want to wash up. I feel like I've picked up a second skin made of dust on me."

"Then you two are lucky," Jude said. "Before I saw off our hired hands, I had them do a little extra chore for you."

Samantha's face broke into a wide grin as she saw what Jude had rigged up for the two of them. Next to the vardo, Jude had erected a special tent with a washing tub. Next to it sat a pair of small water tanks, one on a stand heater. The tent itself was just spacious enough to hold a small dressing table, a decorative screen and a small settee with an oriental carpet spread out on the ground providing the ambiance of a proper ladies dressing room.

Charlotte let out a girly squeal and hugged Jude tight. "Thank you! You do know how to take care of us."

"Now, don't get all sentimental on me," he grumped. He walked off, calling over his shoulder. "I'm going to secure our new funds in the freight wagon."

"And I need to put the horses away for the night," Samantha said. "Need to sponge them down and give them a ration of grain.

"Maybe we could give them an extra ration?" Charlotte ventured. "They all did so very, very well today."

"Not a bad idea," Samantha said, and she led the two draft horses off toward the canvas lean-to that served as a temporary stable for the livestock. Jude, in his amazing efficiency, had already had the area mucked out. New straw had been laid for the bedding.

She heard the two men before she saw them.

The crackle of boots on the straw. The nervous sounds of the animals as they scented someone unfamiliar. She turned, backed into a defensive crouch as two shapes appeared, shadows against the firelight in the distance. One was fat, barrel-shaped. The other was tall and spindly.

Zeke's voice came from one darkened face.

"Nice show y'all put on for us today."

"Ayup," Ezra's voice sounded in kind. "Even put out posters tellin' us where to find ya."

Samantha glanced around. Nothing to fight with. She drew herself up, tried to sound threatening. "*Vous...trespasser! Sortez, maintenant!*"

She pointed imperiously for them to go.

Zeke spoke again, as he stepped closer.

"Don't know what you're saying, I am a guessing that you is wantin' some of this." He grabbed his crotch and waggled his hand suggestively. The other man giggled, but blocked Samantha as she tried to bolt around him.

"Jude!" Samantha cried out, as Zeke grabbed her arm.

Samantha fought like a wildcat, thrashing and scratching with her nails. She heard a curse as one of her swipes hit home. But they had the strength of two against her one, and they forced her down onto the ground. Around them, the horses stamped their feet and whinnied at the commotion. She continued to struggle, as much against the fetid stench of the men's' bodies as their hold on her.

"Hold her, damn it!" Ezra cursed, as he fumbled with his belt.

The *snap* of a whip rang in the air.

Both men looked up. Charlotte stood at the open side of the lean-to, her bull whips a blur of motion. Her eyes glittered, dangerous and steely. She spoke, punctuating her words with a gunshot *crack* of the whips.

"Let her up! *Now*, you son-of-a-bitch!"

The men didn't move. Pitilessly, Charlotte lay into them. Her leather whips cut through cloth and bit into flesh. Samantha felt a warm spray of blood across her hand as Ezra rolled off of her with a pained whimper.

Zeke got up, protecting his face with his raised arms. Charlotte hit him with two more cracks. Welts sprouted like mushrooms after a rain on the man's forearms. With a roar, he charged towards Charlotte, seeking to bowl her over with his bulk.

Charlotte stumbled backwards, trying to get out of the way. Too slow. Samantha fought to get to her feet. Hoping that the man wouldn't be able to reach Charlotte. Knowing better.

The wooden end of a rifle butt rammed Zeke's face with a dull *crunch*. The man staggered backwards and sat down hard, blinking stupidly as Jude stepped in front of Charlotte. Blood ran in a torrent from both of Zeke's nostrils, forming a filmy mustache on his upper lip.

"You boys had better leave," Jude intoned. Without missing a beat, he rotated his rifle so that the business end pointed at the two men. "While you still can."

Samantha's elation at Jude's arrival was cut short as she heard the *click* of a revolver hammer. Jude froze. Charlotte glanced off to one side, where the lean-to obscured Samantha's view, and let out a gasp.

A new voice cut the night. One with a heavy, molasses-thick drawl.

"Hold it right there." The voice's thick Southern drawl cut 'right' into 'rat'.

The third man finally edged into view. A strong, calloused hand pointed a Colt at Jude's head. Soulless eyes peered from under the low brim of a shabby felt hat. A blond mustache framed a weathered pair of lips, ingrained in a hard, leathery face. The firelight caught on a set of worn brass buttons, and

Samantha realized that the man wore the rumpled uniform of a Confederate cavalry officer.

Samantha heard Jude make a strange sound.

It wasn't loud.

A gasp of fear had come from the man's lips.

CHAPTER TWENTY-TWO

"Lissen up, burr-head," drawled the cavalry officer, "You let my boys be. Else when I'm done, there won't be enough left of you to snore."

Jude swallowed hard. He dropped the rifle by his feet.

Ezra got to his feet and brushed straw off his ragged trousers. "They done bushwhacked us, Captain."

"Shut up." Ezra and Zeke cringed, though the man's voice had hardly changed volume. "All you had to do was find their cash box. But no, you two had to go an' let your peckers do the thinking. Now, go find that damn box 'fore I tan both of your hides."

"But..." Ezra stumbled into the light, showing the cuts that Charlotte's whip had made across his shoulders and arms. "Lookee what the girls did to us!"

Zeke got up and did the same. He spat out a bloody tooth into his palm. "And look what the Negro done to me!"

Shadow hid the captain's expression. But his angry exhale, the set of his jaw, made Charlotte's blood run cold.

"Well now, that's somethin' else entirely." His arm came up. "If you'n laid a hand on my kin, then there's payment to be made."

Someone threw the side of the lean-to's cloth back with a *fwap*. The man who stepped out into the light wore a gentleman's summer suit with a black string bow tie at his throat. An absurdly large, six-barreled gun projected from his right hand like a miniature Gatling gun.

"May I be so bold as to interject myself?" The man smiled, and his eyes gleamed like polished black buttons beneath a mop of gray hair. "I don't take too kindly to men taking undo advantage of women folk."

"Stranger," the Confederate captain gritted, "This don't concern you. Just a bit of nuisance between my boys and this here nigger."

The newcomer's lips thinned with distaste below a bushy mustache. "Then I am looking to make that my nuisance, friend. And my finger's getting mighty tired of holding this trigger without finishing its journey, if you follow my meaning."

The captain hesitated, and then cocked his head in Jude's direction. "Even if you do shoot me, there ain't no way I can miss your friend. Not at this range."

"That's a fair bargain. See, I'm holding a pepper-box here in my hand. Six barrels with a shot spread that a riding preacher would envy. There's no way I can miss all three of you miscreants. Not at this range."

The captain squinted at the newcomer, trying to read his eyes. He lowered his pistol. Zeke and Ezra glanced at him, fearful, like dogs looking for permission to bolt.

"Now, kindly exit stage left," the man said. "And a pox on you, if you ever think about visiting Hannibal township ever again."

A final hostile glare between the two. A toss of his head, and the captain disappeared into the night, followed by Ezra and Zeke.

Jude picked up his rifle and turned to watch the darkness. Nobody moved, or even seemed to breathe for the next minute. Until a very strange sound came from the newcomer.

Laughter.

"Sweet mother of mercy," he gasped, as he lowered his barrel-heavy weapon. "God grant me never, ever to have to do anything so confoundedly stupid, or so-help-me, I will start running for Congress."

Samantha could do nothing but stare for a moment. Charlotte found her voice first. She stepped forward, grasping the man's hand.

"Why, we owe our lives to you," she said. "Thank you, Mister–"

"Clemens, Sam Clemens," the man said, bowing elegantly and bestowing a kiss on Charlotte's hand.

"Thank you, Mister Clemens," Samantha added, as she came towards him and also received a peck on the hand. "You pulled our bacon out of the fire!"

"True," said Jude, who hadn't stopped scanning the perimeter of the campsite. "Part of me wished that you'd pulled your trigger, though. Might have been worth meeting my Maker, if I had those three as my honor guard."

"You'd trade your life for three worthless ones?" Clemens said, raising one bushy eyebrow. "I dare say those were just common ruffians. One of whom happened upon a stash of Confederate clothing to keep himself warm on a cold night."

"That may be."

"And on top of that, I was afraid they'd have called my bluff." Clemens held up his pepper-box. "Not too many people have seen these in action. That's for a good reason. They don't fire in a spread. Only one shot at a time, and one must cock the pistol after each shot."

"So it's not like a Gatling gun?" This from Samantha.

"Not in the least. One shot, and they'd have been on us." Clemens considered the weapon one more time. "But it does have an intimidating aspect, does it not?"

"I'd say so. We do owe you, Mister Clemens. Big time."

A snort and a wave, dismissing the idea. "If you feel you owe me anything, then you can grace me with an interview."

"Wait, what?"

"Well, that *is* what I came out here for after your show. I'm not nail-headed enough to be a lawman, nor am I prone to excessive acts of heroism. I pen a column for the *Hannibal Gazette*, and I while my French is horrible to non-existent, my gut tells me that neither of you will have a problem *avec parlez-vous American*."

The two women traded startled glances. Samantha felt her stomach sink like a lead weight. So soon into their journey, and someone had seen right through their deception.

CHAPTER TWENTY-THREE

"Come now, I didn't mean to give the two of you the quivers," Clemens said expansively. "I won't turn your covers back. You think any of the showmen out West are exactly who they say they are? Hellfire, I once covered Buffalo Bill's Wild West show, the one with an entire tribe of 'gen-yoo-ine' Sioux Indians, and you'd never believe what I found out about them."

"What was that?" Charlotte asked.

"Well now," Clemens said, looking satisfied with himself, "you'll have to give me that interview to find out."

"We can do better than that," Samantha said. "Give us a moment to tidy up, and I think we can give you an interview and a dinner."

"Mighty fine of you to do that for an old reporter. I accept, and I'll wait by your campfire, as patient as a stone, till you're ready."

"You go on ahead," Jude said, though his eyes didn't leave the tree line. "I'm going to keep watch from the freight wagon tonight. Just in case."

The two women retreated to the washing area next to the vardo. It took the better part of an hour, but they were able to scrub down and change into fresh clothes. Washing might have gone faster, but Charlotte insisted on checking Samantha for wounds. She found none, save for the start of a ring of bruises where one man had grabbed Samantha's wrist. Samantha drew Charlotte in for a kiss and a shuddery hug.

"I owe you one, Char." Samantha whispered.

They brought their cooking gear out to the fire, where Clemens waited patiently. The man sat, feet propped up on a nearby stump, puffing away at a corncob pipe as if he hadn't a care in the world. However, his pepper-box remained at his side, and every now and again, his gaze would alight on where Jude sat silent watch from the freight wagon.

"It's humble fare tonight," Charlotte apologized, as she opened a container of dried peas. "Ham and pea soup is what I had planned."

"Sounds like a rib-tickler," Clemens said. He leaned forward and grasped one of the dried peas, studying its wrinkly green surface. "The army used to call these 'desiccated' vegetables." He snorted. "More like 'desecrated' if'n you ask me."

Samantha looked up from where she set up the cooking pot. "You do have some amusing turns of phrases, Mister Clemens."

"If I'm in a profession that buys ink by the barrel, I should certainly hope I have some talent. Speaking of that, you two are mighty impressive as well. I ain't seen any finer riding and shooting. Might even give Annie Oakley herself a run for her money."

"And you're quite the flatterer, as well."

"Guilty as charged. Don't tell my publisher," Clemens said, as he removed his pipe and blew an elegant smoke ring. "That'd be a long-distance telegram, in any case. Only people I could get to publish my books are all the way across the ocean, in London-town."

"You write books?" Charlotte said, interested. "I'd like to hear about that, if you don't mind sharin'."

"I don't mind at all, though I fear to bore such nice young ladies."

"We're of a literary bent ourselves," Samantha said. Inwardly, she relaxed. Having Clemens talk about himself allowed her time to think up a good story to give him on the 'origin' of *La Femme Exhibition Extraordinaire*. She rummaged in one of the straw-padded sacks they'd brought over, and came up with the bottle of wine she'd been looking for. "And as you were our savior tonight, I hope you'll join us in a sip or two."

The man's eyes gleamed. "Be a dandy if'n I didn't."

After a quick hunt in the vardo for a set of goblets, Samantha served up three full glasses and Clemens provided the toast.

"Ladies, may you live long, love often, and laugh twice as much."

Given how the evening had started, the rest of the time passed amazingly quickly and pleasantly. Clemens explained how Halley's Comet had swung through the heavens when he'd been born, and that he expected to leave when it came around again. How he'd been a riverboat pilot, and how his book's main character, 'Tom Sawyer' came about.

Afterwards, save for a quick break to run a serving of soup out to Jude at the freight wagon, Samantha regaled Clemens with a story of how 'Dominique' and 'Veronica' now traveled across the state of Missouri in exile from their beloved home country. That exile having been perpetrated by their mother company, *La Belle Carnivales Française*, due to a horrible, bloody accident that had happened during one of their acts.

"Which act?" Clemens said, as he scribbled notes on a tiny pad of paper. "The one with the whips, or the one with the guns?"

"Oh, I really can't say," Samantha said coyly. "That way, whoever reads your story will have to come...and stay on edge, no matter which one of us in on stage."

Clemens chuckled. "You need to meet Monsieur 'Buffalo Bill' someday. You've got the same carnie sense of advertisement."

"Speakin' of," Charlotte reminded him, "What did you find out about the Indians on Bill's Wild West show?"

"Well, back when I saw his show outside of Chicago, the climax of his grand finale was a 'real life Injun raid', complete with 'terrifying members of the nation of the Sioux'! And it was grand, all right," Clemens said, with a fragrant puff of his pipe. "Must've been three, four dozen copper-skinned savages, all jumpin' and hollerin' with their tomahawks and feather headdresses. Of course, I'd slipped out of the audience section and got down close to where I could hear some real Indians converse. And you know what I heard one of the braves say?"

Samantha and Charlotte shook their heads.

"Faith and begorrah, Seamus!" Clemens said, in a flawless Irish accent. "Any more o' this prancin' around, covered in greasepaint, and I'll melt away into a wee spot of butter!"

The two women burst out laughing. Clemens finished up his last puff of tobacco, and discretely knocked his pipe out behind his seat.

"Much as I enjoyed tonight, I must bid you *adieu*," he said, as he stood to leave. "My column on you two will be my last for the paper. Tomorrow afternoon, I take the ferry back across the river. I've got a new house and a lovely wife waiting for me in Connecticut. To my chagrin, I've found that I've become quite the Yankee."

"We're heading different ways," Charlotte said, "But I hope you'll see our show again."

"I hope so as well! I must say that when I watched your equestrian performance this afternoon, it made me feel like I sat in on one of King Arthur's tournaments itself. Very impressive, yes very impressive."

Clemens hesitated for a moment, and then pulled a sealed envelope from his suit's inner pocket. He pressed it into Samantha's hand. She looked at him, questioningly.

"We're not charging you for dinner, Mister Clemens."

"I figured as much," he said, with a twinkle in his eye. "It's just something I chanced to find in town this afternoon before I came to your show."

He bowed, kissed both of their hands again, and set off with a hearty goodbye to Jude. Jude returned the farewell silently with a raised hand.

"What a fascinating fellow," Charlotte mused, as Samantha opened the envelope. A freshly printed piece of paper lay inside, folded three times in order to fit inside the envelope. Samantha smoothed out the paper, and then let out a breath that was equal parts shock and laughter.

A likeness of her and Charlotte adorned the top half. Below, the text had been printed in fresh black ink.

$100 REWARD OFFERED
For information on the whereabouts of
SAMANTHA WILLIAMS and CHARLOTTE HARTE

A thorough description of the women followed, punctuated with an authoritative flourish: *Contact the Pinkerton Detective Agency, Chicago Branch.*

At the very bottom was a handwritten scribble.

I won't tell a soul.
Very Truly Yours,
- Mark Twain

CHAPTER TWENTY-FOUR

Over the next week, Jude led the small group along Missouri's back roads, trending towards the west, and staying well away from the rail lines. The days got hotter, though by far the nights were the worst. No one bothered them, but the dual threat of the Pinkertons and a repeat appearance of the cavalry officer and his two friends loomed in the back of everyone's mind.

The duo making up *La Femme Exhibition Extraordinaire* remained hard at work as well. Two more performances during the week – both held on the outskirts of towns, and during prime daylight hours – kept their cash box from getting too light. Samantha's expertise with her guns and the horses improved markedly, while Charlotte's newfound confidence in her talents continued to grow as well.

Yet the daytime shows made the problem with the heat worse. Outside of town of Moberly, Charlotte saw off the last of the audience who wanted autographs and all but threw herself onto one of the beds inside the vardo.

"Sam," Charlotte said, "I feel like one of those Irish Indians that Mister Clemens talked about. I'm darn sure goin' to melt into butter at this rate. Ain't there a swimmin' hole around here?"

Samantha wiped one sweaty brow as she leaned into the vardo. "There's a stream nearby I used to water the horses earlier today. I think there's a spot we could use."

Charlotte raised her head. "Think it's safe?"

In reply, Samantha patted her holster. "It better be. We can take turns bein' on the lookout."

Charlotte shook her head with a smile. She gathered up soap, towels, and a change of clothes for each of them.

"Jude, we'll be back in a bit," Samantha said. "We need to go cool down, and wash up."

Jude frowned. "Just be careful. I think we lost our trio of friends, but one can never tell."

With that, the two women wandered down into the nearby copse of trees. The sound of running water perked up Charlotte's spirits. Just upstream from where Samantha had watered the horses lay a deep pool of clear water. Wild honeysuckle perfumed the air, and the willow trees perched at the pool's edge as if poised to dive in themselves.

Charlotte shed her clothes and waded in. Samantha tossed her a bar of lavender-scented soap and a washcloth. Next, she found a nearby boulder to crouch on.

"You like getting up that high?" Charlotte asked, as she soaped up.

"Better view from up here," Samantha replied. She allowed her gaze to wander over her lover's taut limbs, flat belly, and dark triangle of hair, framed in ivory suds. "Much better view, as a matter of fact."

Her ears picked up the thud of horse hooves. The pace wasn't fast – more of an ambling walk – but she brought her gun up to where she saw movement at the far side of the pool.

"Something wrong?" This from Charlotte.

"Someone's coming."

Before they could say anything else, a figure on a small gray horse emerged from the bushes. To Samantha's surprise, it turned out to be a woman in a black velvet riding habit. Her outfit came complete with a top hat, garnished with a white plume of feathers.

The woman squinted at Charlotte, then at Samantha. Then at the gun in Samantha's hand.

"Beg pardon for the intrusion," she said, in a voice not unlike Mrs. Pleasance's. "And kindly don't shoot me. I've got some boys with me that might take offense at that."

Samantha lowered her gun, though she remained at the ready. "Pardon us in return, then. We've had problems on this road."

"I can sympathize," the woman said. She doffed her hat, letting a tangle of dark hair spill out, and spoke more warmly. "I'm Maybelle Shirley. We're just passing through."

"So are we. Technically, we're from France," Samantha said, lamely. "I'm...Veronica. My friend in the pool there is Dominique."

"And a right come-ly friend at that!" a male voice came from off to Maybelle's side. Charlotte let out a squeak and dove for the cover of some reeds as four men, each covered in dust from hard riding, appeared next to the woman's horse.

"Damn straight," said one of the other men, "That is the Lord's truth!"

Maybelle's voice cut like the crack of Charlotte's whip. "Cole! Jesse! All you boys shove on and quit violatin' this lady's privacy!"

A chorus of "Yes'm", "Sure", and "Gawdamns" rose up, but the men followed Maybelle's orders. Red-faced, she spread her hands in appeal to Samantha.

"Men! I swear, the whole damn sex is more trouble than they're worth, some days." She looked longingly at the pool herself. "It is powerful hot today, though. Is there enough water for three?"

Samantha found her mind racing. Maybelle and her friend's names were vaguely familiar. Too familiar. But if they'd meant her any harm, it surely would have taken place by now.

"Well," Samantha said, "If you're sure no one else will bother us..."

"Not with my boys on the prowl, no." Maybelle slipped off her horse, led it around to the near side of the pool, and slipped out of her clothes with all the body modesty of a cat. She waded into the water with one final remark. "They won't come back to spy on us skinny-dipping, neither. Last man who did that with me got sent home with a bullet-nick on his pecker."

"You sound like someone who knows what's what," admitted Samantha, who followed Maybelle's lead by disrobing and entering the pool. Charlotte came out from the reeds and offered the soap and washcloth to Samantha. Maybelle paddled off to one side, splashing her face with the cool water.

"Well, I know some things." She snapped her fingers. "That's right. You two are the ones I read about in the paper. It said that..."

A quiet, tense moment hung in the air before Maybelle finished.

"...It said that you'd been exiled from France for killin' someone by accident."

"Oh, yeah. That." Samantha said, as she scrubbed herself down. "That story...it's something of an exaggeration."

"Exaggeration, that's a good one. Tell you what else is funny, though. That you two French girls, when I look at you up close, got more than a passing resemblance to the pictures that the Pinks are nailin' up all over the place."

"The 'Pinks'?" Charlotte asked.

"Pinkerton's Detectives, honey," Maybelle said calmly. "Reason you ain't seen them is because the posters just went up in all the towns east of here, and you're headin' west."

"I'm guessing that the 'Pinks', as you call 'em, must be nearby, then," Samantha said, forcing herself to keep her voice calm. "Did you send your boys off to collect the reward?"

Maybelle stared at her for a moment and laughed.

"My boys? Goin' to the *Pinks?* Hell should freeze over 'fore that happens." She leaned forward and spoke conspiratorially. "Not when the Pinks killed one of 'em, and we took down one of the Pinks in turn last week."

Samantha's thoughts fell into place like a jigsaw's pieces. *Cole Younger. Jesse James.* She glanced at the woman who swam nude next to them.

Belle Starr.

CHAPTER TWENTY-FIVE

"You're the bandit queen?" Samantha asked, incredulous.

"The one and the only," Maybelle agreed. "Don't worry, my boys only rob banks."

"Ah," Charlotte said, unsure of what to add.

Maybelle shrugged. "It's where the money is. Least that's what Jesse and Cole say. Me an' Cole, we have a little thing between us. My husband got himself killed two years ago, so every now and then Cole and I get together and get 'caught up'. But now y'all see why I don't want involvement with the Pinks any more than you."

"Looks like we're both tryin' to keep a low profile," Charlotte said.

"Yup. And like I said, you got nothin' to be scared of around here, not while my boys are on the prowl."

"I just wish we'd not run afoul of that fellow, the one in the cavalry officer's uniform."

Maybelle sat up with a splash of water. She sputtered and coughed for a moment before she spoke again.

"Cavalry officer? In these parts?"

"Why, yes. We had a run-in with a fellow who wore a beat-up Confederate cavalry uniform. He and his 'friends' came close to gettin' their heads blown off for tryin' to rob us, and worse—"

"You're sure it was a Confederate uniform?" Maybelle said, cutting Charlotte off. "The man...short blond hair and mustache? Face looks like a sunburnt boot?"

"Sounds like him, fair enough. The two thugs with him called him 'Captain'."

Maybelle cursed. She stormed out of the water, wrung her hair, and began throwing her clothes on, tugging the stubborn fabric over her still-wet skin.

"Miss Shirley," Samantha said, taken aback, "What's wrong?"

"What's wrong?" She turned and spoke to them, but didn't slow down in putting her clothes back on. "I'll tell you. That man you bumped into is Captain Clark Quantrill, formerly of Quantrill's Raiders. *Now* does he sound familiar?"

Charlotte gasped. "I remember readin' about him when I was a child. He'd take to killin' whole families during the war. But he was killed by the Union Army, or was supposed to be! And even so, the war's over, what would he have to fight for?"

"Honey, the only war Clark Quantrill ever fought in was himself against the world. My boys Jesse and Cole…they were with him during the war. And they cut out because he'd gone plum crazy. Crazy, and mean enough to fight a rattler and give him the first bite."

"Well…it was over a week ago that we saw him," Charlotte said hopefully.

"A week, you say?" Maybelle pulled on her boots and jammed her hat back on her head. "Maybe…just maybe, he's forgotten about you. I don't think he'd sit back a week and let you just waltz on your way. But my boys, the Captain ain't goin' to forgive them. Not for cuttin' out on his outfit. So we're goin' to be on our way."

"Best to you," Samantha said, nodding. "Thanks for telling us about Quantrill."

"You'd have found out sooner or later," Maybelle said, as she mounted up. "As for me an' the boys? You just watch the papers. We're gonna make history!"

She spurred her horse into motion, and then disappeared into the woods.

※ ※ ※

Back at the wagons, Jude listened as Samantha related the encounter with Belle Starr and 'her boys'. His face went gray as slate at the revelation about Captain Clark Quantrill. Without another word, he lifted the seat of the freight wagon and pulled out a map.

"That man's trouble," he said soberly. "Army kept it out of the papers, but we never could state for certain that Quantrill's Raiders had been stamped out. Our best bet is to strike out for the northwest, using only farm tracks and back roads."

"But we've seen neither hide nor hair of them for a week," Charlotte objected.

"Would you rather take a chance of meeting them again?"

Charlotte looked as if to retort, then shook her head.

"The second place that Missus Pleasance wanted me to take you two was the Golden Goose saloon." Jude said, as he spread his map out on one of their fold-up tables. He jabbed a spot in the upper left quadrant of the state. "Right here, just outside Kansas City. That's Miss Brenda's place. Fine liquor, finer women, if you don't mind me saying so."

"Let me guess," Samantha said, "It's one of the businesses that Missus Pleasance helped set up, right?"

"Sure enough. She'll have enough security to keep anyone outside. Means that you two will need to figure out a way to do your act indoors. And we'll need you to perform, I'm afraid. Call it another two, three day's drive to get to the Goose, and we'll need to fill the feed bags again."

With that, the trio started breaking down the camp in the bright afternoon heat. Charlotte, with sweat streaming anew down her face, spoke ruefully to Samantha as they hitched the draft horses back up to the vardo.

"Guess I sure caused a ruckus from my wantin' a bit of cool water."

"There's no need to be sorry," Samantha replied, placing her hand on Charlotte's. "The way I see it, you may have just saved us all."

CHAPTER TWENTY-SIX

The cavernous interior of the Golden Goose swam in a haze of cigarillo smoke. Rich tobacco, warm beer, and cheap perfume made a pungent mixture. Samantha tried not to sneeze as she pushed through the saloon's swinging doors. She, Charlotte, and Jude garnered some semi-interested glances as they made their way across the floor.

Unlike the sounds of the kitchen or the grand piano back at Mrs. Pleasance's Social Club, here the air was rent with loud conversation, laughing women, and the *tak-tak* of an ivory ball as it bounced along a turning roulette wheel.

The trio made their way across to where the saloon keeper wiped up the bar. He gave them a suspicious glance until Jude spoke, softly, but without the wheedling submissiveness that he'd feigned back on the ferry to Hannibal.

"I'm looking for Miss Brenda."

The reply was gruff, suspicious. "Who wants 'er?"

"Tell her Jude's here. I'm direct from Missus Pleasance."

Begrudgingly, the man put his cleaning rag aside and disappeared to a room behind the bar. Jude indicated a table off to the side and away from the rest of the patrons, where he could observe the rest of the room. Samantha and Charlotte took their seats, watching carefully as the ruckus continued around them.

"Busy place," Samantha ventured. "Loud, too."

Jude nodded. "Miss Brenda charges a fair price for liquor, or ladies. It's louder, rougher than Missus Pleasance's. But this here's the wild edge of the frontier. Sharing a border with 'Bloody Kansas', not Illinois. Makes all the difference."

A woman's happy cry cut the air like a soprano blade. "Jude Davis! It *is* you!"

A heavy-set woman with snow white hair piled high on her head, cherry-red lips and bright blue eyes came around the bar and over to their table. A black velvet ribbon with a cameo of

Leda and the Swan graced her ample throat. Jude stood up and stretched his arms open wide.

"Miss Brenda!" he said, hugging her, "Ain't you a sight for sore eyes."

"You old son of a gun, Jude! Why didn't you tell me you were on the way?" She looked past him, her gaze settling on Samantha and Charlotte. "What have you brung me this time?"

Jude chuckled. "That'll take a bit of explaining. We had best go to your office."

She looked at him, a question on her lips. "Why, of course. Right this way, ladies and gentlemen."

With that, she led them back around the bar, trailing the scent of gardenia perfume in her wake. But as soon as they had exited, a greasy-looking man marked where they'd gone, and slipped through the swinging doors with the air of a man on a very specific mission.

※ ※ ※

With the bright glare of the setting sun in his eyes, Matthew Slade tipped down the brim of his hat as he rode into the town of Moberly. Slowly, stiffly, he got off his horse. His head ached from the last traces of his bullet wound. His groin ached from the rather...enthusiastic attempts of Mrs. Pleasance's best girls to convince him to stay another day or two.

Slade took off the last of the bandages the fool doctor in Pleasance had wrapped around his head and tossed it aside with a curse. His mustang nickered at the big man's grumbling. Slade patted the horse's side affectionately.

"You go ahead and laugh, big fella," he said. "At least no fool of a doctor's going to put one of your hooves in plaster..."

His voice trailed off as he caught sight of a sun-browned poster nailed to one of the posts of a nearby building. Absently, he untacked his mount and snatched up the piece of paper. He'd been seeing these since arriving in Hannibal a few days ago, but he'd never paid much attention to carnies. Let alone to something as ridiculous-sounding as *La Femme Exhibition Extraordinaire*.

That said, something had nagged him about these posters. These performers were heading in the same general direction as his quarry. And his quarry had done something that no fugitive had ever done in all his years with Pinkerton: leave absolutely no trace of their passing.

"Unless *this* is the trace," he said to himself, as he thought back to the Williams house in Chicago. The open, clean stable in the back that obviously belonged to Samantha. "If one of you knows how to ride, and the other knows how to use…"

He turned on his heel and saddled up again. His mind raced down each of the roads from Moberly, working routes on the map he'd burned into his mind.

Say the girls were working their way west…as a carnival act. Then they'd have to hit the places large enough to ply their trade. Large enough so that they wouldn't look that out of place.

Slade tugged the mustang's reins. Kansas City, he'd bet. And Kansas City had a telegraph line where he could get the word out to the rest of the Pinkerton network. With a nudge of his heels, he set his mount on the road west out of town at a full gallop.

✷ ✷ ✷

Though the furniture was different, the wallpaper in Miss Brenda's office was a near duplicate of the red velvet type in Mrs. Pleasance's Social Club. It somehow put Samantha more at ease while dealing with this new woman. Together, she and Charlotte quickly sketched out their reasons for travelling, Mrs. Pleasance's interest in their journey, the basics of their show, and how they'd share the revenues with the Goose.

Miss Brenda poured herself a glass of whiskey and downed it in one shot. "I'll admit, I'm intrigued a mite, Samantha. Or should I call you 'Veronica'?"

"It's probably best we stick to stage names while we're here," Samantha replied. "Fewer problems that way. And in public, we're going to limit our English, use some French."

"Ah, that fancy talk always sways the men out here. Anything exotic does, really," She poured herself another shot and thoughtfully swirled it around in the glass. *"La Femme Exhibition Extraordinaire*, eh? How're you going to do your horse-riding tricks in my saloon?"

Charlotte grinned. "Actually, 'Veronica' an' me, we've been working out a way to change up our act a bit for you this evening. Play to the audience here, 'specially if they have a taste for the 'exotic'."

"I like the sound of that."

"I just hope we practiced it enough," Samantha admitted. "Otherwise, I'm going to be mighty sore afterwards."

Miss Brenda put her glass down with a clink.

"Okay. Now you two have me curious. What do you have in mind?"

Miss Brenda's eyebrows rose as they told her.

CHAPTER TWENTY-SEVEN

Samantha, dressed up as Continental showgirl 'Veronica', shot out the last candle. The smell of gun smoke hung thick in the air of the Goose as the crowd of surly ranch hands and cattlemen broke into a chorus of cheers. Samantha chuckled to herself. Right now most of them were so drunk and hard-up that they'd applaud anything with feminine features on the stage.

She sheathed her pistol back in its holster as 'Dominique' returned to the stage, strutting in alluringly, to a smattering of wolf whistles. She'd already wowed them with her whip cracking. But now, they were going to try something new.

"Maintenant," she trilled, in her bad French, "We 'ave for you...ze *grande finale!*"

Dominique led Veronica over to one of the stage's columns. She had Veronica face the column, legs slightly spread, then instructed her to raise her hands above her head. The men watched, intent, as Dominique took her partner's hands and loosely bound them to the column with a length of bright handkerchief.

The largest, heaviest bullwhip of the evening unspooled from her hand as Dominique stepped back ten feet. She turned to the crowd once again.

"If you please, *mes messieurs,*" she said, "Count out loud ze *nombre* of times that I strike!"

A strangely excited murmur from the assembled men.

Dominique cocked her arm. With careful precision, her whip *cracked*, tearing a strip of cloth across Veronica's back. Samantha gasped – the blow hadn't been a light one – but the leather corset placed strategically under the dress deadened the blow.

"*One!*" The men stamped their feet, eyes riveted to the scene.

Another *crack*. A filmy strip of cloth fell to the floor.

"*Two!*"

A third *crack*. Another strip of cloth fell to the floor.

"*Three!*"

Dominique's arm rose and fell four more times. Veronica's dress lay tattered, and on the final blow, the entire garment slid to the floor, leaving the woman wearing only the shiny corset.

"*SEVEN!*" The men jumped to their feet, whistling and applauding. The stage jingled as silver dollars showered down on its surface.

Weakly, Samantha and Charlotte made their bows and hurried backstage.

"Sam! Speak to me!" Charlotte cried, her fingers running up and down Samantha's back.

"Stop being silly," Samantha said, though her tone was gentle. "I'm fine, the corset protected me. Just like it did in practice. I'm just...*whoo*. That. Was. Intense."

"I don't know what I'd do if I'd hurt you," Charlotte said, her face as flushed as her partner's.

"Oh, I figure you could make it up to me," Samantha said, with a playful grin. "Say, later tonight."

They heard Miss Brenda approach before they saw her.

"Where are they?" the woman demanded. When she spotted the two women, she came up and threw her arms around each of them, planting gardenia-scented kisses on their cheeks. "You two just gave me the best night I've ever had here! Old Man Moseby, the town alderman, he was in the back row and he nearly creamed his drawers! Please, tell me that you're goin' to be staying in Kansas City for a while."

"Oh, I don't know," Samantha said. "We need to be on the road..."

"Nonsense! At least stay a week, rest up your horses and mules. I'll have your friend Jude talk some sense into you." Miss Brenda stuck her head back out through the curtain, to a chorus of drunken cheers. "Oh, quit it, the lot of you! Show's over! Ned, get back here!"

In a moment, the man they'd seen tending bar earlier joined them backstage. Miss Brenda, still aglow with excitement, spoke to him rapid-fire. "Ned, where'd Jude go off to? I need him to convince our rainmakers to stay here and make it downpour for a week!"

"Where is he?" Ned scratched his temple in puzzlement. "He went out back to the stable during that last...well, *arousing* performance. You should know."

"What? Why should I know?"

"Someone passed me a note. Looked like your handwriting, Miss Brenda. Said he had to handle one of the horses before its shoe got thrown. I passed it on to him, and off he went."

"Stop the nonsense, Ned. I didn't send you any note. Why would I, when I can holler for you from across the saloon?"

But Samantha wasn't listening anymore. Though clad only in corset and pantaloons, her gun belt still hung at her waist. Her face pale, she pushed through the backstage exit. Cold night air sent goose-pimples rippling up her arms. Charlotte dashed after her.

"Wait!" she cried, "You didn't get a chance to re–"

Her words were cut short as they drew close to their two wagons. They heard the dull strike of fists against flesh. The *snap* of bone. Jude howled in agony. Samantha came around the side of the vardo, dreading what she would find in the murky light of the stable's gas lamps.

Jude lay face down on the dirty floor of the stable, groaning. Blood pooled around his body. One arm and one leg sprawled out, each bent horribly the wrong way. Ezra, Zeke, and Captain Quantrill stood around him, laughing. Quantrill gave Jude another vicious kick to his stomach, causing the man to wheeze in pain.

"Jude!" Samantha screamed.

At the sound of her voice, Jude looked up from the ground.

"Mind me..." he said weakly. "Run! *Run!*"

But this time, Samantha didn't listen.

"Get away from our friend!" she gritted.

"Your 'friend'?" Quantrill drawled. "I don't see nuthin' here but a dead nigger."

In a flash, the cavalry officer drew his .45 and pointed it at the man at his feet. A *bang!* and Jude lay still.

Charlotte shrieked. The sound faded into the background, like a train entering a dark tunnel. All that filled Samantha's awareness was a heightened focus on the three men – the three monsters – that filled her vision.

"Looks like the whores have arrived too late," chortled Zeke.

"Aw, she's gonna cry now!" Ezra grinned in turn.

Samantha's hands moved on their own accord. Not as fast as Quantrill, but with the element of surprise. Both guns slipped into her palms. She squeezed the triggers in a blur. Seeking to annihilate anything in her way.

Four shots erupted from her pistols.

Two bullets punched through Ezra's throat. His windpipe erupted in a gory spray.

Another slammed into Zeke's chest. The fat man made a strangled cough as his lungs filled with blood. He fell forward, next to Jude's body.

A *spang!* as Samantha's last bullet shattered one of the vardo's lanterns. Oily shards of glass pelted Quantrill. He cursed and danced a step back.

Samantha's fingers continued squeezing, squeezing the triggers, but nothing happened.

Her guns had run dry.

Which is what Charlotte had been trying to tell her. She hadn't reloaded after her trick-shooting act.

Quantrill's eyes glittered in the light as he saw Ezra and Zeke lying still. He let out a cry of rage. But it was drowned out by the *boom* of someone else's gun. The whine of bullets filled the air around the former Confederate. He snarled, fired back, and then fled into the darkness.

Charlotte dropped to her knees next to Jude's body. Samantha followed suit. They ignored the sounds of shouting, approaching men, and turned Jude over.

His face had been pulverized. Jagged stumps of teeth and swollen eyes leered at them. The bullet hole in his back bubbled gore. Samantha put her fingers to his throat, hoping against hope.

Her voice was a whisper.

"He's gone, Char."

Charlotte let out tiny, pitiful sob.

Before she could speak, the two heard a sound which they had come to dread. The click of a revolver hammer being thumbed back.

"Stand away," said a gruff voice. "Keep your hands away from your guns, and hold em' high where I can see 'em."

CHAPTER TWENTY-EIGHT

The voice that spoke had the deep, no-nonsense growl of the law backing it up. And it broke the two women out of their shocked state. Together, they stood up and turned toward the voice. Hands open and out to the side, and then held high as instructed.

A man with craggy, sun-burned features and a full, well-kept handlebar mustache approached them, a long-barreled Colt held in one wiry hand. His long, black duster made the polished badge on his chest gleam.

"Yes, I'm the Deputy Marshal," the man said, noticing their glances. "Either of you hurt?"

Speechless, the two shook their heads.

"Fine." His eyes swept the scene of carnage before him. "What the hell's going on here?"

"These two," Samantha said, indicating two of the dead men with a nudge of her boot. "Murdered our friend. They tried to rape and rob me earlier."

"Who shot 'em?"

"I did."

The Marshal calmly surveyed her. To his surprise, he could tell that she felt no remorse. Her expression looked more like one relieved. Like some private demons had been laid to rest. Almost in passing, he noted that she'd gotten into the gunfight – and won – wearing little more than a well-scuffed corset and a pair of gaudy pantaloons.

A puzzled frown crossed his face. Who *were* these women?

"They got what they deserved, Marshal," Samantha went on, more forcefully. "Jude here was unarmed. There were three of 'em. Beat and shot him to death just as we came running."

A groan came from the fat man lying on the ground. The Marshal dug his foot under the man's shoulder and turned him over. Recognized him. His expression mimicked someone who'd just turned over a rock to find a mass of squirming grubs.

"You know, little lady," the Marshal said, "When you shoot a man, make sure you're not sloppy about it. Always finish the job."

He raised his long-nosed Colt and pulled the trigger. Both Samantha and Charlotte started as the thunderous report echoed in the street. The groaning stopped. Without another word, the Marshal looked over their two wagons. Saw that the damage to the vardo was minimal.

"These yours?"

"Yes," Samantha said, forcing herself to speak. "They are."

The Marshal holstered his weapon but looked out to where people had started coming out onto the street. Gunfire brought out the curious. But it usually took a little while. Nobody wanted to get in the way of loaded personal arguments.

"Load your man up and get out of town."

Charlotte and Samantha stared at him.

"As it stands, this is a clear case of self-defense," he explained. "I understand. It's the way we do things in Dodge City."

"But–" Samantha started to say.

"But that ain't here. 'Less you want to be stuck in court for the next couple of months, you two better rake and scrape it!"

Charlotte looked to Samantha, her eyes pleading.

"Jude...he's so gray lookin'." she whispered, shaking. "And...I ain't never touched a dead man before."

The Marshal grimaced, but he stepped in. "I'll help you."

Samantha nodded, trying to tamp her emotions down. Forced herself to grab Jude's arms as the Marshal grabbed his legs. Though limp, something grated like broken pieces of china in one arm, making her shudder. Charlotte opened up the rear door of the vardo, snatched a pair of jackets for her and Samantha, and then lowered the entry steps. Jude was heavy, dead weight, but they only had to carry him a few steps. His body made a sickening *thump* as they slid it onto the vardo's floor.

The Marshal turned and went out to the street.

"That's right," came his voice, as he spoke to the first few passers-by. "All the excitement's done with. Go back to your homes, show's over."

The show's definitely over. Charlotte grimaced, trying to hold back tears as she climbed up and took hold of the vardo's reins. Samantha pulled on the jacket that Charlotte gave her, and then proceeded to hitch up the mules.

"Charlotte," Samantha said, as she swung up into the freight wagon's seat, "Let's get going. Just follow my wagon."

"Get going? But...where to?"

"I don't know..." A labored breath. "Not back east. Don't want to go through the rest of Kansas City to the west, either. North, then."

A snap of the reins, and they began. They resolutely refused to look at the small group of people that gathered around the Deputy Marshal, demanding answers. But no one stopped them as they headed out of the city limits at a careful, measured pace.

Samantha listened to the sounds of sobbing that came from the vardo behind her. She didn't dare look back, not without giving in to her need to cry out in rage and pain. Her eyes stayed dry and burning with the need for sleep, but she kept the wagons relentlessly on the road until the bright stars overhead faded with the barest hint of the approaching morning.

"Up ahead. Pull up by that big tree," Samantha said, her voice a dry croak.

Sunrise streaked the sky pink as they pulled over, coming to rest underneath a large, gnarled oak. To Charlotte, it looked as if its limbs stretched out to welcome the weary and burdened.

Samantha got down from the freight wagon and then helped Charlotte down from the vardo's seat.

"How are you doing? I know it ain't fine and dandy out here, but..."

"Oh, I'm as fresh as a daisy," Charlotte replied. But her voice was thin, her tone flat. "I got to tell you...I ain't never been this tired."

"After we get Jude buried, we can stop for a bit. But we need to put him to rest before the day gets too hot."

The two women swallowed as they opened the vardo's door, trying not to flinch at the sight. The dim lighting of the stables had hidden the worst that had been done to Jude's body. Worse, the vardo's floor carpet had soaked up their friend's blood and had dried, sticky and clotted.

Charlotte put her hand to her mouth and swayed as if she were going to faint.

"I can't do this myself," Samantha warned.

Inspiration struck. She stepped up into the vardo, carefully made her way around Jude's still form, and then wrapped the carpet up around him. She removed one of the curtain ties from the window and secured the carpet with it.

Charlotte snapped out of it once the corpse's identity had been hidden from view. It ceased to be her friend, at least slightly. She reached out with both hands, closed her eyes, and grabbed the body's ankles.

Together, the two women got Jude out of the vardo for the last time. Samantha pulled a pickaxe and shovel out of the freight wagon. Jude's old tools. Luck smiled on them one last time as they found a patch of blessedly loose soil just beyond where the oak spread its tangle of roots. Though the work was slow, the two dug through the morning, not speaking a word to each other, until the hole was deep enough. One more strained lift, and Jude was placed into the earth and then covered.

"Char..." Samantha said, "Can you...please say something? A prayer? My mind...it's gone all blank. And Jude...he deserves something. Something nice."

Charlotte thought for a moment. "My daddy didn't take us to many funerals. But I can try." She cleared her throat, and spoke quietly. "Father, into your hands we commit the spirit of our friend, Jude Davis. I...we have faith that you will know the goodness and kind measure of this man, who protected us as if we were his own kin. Bless him and let him ascend to be with you in heaven. Amen."

Samantha let her tears flow. They fell with a dull patter to the dry ground. She placed her arm around Charlotte's slim shoulders.

Charlotte's tears began too. "Was that nice?"

"Very," Samantha choked out. "Very nice. I think Jude would've approved."

Bone tired, they unhitched the teams and set them to graze. Then, sweat-stained, blood-spattered, and earth-grimed, they collapsed on a blanket hastily laid on the ground under the big tree. The sun had moved high in the sky before they woke.

The waking wasn't slow, and it wasn't pleasant.

The muffled sounds of movement, the intake of someone's breath.

A chill ran up Samantha's back as she realized that someone stood over her. Opening her eyes a mere slit, she slid an arm towards her gun belt.

Only to have her hand stepped on by a moccasin-clad foot.

CHAPTER TWENTY-NINE

Matthew Slade strode into the Golden Goose and spied his quarry at the card table. The man, who sat with his back to the wall and eyes on the swinging doors, spotted him as well. A twitch of the handlebar mustache and the Deputy Marshal sat up.

"Cash me out, boys," he said. As soon as he'd gathered up his belongings, the Marshal indicated with a wave of his hand that Slade should join him at the bar.

"Looks like you were expecting me," Slade said, as he did so.

"One of the boys saw you goin' in to my old office." A shrug. "Plus, you look like you're a working gun. I'm guessing that you're one of the Pinks."

Slade grimaced at the term, but nodded. "That's right."

"I don't mean no disrespect. Just the term I've heard out here." The man gave Slade one more hard glance, and then extended a hand. "Wyatt Earp. Formerly Deputy Marshal of this little piece of Kansas City."

"Your reputation precedes you," the reply came, after a hearty handshake. "Matthew Slade, Pinkerton's Chicago branch. And I thought you were still Deputy Marshal."

"Not as of noon today, no." Earp signaled to the bartender and held up two fingers. In a moment, the man brought over a bottle of rye whiskey and a pair of shot glasses. "Marshal Wheeler got in a scrape-up a couple months ago, hurt his leg. I owed him a favor, so I came in for a while. Now that he's back in the saddle, all I have left to do is turn in my badge. Let's drink to that. You look like a thirsty man, in any case."

"You're on," Slade said, as Earp poured. He took the glass, tossed it down. The drink's bite made him grimace through his teeth.

"Clears the hair outta' your throat don't it?" Earp said, as he downed his drink in turn. "Well, if I'm off my usual pasture, so're you. What brings a Pink – sorry, a Pinkerton man – out here to the dust-side of Missouri?"

"I'm looking for two young women. Their family wants 'em back. From what Marshal Wheeler told me, you bumped into them."

Earp listened to the description Slade gave, and nodded. "That's them, right. They're travelin' a lot fancier. Got this big red gypsy wagon with gilt trim, but it's them. My trail did indeed bump into theirs. Night before last, it was. And they're in for a whole heap of trouble."

"How do you mean?"

"I don't know anything about this. *Officially*, that is. You cotton on to what I mean?"

"Straight up," Slade agreed.

Earp got up and brought a newspaper back to the bar. He turned to the front page, where a picture of two men lay in a pair of hastily made coffins.

"See these two?" He tapped the picture with his finger. "That's Ezra and Zeke. I knew 'em as rustlers, horse thieves, general low-lifes."

Slade nodded, not comprehending. "Anything I should know about 'em?"

"Two things. First, they're the younger brothers of someone you ought to know: Clark Quantrill, of the self-same Raiders."

Matthew Slade sat up straight. "So Quantrill's kin are still out there. What about Clark himself? Kept hearing rumors back in Illinois, but nothing solid enough to sink your teeth into."

"Ain't rumor no more. I *saw* the sonofabitch. Took a shot at him, but he skedaddled. He'll be back, count on it. But not here. Only where your two girls are."

"How's that?"

"Who do you think done in his kin?" Slade stared, dumbfounded, as Earp continued. "I've been talking to Miss Brenda, the lady who runs this place. She says that one girl throws a mean bullwhip, while the other's the deadliest pistoleer since Wild Bill Hickok."

"Those two...my client didn't hint at *anything* like that."

"Maybe your client don't know those girls like he thought," Earp pointed out. "Anyways, I sent those two on the trail out of town."

"Why?"

"Because Quantrill's crazy. He's burned whole towns to the ground," Earp pointed out. "If those two got holed up here, there was bound to be killin'. I'm overdue back in Dodge. And Wheeler, God bless him, ain't up to takin' on the likes of Quantrill."

"But you think those girls will be up to it?"

"Slade, you don't know these parts like I do," Earp retorted. "West of here, the prairie goes on and on. You could toss Illinois, Indiana, and Ohio out there, and still have room left over. It'll take a damn good scrape of luck for Quantrill to find those girls in all of that."

"Or me," Slade grumped. He put his shot glass down. "Thank you for the news."

Earp tipped his hat. Slade turned on his heel and made for his horse. His mount was tired, but he had to make a final sweep through the outlying areas of Kansas City.

The last chance he had, before his quarry disappeared into the ocean of grassland ahead.

CHAPTER THIRTY

A hard rawhide sole bit into the skin on the back of Samantha's hand, pinning it in place.

At that moment, Charlotte cried out.

"Sam!"

Samantha sat up. She cried out in turn as she stared up into the painted face of a half-naked man wearing buckskin leggings. His coal black hair hung plaited in long braids, while a breastplate adorned with carved bone covered his chest. He held a spear decorated with feathers and long hair in one strong hand. A second brave, also armed with a spear, stood over Charlotte.

A stray breeze made something flutter at the man's waist. A string of fleshy, tanned flaps that hung from a belt.

Oh my God.

Scalps.

Wordlessly, the brave held up Samantha's guns. He'd already slipped them free of her holsters as she'd slept. He shook his head and tucked the weapons in a pack. Two more braves came riding up on a pair of painted horses. Their conversation was terse, with a great deal of gesturing and pointing to the two women.

"What d'you think is goin' on?" Charlotte asked, her voice full of fear. "What're they goin' to do with us?"

"Hush now," Samantha said, trying to keep fear out of her voice. "They've got our guns, and we're not going to outrun them with our two wagons. Let's sit tight, see what they do."

"They goin' to take our scalps?"

"Doubt it. They do that to men mostly."

"Mostly?"

"I don't know! But they'd have taken ours already if they were goin' to!"

One of the braves leveled his spear at them.

"*Inila!*" he said sternly, drawing a finger across his mouth. "*Inila, wayela-tah!*"

The two women took the hint and lay quietly, until the discussion among the warriors had been settled. Their horses were brought back and hitched to the wagons. Next, the braves pushed Charlotte and Samantha back to their spots on the vardo and the freight wagon. But this time, a warrior sat next to each of them, and it was the Indian who held the reins.

"*Sukawa*," said the brave in the lead, and with a *thwack* of the reins, the wagons jerked forward, off the northerly road and into the grasslands to the west.

Even through the dust and the rising heat of the day, Samantha could smell the earthiness of the brave's leather outfit. It wasn't unpleasant, but it was completely foreign to her senses. A foreboding chill crept in from all parts of her body. Her stomach lurched with something akin to nausea from fear, but surprisingly, a strange excitement lingered as well.

The rest of the day passed in complete silence. Suddenly, they rounded a bend and Samantha's eyes took in a view she never expected. Several hundred tepees spread out along a lightly forested creek bed. Buffalo skin sides shone glistened and tan in the late afternoon sun. Campfire smoke wafted high into the evening summer sky, and she breathed in the smell of cooking meat.

From behind her, she heard Charlotte's voice. "Sam! Have you ever seen the like?"

"Never," she replied. The brave next to her scowled, and she quieted.

Women and children from all over the village came running from their tasks to see the brightly colored wagon. The commotion as the villagers came to stare and chatter at the sight of the two young women continued to grow, until the braves had to shout and gesture at the crowd to let the wagons through.

They continued in a straight path to the center of the encampment where a large tepee stood, decorated with bright colors and quills. A lodge pole stood outside, hung with masses of bright feathers, beads and human hair. With rough signals, the braves gestured for Samantha and Charlotte to get down from their wagons.

"God, I'm scared," Charlotte said, teary eyed. "Why don't they just kill us now?"

Samantha put her arm around Charlotte and pulled her close, kissed her cheek. The braves watching them noted it, though their expression seemed to be one of astonishment, not hostility. Samantha glared back at them, defiant.

"I'm scared too. Remember that I love you. No matter what, we're together for this."

A man ducked through the low opening in the side of the tepee out into the sunlight. He wore a rough cloth shirt overlaid with a brace of bead necklaces. His leggings, from waist to moccasins, had been beautifully decorated in trade beads and stained quills.

His face was young; it had been wizened by sun, wind, and great sadness. His hair framed his visage in long plaits, braided with brightly colored cloth and a single eagle feather. The braves around them bowed in reverence, instantly elevating the status of this one man.

"*Tatanka Iyotaka*," he said, in a magnificent deep rumble of a voice. He pointed to his chest and repeated himself, this time in halting, but clear English words. "Chief Sitting Bull."

He gestured to himself again.

"Chief of all Sioux Nation. You?" He pointed at them, firm command in his gesture.

"Samantha Williams," Samantha said. She indicated Charlotte and added, "Charlotte Harte. From Chicago."

Right then, Samantha's stomach growled. She looked up, embarrassed. She hadn't eaten anything since before last night's performance, and her stomach wasn't happy about it.

Sitting Bull let out a baritone chuckle. He made a motion for the women to get up and follow him into his tepee. Two Indian women did so as well. A small fire smoldered in the center of the tepee. Off to one side, a buffalo hide hung, stretched on a wooden frame.

Sitting Bull made a motion for Samantha and Charlotte to sit, while the two Indian women handed them each a bowl with chunks of cooked meat and a piece of flat bread.

"Eat." Sitting Bull directed. He took his spot and sat opposite them, as one of the Indian women handed him a smoking pipe.

Too hungry to care about dying just at the moment, the two women set upon the food with a ravenous appetite. Sitting Bull took a long puff and spoke again with his magnificent voice.

"I speak some English. Not much. I must know. Who man you bury?"

"He was our friend," Samantha replied, between bites.

"He black man. You white woman. How you friend?'

"Jude was a man," Samantha said, careful to answer using simple words. "His color did not matter. I killed for him. He would have done the same for us."

"You his women?"

"No! Friends."

Sitting Bull sat back and watched the two women as they finished the bowls of food.

"Why you travel alone? No soldiers."

"We are wanted by Pinkerton. We can't go to soldiers."

"Why they want you?"

"We have run away from my father. He wants me to marry an old man."

Sitting Bull gave a long puff at his pipe. "You not do what father want?"

"No!"

"That is not good thing."

"It *is* a good thing. I want to be with Charlotte." Samantha made a gesture from her heart to Charlotte, and then hugged herself.

Sitting Bull nodded sagely, as if confirming a thought of his. He got up and walked over to where the painted buffalo hide hung in the smoky air, and then turned it to face them. Painted symbols crisscrossed the hide's surface.

"You part of vision." Sitting Bull stated plainly. He pointed to the beginning, where figures of horses and buffalo overlapped each other. "Many buffalo. *Hunkpapas* very happy."

His finger traced the next set of figures. Jagged lines, drawings of bullets, bodies, shining lumps of rock.

Sitting Bull's voice echoed a deep sadness and grief. "White man came for yellow metal. Many die. On both sides."

Then he pointed to two figures painted in blue. Two women. They stood next to a bright red wagon. His finger came to a stop.

"Here. You."

The blue figures were holding hands.

CHAPTER THIRTY-ONE

"Whoa there!" Matthew Slade said, as he pulled hard on his mount's reins.

His mustang let out an annoyed snort and shook his head, but came to a stop. The evening star gleamed over the horizon in the clear sky, and night was coming swiftly on. Another few minutes, and Slade might have ridden right on by.

But he'd seen something.

A fresh mound of earth just off to one side of a lonely road. Not a rough heap of dirt tossed up by a farmer. A rectangular scraping of soil that, to his trained eyes, had been tamped down again.

A shallow grave.

Quickly, he dismounted and led his horse in a wide circle around to one side. He paused underneath the wide-spreading branches of a nearby oak tree. The soil near the grave bore the smeary remnants of tracks and movements.

Slade's eyes struggled to unravel the patterns. A pair of wagons had come and left. Two people had dragged something heavy through the dirt and into the grave. He paused, wondering if one of the girls had been buried here. He didn't relish the thought of disturbing her grave, but his client would want to know.

He shook his head. No, the footprints next to the drag marks were both small. Delicate. Female. Earp hadn't talked about anyone besides the Quantrill brothers being killed, but the girls had definitely buried someone out here.

His heart froze as he found one more print in the dirt: a man-sized moccasin print.

The wagon tracks led here but did not continue along the road. Instead, they vanished into the grasslands beyond. Slade took off his hat and stood quietly for a while, thinking. Not a few of Pinkerton's finest would have ridden back to town and telegraphed the client that the quarry was gone for good.

Yet Slade's mind echoed with one of Earp's comments. *I've been talking to Miss Brenda. She says that one throws a mean bullwhip...the other's the deadliest pistoleer since Wild Bill.*

"So the Indians took you two," he said, grimacing. "But I don't think you two are done, not for a long run yet."

Slade got back on his horse. Turned back the way he came and set off at a gallop towards the twinkling lights of Kansas City. His next telegram wouldn't be one excusing defeat.

He'd put each and every agent in Kansas on alert. His quarry was out there. Like a gopher hidden in a field, it was only a matter of time before the two girls popped up for him to collect.

※ ※ ※

Sitting Bull remained silent, his proud figure wreathed in fragrant pipe smoke. His expression was serene, inscrutable, as Samantha got to her feet. She went over to the painted buffalo hide and extended a hand. She reached out, nearly touching the two blue figures painted on the hide.

"I don't understand," she said.

Sitting Bull exhaled, blew a ring that Samuel Clemens would have turned green with envy at and spoke calmly. "That is fine."

Samantha scowled. "It is?"

"Yes. One cannot understand all of any vision. They are great things. Mysterious things."

"So...if I may..." Charlotte spoke, her voice sounding small in the confines of the teepee, "What does this mean for us? What plans do you have for us?"

"Tonight, you sleep here. In sacred teepee." Sitting Bull stated. "Tomorrow, at first sun, you are free to go."

Charlotte cocked her head, as if unable to believe her ears. "Why?"

"Vision." Sitting Bull pointed at Samantha and Charlotte in turn. "You, and you. Of third kind."

"Third kind? What is third kind?"

"Not just man, not just woman. Third kind. Big magic."

Samantha and Charlotte just looked at each other, confused, but hesitant to ask further.

"You leave sun come up," Sitting Bull added. "You leave sun come up. Take all with you. My braves go with you for one sun. Then they return."

Samantha turned to face Sitting Bull. "I...don't know what to say. Thank you."

He made a motion with his arms. The two Indian women came to his side, helped him rise. "Do not thank me," he intoned. "Vision tells us. We all have part to play in life. We meet on road at dawn, part by sunset. That is your path. Apart from us, together for you."

He inclined his head towards them. Without another word, he and his two assistants left, allowing the tent flap to shut behind them.

Charlotte got up to stand by Samantha's side. She regarded the two figures on the buffalo canvas silently. She slipped her hand into Samantha's and squeezed. Samantha squeezed back.

"Big magic," Charlotte mused. "If my Daddy only knew."

"Maybe," Samantha said, "Big magic is what they mean by love."

"That's good enough for me." Charlotte smiled, and together the two women gathered up the pile of fur blankets that had been left in the teepee. They lay down together, hips and hands touching. Charlotte shook her head. "God almighty, Sam. Between last night...what happened to Jude...bein' brought here...my nerves are feelin' shot through. I don't think I'll ever be able to get some shuteye."

"I know what you mean," Samantha agreed. "But maybe we can close our eyes, try to nap a little, at least."

Charlotte nodded. Fingers interlaced together, the two closed their eyes.

In less than a minute, the teepee filled with the sound of the two snoring.

CHAPTER THIRTY-TWO

Morning came, cold and clammy. Samantha woke to the sounds of activity outside their teepee. She blinked as she saw wisps of steam float by overhead. With a yawn, she sat up to see Charlotte kneeling nearby, sipping delicately from a shell-shaped drinking bowl.

"Mornin', Sam. Join me for breakfast?" Charlotte asked, and a wan smile crossed her face for the first time since they'd arrived in Kansas City. She indicated a wooden platter, laden with strips of dark meat and a pile of blood-red berries.

"I think I will," Samantha said, as she set the fur blankets aside. Much to her surprise, she'd slept as well in the teepee as she had when swaddled in Miss Pleasance's best bedding.

"The two Indian ladies – squaws, I think you call 'em – just brought a couple of water pots. Near as I can tell, the warm stuff is for us to wash up. The hot stuff is for drinking."

"Just water?" Samantha asked, but Charlotte handed her one of the shell-shaped bowls, which held a honey-colored, herbal-smelling liquid.

"It was, but I remembered that I had a couple sachets of chamomile tea stuck in my pocket."

Together, the two tasted the dry meat strips, puckered lips over the tart berries, and finished off the tea. They had just finished washing as well as they could before the teepee flap was thrown aside. Sunlight flooded in, framing one of the Indian women. She beckoned to them, and they came outside, blinking in the strong morning sun.

Around them, the people of the village bustled with the business of the day, ignoring them. Either their novelty had worn off, Samantha thought, or Sitting Bull had decreed that no one should bother them. A pair of braves, younger and brawnier than the two which had brought them to the encampment, stood before them. One of the men, who bore an old scar across one cheek, stepped forward and spoke.

"I speak some of your English," he said curtly. "We guide you from here. For one sun."

"Thank you," Samantha said. "You...ah...I guess you know who we are. Who are you?"

"I am called Has-No-Horse," He pointed at his taller, lankier companion. "He is Loud Thunder."

Samantha looked over to where their wagons had been drawn up, horses and mules hitched. The animals looked as if they'd been properly rested, watered, and fed. She climbed up into the freight wagon's seat while Charlotte did the same with the vardo.

To her surprise, instead of joining her, Has-No-Horse walked away and came back astride a beautiful bay-and-white pinto. Loud Thunder followed suit on a similar looking black and white spotted mount. The horses were decorated with feathers twisted up in their mane and tails. Painted symbols on their shoulders and flanks added color to the already colorful markings.

"We leave now, Big Magic," Has-No-Horse said, and with a kick of his heels, he set off, leading the way. As before, the people around them carefully made way for their little procession. After the freight wagon jerked into motion, she eventually pulled alongside Has-No-Horse's mount.

Samantha swallowed, and then carefully ventured a question that had been on her mind since last night.

"Has-No-Horse...I needed to ask something."

The brave grunted, nodding.

"Um...we may be 'Big Magic', but magic alone won't protect us. Do you have our guns?"

"Yes. Your weapons inside red wagon," he said, tossing his head in the direction of the vardo. "Now quiet. You talk too much."

Samantha's lips curled as she considered a retort, but wisely, she decided to stay silent. However, the feel of the two women being kept 'under guard' faded as the morning wore on. Instead of bracketing the pair of wagons, the Indian braves instead rode ahead as outriders, always a ridgeline or two ahead of the steady, plodding pace of the wagons. Eventually, the sun broke through the gray banks of clouds, and the smell of wildflowers from the rolling fields around them rose up, heady and strong.

The remainder of the morning went similarly. Except for a single stop, when Has-No-Horse and Loud Thunder spoke quietly together of the path ahead, the Indian braves had little to say. Charlotte and Samantha took their cue from the two, and spoke in hushed tones. The warriors guiding them grew more agitated as the day drew closer to noon. Samantha saw that they hung closer to the wagons. That they circled back around, watched more carefully.

"Is it just me, or are our friends getting mighty antsy?" Charlotte said, as quietly as she could manage from her perch on the vardo's seat.

"Not just you. I'm seeing it too." Samantha said. Her voice cut off as the wagons crested a ridge. Stretching out before them, the land flattened out into a golden sea of grass, slashed in two by a wide, rushing river. Beyond it, the grasslands trailed off into scrubby woodland. On the western horizon, she made out the hint of brown-shingled roofs and the skinny profile of a church steeple.

"We have guided you," Has-No-Horse said, as he brought his mount to a halt by Samantha's wagon. He swept a hand towards the fast-running water. "This is the Big Blue river. To cross, you must take ferry. One sun's ride north."

"You have our thanks," Samantha said, hurriedly. "But please, wait one moment. We saw that you and Loud Thunder are worried. What is wrong?"

A look passed between the two braves. Loud Thunder shrugged in disinterest.

"Confusing signs. Many horses on the move. Far away, but not far enough." Has-No-Horse said carefully, as if picking and choosing from his limited number of alien words. "Some move north. Move together, in step. Cavalry soldiers."

He practically spat the last sentence.

"Some move north...and others?" Samantha prompted.

"Others move north and west. Towards ferry. Strange."

"Why strange?"

"Hear metal-on-metal. Of guns and rifles carried. But not in step. Not soldiers. Something else." He tugged at his reins. "We go now. Sitting Bull has spoken. Gives you his blessing to you both, Big Magic."

Again, the two women thanked the braves. They nodded curtly, and with a whoop, they disappeared down the rear slope of the ridge. Samantha listened to the pounding of their horse's hooves until they faded into the distance. Suddenly, the day felt lonely, vaguely threatening.

And it finally hit Samantha. For the first time since they had left Mrs. Pleasance's, they were completely on their own.

CHAPTER THIRTY-THREE

"We ain't takin' the ferry? What kind of horse dung is that?" Charlotte demanded. She turned back to where they had stopped the wagons, on the east bank of the Big Blue River. Peevishly, she watched the fast-moving water flow by with a look akin to hatred.

"Just what I said. We're not heading that way," Samantha said. She jabbed a finger at where they'd spread out the last remaining western map they'd found in the vardo. "We're just south of Marysville. It's got the only ferry over the Big Blue in this part of Kansas."

"So?"

"You heard Has-No-Horse. Someone's on the move out that way. If it's not the U.S. Cavalry, then there's only two possibilities. Care to guess?"

"Pinkerton," Charlotte said sourly. "Or Quantrill. The way our luck runs, he's got himself a mess of friends."

"Precisely. So if we're going to cross, we better do it now, before it gets too late." She paused, waited for Charlotte to step away from the river and looked her in the eye. "We need to switch places. I'll take the vardo across first. You'll bring the freight wagon over afterwards."

Charlotte stared at her, stunned. "But...I can't drive them mules!"

"You can, believe me. The mules won't be any harder to drive than the draft horses." Charlotte put her head down and bit her lip. Samantha continued, trying to sound firm, but understanding. "The vardo's lighter, and it's watertight. Plus, the draft horses are taller. They'll have to do less swimming, if it comes to it."

"Okay," came the sullen reply. "Then what? It sounds like you're givin' me the shorter end of the stick. The heavier wagon and the smaller mules."

"It's not the shorter end. Once I get across, I can unhitch the two draft horses and help you if you need it. So you just wait until I signal you that it's time for you to start across. Okay?" Samantha waited, but Charlotte didn't reply right away. Finally, almost imperceptibly, she nodded her head.

Samantha got into the driver's spot on the vardo and lined the horses up to cross. The draft horses looked unperturbed by the crossing ahead. From the rear of the vardo, the two riding horses nickered nervously at the sound of the rushing water. Charlotte followed Samantha's lead by climbing aboard the freight wagon. Reins held listlessly in one hand, she stared straight ahead into the distance, as if transfixed on the distant horizon.

Samantha moved the heavy draft horses out and into the river. The chill water rushed around the edges of the vardo with a *hiss*. The water crept up, up and still further up to near the tops of the wheels.

She felt a nervous trickle of sweat trickle run down her back as they reached the halfway point and with a jolt, she realized that the horses were swimming. The vardo bobbed up, wheels scraping the occasional stone. The horses both in front and behind the vardo whinnied and strained, their strong legs kicking in the water's flow.

And then, the draft horses got through the deepest section. The vardo's wheels touched the bottom, and even the smaller riding horses were able to find their footing. Puffing and snorting, both pairs shook the water from their coats as they emerged on the far bank. The vardo dripped both water and mud, but it appeared undamaged.

Not wasting any time, Samantha climbed down off the wagon. She took a coil of rope out from under the seat and unhitched the two draft horses. Carefully, she led them back to the river's western edge, slightly upstream from where Charlotte watched her, and then turned the animals so that they faced away from the river. She tied an end of the rope to the singletree bar that hung from their traces behind them, and held the rest of the coil in one hand.

"You're going to end up swimming!" Samantha shouted, as loudly as she could. "But you have to keep going forward, no matter what! I can get to you if you need help, just keep coming!"

Charlotte stared at her, glassy-eyed, but she set her jaw and cracked the whip. The mules moved out and into the river. For the first minute or two, Samantha hoped against hope that her help wouldn't be needed. But as the freight wagon reached the middle of the Big Blue, the smaller mules brayed with panic as their feet lost contact with the riverbed.

The current caught the bulky freight wagon and turned it. With a groan, it began to jack-knife and swing downstream. Her arms shaking, Charlotte cracked the whip again, letting out a scream as she felt the powerful current wrench the wagon around.

Without hesitation, Samantha looped the coil of rope around her head and shoulder and dove into the river. The numbing cold of the water felt like nails driven into her skin as she moved through the current, thrashing her way towards the midstream. The iron taste of minerals and mud filled her mouth, and she spat, gasping, trying to keep her head above the water. The current grabbed her, tossed her around like a rag doll, but pushed her downstream to where the freight wagon listed to one side at an alarming degree.

Samantha grabbed onto the wagon's rear panel. The water slammed her against the wagon, sending pain searing into her like a knife blade as she grabbed at whatever she could to keep from being pulled under. Water gushed down her windpipe for a second as a wave blinded her. For a second, the terror of drowning almost stilled her hands.

She forced herself to focus. Pulled herself upright, braced her side against the wagon, and managed to pull the coil of rope, dripping, over her head. With numb fingers, she tied the rope to an iron ring set into the wood, where a grease bucket had once hung.

With the last of her strength, she pulled herself up and over the lip of the wagon's rear deck. Boxes and gear fell with a clatter around her as she landed inside the wagon's damp bed. Coughing, she got to her hands and knees. The wagon still listed dangerously, but it hadn't tipped any further. Samantha looked up, to where Charlotte half-sat, half-stood in the driver's seat, thrashing her whip with abandon.

Eyes aglow with fury and panic, Charlotte cursed and swore at the mule team like a veteran skinner, using words that would've made her mother faint dead away. But the fear-crazed animals continued to inch forward, swimming against the current in the same direction. Samantha stared, impressed, but she knew that they would tire soon. She stood up and shouted at the top of her lungs to the draft horses on the far bank.

"Pansy! Daisy!" Samantha called, using the draft horse's names, *"Git up!"*

The big mares set their feet into the ground and dug in to keep from being pulled backward into the river. They see-sawed back and forth, trying to gain leverage in the soft dirt.

And finally, they found purchase. Their hooves dug in and they moved forward. A few seconds later, the mules also found the river bottom. Steadily, they bore on, straightening out their course. With a *creak*, the freight wagon lurched onto the far bank.

"Whoa there!" Samantha cried, and the two draft horses halted. The mules followed suit, blowing and coughing up water with rude, unhappy sounds. She stumbled her way up front, spattering drops of cold water as she made her way to sit next to Charlotte.

The younger woman continued to stare forward, glassy-eyed. Her skin had gone ashen, giving her face the look of a porcelain doll. The reins dropped from her hands, stained red with blood. She spoke in a pained whisper.

"I don't know how to swim."

Samantha put one hand on hers. "I didn't know. But we have to—"

Charlotte shook off Samantha's hand. A shudder ran down the length of her body. Color suddenly infused her cheeks.

She leaned back, and then slapped Samantha hard across the face.

CHAPTER THIRTY-FOUR

Samantha's cheek stung with the blow from Charlotte's leather gloved hand.

But that was nothing compared to the stab she felt to her heart.

Charlotte's face flushed from sun-bronzed tan to sunburned red. Her voice shook as she angrily declared, "How dare you, Sam? How dare you put me in such...I could've..."

"Drowned," Samantha said wearily. "I told you, I didn't know. Came close to drowning on my own out there. But we—"

"Don't touch me!" Charlotte leapt from the wagon and stumbled to the base of a nearby tree. She sat down. Pulled her legs in tight to her chest, wrapped her arms around them.

Charlotte laid her forehead on her knees and cried. A strange, hysterical kind of crying, punctuated by an occasional hiccup.

Samantha felt as if the chill from her wet clothes had frozen her in place. She stared helplessly at Charlotte, words all jumbled in her mind, unsure of what to do.

How could Char ever think that I would knowingly put her in danger? I'd rather die first.

A tremor ran through her body at the thought it might come to that.

Stiff, bruised, and battered, Samantha limped away from where Charlotte continued to cry. She clambered aboard the vardo, peeled off her soaked clothes and into a set of dry ones. Next, she went to untie the two draft horses from the freight wagon, and then tend as best she could to all the horses and mules, leading them in pairs further up the bank to allow them to dry off and recuperate in the sun. It was a sign of her weariness that what normally engaged her a few minutes to complete took more than a half-hour.

At the last, Samantha led their two riding horses, Jubilee and Patches, up to the top of the bank to let them rest and graze.

Jubilee nuzzled her, and Samantha leaned against her mount in return, feeling her reassuring solidity.

"You've been gettin' it easy so far," she murmured, stroking the horse's mane. "No pulling heavy wagons, and we haven't gotten to riding you and Patches, except for our shows."

She cast a glance down towards where the river still swirled over the rocks.

In all this time, Charlotte hadn't moved.

Samantha waited a while, let the sun warm her, stiffen her resolve and drain the worst of the weariness away. She sighed, and then went to approach the figure curled up at the base of the tree.

"Char?" she ventured.

No answer.

"Char, honey?"

Charlotte's voice was a whisper above the gush of the river.

"We should never've done this. Any of it."

"We had no choice," Samantha said. "We had to get across."

Charlotte finally raised her head. Her face had lost its flush, but her skin was rimed with grimy dust and tears. Her eyes, bloodshot and watery, shone with anguish.

"No, Sam. *We* didn't. *We* didn't need to get Pinkerton after us. *We* didn't need to get Clark Quantrill after us. *We* didn't need to kill two men back in Kansas City. *We* didn't need to get Jude, poor innocent Jude...murdered."

Charlotte stopped and took a ragged breath as she continued, more softly.

"You were the one that needed to leave home. It was you that convinced me to prove my love for you by coming out here. You got Jude killed and made us fugitives. And it was you that almost got me drowned."

Samantha stared for moment. She stood up and dusted the seat of her pants off. She returned back to the vardo and found where the braves had safely stashed her guns. Her fingers gripped the leather of the gun belt and holsters like friends long missed. She strapped the belt on, checked that her guns were fully loaded.

A feeling of something close to comfort eased into her. The routine of the familiar. The smell of leather and gun oil in the confined space of the vardo. The heavy, balanced weight of the metal on her hips. It was a heady mix that buoyed her spirits. She found Jude's last map, unfolded it, and stepped outside to take a look.

West of where they crossed the river lay the town of Palmetto, Kansas. Under the dot that marked the place, she saw where Jude's sharp-edged handwriting had noted: *Jacks or Better Saloon. 'One-Eyed' Jill Sinclair. Ltr from E. Pleasance in frt-wgon strongbox.*

She stepped up into the freight wagon, located the strongbox, and found a letter from Mrs. Pleasance introducing them. Samantha also found a dwindling pile of coins, all that was left of their cash. They'd fled Kansas City without stopping to collect their pay.

She let out a breath. Knowing now what she had to do and say, she quietly walked to where Charlotte still sat. She squatted down in front of her so that there was no missing the seriousness in her eyes.

"You don't need to talk to me if you don't want to," she said plainly. "Just listen. I couldn't marry Percy Hanover. If I had, I'd have ended up dead, even if by my own hand. And yes, I wanted you to come with me. I love you, Char. When we started all this, when I saw you waiting for me by the bridge, my heart sang. But yes, it was selfish of me to ask you to come. Maybe it was a mistake. Maybe I should have just left by myself."

She paused, but it was only for a moment. The words were coming now. Hard to pull as cheatgrass at first, now they tumbled out like ore down a chute.

"It's never been my intent to put you in harm's way. God knows I would die first. Jude was my friend too. But I am not responsible for men's hatred of one another. I had no choice but to kill those two men. If I hadn't, what they would've done to us would have been worse."

Charlotte didn't speak. But her eyes focused on Samantha to the exclusion of everything else. Even if it hurt to hear the words, she was listening. Samantha was sure of that.

"It was just plain bad luck about Quantrill. I had nothing to do with that. As far as the Pinkertons...well, we don't choose who our fathers are. When I was little, before my mother died, I saw how he broke her, shaped her to his will. That's what the world wants for people like you, people like me. While I still have breath, I won't let that happen to me. To us, Charlotte. To us."

And with that, Samantha stood up. "But for now, you need to get up and help me get the teams together. We need to get to the town we saw in the distance. It's the last place that Mrs. Pleasance directed us to. So the way I figure it, we need to get on with our show. Honor the contract that Mrs. Pleasance trusted us to keep."

Charlotte didn't say anything.

But she got up. Stiff from sitting so long, she stretched, vertebrae popping. Samantha offered her a fresh handkerchief. Charlotte took it with a tired nod and then wiped her face clean of the worst of the grime and tears.

Without another word, she pushed past Samantha to where the draft horses waited.

CHAPTER THIRTY-FIVE

The 'Jacks or Better' saloon sprawled like a seedy ranch block house at Palmetto's edge. Even though the place was practically empty in the mid-afternoon heat, Samantha and Charlotte entered warily and turned their backs to the large common room as little as possible while they waited to be shown into the owner's office. Mrs. Pleasance's Social Club, with its kitchen smells and tinkling piano, had been almost homey. Between the cigarillo smoke and the sound of the roulette wheel, the Golden Goose in Kansas City had also retained a rustic, gambling-house charm.

But the current establishment had a rougher, grittier feel. Instead of the Social Club's fine marble-topped bar, a scarred wooden counter stretched along one full side of the saloon, designed to let entire gangs of cowboys and frontiersmen get to their drinking as quickly as possible. The cigar smoke in the air smelled rawer. The women noticed large brass spittoons parked at regular intervals along three of the four walls. And instead of a roulette wheel, a small sea of tables packed the center of the room, laid out for card dealing.

Two men, each unshaven and heavily muscled, showed Charlotte and Samantha around back to a grimy hothouse of an office. The women sat, uneasily eyeing the men as they took up positions off to the side. A tall, heavyset woman bustled around the office, only noticing that she had company as one of the men cleared his throat.

Samantha raised an eyebrow as she looked at the saloon's owner. One-Eyed Jill had crammed her robust frame into a bright red and black striped satin gown. Her hair was the color of soot, as was a large beauty mark at the corner of her crimson-rouged lips. And her moniker wasn't misleading – the woman wore a velvet patch adorned with diamonds arranged in a heart shape over her right eye.

"'Fraid you got the wrong place, ladies," Jill said brusquely. "Appearances to the contrary, I don't run a brothel out of this here establishment."

Samantha nodded. She glanced a final time at the men who lurked off to the side, swallowed hard, and spoke up.

"Miss Sinclair? My name is Samantha Williams, and my companion here is Charlotte Harte. We're not looking to ply those kind of wares here, but we are looking for a place to perform. Missus Elvira Pleasance sent us here for that."

"She did?"

"Yes, and she sent us with a letter of introduction." Samantha handed over the paper, which Jill quickly skimmed. Her hard-edged expression gave way to a smile. She extended a hand, which Samantha gratefully took.

"Pleased to meet you both. And do call me 'Jill' from now on. Elvira and I don't see eye-to-eye on plying the woman's trade on the frontier, but she taught me all I know about runnin' a whiskey joint. How's that old cow doin' anyway?" A puzzled look swept over her face, her eye searched the room. "And I don't think that she'd sent you all this way alone. Where's Jude?"

Samantha grimaced. "Jude's dead. I haven't wired Missus Pleasance about that yet."

Jill sat down abruptly, as if she'd run short of air. A tear came to her one eye. It washed over the rim and threatened to leave a black trail down her cheek. Her hand came up and wiped it away.

"I'm sorry to hear that. He was a good man, a damn good man. What happened?"

"He was bushwhacked by some fellows carrying a grudge from the war," Samantha said, skirting the edge of the truth. "Took three of them to get the jump on Jude."

Jill shook her head. "I'll send a wire to Elvira in the mornin'. But I sure hope they get 'em that done it."

"They got two of them so far," Samantha said quietly.

"Then let's hope the last one is reunited with the devil as well." After a few moments of silence, Jill spoke again. "Well, whatever Elvira Pleasance sent you out here for, she must've felt it was important. And her letter says you two are 'French' performers, that right? Which one of you does the whip act?"

"Why, that would be me," Charlotte said, speaking up for the first time. "We've put a twist into our act, tried it out at Kansas City. Left the men in the audience howling like wolves and panting for more."

"Hm." Jill steepled her fingers for a moment. "If they're howlin', then they're goin' to be thirsty as well."

"That they would," Samantha put in. "I can guarantee that if you give us the stage for this evening, we'll have more than enough coin to split between us."

"I like that right well," Jill said firmly, settling the deal. "You two can take the upstairs room for the time you're here. I'll make sure that your horses get taken care of, too. Won't be too much, but keep in mind that it'll come out of your cut."

"Wasn't expecting it otherwise."

"It can get to be a rough crowd here. That's why I got rough an' rowdy in turn."

"You did?" Charlotte's brow furrowed. "I don't understand."

Jill indicated the two men. "I needed a couple of bruisers to watch over things. The one on the left is nicknamed 'Rough'. Rowdy's the one on the right."

Each man nodded in turn. Samantha couldn't resist cracking a grin at that.

"I like the way you think, Jill. And Charlotte there – Dominique, I should say – she's not exaggerating. You'll get a few wolf whistles tonight."

※ ※ ※

Whistles? Samantha thought, as she strutted backstage, her emptied guns still smoking from her trick shots. *I was wrong, Charlotte right. It's a right pack of wolves baying at the moon tonight.*

The saloon was packed to near-overflowing with cowboys, most fresh off the cattle trail leading up from Texas and into Missouri. Howls and cries for 'more!' rocked the rafters. Despite the noise, the crowd behaved themselves as Rowdy and Rough positioned themselves off to the sides of the stage, each with a shotgun in hand.

Samantha turned around and faced the wall as Charlotte laced her into the corset. Her breath whistled out as the protective covering came together. Charlotte yanked at the laces with an added strength this evening.

"A bit...tight...isn't it?" Samantha asked, panting.

"Do tell," was all the response she received.

Once again, Charlotte – in her guise as Dominique – led Samantha out and positioned her against a handy column.

"*Maintenant*," she shouted, over the roar of the assembled men, "*Ze grande finale!*"

Dominique unspooled the bullwhip and tasked the crowd to count. Her whip *cracked*, and the men gasped, held speechless by the spectacle, counting from one to seven as a singular, mesmerized crowd.

Only the count didn't stop. Samantha gasped as Charlotte continued with another cutting blow, one that made her jump. The impact rattled her body as 'Dominique' bore down again and again.

"*Eight!*" the assembled men cried. "*Nine! Ten!*"

At twelve, Samantha risked a glance back. Charlotte's cat-grin didn't seem full of mirth, but it did look satisfied.

A final crack. "*THIRTEEN!*"

And with that, Dominique let the whip come to rest. She bowed deeply, to the cheers of the crowd. The curtain came down amidst the deafening jingle of thrown coins. Charlotte coiled up her whip, strode to Samantha's side, and pulled back the few tattered fragments of cloth on the woman's back.

Charlotte let out a gasp as she watched blood ooze from between the tightly woven corset laces.

CHAPTER THIRTY-SIX

Charlotte led a gasping, quivering Samantha backstage and towards one of the building's walls. Positioned Samantha so that she could begin unlacing the corset's bonds.

"How…do I look back there?" Samantha asked, as she felt the corset begin to release. The skin between her shoulder blades burned dully, like metal left out in the noontime sun.

"Striped. Not bad. Only broke the skin in a couple spots. Stay still, I'll take care of it right away."

Samantha pressed her forehead up against the wall's cool wood. She heard Charlotte rummaging around in one of their bags. The *pop* of an unstoppered cork. She let out a hiss as Charlotte dabbed a cloth doused in alcohol across the open scratches.

"I guess…you made your point." Samantha said, as she continued to face the wall. "How you felt…about today."

The reply was weary, but held no trace of anger. "It's never been my intent to put you in harm's way," Charlotte said, mimicking what had been said earlier. "Well, maybe at first I wanted to punish you. For today."

Charlotte peeked around a corner, saw Jill's two strong-arm men herding the audience back out into Palmetto's streets. A single quartet of men remained at a table off to the side of the bar, playing cards and drinking. She turned her attention back to Samantha.

"And did you? Finish punishing me, I mean."

"I think so. I'm still working it out. Got a lot of it out tonight on stage."

Samantha pushed away from the wall to face Charlotte. Together, the two women took their time and slipped out of their costumes, wiped off their stage makeup, and pulled out a change of clothing. Charlotte picked out a plain cotton frock, while Samantha slipped into a set of men's trousers, shirt, and leather vest she had grown to favor.

"You'll come up to the room tonight, then?" Samantha asked. "I made the bed earlier, while you were getting ready for the show."

"I'll come up. Eventually. I'm tired, but not sleepy. Restless, if'n that makes any sense. I want something to drink, calm my nerves."

"Well, I need to stay here for a bit, until Jill comes back with our cut for tonight's entertainment. Whatever you get, bring it back to the room, I'll see you there."

"I may," Charlotte said, and the two women traded a look. "I'll be back...when I'm back."

"Okay," Samantha acknowledged.

Charlotte didn't bother with a reply. Instead, she went around to the stage room door and emerged in the common area. The scents of tobacco, whiskey, and freshly tanned leather hung thick in the air. She came up to the bar, where the tender was doing his best to scrub out the latest batch of stains. He looked up, recognized her from the evening's show, and spoke respectfully.

"What'll you have, Miss?"

Charlotte considered. Without hesitation, she dropped her made-up French accent and spoke direct. "What d'you got that's not whiskey? And do you have any food to go with it?"

"Ma'am, we do our own home-style brew here. Mind you, it's at room temperature, but if you don't mind that, I can rustle you up some brisket to go with it."

"That'll be fine. Bill it to my room. The one up there." Charlotte leaned to one side and pointed towards the door at the top of the stairs.

The bartender nodded and poured her a frothy glass of beer. Gratefully, Charlotte tipped the glass back and felt the blessedly warm flush of alcohol pink her cheeks. Off to one side, she watched as the card players called it a night, waved to Rowdy as they exited the swinging doors.

All but one. Specifically, the one who'd played the entire game with his back to the wall and his wide-brimmed hat tilted low over his face. She tried to hide her astonishment as he got up. Whoever he was, his build was what her mother would have called 'a long drink of water'. Thin without being scrawny, the man's long legs easily made him the tallest man she'd seen since leaving Chicago.

He pushed the brim of his hat back with one leathery thumb to reveal a lined, haunted-looking face framed by long curly locks of reddish hair and punctuated by a long, sweeping nose. His mustache arched downwards with a healthy dollop of styling wax. Though a pair of ivory handled pistols peeked out from a sash around his waist, Charlotte felt oddly unconcerned. The man's eyes were curious, not hostile, and she allowed herself another long drink of beer as he approached and stood at the bar next to her.

His voice sounded kind, and as smooth as polished saddle leather.

"Pardon me, *mademoiselle*. Or, perhaps I should say, 'ma'am'. May I join you for a nightcap?"

Charlotte paused for a moment. Glanced towards the stage, where Samantha would surely be emerging from in a few minutes. She returned her attention to the man in front of her, and allowed her southern drawl to drop to a sultry depth.

"Why, I'd be ever so pleased to make your acquaintance. Dominique is my stage name, but y'all can call me Charlotte." On an impulse, she extended her hand toward the man.

Not missing a beat, the man took it and raised it to his lips. Delicately, he planted a kiss on her knuckles. She smiled at his manners, and only the warm scent of freshly cooked beef was able to distract her attention. The bartender placed a plate with a small heap of thinly sliced brisket before her, and then glanced at Charlotte's companion.

"What'll you have, Mister Hickok?" he asked.

"Another Taos Lightning, for the trail," the man replied. The edges of his moustache perked up a little as he smiled, watching Charlotte's wide-eyed reaction.

"You wouldn't be the one that all the books talk about back East, would you?" she asked breathlessly, "Wild Bill, that is?"

"Yes. Some folks call me that. Won't you just call me Bill?"

"All right, 'Bill', I'll just do that. But…what're you doing in these parts? I thought you were travelin' through the Midwest with Buffalo Bill Cody's show."

"I'm out here tryin' to sort out some things in my head," Hickok said, with a shrug. "I find it easier to do that out here. More space to think."

The bartender slid over a glass filled with a dark, oily-looking liquid. Hickok picked it up and drained it in a couple of swallows. His eyes twinkled as he added, "The liquor's better too. As are the ladies, if you don't mind me saying."

Charlotte let out a loud giggle, one she was sure would carry across the room. As if in response, the *slam* of a door rattled the wall next to the stage. Hickok watched with interest as Samantha stalked over towards the bar, eyes glowering.

As she made her way over, Samantha listened as Charlotte let out another merry laugh. She knew it was done on purpose, but it still twisted her gut. For the first time ever, jealousy's green-eyed presence had made its way into her heart.

She came up to where Charlotte stood, unconcernedly chewing a slice of brisket. Samantha's hands rested on her hips, feet spread apart. Hickok made no move, but his eyes didn't leave the woman's face. Or her hands.

"Well, good time for you to show up," Charlotte said, as she finished off her beer. She burped delicately into the back of her hand, and then motioned between the three of them. "Bill, this is 'Veronica', though she normally goes by Samantha. Sam, this is Bill. Specifically, this is 'Wild Bill' Hickok. You may have heard of him. Why, I reckon you might have—"

"Excuse me, Charlotte," Samantha said, interrupting. "Is this man bothering you?"

"No. No, he's not." She returned Samantha's glower coolly.

"I'm going to bed now. You coming?"

"In a minute. I haven't finished talking to this nice gentleman." She flashed a smile at Bill.

Samantha opened her mouth to say something to Hickok. His countenance hit her all at once. From the wild locks of hair to the deceptively easy way the man stood, hands within quick reach of his guns. She thought better of it. Without another word, she stomped off towards the stairs.

Hickok didn't take his eyes off of her until she'd vanished up the staircase.

"Interesting," he remarked. "Your friend's a mite protective. Possessive, almost. She's quite the mother hen to you, ain't she?"

Charlotte flashed Hickok a beguiling, teasing smile.

"Actually, where I'm concerned, she's more of a *rooster*."

Hickok sat back as if someone had punched him in the gut.

He looked toward the staircase. Back at Charlotte. He put his hands up.

"Okay…I get the picture." He got up and doffed his hat. "I believe this is my cue to leave. However, Jack's is about the only place a man can get a warm breakfast in this town. At least one who ain't busy punchin' leather on the hoof. And I'd like to know what you two are doing out in these godforsaken parts as well. Perhaps I will see you down here?"

"I'd bet on it, Bill," Charlotte said, favoring him with an ingénue's smile. "I'd put a whole pile of chips on it, as a matter of fact."

CHAPTER THIRTY-SEVEN

Though the morning sun lit up the landscape, it did little to illuminate the cavernous interior of the saloon. Rather, to Charlotte's eyes it simply highlighted how gloomy the place looked. Still, the smell of tobacco and cigar smoke had been replaced by the wholesome scents of frying pork and freshly laid sawdust. She straightened her dress, a pretty outfit bearing the pattern of blue cornflowers, and came down the stairway.

A few of the saloon's regulars sat at the scattered tables as the bartender circulated around, passing out plates of hot food and doling out steaming cups of coffee from his battered steel pot. At the far side of the room, five men sat around one of the tables, intent on their poker game. Hickok, his long frame seated in the chair against the wall, lounged behind a miniature mountain of chips. She made a small wave to him, which he acknowledged with a nod.

Rather than bother the man when he was so deep into his game, Charlotte came back to her prior spot at the bar. With a practiced hand, the bartender swept on by, leaving a hot steel plate piled with ham, cinnamon-sprinkled apple chunks, and eggs done sunny-side up in his wake. Grateful for the repast, she dug into the food with a will after the bartender's second pass, when he dropped off a fork and a tin cup filled with steaming coffee.

"*Merci*," she said, deciding to be a little more careful with her English speech in the daytime. "Veronica…she is where, Monsieur?"

"If you mean your woman friend, she paid up for your room and board through this morning, and then went out to check the horses. Said she'd be back very soon, I believe. Hard to make out your ladies' French, if you don't mind me sayin'."

Charlotte let out a very Gallic snort as she tried to suppress a laugh. She returned to her food, polishing off the entire plate. Idly, she wondered if she should ask for seconds on her coffee, when a man's thick, grubby hand slammed onto the bar top next to her, pinning a stack of dollar coins under the palm.

The hand came part and parcel with a husky man in a ranch foreman's outfit, complete with a weather beaten leather vest, sun-faded hat, and a shirt that might have been red a few dozen washings ago.

"Looks like Jill finally decided to see the light," he chortled. His other hand reached out to stroke Charlotte's cheek. "It's 'bout time she got in some painted cats for us horny cowpokes. And she got us some high-class tail, too."

Charlotte drew back from the man's hand. "*Ne me touchez pas!*"

"Aw, you don't got to be like that. I got cash on the barrel right here, enough to buy me a 'French'. A 'French' from a Frenchie, I like that. Matter of fact—"

"That'll be enough, Cooper." Hickok's quiet, deadly voice sounded in Charlotte's ear. Startled, she looked off to her side. Hickok had moved so quickly, so quietly, it was as if he'd *materialized* next to her. "The lady's not interested."

"A lady? In the Jack? Hell, I don't think so. Just whores."

"Cooper, listen up," Hickok said. But the man ignored him and just spoke louder.

"Hell!" Cooper swore, "You just stepped into the middle of my talks for this cat's services. I need 'em right now, my trouser snake's been burnin' for one since I left Cimarron."

"And you just interrupted my morning's poker game. There ain't goin' to be any whorin' here, not so long as Jill runs the place, and you know that. If you're in such need, then go out back and take matters into your own fool hands. That is, if you can *find* it down there."

Cooper's face flushed red, as if he'd stepped into a steam bath. He uttered a curse and stepped forward. His hands balled into fists and he brought them up in a boxer's stance.

Hickok pulled one of his guns.

Before Charlotte could blink, the gunfighter moved to pistol-whip Cooper into submission. The revolver's barrel was a silvery blur as it connected with the man's skull. Cooper slumped to the floor with a groan and lay still.

Charlotte stared, open-mouthed. Hickok gave the gun a twirl and slipped it back into place in his sash. He tapped the gun's ivory grip meditatively.

"Colt '51 Navy Revolver. All sorts of uses. 'Specially for puttin' holes in things."

"I could very well see that," Charlotte said, flustered.

"Cooper's a whey-belly, but he didn't quite deserve that. So I buffaloed him." He snapped his fingers, got the attention of the barkeep, who'd been frozen in place, watching, as soon as Hickok had crossed the room. "Bert, grab me a shot of red-eye. Bring the lady a Mule Skinner. She needs something keener on nerve-settlin'."

"I...I'm not sure that something with that name is goin' to help."

"I'm no country doc, but it should," Hickok said, as he patted her hand reassuringly. Then, self-consciously, he removed his hand from hers and stuck it in a pocket. "A 'skinner' is a shot of whiskey, sure enough, but it's cut with blackberries."

The two drinks arrived, one a large mug filled with clear whiskey and the other a shot-glass smelling of rotgut overlaid with ripe berry. Charlotte picked up the glass and sipped at it delicately as Hickok helped the bartender drag the unconscious Cooper outside. Hickok pulled the man's guns and set them behind the bar counter without comment, and then returned to the card table. To her surprise, Hickok turned in his cards, cashed out his winnings, and came back to the bar.

"Bill, I guess I owe you my thanks," Charlotte said carefully. "There's not much I have that I can repay you with for your kindness."

"You don't need to pay me for anything," Hickok said, smoothing out one side of his moustache whiskers. He picked up his drink and added, "Unless you'd be willin' to tell me a bit more about what brought you and your 'lady friend' out Palmetto way."

"After what you just done, I should. Besides, I don't get much chance to talk with anyone ceptin' Sam and Jude."

"Jude?"

"Oh!" Charlotte raised her hand to her mouth for a moment. "I'm sorry. You wouldn't have known. Jude had been our hired man. Had been our friend. He was killed back in Kansas City. It's why…well, it's why we've been travelin' on our own since then."

"Travelin' alone, in these parts? Don't rightly know if I'd call that brave or foolhardy."

"I'd venture it's a bit of both. Truth is, I've never given it much thought, everything's been happenin' so fast to Samantha and me." She took another sip of the Mule Skinner, felt the blackberry-flavored burn going down her throat, coursing into her veins.

"You two have…ah…'known' each other a long time? I mean, as…um…friends?"

Charlotte pulled out her beguiling smile again. "No need to dance around it too much, Bill. We've been together around four years. Left Chicago together some weeks back. Sam's daddy is a right old creep, wanted her married off whether she said *yea* or *nay*. So – off we went!"

Hickok took a swig of his drink. "That said, where are you all goin' from here?"

"Well, Sam wants us to go to San Francisco."

"Hickok's eyebrows rose. "San Francisco? As in California?"

"We hear that we'll be able to live the way we want to out there. We got us some backing to set up a social club out there."

"Hm." Hickok said nothing for a moment, absorbing all that he heard. "It sounds like it was Sam's idea – Samantha's idea – to leave Chicago when you did. And it was also her idea to head for San Francisco."

Charlotte nodded, unsure of Bill's line of questioning.

"So if you don't mind me askin'," Hickok said directly, "Do you always let Samantha do the thinkin' for you?"

CHAPTER THIRTY-EIGHT

Wild Bill Hickok's question hung in the air before Charlotte like a loaded gun. She gaped at him a moment, then spoke up firmly.

"Why, no sir! It's just that..." Charlotte gestured helplessly as Hickok continued.

"I don't mean to ruffle anyone's feathers, but how much does Samantha know about where y'all are heading? It's mighty rough country west of here. Rough for anyone, much less two young women. And there's been Indian trouble. The entire Lakota Nation is on the move. So's the U.S. Cavalry. And that's stirred up all the other tribes to boot. Probably be killing there, before all is said and done."

"If there is, then it's our country's fault for not leaving Chief Sitting Bull alone!" Charlotte replied hotly. "I'd never imagine that he'd go out of his way to harm anyone, not unless his people were at risk."

"You'd never imagine that of him? You talk as if you know him."

"Well, we do. Sort of. We stayed with his tribe for a night."

Hickok choked on his drink. Charlotte continued, trying to reassure him.

"Really, they're fine people. Treated us well. Called the two of us 'Big Magic'."

Hickok sat back and stared a moment. "Christ almighty, I can't say as I'm not impressed. Miss Charlotte, most men wouldn't have been let loose, at least not alive. You two stayed overnight in the camp of the most feared war chief of the Plains. And you came out completely unharmed."

"A lot of that was Sam's doing, as well. She kept her wits about her, helped me do the same." Charlotte shook her head as she thought about Bill's original question. "As for what Sam does...well, I don't have much of a head for things out here. Out in the wild side of the frontier, I mean. Sam is awful smart. Tough as nails, too. She takes care of me, ceptin' just now. But then *you* were here."

She stopped.

Bill had been there. And his presence had come in handy.

Mighty handy.

"Mister Hickok," she ventured, "Now you know why we're out here. I can only guess at what y'all are doing. Aside from getting 'space to think'. Which way are you heading?"

Another pull at the long handlebar mustache. "I'm heading west. Not out to California, mind you. But there's only so many roads a wagon can take out of here. Depending on when you two leave, I'll be either ahead of you, or followin' your trail dust."

"That you might…" Charlotte began. Then, impulsively, she leaned forward, speaking almost conspiratorially. "But you could be of so much more help to me. To us, I mean. If you chose to travel with us, instead of just in the same general direction."

"I reckon I could," Hickok said, slowly, cautiously. "But…"

"But there is the question of compensation," Charlotte agreed. "I don't rightly know, don't know your rates. Or how much cash in is our box. Maybe we could work out something on credit."

"Pshaw, that's not what I meant. I'm no hired gun. If we travel together, it'd be just two parties doing so for safety, and to share the duties of shootin' game to put in the stew pot. No, my concern is what your Samantha is goin' to say. And I can pretty well predict it."

At that moment, Samantha burst through the swinging doors of the Jack. Her chest heaved with exertion, as if she'd been running.

"Speak of the devil," Hickok said. A look of annoyance crossed Samantha's face as she came over to speak to Charlotte, but the woman ignored him.

"Char, we've got to get a move on. Palmetto's not going to be safe for much longer."

"Good mornin' to you too, Sam," Charlotte said, archly. "Now, what's gotten you worked up into a fine lather?"

"Down at the stables. I was checking on Patches and Jubilee. Felt like someone was watching me. I looked up, saw this scrawny hayseed of a fellow just staring at me. Like he was looking extra-close to make sure it was me. I called out to him, but he took off, mounted a horse, and galloped out of town as fast as he could. On the north road."

"Someone's headin' up to Marysville to raise the alarm," Hickok observed. "Unless the U.S. Cavalry has you on their mission board, I'm afraid I got my spurs tangled up over this one. Who's after you two?"

Charlotte downed the last of her drink. "More like, who *isn't* after us?"

"Listen, Mister Hickok," Samantha said firmly, "This isn't any of your business. Step aside and let me handle my own wagon."

Charlotte stood. Her voice cracked like one of her whips.

"Who says that this ain't none of his business?"

Samantha froze, stunned. "Char, I'm telling–"

"No. I'm the one doing the tellin' this time. I've asked Mister Hickok to accompany us."

Samantha glared at Charlotte. "You did what?"

Charlotte glared back. "I have just as much say about who comes with us as you. With Jude gone, we need someone who can protect us."

"*I* can protect us!" Samantha jabbed her thumb to her chest to punctuate the retort. "What makes you think he can protect you more than I can?"

Charlotte's reply came from between gritted teeth. "Because. He's. Wild. Bill. Hickok."

"So what?" Samantha shot back. "You know them dime novels are all a pack of lies. Fancy tales made up by writers sittin' around a typewriter in a comfy office."

A smile crept across Hickok's face.

"If I may get a word in, before you two put me out to pasture…" he interjected, "I can prove that I'd be a better travelin' companion than a spur-buttoned side jockey."

"Bill," Charlotte said, "I already said that you're comin'."

"I know, but I think your friend and I still need a talk. You know. Man to man." A smile crept across Hickok's face. Samantha did not return it. "A moment, Miss Samantha?"

Hickok turned on his heel and moseyed through the saloon's swinging doors as if he had all the time in the world. Samantha glowered at Charlotte once more, and then followed Bill outside. Charlotte trailed behind, staying on the saloon's front porch as Hickok and Samantha walked over to a vacant cattle lot next door.

Hickok took a pair of silver dollars out of his pocket and threw them high into the deep blue sky. With an ease born of long practice, he drew one gun in a single fluid motion. Two squeezes of the trigger. The coins made a painful-sounding *ping* as the bullets hit them.

Samantha crossed her arms. Her jaw remained set and her expression blank.

"I do those tricks every time Char and I perform. I don't see why you should come along."

In reply, he dug into his pocket, found three more silver dollars. Flung all three into the air. Three shots, three more *pings*. The coins arced away as the bullets found their mark.

"Impressive," she said, in a tone that managed to convey the exact opposite. "Well, if that's all you have to offer…"

"Not quite," Hickok said. "Between whoever's after y'all, and the rogue's nest of bandits and Indians west of here…you're going to need someone who knows how to win a gunfight."

"Still don't see no reason. I can protect us. I can shoot a damned gun."

"Of that I have no doubt. But I didn't say 'I know how to shoot a gun'. I said: *I know how to win a gunfight.* There are rules you need to learn. If you let me, maybe I can teach you."

"You?" Samantha snorted. "How?"

"Easy. Imagine that I'm a hired gun, sent by your nemesis to take you back to Chicago, in a pine box if necessary. Got that?"

Samantha nodded. "Okay."

Hickok's voice rose to a commanding bark.

"Then draw, or die where you stand!"

Wild Bill's gun leapt into his hand. Barrel pointed at Samantha's temple. Charlotte, watching from the porch, let out a gasp. As did Samantha.

Her hand had only slapped her trouser leg. She'd left the gun belt in her room.

"Rule number one about winning a gunfight," Hickok stated dryly. "Bring a gun."

Samantha felt the heat of embarrassment rise to her face, along with a bitter taste in her throat. The realization hit her hard, as if she'd been thrown from her horse. That if Hickok had wanted to kill her, right then and there, she'd have been traveling home first-class. In a coffin.

She turned and walked back to the saloon. Stopped as she came up to Charlotte. Samantha's voice came out in a dazed tone just a hair above a whisper.

"I'll go pack up our things. Tell Hickok to do the same with his stuff. He's coming."

Samantha didn't wait for a reply. She pushed through the swinging doors. Without Jude, she didn't really know what to do next. But she couldn't let Charlotte know that. She had to be strong or she might lose her too.

If she wasn't already losing her.

CHAPTER THIRTY-NINE

One-Eyed Jill drew Charlotte and Samantha into her more than ample bosom. The strong smell of musk along with the hug took their breath away. She let out something akin to a sob.

"Well my honeys, you put on one hell of a show. If you're ever back this way you'd be more 'n welcome." She pressed the agreed-upon pouch of coins into Samantha's hand, gave Charlotte a last peck on the cheek, and then stood back as the two young women got up into each of their wagons.

"I won't ever forget you, or the Jack." Charlotte said.

"Thank you Jill," Samantha added. The seat of the freight wagon creaked as she sat down. "I wish we could stay longer, but…"

"…But you got business out west which ain't done yet. I understand." Jill cast as keen a glance as she could with one eye at Hickok, who sat astride his horse, watching the proceedings. "You keep these two safe now, Wild Bill!"

"Don't you fret none, Miss Sinclair." Hickok replied sagely. He tipped back the wide brim of his cowboy hat and gave her a direct look. "I'll make sure they travel the lonesome spaces with me and come out the other side."

Samantha picked up her set of reins and gave them a slap.

"Git up, mules!"

The wagons started up with a clatter of hooves and wheels. Hickok spurred his horse to a gentle trot, easily keeping pace with the wagons as they swung onto the road heading west. The lone rider and two wagons kept up a steady pace for the next few hours, kicking up dust as the sun rose behind them and the day grew warm.

The road petered out into the isolated ruts of wagon tracks in the dry, tar-black soil, but the gentle rolls of the land hardly slowed them. Trees faded into insignificant, dusky green points that punctuated the prairie. At times, to Charlotte it was as if they sat atop a pair of small ships, adrift on a golden sea of grass.

Lunch was eaten on the road, with only a quick stop at a watering hole for the animals. Hickok waited until both the wagon teams had drunk their fill. Only then did he bring his mount, a glossy-maned sorrel the shade of a new copper penny, over to the cool water.

"Nice horse," Samantha commented. "He looks well taken care of."

"Buckshot and I have been through a lot of this country over the years," Hickok replied. "I take care of him, I figure he'll take good care of me."

"By 'this country', I'm hoping you mean 'from around these parts.'"

"More or less," Hickok hedged. When he didn't volunteer any more information, Samantha pressed on.

"What I mean to say is, I'm thinking about our next stop. On the way out towards California."

"Well, I wouldn't want to opine on such matters. It might be thought too forward."

Samantha snorted. "I realize that things are a bit…delicate…between us, Mister Hickok. But while I'm not deferring to *you*, I am deferring to your knowledge of the land. Be foolish of me not to ask you, wouldn't it?"

"I'd say that's both straight and true as a wagon's tongue," Hickok said. "I have some ideas, for sure. But it depends on a couple of things. For starters, our supply of victuals, and ready cash. I know you're not hurtin' for the latter."

"We're not bad on the former either," said Charlotte, who'd come over to join them. "I do believe we could easily stretch for a fortnight's worth of suppers for three."

"Then that brings me to my next, and more important question," Hickok continued. "Who exactly is tryin' to put a spoke in your wheels? If I had to venture a guess, I'd say it was the Pinks that you're on the run from."

Samantha stiffed. "That so obvious?"

"Nope. Just makes sense given what Charlotte told me about your father wantin' you back. Pardon me for saying so, but young ladies from the city don't normally learn how to ride, let alone shoot, unless they're from money. I figure that if your father has the greenbacks, that's who he'd hire to bring you back."

"You're spot on. But only for part of it. You hear about our friend Jude?"

"Only that he got put toes-down back in Kansas City. I doubt that was the work of the Pinks. They don't do that to folks, normally."

"It wasn't the Pinks. It was *Clark Quantrill*."

Samantha waited for a reaction. Charlotte breathlessly watched Hickok's face, which remained poker-table placid. The man moved his jaw as if he was chewing tobacco.

Charlotte cleared her throat, broke the silence. "If that worries you, Bill, maybe we can…"

"Worried? Hell! I wore Union blue during the war. Went up against Quantrill's Raiders more than once. My detail went through the ashes of Lawrence, Kansas when he was done torchin' the place. Nasty stuff."

Hickok looked away, spat on the ground.

"I seriously doubt that Quantrill's still kickin' up dust after our cavalry went after him. Sure, there could be someone who's playing the part. Clark Quantrill and Bedford Forrest, they're like bogeymen all over the Border States. Eat your greens and say your prayers, or they'll come gobble you up like chicken feed."

"He seemed real enough to me," Charlotte said quietly.

"If he is, then we'll deal with it," Hickok said. "But let's play it down the straight an' narrow. Say that we got Pinks 'round here. Maybe Quantrill, or someone claiming to be him. I say that we cut cross-country, get off the beaten path. Helps muddy up our tracks for anyone comin' west from Palmetto."

"I like what I hear so far," Samantha said.

"I'm thinking that we head north-by-west next. Fourteen, maybe fifteen days out we'll cross over to Nebraska and into someplace I know like the back of my saddle – Rock Creek

Station. We can resupply there as well as put an ear to the ground for any news of the Pinks. Or Quantrill, for that matter. It's your call, Miss Samantha, but that's what I would do."

A nod of agreement, and the matter was settled.

Up ahead, the grassland gave way to a dry streambed. Hickok scouted a way for the wagons to turn down the rocky path and then waved them ahead. Jouncing with the noise of creaking wood and clattering containers, he led them for several hundred yards off the main path until the wheels returned to soft prairie dirt.

They continued on without incident, trampling wagon-sized wedges in the vegetation before them. The dry, nose-tickling smell of straw and wildflowers filled the air around them in a bronze haze. Eventually, the scent faded as the ground grew harder and the vegetation shifted to a pale green carpet of short, sturdy buffalo grass.

It wasn't until the sun began to sink in earnest ahead of them that Samantha called a halt for the day. They pulled the wagons into the meager shade of a scraggly copse of trees. As had become part of their routine, Samantha took care of the horses and mules, ensuring that all of the team got fed. Hickok ground-tied his mount and watched with a certain amusement as Charlotte set up the cooking supplies and prepared to light a fire.

"Something strike your funny bone, Bill?" Charlotte inquired, as she pulled out one of the cast iron pans. Samantha looked up from where she worked with one of the mules. She wandered on over as Hickok spoke.

"Well, unless you got something fresh that needs fryin' up, I was thinking of putting some fresh meat on the skillet." Hickok snapped his fingers. "Miss Samantha, how are you at shooting things? I mean, besides putting holes in a deck of playing cards."

She stopped tying the lead line of the last mule and gave him a look. "Are you asking me if I know how to hunt?"

"I reckon so." He pulled off his gloves, slapped the dust off his buck skinned clad leg with them. "Curious how you shoot, outside of a show ring, that is."

Samantha cocked a grin at him. She found that she liked the challenge. Hickok wasn't trying to take charge so much as see how good she was. See how much there was to teach.

"Well, I don't suppose there's any grizzly bear out here that I can bring down for you."

"Not hardly! Aside from bison, this is varmint country. I'm thinkin' rabbit. Seen a whole mess of them out there, and this is when they get most active."

"Never done that before, but I'm up and ready for it."

"It's easy. Walk out slow from here. Wait a bit. Look for the critter's eyes. A rabbit's round, dark eye is easiest to spot. When you see a rabbit you have to let out a whistle."

"What do you mean 'let out a whistle'?"

"Just that! That old rabbit will just stop what he's a doin' and sit up and look at you." He made a pistol out of his hand and forefinger, took careful aim. "That's when you pop him."

Samantha looked uncertain. Hickok frowned.

"Don't tell me that you're concerned about puttin' a bullet in a rabbit, now."

"It's not that," Samantha said, embarrassed. "It's just…how do you *whistle?*"

CHAPTER FORTY

The ends of Hickok's moustache twitched as he digested Samantha's statement.

He lifted up his right hand and showed her his thumb and middle finger, tucked the others into the palm, and then placed the two in the corners of his mouth. Curled his tongue around the back of his teeth and blew.

A shrill single note came out.

"Like that," he said.

Samantha did as he instructed. Her first attempt came out as a slobbery *phhhbbbt!* sound.

Charlotte watched, arms hugged to her sides to keep in her laughter. No one ever really showed Sam how to do anything. Hickok traded a glance with her, eyes twinkling. A few more tries, and Hickok deemed Samantha's whistle to be good enough.

"If that don't get them to sit up, then it should rightly frighten them to death," he stated soberly. "Now, if you'll take my advice some more this fine evening, I've been looking over your firearms. We need to swap out some gear."

"You mean my pistols?" Samantha asked.

"I daresay, but that's for later. No, the first problem we got to solve is your rifle. Charlotte, if you'd be so kind, I'd like to trade you what you've got up in the vardo for what I'm carryin'." Without waiting for a reply, Hickok went over to his horse's heavily laden saddlebags. Charlotte glanced at Samantha and got a nod in the affirmative. She pulled out Jude's rifle from where it sat near vardo's seat.

Hickok squinted at the gun, and then took it in his free hand. Hefted it with respect. He held it aloft for the two women to look at.

"This here's what we used to call a Yellowboy," he said proudly. "A gen-you-wine Winchester original, the old '66. First decent lever-action piece the army got. Damn shame it came out the year *after* the war. And it's the wrong gun for what you need right now."

"What's wrong with the rifle? It seems a damn fine one to me," Charlotte said, defensively. It had been Jude's gun, and irrationally, she felt a little protective of the firearm.

"No argument, this here's a fine weapon," Hickok said quickly, sensing the hostility. "But it's still chambered for a .44. Very powerful, but a lot of kickback. I'm guessing that if this belonged to Jude, then he was a fair-sized, strong man."

"That he was," Charlotte admitted, her mood calmed.

"And he likely outweighed both of you by a good amount. I want you to take this instead." Hickok handed Samantha his own rifle. She grasped it in her hands, felt the smooth wooden stock under her palms. "This one's a Winchester '73. It uses a lighter bullet. Just the thing you need for huntin' small game. And it'll hold steady enough for you to use in defending yourselves."

"I prefer my pistols," Samantha said, sounding unconvinced.

"Didn't mean you. I meant Charlotte." Hickok rubbed his chin as he regarded the slighter of the two women. "Yes, Charlotte, you need to get used to the rifle. Your whips look good on stage, but they're not goin' to outrange a Winchester. And Miss Samantha needs backup."

"I see what y'all mean, Bill," Charlotte admitted. "I'll do it."

"Good. But right now, we need meat for the table."

And with that, Hickok walked Samantha out to the edge of their camp. He stayed at her side as their eyes slowly adjusted to the dimming evening light. Neither spoke a word as the sky shifted from bands of rusty ochre to violet. High above, the bright dot of the evening star gleamed, an icy crystal in a sky of Concord-grape purple.

A little gray-brown shape moved off to one side. Samantha saw the eye of a rabbit in the distance, shining like a ripe blackberry. She flubbed the whistle the first two times, but on the third, a passable trill escaped from between her fingers and lips.

The rabbit sat up.

Samantha shouldered the rifle. She squeezed the trigger.

She swore that the hair on the rabbit's ears had been ruffled by the bullet's passage. But the animal scampered off, having only received a scare. Samantha bit back a curse.

"Not bad for the first shot," Hickok observed. "Remember, you're a pistol fanner by trade. Takes time to get used to the rifle. It'll be easier if I ain't ridin' shotgun on you. 'Specially since I don't actually have a shotgun."

Samantha, her competitive spirits roused, nodded in agreement. "I can take it from here, Mister Hickok. See if I can't nab something for supper."

Hickok tipped his hat to her. "Carry on, then."

The campfire bloomed bright red and orange behind them as he stepped away. He watched Samantha take a few more paces, stop, and whistle again. She moved further out to a small rise, then faded out of sight.

Hickok looked back to where Charlotte busied herself making the campfire meal. He stroked an end of his moustache between his fingers, thinking about what he wanted to say. It was a delicate subject, but he doubted he'd get a private audience again. He sighed, returned to the wagons, and sat down on a fallen log next to the fire.

"Charlotte," he said, "The fire'll catch just fine without you fussing over it. I want to talk to you for a moment, while we have the space to ourselves."

"Why sure enough," she said, with an innocent shrug. She gave the fire one last poke, and then came to sit near him. "What did you want to talk about?"

"I've only known you a short time, but it's been long enough for me to take a shine to you."

Charlotte crossed her arms with a dark scowl. "Bill, I'm sorry. I'm with Samantha. She can be a right pain in the caboose, but that don't mean I want a man."

Hickok took off his hat and ran his hand through his hair. "Not what I meant, not at all. I don't have that kind of interest in you. If anything, you make me think of my youngest niece. I'd suffer slings and arrows till Judgment Day before I let anyone hurt her."

"Then whatever are y'all talkin' about?"

"I done told you that I was out here to get some space. For thinkin'. But I didn't say about what. It's...well, it's because I done got married a couple months back."

"Congratulations," Charlotte said, though Bill's face looked drawn as he spoke. "I mean...well, it's supposed to be somethin' to congratulate you on, ain't' it?"

"I suppose," Hickok looked into the fire as he continued, his voice gloomy. The crack of a rifle echoed in the distance behind him. "The woman...my wife, I should say...kind of backed me into the corner on it. Said that the child she had was mine. And it could be, could be. The thing is, the marriage – this mystical union that God's all-fired-up about – wasn't really my idea. Hell, wasn't my idea at all."

"I...maybe I'm missing the point you're tryin' to make."

"Just this." Hickok reached into his coat pocket and pulled out a small leather coin pouch. He reached out and took her right hand in his, turned it palm side up. The pouch jingled as it set in her palm. "Take this. Rock Creek is on the stagecoach line. This'll let you to buy a spot on the mail run to Omaha. From there, you can hop on a train back to Chicago. If that is what you want."

Charlotte couldn't believe her ears. She stared at the weathered looking leather pouch, feeling the weight of it.

"Why would you do such a thing?"

"You never quite answered my question back at the Jack: Do you always let Samantha do the thinkin' for you?" He let her hand go, reluctantly. "Guess I felt like I went an' got buffaloed into a marriage I didn't really want. The meddler in me doesn't want anyone else to have to go through the same."

"I...don't know what to say."

"You don't need to say nothing. I just want you to think, decide if you're truly committed to this relationship. Before we go much further into *terra incognita* out here. Or get yourself killed for something that you didn't have the final say in."

Charlotte stared into the fire and didn't speak for a while. In the distance, she heard two blasts of a rifle. She tucked the pouch into one of her pockets, hurriedly, secretively. When she spoke next, her voice was a mere whisper.

"Bill, y'all really think that we could be killed?"

"All I can say is...that I am going do my best. To see that don't happen."

Their sober thoughts were interrupted by the pounding of approaching feet and a victory whoop as Samantha returned. She posed dramatically, with rifle muzzle over her shoulder.

And three fat rabbits dangling from her outstretched hand.

"All right," Samantha crowed, "Who gets to clean this fine bounty I so ably provided?"

Hickok took the rabbits and addressed Charlotte in a theatrical, arch tone. "Get thee a pot, and prepare a feast for your hunter returned from yon forest with the king's bounty. I shall get myself scarce and henceforth to clean it."

With that flourish, he set off downwind from the camp to prepare the meat for cooking.

The sound of Charlotte's laughter rung like music in Samantha's ears. It had been a long while since she had heard it delivered with such abandonment. It sounded sweet, and childlike. With it a promise to be made and one to be given.

CHAPTER FORTY-ONE

Charlotte placed the skinned, prepared rabbit meat at the bottom of a Dutch oven. She slid roughly cut pieces of onion and turnips into the pot, along with a chunk of salt pork for flavoring. With that, she secured the oven's heavy iron lid and then placed the pot directly onto the campfire's glowing coals. For added measure, she built the coals up around the pot's base and even used a pair of iron tongs to balance some of the coals atop the lid.

Samantha set out the pull-down table from the freight wagon, and then followed it up with a set of three wooden benches. She placed out a bottle of wine, a trio of glasses, and beckoned Hickok to one of the benches with a wave of her hand. He sat himself down, as did Charlotte, while Samantha poured.

"Shall we toast my first-ever rabbit hunt?" she asked, raising her glass.

"I'd say 'yes' to that!" Charlotte replied.

"Darn straight," Hickok chimed in. They clinked their glasses together, and down the hatch the liquid went. Hickok smacked his lips, dug in his pocket, and came up with a deck of travel-stained playing cards. "Well, now…we've no doubt got a couple hours 'fore those rabbits are properly done. How'd you two like to learn to play poker?"

"I'm game," Samantha said, and Charlotte nodded in turn. "We know some of the card games, at least what they play in Chicago. Is poker anything like whist?"

"Naw, it's a lot different. And a lot more fun. You need to know how each hand of cards ranks against another," he explained, as his hands moved effortlessly, shuffling the cards in a blur of motion. "You have what's called a 'high card'. That means when nothin' matches up, then the one with the highest card wins."

"I follow you so far."

"When you pair up, it means that you have two cards of the same value. Then there is two pairs." Hickok laid the cards on the table with a *slap* as he spoke. "Three of a kind beats two pair. A straight is when you have five cards in sequence. A flush is when all five cards are the same suit. A full house – what some cowpokes call a 'full boat' - is when you have three of a kind, plus a pair. Then four of a kind and the straight flush, all five cards of the same suit in a sequence."

Samantha and Charlotte looked at the cards, brows furrowed.

"I know it's a lot to take in all at once," Hickok said. "Best way to get familiar is to play!"

The next hour-and-a-half went by with no interruptions to the game. No interruptions, that is, save for Samantha grabbing a second bottle of wine to share out. And the questions the two women would pepper Hickok with regarding one of their hands, or the general rules of the game.

It was only with some reluctance that Charlotte called 'time' on their latest hand – which, as with every earlier one, Hickok had won with ease. She pulled out a set of tin plates and gave each of them a generous scoop of piping hot stew. Conversation halted as forks dug into tender chunks of meat and vegetables.

"Mister Hickok," Samantha said, as she polished off her second helping, "What else were you planning on 'swapping out' with me? I mean, about our guns?"

"Your revolvers," Hickok said, as he used the tines of his fork to spear one last chunk of rabbit meat. "Just as that rifle you had was too heavy, your guns are too light. I'm guessing that your Colts don't pack more than a .22 cartridge. Don't get me wrong, now. That's fine to use in your show."

"They're designed for trick shooting," Samantha admitted. "But they did well enough in a tight spot. Killed two men with them. It's why we had to skedaddle out of Kansas City."

"One man," Charlotte pointed out, though not unkindly. "That marshal had to finish him off, the way I recollect."

Hickok looked Samantha over with a newfound respect. "There's not many men who'd come out of a killin' without a shake or rattle."

"I didn't have much choice," Samantha demurred. "It was us or them. I didn't like it, not exactly, but they damn well deserved it for stomping our friend to death."

"No doubt, no doubt. But let me find something out. During that fight, say that you were standing where you're sitting now." Hickok got to his feet. "I'll step backwards until you tell me about where the men you shot were standing, okay?"

Samantha nodded. Hickok took a step back, and then another. He took a half-dozen more paces until Samantha said 'stop'. Charlotte nodded in agreement.

"That looks about right to me, Bill."

"If so, that's what I thought. Damn close range, damned close."

"We did sort of run right up on three of 'em," Samantha said sheepishly. "They weren't expecting us, and they sure weren't expecting me to pull my triggers. Nailed two, missed one."

"That one *will* expect it from now on," Hickok said gravely. "I ain't knocking what you did, mind you. That took guts and gumption. But even so, had those two been wearing heavy leather, I'm not sure the guns you had would've done the job."

"What's your suggestion?"

"Pack your old guns away until you have a show to do. I got an identical pair, only these use the same bullets you got for your Winchester."

"You don't think that's still a tad light?"

"Not for someone with your skills. Hell, my Navies only take a paper-cartridge .36. So long as you put metal on target, your new guns will scratch anyone's board."

Samantha rubbed her hands together. "I'm ready to go and grab the bull by its horns right now."

Hickok shook his head, and his finger followed suit. "On the 'morrow, Miss Samantha. Never touch a firearm if y'all can help it, once you've had more than a few swigs of the firewater."

"Even if it's wine?" This from Charlotte.

"Even so. I'm not exactly lookin' down the neck of the bottle, but the guns will wait for the sunrise. For now, I bid you both *buenas noches*."

In the gloom of the shadows, they watched him remove a bedroll from his mount's pack, and then set it up, just at the edge of the light cast by the fire.

Samantha reached her hand out to Charlotte. Hoped that even after the events of the past two days, she would take it. The night sounds magnified and the seconds ticked by in what seemed to her to be eons.

Charlotte's delicate fingers slid into her anxious palm.

Squeezed. Sent a wave of love and hope directly into her as if a bullet had found its mark.

Samantha brought the clasped fingers to her lips and kissed them tenderly. The lantern hanging on the eave by the vardo's door lit the way as the two made their way up back steps and into the waiting coach. Once inside, Charlotte folded into Samantha's arms. She looked up at her partner, pleading.

"Sam, it's been awful not bein' with you. I'm so sorry. I've been actin' like a spoiled little fool."

"You've got nothing to apologize for." Samantha's hand went to Charlotte's face. She brushed back a loose russet curl.

The pressure of their bodies, held close together. The smell of the cooking fire, mingled with the scent of lavender soap and sun-dried linen. It made their passion rise up into a burning need. A need that demanded immediate quenching.

"Char," Samantha murmured into a porcelain-delicate ear. "I need to love you."

Nothing else needed to be said.

Charlotte kissed her, at first delicately, then with wild abandon, her shaking fingers fumbling with the buttons on Samantha's gunpowder-stained shirt.

CHAPTER FORTY-TWO

A distant *rumble* rocked the vardo.

Samantha's eyes came open in a jolt. She gasped, quickly assessed the situation. Dusty shafts of light, shot with gold, filtered through the slits in the vardo's windows. Dawn, then. The blankets lay piled over her, as did Charlotte's soft, nude body.

The sound came again. Like the rhythmic pounding of a locomotive.

As carefully as she could, she half-rolled Charlotte off to one side and slid out from under her warm frame. Due to the drink, the lovemaking, or sheer fatigue, Charlotte barely stirred beyond a low mumble and a key-change in the sound of her snoring.

Samantha pulled on a fresh shirt, trousers, and boots. Again, the distant pounding, hammers on the dirt of the tabletop flatness of the prairie. She forced herself to remain calm, to tug on her boots and strap on her guns.

She threw open the rear door of the vardo. A blackened iron coffeepot sat atop the campfire's remaining coals. Hickok stood a few paces further off, gazing into the distance. He lifted a steaming mug to his lips and took a swig before he spoke.

"Mornin', Miss Samantha," he said. "I hoped that you'd get up in time to see this."

"What—" she began, and then her breath froze in her chest as she saw it.

Her brain had simply refused to acknowledge the image until she paid attention. Had simply told her that the mass of brown towards the horizon was simply low-lying cloud, or the remnants of a huge prairie fire. But the mass moved. It made a low, almost mournful sound of thuds and clops that fuzzed out over the distance into a general, low-level rumble.

She squinted, picking out the shaggy hides and hooves of the individuals at the edge of the herd. But the rest simply merged into the mass, and her eye couldn't follow. She caught the barest hint of a dull, musky, animal smell on the wind. She remained frozen in place, a witness to this explosion of life on the quiet expanse of grassland, until the herd diminished in size and vanished over a rise to the south.

"It's not as common to see this as you'd think, not anymore," Hickok said, in a hushed, almost reverent tone. "Time was, you'd see a herd like that take a whole day to pass you by."

"You never hunted one?" Samantha asked, as she stepped down from the vardo. She saw that Hickok had placed one of the benches close by. Something gleamed atop it.

"I took a hide or two when I needed the money. But there ain't no sport to shoot something that big, that slow. A man would let his aim get soft if he did that sort of thing." He paused, gave Samantha a look. His eyes twinkled. "Or woman, for that matter of fact. See what I've got for you on that bench over there."

Samantha walked over towards the fire. A freshly washed tin coffee cup sat gleaming atop the bench's polished wood surface.

So did a polished, oiled set of Colt pistols.

"Mister Hickok…" she said, "I think I owe you for these. Big time."

"Only thing you owe me is learnin' how to use them. Keep that lady of yours safe and I'll consider it payment in kind."

"When do we start?"

"You know a better time than the present?" Hickok said, and then held a hand up. "No, that ain't quite fair. Swap out your guns, get a mess of coffee in your gut, then come join me."

Her pulse quickened with excitement. Samantha carefully stowed her trick-shot caliber Colts back in the vardo, replaced them with her new weapons, and then poured herself out a cup of coffee. She grimaced at the taste – the man liked his brew strong, and he didn't mind a smidge of bitter grounds in it – but she gulped it down hurriedly.

Hickok had set out the remaining wooden benches, one at a half-dozen yards, the other at near triple that. Sets of empty cans and bottles, including the pair from last night's meal, had been set out as targets.

"I can understand the farther targets," she said, frowning. "But why put one of the benches so close?"

"It's 'cause you need to learn to shoot at the distances that you'll be killin' a man," he said plainly. Samantha stared at him, but he nodded in emphasis and went on. "You want to know one thing the dime novels got wrong? You don't always get a nice, pretty gun duel at twenty paces out on Main Street. You get shootouts in the saloon. In a pool hall. Even someone's stable."

"I get your point," she said, thinking back to Jude's death.

"It's why you never let someone who's threatening you get inside arm's length if you can help it." Hickok waved his arm and then added, "Enough with the jawboning, give your new pieces a try. Stick with a one-gun draw for now, but try 'em both."

He stepped back to one side and watched without comment as Samantha began practicing her draw. Two of her first six shots merely clipped the top of one bottle; after figuring out how the weapon shot, she adjusted, and a series of *bangs* and *plinks* echoed across the prairie. She did the same with the second gun, with roughly the same results.

"Hold up," Hickok said, as Samantha stopped to load. "That was good, damned good. What did you learn?"

"A bit more kick in these guns. Made me shoot high at first. But I got it now."

"More powder behind those bullets, so it figures." Hickok intoned. "Now, let's try something else. I know you got a natural's feel for trick shots. See how you are on speed."

"How do you want to test that?"

"Simple." Hickok stepped up to Samantha's side, and then pointed to the far bench. "I'll take the bad ol' can on the left. You go for that bottle on the right, he's got a mean glint to him. When I say 'draw', got it?"

She finished reloading, got into position, and nodded.

"Then *draw!*"

Their arms went into a flurry of motion.

CHAPTER FORTY-THREE

The report of their guns *cracked*, one almost atop another.

Hickok's can flipped into the air with a tinny sound.

Samantha's bottle remained untouched. She cursed under her breath.

"No cursing needed," Hickok said magnanimously. "You were fast, damned fast. Practically outdrew me, on the very first try. Never seen that before. But it was close enough that if we'd been dueling, I think we'd both be takin' the big jump. Save for one thing."

"That I didn't hit what I was aiming at," Samantha said.

"That's right. Remember, fast is fine. But accurate is *final*."

Another curse, this time from behind them. They looked over their shoulders to where Charlotte poked her head out the vardo's door, squinting blearily into the sunlight.

"Is Quantrill attacking us? What're you two shootin' at?"

"Cans and bottles," Samantha called back. "Just preparing."

"And we'd best make this a habit," Hickok said. Every morning without fail. You and I start by cleaning our guns. Then a minimum of one hour of practice."

Samantha let out a groan. "Every single morning?"

Hickok holstered his weapon. "If you're right about Quantrill, then he's been practicing for over ten years. And that's only counting the time spent after we ended the war."

She thought on it. "Point taken."

"Thought it might be."

"Char!" Samantha called, "Come on, we got to put some more miles in today."

Hickok chuckled, but didn't say anything as Samantha and Charlotte swung into action, getting the day's chores started as the sun lifted off the edge of the eastern horizon. Together, the two put breakfast together, made sure the animals had been watered, and stowed everything away in admirable time.

The next two weeks settled into a similar pattern. Whether bright prairie sun or muddy rain shower, the trio continued in their journey across the endless flat expanse of grass. The freight wagon normally led the way, followed by the vardo. Hickok, mounted on Buckshot, accompanied the small caravan in the outrider role, scouting ahead for most of the day, and then making a complete sweep of the area whenever they stopped for the night. Charlotte's dinners were unexpectedly sumptuous, as they were supplemented by Hickok or Samantha bringing in fresh rabbit or fowl. At least two hours of poker would follow. Sleep would be broken every morning at the break of dawn – followed quickly by the *crack* of pistols and the deeper *bang* of the rifle.

By the third day, Samantha managed to coax Charlotte into joining them, in order to practice shooting with the Winchester. Hickok had Charlotte practice shooting mostly from two positions: kneeling behind an object, and lying prone on the ground. When she asked why, Hickok's reply was to the point.

"Because if you two get in a scrape with any beast on two legs, that's how you should fight. Rifles are heavy. They slow you down. You're best making yourself less of a target, protectin' your vitals."

"And steadying my shots back?" she guessed.

"Damn straight! Whoever's attacking you, make 'em come at you through a hail of bullets! At the very least, it'll rattle them enough into shootin' blind."

It took some practice, but while Charlotte couldn't match the other two for speed with the rifle, she became a passable shot. At the end of the week, when she bagged her first pheasant, Samantha broke out a new bottle of wine and both she and Hickok took over kitchen duties for the evening.

For her part, Samantha found that her accuracy got better and better – but that try as she might, she could never quite beat Hickok's legendary quick-draw.

She watched him one cold, gray morning, during one of the rare times he target-shot by himself. His hand moved in a blur of motion when he shot. Abruptly, she realized the depth of the man's expertise. And his abilities as a teacher. Hickok wasn't slightly faster than her. He was *much* faster. But he was able to vary the speed of his draw to make her feel that she was only a split second behind. Just enough to encourage her.

The man's lessons ranged from the subtle to the knuckle-skinning raw, as well.

"Mister Hickok," Samantha said, at the start of one of their practice sessions, "You talked about rules to winning a gunfight, back in Palmetto. How many rules are there?"

"Well, that depends on who you ask," came the reply. "Me, I always thought that there were only three that meant a damn."

"You taught me the first. I want you to teach me the rest."

"In due time," he demurred. His spread his hands in an expansive gesture. "When you're ready, we'll talk about the others. But only when you're ready."

Samantha scowled. "I don't like to be patronized, you know that."

Charlotte sat up from where she was relaxing against the side of the vardo. She'd heard that tone in Samantha's voice before, and it did not normally bode well.

"Didn't mean to be." Hickok said, watching Samantha carefully. "But you ain't ready."

"Who says? I can't outdraw the great 'Wild Bill' yet, but I can put metal on target."

Something hard glinted in Hickok's eye. His long, full nose twitched as he stepped up to loom over Samantha.

"You think you're ready? Fine." He half-turned to speak to Charlotte. "Here's what you're goin' to do. When I call 'draw', you count off twenty seconds to yourself. When you're done, you shout 'time' as loudly as you can."

"Yes, I'll do that, Bill." Charlotte said, nervous. She wasn't sure what Hickok was getting at, but it put a flutter in her stomach.

"Now, Miss Samantha," Hickok pointed at the targets they'd set up for the day. "We got a half-dozen targets out there today. They're not bottles and cans no more – they're gunmen. In those twenty seconds, you better hit 'em all, or they'll put a nasty hole in you."

"I'm ready," Samantha gritted. "I've done this number of targets before."

"Then...draw!"

Instantly, Samantha drew one of her Colts. She got off two shots. A pair of bottles shattered. She shifted her aim to the next.

And Hickok drew his own guns. Pointed them at the ground. Squeezed the triggers.

Dust erupted from the ground next to Samantha's feet. She danced a half-step back in shock. Her shot went wild.

Hickok pointed his guns skyward. Another pair of shots, this time by Samantha's ears. Her head rung. The stink of powder, flooded her nostrils. She coughed.

Hickok shouted in her ear, deafening her. *"What're you waiting for? Shoot! God damn your eyes, woman! Shoot!"*

She shot. The next one missed. The fifth hit. The sixth tagged nothing but air.

She was out. Hickok stamped at the dirt around her feet. Screamed in her ear. Fired into the air again, coating the side of her face with greasy black smoke. She tried to re-holster the empty gun. She fumbled it into the holster. Pulled the other gun out.

Squeezed the trigger. Another miss.

"Time!" Charlotte screamed.

Hickok's voice was quiet. "I'm sorry I had to do that. But every tenderfoot gun-fanner thinks that blowin' away targets that don't shoot back makes them an expert. Ain't so. Gunfights are a lot noisier and plum full of all kinds of chaos." He blew out a breath, made the curls of his moustache flutter. "Do you still think you're ready for a gunfight?"

Samantha looked at the ground. "Not yet."

"Then there's time," Hickok said. "Time to get you to that point."

He clapped her on the shoulder and got a weary nod in return. Hickok went over to the pull-down table by the freight wagon, took out his guns, and set about cleaning them.

Samantha looked at the remaining three targets. Her eyes narrowed. She holstered her remaining loaded revolver. Thinking.

She dropped, rolled, and came to one knee. Drew the revolver in one smooth motion.

The remaining targets shattered and twanged at each of her shots found their mark.

Charlotte came to her. Samantha looked at her, a question on her lips, but the younger woman shook her head.

"Remember, I love you," Charlotte said. She put her arms around Samantha and gave her a full-on kiss.

Samantha re-holstered her gun. A broad grin creased her sun-browned face.

The small caravan made good time for the remainder of the day. Dinner passed without mention of the morning's lesson. So did the evening's poker hand.

Only one thing changed.

That night, as Hickok bedded down under the bright prairie stars, he felt a lump under a corner of his blanket. He reached underneath and pulled an object out. He bit back a laugh as he glanced back to where his two female companions slept in the vardo.

Charlotte had given back his coin pouch.

And, not coincidentally, she'd also given him her answer.

CHAPTER FORTY-FOUR

Over the next couple of days, the wagons rolled through a new, hostile-looking landscape. The air felt drier, left the taste of dust in their mouths. The carpet of buffalo grass grew patchier, like an unkempt rug, and was soon replaced by clumps of thorn bushes and jagged outcroppings of gray rock. The pool-table flatness vanished as the landscape rumpled into low hills and ravines.

The small squeak that came from the movement of the freight wagon turned into a squalling, groaning sound as the little caravan began to move up and down the varied slopes. Samantha traded a look of concern with Charlotte. But after a half-hour with no respite except for the sound escalating in volume, Samantha could no longer afford to ignore it.

"Whoa mules!" Samantha brought the team to a halt, tied the lines around the brake handle, and jumped down off the wagon seat. She knelt and inspected the axles supporting the wagon's bed. A curse rolled off her tongue. "Of all the god-damned bad luck!"

Hickok had been in the lead, but he stopped when Samantha had called 'whoa'. He nudged his horse to turn back towards the wagons.

"What's the problem?"

"I'm hearing bad sounds coming from the wheel hubs. Or the axles."

Hickok swung down off his horse and inspected the wheels himself in turn. "When was the last time you two greased these wheels?"

"Greased the wheels?" Samantha's blank look said it all.

Hickok sighed. "Do you have any grease with us?"

"I don't think so." She looked to Charlotte, who shook her head in the negative.

"The dip you took gettin' across the Big Blue must've washed away all the grease on the wheel spindles." Hickok sat back on his haunches. "Well, I hate to be the one to say it, but the axle on this cowchip schooner ain't going to last much longer. It's about rusted through."

"Bill...what are we goin' to do?" Charlotte said, her voice tense with worry. "Don't we still have a ways to go?"

Hickok squinted at the hills ahead. "I'm dead sure that we're in the Wildcat Hills right now. Call it another twenty miles north and west to Rock Creek. We'll just have to see how long that axle lasts. Maybe long enough to get us to town, if lady luck is feelin' generous."

From there on, the party tried to keep an even pace. The sound got worse on the up and down slopes of the hills, so they picked the flat bottom of a dry gully to run the wagons along and prayed for the best. Samantha steeled herself against the growl of the metal as it wore away. Each groan it let out caused made her stomach give a twinge.

The next few hours wore by in painful silence, as each member of the party listened to the complaints from the freight wagon's axles. Finally, as the sun approached the horizon and the light turned copper-red, the wagon's rear axle gave way.

The tortured metal let out one last cry of anguish as it broke and the wagon came to a grinding halt. The left rear corner of the wagon sagged, and containers of feed and dry goods spilled out into the ground.

The mules continued to strain forward until Samantha called out 'Whoa'. She looked around skeptically at where they'd come to rest – surrounded by a ring of hills covered in alternating swaths of dry brush or loose dirt. She pulled the reins up and over the backs of the mules. Hickok rode off to one side as the vardo caught up with the halted freight wagon.

"Charlotte," Hickok instructed, "Back your vardo up to the wagon. Y'all want to form a right angle over here."

Samantha saw what the man had in mind. She got down, unhitched the mules, and then led them into the triangle made by the two vehicles. Next, she went around to the vardo and began to untie her riding horse, Jubilee, from the back hitch.

"Hold on there," Hickok cautioned. "Where do you think you're going?"

Samantha paused. "I figured that I'd need to go get help. Or at least accompany you."

"You need at least two armed people to protect these wagons, and I'm the only one who knows the way to Rock Creek Station. You two will have to stick it out till I get back."

"Damn it all," Samantha grumbled. She struck the edge of the vardo with the palm of one hand in frustration. "You're right, Mister Hickok. How long you plan on being gone?"

"Can't be much more than fifteen miles to Rock Creek. But I need to rustle up a wagon jack, maybe a couple extra hands to fix this. With luck, I'll be back the next mornin'. In the meantime, you two should unload as much of the freight from the wagon bed as you can."

"What about tonight?" Charlotte asked. "Any advice?"

"Yes, but you won't like it. This ain't the safest country to be stranded in. There's Indians out here – from tribes who'd just as soon shoot Sitting Bull. And they won't care a lick that you two are 'Big Magic'. So for tonight, I want you two to sleep away from the wagons." He pointed at a small cluster of rocks a couple dozen yards up the gully, on slightly higher ground overlooking the wagons. "Up in those rocks would be good. Take the extra guns and ammunition up there with you. And no lighting a camp fire."

"Up in the rocks? What about the mules, the horses?"

"Put the stock inside the wagon triangle. Make a rope corral. If anyone comes along, they'll be looking there, not up at those rocks. That clear?"

"Clear as crystal, Mister Hickok," Samantha said. "Just don't forget about us out here."

"As if I could." He tipped his hat to them both. "Daylight's burnin', and it's rough, slow-riding country between here and Rock Creek. I better go."

With a kick, Hickok spurred Buckshot into a lope and disappeared down the gully. The dust trail kicked up by his mount spiraled into the dry air, until it too faded into nothingness. Charlotte looked at the stony outcrops that surrounded them. The waning sunlight cast ominous shadows. She shuddered, and wrapped her arms around herself as if to ward off a chill wind.

"Sam, I hate to say it, but I think I'm a bit spooked."

"We'll be all right." Samantha patted her new Colts meaningfully. "I won't let anything happen to us. Let's start by unloading the wagon before it really gets dark."

※ ※ ※

A chill evening wind blew up, pushing dirty gray clouds across the blue-black sky as Hickok rode into Rock Creek Station. The town looked much like Palmetto, with a scattering of dry good stores, a saloon or two, a branch of Wells, Fargo & Company, and a stagecoach stop intermingled with humble family homes. Lantern light flickered from behind curtained glass windows; people were still awake, but no one wanted to be out in the cold breeze.

Hickok stopped to consider for a moment. Men could be found at a dry goods store, but those were closed this time of day. Rock Creek had a sheriff's office, but his gut told him not to go there unless all the other options had been used up – his traveling companions wanted to stay low to the ground. Looked like he'd have to go to the usual place: the town watering hole.

He tied up in front of the most crowded, noisy place along the main street, a sprawling saloon-house called 'Aces and Eights'. Hickok pushed through the swinging doors and was greeted by the sight of steer horns, spurs, and saddles adorning the walls, the smell of chewing tobacco and cigar smoke mixed with whiskey, and the sound of a rowdy card game.

His fingers twitched as he saw hands of poker being dealt out, but only for a moment. Charlotte and Samantha were depending on him. He worked his way through the bustle of townsfolk and ranch hands, made his way to the bar, and waved to the apple-cheeked, heavyset man behind the counter.

"Bill!" the man said, extending his hand, "How good to be seein' you back in the 'Creek! You finally decide on settlin' down here?"

"Good to see you too, O'Dell." Hickok returned the handshake warmly. "I ain't stayin', more like passing on through."

The bartender made a porcine grunt at that. He picked up a tray of used, empty beer steins and set it aside. "That's just what your friend said."

Hickok gave O'Dell a look. "Not many I'd call 'friend' out here. Do you mean—"

"I mean, Mister William Frederick's in town. Stayin' at the Red Dog hotel, just down the street."

"Is that right?" Hickok considered. "I may have to see him. But first, I got to throw a wet horse blanket on the merriment for a bit. Got an emergency that needs tendin' to."

"Sure thing, Bill." He pulled a small hammer from his pocket and tapped it on a large brass bell that sat on the counter top. The patrons cheered, until O'Dell quieted them down. "Sorry boys, nobody's buyin' for the house this time. What we got here is the real-life Wild Bill Hickok, and he needs to make an announcement!"

Hickok turned to the crowd and drew himself up. His voice rung in the still, smoky air.

"I got an emergency here," he stated. "Got two women stranded in a broken wagon, way out in the Wildcat Hills south and east of here. I'd call it 'bout fifteen miles. I need two men and a wagon jack to head out at first light. Anyone want to earn some cash for helpin' me out?"

A murmur ran through the crowd. Sounds of people chatting excitedly. Until a voice, one with a low, ugly drawl, cut through the noise like a mill saw.

"I'll send any man fool enough to take up that offer home. In a pine box."

For the first time in his life, Wild Bill Hickok felt the blood drain from his face. The man who stepped out of the shadows by the door wore a shabby gray hat and uniform, both trimmed to a cavalryman's cut. Soulless eyes gleamed in the light of the saloon's lanterns. Hickok recognized the weathered face, with its high cheekbones and strong, jutting jaw.

"Clark Quantrill," he said, amazed. "So you're still kickin' dirt. Ain't no one gotten around to puttin' you out of your misery yet?"

Hickok's hands moved on their own accord towards his guns.

CHAPTER FORTY-FIVE

"Before you jerk that pistol," Quantrill growled, "You best consider who else you're gonna kill. Like everyone in this room. Like everyone in this town."

"I don't plan on missin' you," Hickok shot back.

"Maybe not. Think you can get all of us? Before we drop you?"

Three more men stepped out to flank Quantrill, two on his left, one to his right. Each wore a travel-stained, dun-colored duster. Hickok noticed that each of the men looked grizzled, older than the green ranch hands and cowboys that sat, frozen, between them. Old enough to have ridden with him before…

And all of a sudden, it clicked in Hickok's mind.

"You've called together Quantrill's Raiders," he said, in a stunned voice. "Damn you to hell, Clark! For Christ's sake, the war's over!"

"*Your* war is over, Jayhawker!" Quantrill spat. "*Mine* never was! You so much as touch your gun, my men will raze this town to the stumps!"

Hickok's palms tingled, but they didn't move any closer to the grips of his revolvers. He and the Confederate glared at each other. No one moved until Hickok spoke again.

"Best you leave now, butcher. Before I change my mind."

"Gladly," Quantrill smirked. "Good luck getting anyone to follow you. And thanks for spillin' the whereabouts of those two girls. Your fool mouth just condemned them to death."

The cavalryman grinned, exposing cadaverous, tobacco stained teeth. He backed out of the saloon, followed by his men. Hickok didn't move until the saloon's doors ceased swinging. He lowered his hands. The crowd let out a collective breath.

"Y'all heard what he said," Hickok stated. "But there are two women out there who need help. I know where they are. Quantrill's goin' to have to search the entire Wildcat Hills. Are there any men here who've got real courage? Any who'll follow me?"

The men closest to him looked into their drinks. O'Dell shook his head. Murmurs of 'Remember Bloody Kansas?' and 'It's suicide'.

Hickok's jaw tightened.

"Right," he said curtly. Without bothering to meet anyone's frightened glance, he strode through the saloon doors and into the brisk night wind.

✳ ✳ ✳

Charlotte sat watch, as miserable as she'd ever been. The granite boulder at her back sucked heat from her, even through her leather jacket. Worse, her stiff spine let out a jolt of discomfort at the slightest movement and her hip bones ached.

The rifle lay across her lap. She yawned and stretched as the sky began to turn the slightest shade of pink in the east. Each of the women had missed half a night's sleep in their nest of cold, mercilessly hard rocks above their campsite. Waiting for something. Anything.

She let out a tiny snort. What a waste of time. As far as she was concerned, they could've spent the night in the vardo's bed. Cozy and warm, with Samantha's firm belly and breasts pressed up tight against her...

...one of the mules let out a bray.

Charlotte peered over the edge of the boulder. Shadows in the brush moved toward the wagons. Man-sized shadows, at that. She watched, horrified, her every sense screaming that this was really happening. Her sleepiness had vanished, as if someone had poured ice water down her back.

She ducked down, reached over to where Samantha lay sleeping. Grabbed a shoulder and shook her. Hard.

"Sam! Sam! Wake up!"

"What?" Samantha replied, her voice groggy and still full of sleep.

"We got company," Charlotte whispered urgently. "Lots of it!"

Samantha rubbed the sleep grains from her eyes and sat up. Her drowsiness fell away as she watched the scene as it unfolded in front and slightly below their position.

The creeping shadows came into better view as the sky changed from dull salmon to rosy pink. Four men with pale complexions and tattered gray clothing entered the campsite triangle. There was more movement, hidden in the brush. Another mule brayed and one of the horses neighed, startled.

Charlotte's voice sounded small and quiet in Samantha's ear. "Is it Indians?"

"No. Either bandits, or Quantrill."

"I'd have rightly preferred the Indians. What'll we do?"

"Once they find the vardo empty, they'll go searching around for the owner. They'll find us soon enough." Samantha reached out, touched Charlotte's cheek. "We have to fight. Have to, while we got surprise. I'm so sorry, Char."

"Don't be, Sam." Charlotte whispered. "I made my choice to be here. With you. I just didn't know that I'd have to grow up so much. So fast."

They kissed. Noses and lips cold, like points of ice, but it warmed them.

"I'll start," Samantha said, drawing her guns.

"No," Charlotte said. "Let me. Rifle's better at this distance, don't you think?"

Samantha could do nothing but stare for a moment, but she nodded. Charlotte set the Winchester up on the flat surface of the boulder. Spotted one tall, hulking figure creep up to the back door of the vardo.

The man touched the door handle. In the early morning light, Charlotte could just make out the blue-steel gleam of a pistol in the man's hand.

Any misgivings she had vanished like smoke.

She lined up her sights.

Squeezed the trigger.

The *bang* echoed off the walls of the gully. Startled birds into flight.

The man gasped, dropped to his knees. His gun went off, firing uselessly into the vardo's wooden step. He dropped, arms and legs twitching.

Charlotte didn't stop to watch the man's death throes. She jerked the rifle's lever, sending the spent cartridge flying. Quickly slid another bullet into the rifle's side-loading gate.

Samantha rose to her feet. Drew both of her guns. Gambling that no one had yet seen the flash of Charlotte's rifle, she unloaded both of her Colts at the shadowy figures below.

CHAPTER FORTY-SIX

Samantha's shots ricocheted and sparked on the rocks. But another found its target. One man's head and arms jerked back and he fell to the ground in a heap. Another cried out in pain and fell over. He crawled desperately towards cover, until the fourth man helped drag him to safety. They left a bloodstained trail that glistened black in the dim morning light.

A split second of silence.

With a thunderclap of sound, a golden halo of gunfire rose up from the gully floor. Samantha threw herself on the ground, trying to shield Charlotte. The volume of fire was incredible, from the higher-pitched *pops* of revolvers to the deep *boom* of a shotgun. Chips of rock showered the women as they did their best to remain under cover.

The fire slackened, then died.

A voice floated up to them. A southern drawl made the air's chill bite harder than ever.

"That wasn't very nice, to shoot my men like that. Missus Williams, Missus Harte, didn't your folks raise y'all better than that?"

"Quantrill!" Samantha cursed.

"And how does he know our…" Charlotte gasped.

"I suppose I should use the stage names y'all put together," Quantrill said, a sardonic tone coloring his speech. "But the Pinks done spilled the beans, putting up their posters right next to yours. Suppose I could earn myself an easy hundred dollars if I telegraphed the right people."

"You just go ahead and do that, you son of a bitch!" Samantha shouted back.

Quantrill *tsked*. "Your parents' money don't interest me. And they would be shocked, plum shocked, if'n they heard the filth that came from your mouth. How did they raise you, anyhow?"

Samantha ignored that. "What do you want from us, then? You can take what you like from our wagons, just get it and leave us be!"

A low, evil, gurgling sound. The women traded a glance, realizing that it was Quantrill's laughter. It wasn't a happy sound. Wasn't a sane one, either.

"You remember Ezra?" Quantrill said, "Or how about Zeke? The men you gunned down back in Kansas City."

Charlotte blinked and traded a puzzled look with Samantha. "I can't figure as how Zeke and Ezra had any friends."

"I remember them," Samantha yelled back over the rocks. She paused for a moment as she reloaded both of her Colts, and then added, "The ones that helped you murder Jude!"

"That's nothing compared to what you took from me," Quantrill said. "Those two men were my younger brothers."

Charlotte and Samantha traded a questioning look. Their hands gripped rifle and revolver so that their knuckles stood out in sharp white relief. Quantrill's voice shifted back to the same teasing, bantering tone that it had earlier.

"So why don't y'all come on down here? Save us some trouble. We won't hurt you."

The captain's words were followed by gruff laughter from his men.

"What's he doin'?" Charlotte shook her head. "He's got to know we ain't that dumb."

"Maybe…" Samantha frowned, and then motioned to the far side of their stronghold. "He's distracting us. Watch the front, I'm going to peep over the back."

Charlotte nodded. Samantha moved, crouched as low to the ground as possible, and took three steps to reach the rear of their little rocky outcropping.

"You two still got some mighty fine qualities that'll compensate some for what you did," Quantrill continued. "About the only good thing a woman's good for, 'sides from work at the stove. So what say you?"

Samantha's heart leaped into her throat as she came almost face-to-face with the three men climbing the rear slope of their position.

Two older men with dun-colored dusters and boots, one younger man with a spotted red kerchief. The nearest stood just below her. Closer than the first set of targets Hickok had set out for her. Close enough for knife work. The man looked up, his sun-wrinkled face widening in surprise as Samantha brought up her guns.

Two shots at that range blew the back of the man's skull out. His brains spattered the rocks in a gory spray. A simultaneous cry from the two remaining men. They charged the few steps up the back of the hill.

Samantha didn't flinch. She squeezed her triggers without remorse. The next pair of bullets hit the youngest of Quantrill's men in the chest. The red kerchief flipped up as the man landed on his back, covering his face like a shroud.

Quantrill's men at the front of the hill put up a tremendous volume of fire. Charlotte hefted her rifle and blindly fired back over the top of the rock. Shards of stone zinged and sprayed around her, kicking up sour-tasting, lung fouling dust. She loaded, fired again, and then shoved the next bullet home as the lever kicked out the empty cartridge.

Samantha continued shooting as the last of Quantrill's men came up the slope. The toe of his right boot exploded as a bullet went through it. Sent him sprawling. His gun tumbled out of his hand. He made a grab for it. Had it in his fingertips as Samantha put another bullet in him. A scream, and the man's body tumbled down the slope to the foot of the hill.

More shots. Movement from down below. Samantha dropped. Managed to reload one gun with shaking fingers as Quantrill shouted orders to his men. She glanced at Charlotte, who gave her a dazed, exhausted look. Spent cartridges littered the ground around her like sooty coins.

"I hit a grand total of nothin'," Charlotte admitted. Her voice came out as a dry croak. "But it kept their heads down, so it ain't a total loss."

"You're doing fine," Samantha said, her voice dust-clotted as well. She nudged open one of the remaining boxes of cartridges, grabbed a handful and reloaded her second revolver, all while trying to watch the back side of the hill. "Think we're doing all right so far. You okay?"

"Think so…except…" Charlotte said, in a small voice, "*I got to pee!*"

Samantha fought back a laugh. Of all the inopportune times…

"Fine, I'll cover you."

"But…"

"If you have to go…it's got to be where you are. There's nowhere else!"

As if to emphasize the problem, Quantrill's men sent up a volley of shots. More stinging rock chips rained down upon the two women.

Charlotte groaned. "When's Bill getting back? He must've found some of his friends to help us out by now."

"I'm sure that he…" Samantha's voice faltered as she looked up from reloading her second revolver. "Char, I think someone else is bringing their friends."

Charlotte turned, let out a gasp. Large clouds of dust rose from behind the hills on the gully's far side. Samantha's skin broke out in goose pimples as she heard the shriek and hollers of Indian war cries.

An Indian brave appeared at the crest of the hill, riding a large pinto and carrying a wicked looking spear. He was shaved bald, save for an ebony scalp lock, and his war paint differed from Sitting Bull's braves. Slashes of red and black gave his face a horrific appearance.

He twirled his spear, pointing at the men in the gully, and then called back over his shoulder. Samantha's hopes that it could be Sitting Bull's tribe were dashed as she heard the new, foreign tongue of the Indian brave above them.

"*Tókhi!*" cried the fierce warrior, "*Waniphika, ni! Ankanu, petu!*"

The response from the men at the base of the hill was immediate.

"Indian war party!" "Captain, we got to skedaddle!" "Leave the damned wagons!"

And through it all, they heard Quantrill's insane laughter.

"You whores are dead! *Dead!* Enjoy your scalps, while you still have them!"

CHAPTER FORTY-SEVEN

The brush at the base of the hill rustled and swayed as Quantrill's men ran as fast as they could down the gully. They disappeared around the bend. Samantha listened as the Confederate's men mounted up their horses. Dim sound of hoof beats as they retreated.

"Come on," she said, grasping Charlotte's arm, "We've got to try and make it out of here."

Together, they made a dash down the slippery, rocky slope towards the wagons. In a couple of minutes, the two had made it to their vardo. But the sound of the approaching war party had reached a fever pitch.

Charlotte, her face grim, gripped the Winchester and prepared to use her last rounds. The dust cloud boiled over just as the sun rose over the hills, throwing golden shafts of light into the gully. The whooping war cries became ever fiercer, a crescendo of noise that set their teeth on edge.

Wild Bill Hickok came up over the ridge top at a gallop. He caught up to the Indian brave and gave him a brisk salute as they continued down towards the wagons. And just as the women took in the sight of the two men riding together, an even stranger sight appeared.

A team of two horses strained to pull a buckboard wagon over the broken ground. Bundles of brush dragged behind the wagon on a long rope, kicking up the roiling clouds of dust. A buckskin-clad man wearing a broad-brimmed Stetson gripped the reins. The man's hat brim had been pinned or folded up along one side, allowing a view of his face. His moustache was shorter, nattier than Hickok's, and a single gray stripe of beard covered his chin. Mischief danced in the man's eyes, and he surveyed the scene before him with scarcely concealed amusement.

The two horses and the buckboard came to a stop beside the vardo. Hickok surveyed the scene, then dismounted and came over to the side of the gypsy wagon. The buckskin-clad man and the Indian brave followed suit.

"Are you two all right?" he asked.

"No, we're not!" Charlotte shouted, her voice shaky with indignation. "Y'all just about scared my bloomers off!"

"You don't wear bloomers," Samantha pointed out, before turning back to Hickok. "We're all right. Scratched up some. But in one piece."

"Better than some of these poor devils fared," Hickok said. He went over to where one of Quantrill's men lay dead, next to the freight wagon. "You and Charlotte...you did just fine."

Samantha beamed at that.

"And I think you learned the second rule of a gunfight, all on your own."

"I did?"

"Yeah. If you have more than one gun, you better well *bring* it."

Charlotte shifted the grip on her rifle and squinted against the sun at the new arrivals. "Bill, where are your manners? Who're your friends?"

Hickok indicated the fierce-looking Indian with one hand. "This here is Standing Elk, Shoshone warrior."

The brave stepped forward. He took his fist and brought it to his chest. Charlotte beamed her best smile at him.

"I thought y'all were an entire tribe on the move, Standing Elk."

The brave nodded. His words were brusque, but not unkind.

"To drive away bad men is no great feat. Only one Shoshone is needed."

"Well..." Hickok hedged, "One Shoshone...and some quick theatrics. That's where my other friend comes in. Miss Samantha, Miss Harte, I'd like you to meet William Frederick Cody. Y'all might know him better as 'Buffalo Bill'."

Charlotte couldn't help but let out a squeal of delight.

Bill Cody's eyes twinkled as he heard it. He stepped forward, bowed at the waist, and gracefully swept his hat from his head.

His voice sounded regal, like a player reading a set of well-rehearsed lines.

"Ladies," he said grandly, "I am happy to be at your service. Please call me 'Cody', as I don't stand on ceremony. I hear that you are fellow denizens of the stage. And *l'estage belle Français*, at that."

"Well, now," Hickok said, "About that…"

"Yes, about that," Charlotte interrupted. "Excuse me, y'all. We left our ammunition up top of that pile of rocks. I need to get that. And I need to…go powder my nose, while I'm at it."

With that, Charlotte set aside her rifle. She stepped down from the vardo, and began the hike up. Standing Elk's expression conveyed his puzzlement.

"Cody, we're about as French as Chicago gets," Samantha admitted. "But no matter. I don't know how Mister Hickok managed to pull an ace like you from his sleeve, but I'm grateful all the same."

The showman looked ever so slightly abashed. "Matters of showmanship brought me to Rock Creek Station. I've been trying to convince Standing Elk, and some more members of his tribe, to join my Wild West show next year."

Standing Elk said nothing as Cody shot him a reproachful look. Instead, the brave moved his thumb back and forth over the tip of his index and middle finger, as if rubbing a wad of bills together. Hickok turned away so as not to laugh at Cody's pained expression.

"In any case," Cody continued, "Our friend Captain Quantrill made quite an impression on the town when Bill here came 'round, asking for help. Threatened to blow the town into smithereens, he did. So no one wanted to ride out."

"Everyone remembers him burnin' down Lawrence, Kansas," Hickok said. "It's hard to blame them. We just got lucky that Cody was out this way."

"No, you got lucky that we found enough scrub brush in these hills to drag behind that there buckboard," Cody pointed out. "And that Standing Elk was willing to put on stage makeup to help us pull off our little stunt."

At the latest mention of his name, Standing Elk coughed into his hand. "I must return to my tribe before the sun stands high in the east. And I need to wash. Your 'makeup' feels like wet mud. Smells like bad grease."

"The trials of the stage, my friend," Cody said. He pulled out a wad of cash from his pocket and placed it in Standing Elk's palm. The brave bowed, got back on his horse, and rode off with a *whoop*.

"He seems like a good man to have in a tight spot," Samantha observed.

"True," Hickok agreed, "But I'd hoped that he would stay and help us with the wagon jack. Looks like your repair crew is goin' to just be me and the great-and-dandy 'Buffalo Bill'."

"Yes, yes," Cody said, distractedly.

"Something on your mind?" Hickok asked, as he went to the back of the buckboard. He released the dragging bundles of brush, and then hefted the wagon jack out of the wagon's bed.

"Oh, I just hope Standing Elk can convince more of his fellow braves to join my show," Cody grumbled, as he joined Hickok. "Some damned journalist blew the lid on my 'Irish Injuns', and now the audience is on to me."

CHAPTER FORTY-EIGHT

Working together, Cody and Hickok quickly replaced the spindle and changed out the wagon wheel. Charlotte, once nature had finished calling to her, made two trips up and down the rocky hillside to bring back all of their ammunition. In the meantime, Samantha busied herself with the unpleasant task of moving the bodies of Quantrill's men away from the vardo.

Once the freight wagon had been reloaded, Samantha climbed aboard, took the reins, and gave a hearty 'Git up!'. She held her breath as the wagon shuddered forward with a teeth-clenching *creak*. One revolution of the wheel, then two, then a half-dozen. She gave the rest of the party the 'OK' sign. Hickok saddled up and spurred his horse to lead the way, while Charlotte and Cody fell into line with their own wagons.

While nothing was said outright, a certain tension hung in the air. Guns or rifles were kept close to hand, and everyone kept a careful watch on the gully walls. It wasn't until the afternoon that the group emerged onto the rolling grasslands again. Hickok called a brief halt. Rock Creek Station lay across a tabletop flat expanse of grass in the middle distance.

"Stay sharp," Hickok said. "Just in case Quantrill and his boys come snooping 'round."

No one argued. Samantha quickly watered the animals, while Charlotte passed around a sackful of beef jerky for the group to gnaw on. They saddled up and continued on. With a snap of his reins, Cody brought his buckboard up alongside Hickok's horse and Samantha's wagon.

"You know," Cody remarked, "I got dragged out of bed in the middle of the night over this. I'd like to know why Captain Clark Quantrill has chosen to show up here, way past the time the hangman should've had him doing the Texas two-step. And why he's chosen to go after two such lovely – and rather well armed – ladies."

"Well, I can hazard a guess at the first part," Hickok said. "During the war, Clark's cavalry brigade earned the name 'Quantrill's Raiders'. Kept up a 'partisan' war behind Union lines all through the West. Had a nasty habit of wreckin' anything they came across. And there's the towns they burned down, the folks they slaughtered."

"I suppose Quantrill hasn't noticed that his side laid down their arms ten years ago?"

"The war's still up in his brain," Hickok said gloomily. "Had a stare-down with him, right before I went to find you." He shifted in his saddle and raised his voice to address Samantha and Charlotte. "Quantrill never formally surrendered. He disbanded his men, and the Union Army sent troopers out to hunt him down. The newspapers said they ran him to ground. Seems to me that he's been playin' possum all this time."

"Charlotte and I ran into him when we took the ferry into Hannibal, Missouri," Samantha said. "He and his brothers tried to rob our camp, and they'd surely have raped us as well."

Hickok gave her a sharp look. "Clark and his *brothers?* Y'all forgot to mention that part."

"That's 'cause we just learned it ourselves," Charlotte said, in a wry tone. "In between tryin' to shoot us full of holes, the good Captain was kind enough to let us know."

"We ran into them again outside Kansas City," Samantha continued. She did her best to keep her expression neutral. "They murdered our friend, Jude. We showed up too late to help him. I pulled my revolvers and started shooting. Missed Clark. Got his two brothers, though."

Cody let out a whistle. "You tucked two of Quantrill's brothers in for a well-deserved dirt nap? I don't know if I find that courageous, or foolhardy."

"We didn't exactly get a choice in the matter. Based on what happened this morning, he took those deaths rather personal."

"You could say that," Hickok said. "I counted the muzzle flashes before we rigged up our little bit of misdirection. He brought at least two dozen men to scour those hills on foot to find you. Looks to me like he's calling in all of his chips, bringin' the old Raiders back together. Maybe even with a few youngblood outlaws thrown in."

"Ain't you just chock full of good news today?" Charlotte grumbled.

The freight wagon's rear axle began to squeak again as the wagons finally rattled their way through the dusty streets of Rock Creek Station. Yet what chilled Samantha and Charlotte wasn't the ominous sound that came from the wagon. It was the dead-eyed, hostile stare that the townspeople gave them as the little procession passed by.

"Friendly place," Samantha remarked.

"It ain't that way, not normally," Hickok said. "Word's gotten 'round about Quantrill's threat. The way I see it, we better get a move-on from this town as soon as possible."

"Can't we just rest our weary bones for a short spell?" Charlotte asked, plaintively. "I'm right on the edge of fallin' over."

"The lady has a point," Cody said. "They've been through hell and back, Wild Bill."

"I just don't know who I can trust in this town no more," Hickok said, shaking his head.

"Where trust don't work, sometimes money and fancy talk does," Cody said firmly. He pointed at a two-story brick building on the next block. "I still have a room reserved for the night at the Red Dog. I'll make sure the ladies get it while I see to the horses and wagons. You just rustle 'em up grub and whatever they need to pull up stakes first thing tomorrow morning."

"That's a damn fine plan. I'll meet you at the Dog right smart." And with that, Hickok spurred his horse towards the dry-goods store on the next street over.

"Cody, you don't have to do—" Samantha began.

"I'm afraid I must," Cody said, with a wave of his hand. "Right now, you two are going to be as popular as a wet canine at a parlor social. It'll be for the best if you stay low for today."

Samantha nodded in agreement as they pulled up to the hotel's front gate. The fatigue she'd been fighting since the morning had come home to roost, this time for good. Her head swam groggily as Buffalo Bill persuaded the proprietor to allow his 'stage assistants' access. She murmured 'thanks' as Cody led them to the room, pressed a brass key into her palm, and promised that he'd look after the wagons before he left.

The hotel suite, while not as sumptuous as the one at Mrs. Pleasance's Social Club, came nicely appointed with a washroom, carpets spread neatly across a timbered floor, and a big, brass-framed feather bed.

"I'm so tired, I feel like molasses in January," Charlotte said, as she went to flop on the soft quilt that lay atop the bed. "You go ahead and use the washroom first. I'll catch up after a nap."

"I got a better idea," Samantha replied, as she flopped down next to Charlotte. "I say we both stay dirty a little while longer. While I check the insides of my eyelids for leaks."

"Maybe we'll get lucky, wake up to some hot grub. What d'you think?"

"There's no hurt in hoping." Samantha closed her eyes, lost in thought about what they'd been through. What lay ahead. She cringed at the sour-milk taste of appeasing the blustering anger of her father. He shouted, and she ran from his beet-red countenance. Ran until she saw the prairie ahead of her, golden stalks of buffalo grass undulating in the wind. It went dark. She saw the flash of guns. Smelled gunpowder. Quantrill's insane laughter echoed in her brain.

"Sam," Charlotte said. Again, more insistently. "Sam!"

"What?" she replied irritably. "Char, let me sleep a spell, okay?"

"You have been sleeping. We both have."

Samantha rubbed her eyes, wiped away the grains of sleep sand. Charlotte stood by the room's window, outlined by the gray light of a cold, cloudy morning. Samantha sat up, felt a pain her hip bone. She'd slept on top of one of her guns and hadn't even noticed.

"Guess we *were* tired," she remarked, as she rubbed her hip.

"And the washroom's goin' to have to wait a little longer," Charlotte said, as she sat back down on the side of the bed. "Bill and Cody knocked on the door just now, checkin' on us. We need to meet 'em in the hotel parlor right now."

"What? Why the rush?"

Charlotte looked at her, worry pulling her face drum-tight. "We've got problems. Looks like the freight wagon's broken down again, this time for good. And that's just the start."

CHAPTER FORTY-NINE

Buffalo Bill Cody set the corroded metal rod down on the parlor's table with a *clank*. Hickok and the two women gathered around the table, each holding a mug of freshly brewed hotel coffee. Their expressions were as downhearted as if viewing a body at the undertaker's.

"The good smith showed this to me last evening, after you ladies hit the hay," Cody explained. "The axle just split in two as they started work on it."

"We're not all that welcome here," Samantha said, as she sipped at her mug. "Could the smith - or someone else in town - have done it deliberately?"

"I doubt it, as I was watching the repair work. And it's worth keeping in mind that they may not like you, but they want you gone. Sabotaging your wagon would be the furthest thing from their minds. No, it looks like the piece simply rusted straight through."

"Jude may not have greased it enough," Hickok observed. "Or he got a bad piece of metal. Happens once in a while. But that's bad luck all 'round. How much is it goin' to cost, Cody?"

"Five hundred and change." Cody pronounced.

Charlotte nearly choked on her coffee. "That's darned near highway robbery! It's more than the wagon itself is worth!"

"I would tend to agree, especially given the heavy wear it's seen," Cody said with a nod. "However, that's not just for the one axle. It includes fixing damage to the wagon bed itself, not to mention shoes for all of your horses. The smith thinks a couple look ready to throw a shoe any day now. I looked it over with him, and sad to say, I believe he's right."

"Trust me on this one," Hickok added. "Never skimp on shoes for your animals. We'll need them to make it to our next stop on the way out west: the town of Scott's Bluff. It's right where this state bumps up against Wyoming and Colorado. Call it four day's ride in good weather. From there, you two get to make the final decision."

"About what?"

"About how you're gettin' to California."

Hickok paused to take a drink from his steaming mug. He reached into a coat pocket and pulled out a map of the territory. With Charlotte's help, he unfolded it on the table and weighed it down with the broken axle piece.

"We're here," he said, jabbing a finger at the map. "And over to the west is Scott's Bluff. That's where the road splits. You can take the northern route towards Fort Laramie, follow the old trail over the Rockies into Oregon. Or, swing south and west towards Fort Collins and Denver. You'd follow the rail lines over the next couple of states, get into California that way.

"Which would you take?"

"Depends a lot on whether the passes are open into Wyoming. Or if the Pawnee tribe is feelin' neighborly enough to let travelers pass through their territory. Here's the kicker, though." Hickok fixed the two women with a keen eye. "It's rough, slow country for wagons. You can count on havin' more breakdowns from here out, which we'll have to pay to fix. And if we're slower, then we run the risk of Quantrill catching up to us."

"You think Quantrill's going to be back, then."

"You can count on it. With so many men to feed and outfit, they'll be comin' back to Rock Creek Station. I'll bet hard cash that people in this town will tell them you've been through."

"Well, I appreciate you trying to break the news to us slowly," Samantha said, with a frustrated tone in her voice. "Char, you're not going to like this…"

"…but we need to get rid of the wagons," Charlotte finished for Samantha. "We need to ditch the vardo and the freight."

Samantha blinked. "That's right."

"I came to that conclusion myself this mornin', before you woke up. Quantrill's laugh put a scare in me, and anything we can do to avoid him, I'm in favor of." She sighed. "Even if it means sleeping on the ground again."

"And no more *La Femme Exhibition Extraordinaire*, either. If Clark and his idiot brothers figured us out, Pinkerton probably has too. They'll be on the lookout for our showgirls' vardo."

"The Pinks don't worry me. It's that if we don't have the vardo, we ain't doing shows. If we ain't doing shows, how are we goin' to earn our way to California?"

"I believe I can help you, on both accounts," Cody said smoothly. "That vardo of yours would be perfect for my Wild West show. Selling your broke-down freight wagon should pay for re-shoeing all of your animals. I could take the vardo, the two draft horses, and all of the dry goods you won't need, off your hands for a flat one-thousand dollars."

"That's sound like a square deal to me," Samantha said, after conferring with Charlotte a moment. "But you said you could help on 'both counts'. What about Pinkerton?"

"Well, it occurs to me that the Pinkerton men will be on the watch for that distinctive-looking vardo. As it happens, I'm heading back east for a while to drum up some financial backing. If I take the vardo with me, it'll probably help bemuse and befuddle them."

Samantha's face broke out in a broad grin. "Then you have a deal, Buffalo Bill."

"The smith is already at work shoeing your animals," Cody said. "Shall we head on over?"

Charlotte coughed, meaningfully.

"On second thought...we'll meet you and Mister Hickok there in an hour," Samantha said.

"What's all the lollygaggin' around for?" Hickok said, annoyed. "If y'all remember back, I wanted to get a move-on at dawn. Now it's halfway to noon!"

"Bill," Charlotte informed him, "This may be the last chance in a long while that Samantha and I are going to be able to use a real washbasin and tub. And we plan to take it!"

"Of all the confounded things—"

"Aw, let them be, Wild Bill," Cody said, as he took the sputtering Hickok's arm and led him to the hotel door. "As a matter of fact, it wouldn't do you harm to re-acquaint yourself with the soap and water routine for a bit, either."

"So," Charlotte said, "I checked, the facilities they got here are only big enough for one person at a time. Who's goin' to get to bathe first?"

Samantha laughed for the first time since the gunfight outside of Rock Creek. "How about whoever gets to the room first?"

"Sounds like a fine idea." Charlotte let out a gasp, and then pointed out the window. "What the blazes is *that?*"

Samantha turned, alarmed. "What?"

Charlotte took off like a shot for their hotel room. Cursing, Samantha dashed after her.

An hour later, Wild Bill Hickok paced the wooden sidewalk outside the smith's shop impatiently. He'd already stashed as many provisions, ammunition, and other essentials as possible into the saddlebags and packs for the two mules, his own mount, and the women's pair of riding horses, Patches and Jubilee.

He watched through the shop window as Samantha handed Cody the ownership papers. Nearby, Charlotte stroked the manes of the two draft horses, Pansy and Daisy, telling them that they'd be missed. Finally, Samantha finished tidying up her business and came outside. Cody followed suit, his voice sounding fatherly in the cool morning air.

"My one and only regret," he said, "Is that I didn't get to see you ladies perform in my show. But maybe I'll be able to convince you at a later date?"

"Only if you come out to California."

"Oh, really?" Cody mused, stroking his beard in a meditative fashion. "Then I'm just going to have to look you two up the next time I head out west."

"Agreed, you'll have to do that," Hickok said, his breath ruffling his moustache. "Now, ladies, can we finally head on out of town?"

"Sounds good," Samantha said, and was echoed by Charlotte. The three saddled up, with Hickok and Charlotte leading the way, while Samantha brought up the rear for a change. A pack string rope ran from her mount's saddle horn and tethered the two pack mules to follow behind.

"*Adiós, Bill,*" Hickok called, as they proceeded on their way.

"*Vaya con Dios, Bill,*" Cody replied, with a sweeping bow of his hat.

The women shouted their farewells in turn, and then the town fell away behind them as they headed due west. The flat plains ended and the land rumpled into rock-strewn foothills that seemed to frown upon them as they journeyed up the slope.

Charlotte looked back once more and saw the pane glass windows of the town twinkling distantly in the sunshine. She saw Hickok looking as well, with an expression of loss on his face. But as she watched him, he turned away.

"You goin' to miss your old watering hole?" Charlotte asked quietly.

"Naw. Not really," he said, though his voice sounded sad. "The town I knew back when, they wouldn't have knuckled under to anyone the likes of Clark Quantrill. Now? They're all a little too fat, too prosperous, too scared of losing hold of a dollar." He turned away from Charlotte, leaned over and spat. "Rock Creek's no kind of home to me anymore."

With that last pronouncement on the matter, Hickok spurred his horse along the path as it wound up and into the hilly country ahead.

CHAPTER FIFTY

The weather remained dry, but a brisk autumn wind scoured the landscape and chilled the three riders as they continued into western hills. The two women found that they had to build the fire up at night in order to keep warm. Hickok didn't like it, as it made the party more visible at a time when he wanted to lay low, but he didn't overrule Samantha or Charlotte's decision.

Though deprived of the conveniences of the wagon, only the temperature proved to be a challenge so far. Food came courtesy of Hickok or Samantha's success in flushing out pheasants and quail from the scraggly underbrush. Target practice resumed for the three days they remained on the road. Only this time, the practice went on sporadically throughout the day.

"Try it again," Hickok said during one rest stop. He flung a gnarled pine branch into the air, off to Samantha's left. A second behind him, Charlotte did the same, on Samantha's right.

Samantha pivoted, drew her guns. Two pair of *cracks*, and the branches splintered into pieces. She grinned, pleased with her improving performance. Hickok nodded his approval.

"I do believe you're better than Annie Oakley!" Charlotte said, applauding.

"Shucks, 'tweren't nothin'," Samantha said, mimicking the lawman dialog she'd read in the dime store novels. "Just doing my job, ma'am."

Charlotte laughed, and even Hickok let out a chuckle.

Another day's hard ride brought them to a well-traveled dirt road that led directly up a long, steep ridge. By the time evening was well advanced, they spotted the lights of Scott's Bluff ahead. Just beyond, in the deepening dusk, Samantha could make out the shadowy presence of mountains. She squinted at the half-seen range ahead, trying to make out details.

Hickok cleared his throat, loudly. Called her attention to a man standing at the entrance to town. He wore a hooded winter jacket the same color as buffalo skin, and in his gnarled hands he gripped a shotgun. The man's eyes looked them over dispassionately as he stepped directly into their horses' path.

"Evenin', friend," he said. "You coming to town for business? Or you passing through?"

"Evenin'," Samantha said, with a tip of her hat. "I don't mean any disrespect, but what business is it of yours? Are you the sheriff?"

"The name's Ramsay, and I ain't the Sheriff, I'm one of the town aldermen. The sheriff's been killed as of last night. Lot of strange people in town as of late, too. Me and a bunch of citizens just want it quiet. So we're watchin' who's coming to our fair community."

Samantha hid her surprise. She exchanged a glance with Hickok. His expression was one of concern, but he said nothing. Instead, he nodded at her: *Go on, then.*

"We're not looking for trouble," she said. "Us three are just traveling though."

Ramsay grunted. "You may find that to be a problem. We got a freak snowstorm last week. If you want to continue on, Mitchell Pass is closed. Avalanche."

Samantha paused, let the news sink in. Her stomach felt as if she'd been riding out a storm-tossed sea. But Hickok spoke up next.

"Well, there's closed, and then there's *closed*," he said firmly. "I want to see it myself, maybe there's a way around."

"I think you'll need mountain goats more than horses and mules, but it's your funeral," Ramsay said, shrugging. He stepped out of their way and pointed towards the town. "You'll need to wait 'til morning at least. We got a halfway decent boardin' house. Called the Wagon Spoke. Should do you for the night."

Samantha thanked Ramsay, and they slowly rode into town. There was an air of wary watchfulness among the few people out for the evening. It wasn't until the horses had been tied up at the Spoke that they felt free to speak.

"I don't know…" Charlotte said, "This place feels like Rock Creek Station to me already."

"Something's definitely got the town's dander up," Hickok said, as he rubbed his goatee in thought. "I don't like it."

"Me neither," said Samantha. "Any thoughts for tonight, Mister Hickok?"

"Yes. Keep your door locked, curtains drawn." He considered for a moment, then added, "Keep your guns nearby. And loaded."

※ ※ ※

The massive black shape of the locomotive cut arrow-straight through green stretches of buffalo grass mixed with fields of golden-brown wheat. It slowed, screeching and protesting in timbres that only metallic steam brakes can reach. A jolt, and it settled to a stop by a bustling, smoke-stained station. A large barn-red sign cheerily reminded all of the disembarking passengers that alcohol and tobacco were illegal to bring into the city of Des Moines.

Matthew Slade stepped down off the first-class passenger car and waited patiently for the crowds on the station platform to disperse. Eventually, the salmon-like rush of people ebbed, and a slightly built man approached him. The man wore a dapper gray suit and a starched white shirt, topped with a straw boater hat. Slade extended a hand, which was accepted warmly.

"Gavin, it's damned good to see you!" Slade said.

With an accent that would've sounded at home back in Killarney, Gavin reply came out in a rich brogue. "Aye, likewise to you. Welcome to Iowa, and thank you most kindly for comin', Matthew. Short notice, I know."

"Maybe, but it's never hard to go hoppin' a rail out of Chicago. And the farther I am from the city right now, the better."

"My ears have been hearin' as such, and I don't need my Pinkerton training to figure out why. Problem client is my guess."

"You could say that." Slade cast a glance around before adding, "It's nothing that a bottle of rotgut and two bullets couldn't solve."

Gavin chortled at that. The two men walked towards the station house as yet more people emerged, waiting for the steam engine to take on water and coal before they boarded. Yet despite the bustle around them, Slade riveted his attention on what Gavin had to say.

"I wasn't sure whether to be troublin' you," the smaller man said, as he pointed towards one of the holding areas next to the station house. "But I've been readin' up on your case, the one with the two pretty young cuties that ran off, and I have a lead."

"Let's hear it."

"Oh, it's not for the tellin'. Better if you use your eyeballs."

Slade's breath came out in an explosive exhale as they rounded the corner of the building. There, sitting in one of the freight holding pens, sat the same red-and-gilt trimmed vardo that Wyatt Earp had described the girls using in Kansas City. But he quickly composed himself, considering the alternatives as they walked up to wagon's rear door.

"I know what you're thinkin'," Gavin said. "Anyone could paint a gypsy wagon red. But there's some interesting things about this one that made me draft a telegram to you."

"I'm all ears."

"For starters, the owner says he bought it about two hundred miles west of here, in North Platte, from a man who was travelling south from Canada. The current owner's taking this pretty little wagon back east to put into storage until he kicks off his next Wild West show."

Slade's ears perked up. "Are you saying this show wagon was bought by Buffalo Bill?"

"Aye, and he's lyin' to us about the wagon. He's coverin' the tracks up for someone, that much is sure." Gavin shrugged. "We can't legally search or detain him, but the train to New York he's wantin' only runs every three days. Figured you'd want to see this before he left."

"That I do. Buffalo Bill's a slippery devil, but he's got really good relations with the Indians. And that's where my quarry went to ground – with the Kansas Lakota people." He stepped up to the locked rear door of the vardo. "Question is, where did they pop up again?"

"Technically, 'tis illegal to search that wagon, Matthew. If I see you doing that, I'm obligated to report you," Gavin stated. With that, he turned around to resolutely face the other way. "So I don't want to see you doing it."

Slade dug into his coat pocket and pulled out a lock pick. A couple of minutes of fiddling passed before he was able to persuade the lock to open. The door swung outward with a creak, and he stepped inside. He swept back the curtained windows to let the light in.

Slade had to step carefully around the boxes of dry goods that covered the floor. But up close, he saw that clothes for two women had been neatly folded and stashed in boxes on the bed. The cabinets were jammed with dishes, utensils and medical supplies for both humans and horses.

He raised an eyebrow as he found a set of coiled leather bullwhips in one storage area. In another, he saw a set of revealing feminine corsets. As he turned to go, he spotted the corner of a piece of paper that jutted out from under one of the storage boxes.

He pulled it out, scanned it. Felt his pulse pick up with the excitement of the chase. The quarry beginning to come into view.

"Gavin!" Slade said excitedly, as he emerged from the vardo, "Let's go chat with the station master. I need a map. And more importantly, the latest railroad time table."

CHAPTER FIFTY-ONE

Samantha's breath hung in a gray fog as she exhaled. Her expression took on a grim cast as she surveyed the drifts of snow and blocks of ice that covered the saddle-shaped pass below. Charlotte came up from behind, leading their horses. She raised an eyebrow in a silent question. Samantha shook her head, but nodded towards where Hickok had climbed atop a snow-covered boulder at the side of the path.

He peered through a brass pocket telescope for a moment longer. Let out a single word as a curse. He snapped the instrument closed with a *clack*, and then made his way back down the rocks. Dabs of ice stippled the ends of his mustache, making it droop even more somberly.

"Well, that darn well settles *that*," he said. "I can barely make out the tops of trees down there. And there's more snow on the heights that could come tumblin' down any time."

"Then I guess we'd best not consider this way, not unless there's nothing else on offer," Samantha said, as she took Jubilee's reins from Charlotte.

"Maybe not even then. The way to Laramie is flat-out suicide." He waited until the two women had remounted their horses, and then led the way down the slope, back towards Scott's Bluff. "Means that we'll have to backtrack a bit, take the south fork of the trail towards Fort Collins."

"What about the Pawnee tribe?" Charlotte asked. "It sounded like we could only go that way if'n they were keen on it."

"A fair point. I'll have to ask 'round town to find out what mood the Pawnee are in these days. See if anyone comin' up from Denver had to have a mess of arrows plucked from their backside."

Charlotte gave the man a look. "I swear, Bill, there are times when I don't know if you're pullin' my leg or not."

"So long as we can find out fast, and move on," Samantha added. "I kept the guns out last night. Had a chair up against the doorknob, too. It was quiet, give it that, but too quiet. I didn't like that one bit."

With that grim pronouncement, the entire party spoke little for the rest of the afternoon on the ride back to town. The golden-hued plains and sun-dappled forests of the Midwest had given way to dark green conifers and ice-crusted patches of snow. The patches faded to a gentle sugar dusting as they descended, and then finally vanished as they made their way down a narrow defile into the town's outermost buildings.

Scott's Bluff wasn't a rail hub or a cattle drive stop so much as a trapping and trading post. Because of that, the place had a blockier, more closed-in feeling compared to Rock Creek. But as with the former town, the inhabitants had a wary look. One that hardly welcomed outsiders.

The three had just finished tying up their mounts at the hitching post in front of the Wagon Spoke when the innkeeper, a slight, freckle-faced man, came up to them with a package in hand. He approached them, gave a nervous cough, and then spoke in a high-pitched voice.

"I got a package here," he announced. "For whichever of you goes by the name 'Veronica'."

The two women looked at each other, startled. Samantha spoke up and said, "That would be me. It's my…well, it's sort of a nickname."

Without ceremony, the innkeeper handed over the shoebox-sized package. It *clinked* as Samantha took it. She hefted it, felt its weight.

"Who sent this?" she asked.

"Don't know. A kid delivered it to me just a few minutes ago. Didn't say who it was from." With that, the innkeeper retreated back inside his establishment.

Samantha tore open the brown paper wrapping and opened the box inside. She shuddered at what lay inside. Charlotte grimaced, but her look was one of puzzlement. Hickok sighed. As if he'd known all along what they'd find.

A pair of engraved Colt .45's nestled inside the box. The barrels gleamed, cold and bright. The handles were well worn chunks of ivory. A single sheet of paper lay pinned underneath the guns.

"I don't...I don't understand," Charlotte said. "Who's this from? What does this mean?"

Hickok let out a grunt. "It's from the only person around here that knows your stage names. That's Clark Quantrill. Means he wants to talk."

She rounded on him. "Are you sure? Bill, what in heaven's name would Quantrill want to go on and jawbone about?"

"Don't know what he wants to talk about, but it's him all right," Samantha said. "I'd bet a stack of chips that his gang got in here a day ahead of us. Probably killed the sheriff, put this town so on edge that they're jumping at their own shadows."

"And these here guns?" Hickok said, jabbing a finger at the set of Colts, "They're Quantrill's, special made. He'd only send them here like this because he wants to *parley*, call a truce so we can talk."

Samantha reached inside the box and pulled out the paper. With one hand, she unfolded it and read the spidery handwriting inside aloud.

Meet me at the cabin by Pepper's Rock outside of town come five o' clock. Just the tall skinny gal and Hickok. No one else. No more tricks. Bring my Colts. If you don't show, me and the boys will come into town and get you and the guns. – Q

"What'll we do?" Charlotte asked.

"Ain't nothin' else to do," Hickok said calmly. "The note's very clear."

"Clark wants to talk," Samantha said, her voice tight. "So we'll go."

Charlotte looked up, her face pale as porcelain. She gripped Samantha's shoulders and gave them a shake. "What the hell are you talkin' about? You plan to go out there...and get yourself killed? Or worse?"

"It's not like that," Hickok insisted. "This is an offer to parley. This is the gunfighter's code."

"And you'd trust a snake like Quantrill to keep it?"

Hickok tugged the ends of his mustache, glanced curiously at the bits of ice that came off. "Much as I hate to grant that man some manners…yes, I would."

Charlotte swung back to Samantha, her voice frantic. "Don't go, Sam! I got a bad feelin' about this. Think of me, don't go!"

"I am thinking of you," Samantha said quietly. "Thinking of us. So I'm going. That's final."

"Final?" Charlotte looked at her lover, disbelieving. Tears welled up in the corner of her eyes like moist jewels.

"Yes. I daresay."

Furiously, Charlotte brushed away the droplets. She set her jaw, not unlike Samantha, and stiffened her back. "Then I'll be in our room. I don't think I can bear seeing your horses comin' back here, saddles empty. I just can't…"

Her voice trailed off. She stalked off towards the hotel without a glance back.

CHAPTER FIFTY-TWO

Pepper's Rock jutted from the sea of scraggly pines and sagebrush south of Scott's Bluff like an accusing gray finger. At the base of the rock sat a small lineman's shack, one that had seen much better days a decade ago. A corner of its tarpaper roof flapped loosely in the wind, and the door hung off to the side on a single hinge.

Hickok's horse, Buckshot, came to a halt and gave a worried-sounding nicker. Samantha tugged Jubilee's reins and stopped to watch Hickok lean forward and stroke his mount's mane.

"It's okay, big guy. I feel 'em too."

"Quantrill's men." Samantha didn't even voice her statement as a question.

"Yep. They're out there, lyin' low in the underbrush. They ain't gonna bushwhack us, not unless we do the same to their leader."

"They going to make us disarm before Quantrill shows his ugly mug?"

"Nope. Though I'll bet that Quantrill has at least one of his gang there, guns in holsters. Likely the second-in-command."

"That's close enough to even-odds." Her palm caressed the grip of one pistol. "You want to take Quantrill? I should be able to tag his second-in-command. Or—"

Hickok, in a tone that brooked no argument, said, "Your irons stay in the leathers. A gunfighter's word is his bond."

The sound of movement came from inside the shack. Then a full-bellied man wearing trousers held up by dun-colored suspenders stepped out into the late afternoon sunlight. His appearance might have been comical, had it not been for the magnum-sized holster at his side. The man stepped aside, and Quantrill emerged. His gray overcoat flapped in the breeze, and his weathered face lit up as he saw the two visitors.

"Don't that take all," he said grandly. "If I was a bettin' man, I'd be the fool who's out of the money. Be honest, I didn't think y'all would make it."

"Hobble your lip," Samantha said bluntly. "I'm here. What do you want?"

Quantrill *tsked*. "Manners, Missus Williams. First things first. Did you bring my guns?"

Wordlessly, Hickok hefted the box containing the pistols. Quantrill nodded at his heavyset sidekick, who then stepped forward and retrieved the box. He brought it back and the Confederate cavalryman eagerly holstered his weapons.

"Don't rightly feel *proper* without them," Quantrill drawled. He motioned towards the open doorway. "Come on in, sit a spell."

Samantha and Hickok dismounted and followed the two men inside. The fetid smell of sweat and rancid bacon grease permeated the air inside. Sunbeams filtered through the grimy windows, giving the interior an eerie twilight glow. In the center of the room was a table and a set of chairs, each pitted ominously with knife marks. A trio of tin cups perched on one ragged edge swayed precariously as Quantrill pulled a chair out and sat down.

"Lem," said Clark Quantrill, motioning to his man, "Pour us all a double-sized shot."

Samantha took a seat. Her eyes darted about the shack as Quantrill's second poured a generous helping of an amber-colored liquid into each cup. She glanced at Hickok, who seemed uncommonly serene.

The Confederate Captain took up his cup once the three had been distributed. "This is parley, so let's toast to jawin' over shootin'."

"Hear, hear," Hickok said quietly. Samantha watched him pick up his portion. Though she noticed that he didn't tip his cup back until Quantrill had drank his share. Only then did he toss his whiskey back. Samantha quickly followed suit, and the liquid flared, burning her esophagus all the way down like a torch tossed down a coal shaft.

"We got this here problem," Quantrill began. "The blood that's been spilt between us. Your boy, an' my brothers."

Samantha frowned at how the Confederate referred to Jude, but otherwise remained impassive. Something about a calm, thoughtful Clark Quantrill frightened her even more than the bloodthirsty one. Lem stood silently in the background and poured his boss a second cup of whiskey.

"Y'all got my dander up, y'see. And that got me to callin' in all of my Raiders." He tipped his cup in Hickok's direction, then tossed the contents down. "Maybe we can't charge up the war no more. But we can strike out for the West, same as you, carve out a piece of it ourselves. There's a lot of gold and silver on the move out here. Enough to keep me and my men happy."

"Well, we don't have any gold," Samantha said. "So we can't have anything you want."

"Naw, naw," Quantrill said, shaking a finger at her. "You got two things. First one bein' my peace o' mind."

"What—"

"See, this killin' of my brothers...Lord knows, I've tried to leave it in my trail dust, but I can't." Quantrill let out a dark laugh, a giggle, really. Samantha's skin crawled at the sound. "So I want compensation. And it turns out the second thing you got...is what I really want."

Suspicion bloomed anew in Samantha's eyes. Hickok saw the sudden heat catching fire and moved to control it. He leaned forward and spoke for the first time.

"Stop your fence ridin', Clark. What is it?"

"You ever wonder, Jayhawker? You ever wonder why I burned the entire town of Lawrence to the ground?"

"I'm sure that the fifty families lyin' under the soil would like to know."

The Captain ignored him. His eyes took on a distant look. "Just a month before I rode up to Kansas, the Yankees...the damned bluebellies...they busted their way down into Arkansas. Where me an' Caroline had been living, startin' to raise a family. On one of their raids, they burned my crops, chopped down my orchards, set fire to my house. And she...she never got out."

Hickok's reply was cold. "A lot of us lost family in the war. We all didn't go insane, the way you did."

"Insane?" Another mad giggle. "Seems to be that it was the logical way to start thinkin'. But the plain deal is that my better half was Southern, through and through. Beautiful, and the right sparklin' image of that other girl you got travelin' with you."

Hickok saw Samantha's reaction. The curling of her fists, the warm flush of blood to her face. He tried to signal her with a tiny shake of his head, tried to warn her. But she ignored him.

"No deal." Samantha gritted.

"Did I say you had a choice?" Quantrill asked. "Bring that girl back with you tonight. Bring her back to warm my bed, wear my ring, and earn her keep in my house. An' all will be square between us. If'n you don't...I got twenty rifles backin' me up. Make no mistake, we'll track you down. And we won't leave enough for the *flies* when we're done."

Samantha leaned forward. With a sweep of her arm, she knocked the cups to the floor with a metallic clatter. The fumes of spilled alcohol joined the slick of sweat and bacon grease in the small room.

"God damn you, all men like you!" she shouted. "I'll see you in Hell before I let you touch my—"

Her breath caught. So did Quantrill's. Now it was his turn to sit up. He rubbed his leathery fingers together as if sifting coins.

"Well, now. That adds a whole new pickle to this barrel, don't it?" His eyes gleamed, feral in the dim light. "We got a new breed of slut here...the *un-natural* kind."

"Quantrill—" Hickok warned.

"Oh, this is much better. Much better," Quantrill leered. "I understand now. No deal, I get that. But I wouldn't have it any other way. Now, when I take your woman from you? It's goin' to taste sweet. Twice. As. Sweet."

Samantha leapt to her feet with a snarl. Her chair clattered to the floor. Her hand hovered above her gun.

The barrel of Lem's pistol appeared. So close to her eye that she couldn't focus on it. The fat man was faster than he looked.

So was Hickok. He'd pulled both guns. Had one at Lem's head. The other at Quantrill's gut.

"Miss Samantha," Hickok said slowly, "I'd love for you to blow a train-sized hole in this swine. But you move a muscle, and we're all goin' up in gunfire."

"That's right," Quantrill said, his expression cool and amused. As if Samantha had just objected to the flavor of the whiskey that lay spattered on the floor. "My men hear a gun go off, they'll turn this shack into a lead mine with their shot."

Samantha withdrew her hand. Lem backed off, and Hickok holstered his weapons.

"I returned your guns," Samantha spat. "Next time we meet, you better be wearing them."

Quantrill smiled. "I'm lookin' right forward to it."

She and Hickok backed out the door under Lem's watchful eye. They mounted up as quickly as possible in the fading evening light. Together, they took the road back towards Scott's Bluff at a hard gallop.

CHAPTER FIFTY-THREE

Buckshot and Jubilee kicked up dirt as their riders brought them to an abrupt halt outside the Wagon Spoke. Hurriedly, Samantha and Hickok dismounted and untacked the horses. Samantha uttered a curse, looked off into the distance, and then swung around to address her companion for the first time since they'd left Clark Quantrill behind.

"So, Mister Hickok," she said. Her throat felt tight, coiled like one of Charlotte's bullwhips. "Now that we let the element of surprise slip away, what's the plan? We run, or do we make a stand here?"

Hickok paused, but let Samantha's barb pass. "Been thinkin' on that all the way back here. The way I see it..." He spotted someone approaching from behind Samantha, and his face broke out in a grin. "Well, it'll keep. You got someone incoming."

"What?"

Samantha had only halfway turned, when a projectile in a brown dress hit her, grabbed her waist, and began kissing her furiously. She gasped and staggered back, trying not to fall over.

"You made it! You're alive, Sam!" Charlotte cried, between kisses. "I've been sick with worry, been right awful sick..."

"Okay, okay," Samantha said, planting a kiss of her own on Charlotte's berry-colored lips. Her cheeks began to burn with the same color from the open display of affection. "Come on, folks out here could be watching."

"Let them! Let them watch!" Charlotte said defiantly. But she did stop in her kissing, enough so that Samantha could throw Hickok a 'help me out here' look.

"Ah...if I could interrupt," he said, clearing his throat. "Unless you really want to try seven-to-one odds again Quantrill – and get a lot of folk here killed – then we need to make ourselves plenty scarce."

"But they're sure to be watching this town, the roads," Samantha objected.

"And the country out here, it ain't like the plains," Charlotte chimed in, though she didn't release Samantha from her embrace. "How're we goin' to outride 'em?"

"We can outride 'em if can we outfox 'em," Hickok said. He blew out a breath, made the tips of his mustache quiver. "I got a suggestion, but I don't think y'all will take kindly to it."

Samantha shook her head. "It's suicide to try the pass. Whether we stay in town or make a run for Fort Collins, it means a shootout for sure. What could be worse?"

"For starters, your father." Samantha stared at him a moment, but then nodded at Hickok to go on. "We slip out of town now. Head to the north. Don't take the roads, but we circle 'round, make a beeline for the plains. Then we ride all-out, headin' due east."

"Back to Rock Creek?" Charlotte groaned.

"Nope. Ten miles further. We hit the town of North Platte, puts us smack on the main rail line. From there, we buy a ticket to California, get you to your destination in four, five days."

"But Pinkerton—"

"Yep. Pinkerton. What do you think, Samantha?"

Now it was Samantha's turn to pause. "I like Mister Hickok's plan. If it works, we'll finally be out of the Raiders' reach. If it doesn't...well, should Pinkerton catch us, we get shipped back to Chicago. Maybe get a chance to escape. But if Quantrill catches us..."

She let the answer hang like deadly mist in the air. Charlotte stared, then turned to Hickok and nodded her assent to the plan.

"Fine," Hickok said. "Gather up your things, meet me back here at the hitchin' post in ten minutes. Absolutely no longer than that, got it?"

"We'll be ready," Samantha replied. Hickok dashed off into the deepening shadows. She gently pried herself loose from Charlotte's arms with a smile. "Believe me, Char, I was as scared as you. I don't ever want to put either of us that far into harm's way again."

"Then we'd best get to stuffin' what's left of our bags," Charlotte replied, and together they ran up the hotel's steps to their room.

※ ※ ※

Hickok paced back and forth, snatching glances at his brass pocket watch in the dim light of the hotel's lanterns. With a clatter of boots on wood, the two women emerged from the front door, laden with bags. He stepped forward, took one from Charlotte, and helped lash it firmly into place on her mount, Patches.

"Sorry we're late," Samantha said, her breath puffing steam into the evening's cold air. "Practically had to draw down on the innkeeper to get our bill straight."

"We'll make up the time," Hickok said, as the three swung into their saddles.

"Why the big fuss, Bill?" Charlotte asked.

"Figured we needed a way to distract Quantrill's boys, if they're watching the town. And any of the locals who've been givin' us the stinkeye."

"What did you come up with?"

The gunfighter shrugged. "I set fire to the tannery at the south end."

Charlotte stared. "You didn't!"

The breeze soured, carrying the eye-watering stench of burning cow hide and tanning solutions. Orange flames leaped into sight from a building a couple of blocks down. People began running towards the blaze, shouting alarm. As the ruckus kicked up a notch, Hickok nudged Buckshot into motion. The two women followed suit. They passed out of the north end of Scott's Bluff without anyone challenging them, and they quickly passed into a belt of densely forested hills. Behind them, the sound of chaos continued as the townspeople tried to fight the blaze.

"Easier than you'd think," Hickok remarked. "Thanks to Quantrill, the town council has people all posted along the outskirts, looking out for trouble. Nobody's left to watch for it in the town itself."

Keeping together so as not to lose each other in the darkness, the three carefully picked their way through the underbrush. Ankle-deep drifts of snow crunched under their horses' hooves. A scant sliver of moon rose, giving them precious little light to see by. Hickok surveyed the landscape as they crested one hill, and then motioned to the right.

"Let's start cuttin' back east for the plains now. That-a-ways."

"Good," Charlotte said. "Hope we can make it to someplace warmer soon. I don't fancy sleepin' on the ground when it's this cold."

"There's that, but I'm more worried about this here snow."

"Me too," Samantha remarked. "Makes it easier for Quantrill to track us."

"You don't think that Bill's fire threw 'em off our trail?" Charlotte asked.

"We can pray for that." Samantha threw a hopeful glance at Hickok.

He grimaced and shook his head in the negative.

But all he said out loud was, "We can pray as we ride, then. Come on, this blessed darkness ain't goin' to last forever."

CHAPTER FIFTY-FOUR

Charlotte winced as lightning flashed overhead, followed by the grumble of thunder. The heavens opened up with a downpour that Noah might have felt bracing. She sighed, pulled up the hood on the rain slicker that Samantha had given her, and continued urging Patches to keep up with the group.

The three horses plodded along, plowing through the mud and chunks of mucky prairie grass. The cold rain stung their riders, but the group pressed on. Only a few copses of wind-lashed trees broke up the monotony of the rolling gray landscape. In the distance behind them, the mountains leading up to Scott's Bluff had faded into a dull smudge against the horizon.

Samantha let her mount fall a few steps behind. She pulled her jacket around her body more tightly and held a fist to her mouth. She let out a series of racking coughs. Turned to one side, spat into the brush. Charlotte watched, and then nudged her horse over next to Hickok's.

"Daylight's fading, Bill," she said. "We need to stop, try to find some shelter. And we need a fire. Something to dry us out, 'fore we all die of pneumonia."

"I'm not liking this any more than you," Hickok said. "But I'm of a mind to push on. It ain't safe out here. Quantrill's hunting us, I can feel it."

"We haven't seen hide nor hair of them in the past few days."

"Don't mean they ain't back there. We light a fire, they'll be able to spot us miles away."

"In a half-hour, we won't be able to see further than our noses in this downpour!" Charlotte retorted. "The rain should beat the smoke down. And we need some warmth. Sam's startin' to cough. Bad."

Hickok tipped his hat back. Rainwater sluiced down the rear edge of the brim with a wet patter. He grimaced, but he craned his neck to survey the land ahead.

"Let's set ourselves down for a spell at the next set of trees," he said. "I'm seein' a couple of boulders over there, maybe get us some shelter from the wind, at least."

Charlotte conveyed the decision to Samantha, who nodded her head glumly in agreement. Luckily, the canopy of trees cut the sheets of rain to a steady patter of icy drops. But when they dismounted, the wind came at them from all quarters, pulling and leeching the heat from their bodies. Shivering, Hickok and Samantha did their best to get the horses fed while Charlotte tried to dig a pit to shelter the fire.

The ground gave way reluctantly, squelching as Charlotte dug her spade into the sodden earth. She lay in a bundle of halfway dry kindling and, after several attempts, managed to light it. The heady, familiar smell of the campfire buoyed her spirits just enough for her to stagger through the necessary chore of boiling water for coffee and a dinner of cooked oatmeal and dried meat strips.

Samantha downed the contents of her steaming mug, then held the warm tin surface against the side of her face. Another spasm of coughing. A spit of phlegm into the darkness.

"We really ought to rub the horses down," she said. "If they get too cold, I don't want them collapsing on us."

"I'll see what I can do," Hickok said. He watched Samantha carefully, studying her wan complexion. He moved closer, a concerned look on his face, and began to raise a hand. He stopped. Hesitated. And then quickly lowered it.

"What is it?" Samantha asked.

Hickok looked at her, considering. "Just...don't fret none."

He reached out and laid the back of his hand on Samantha's forehead for a moment. She didn't object. Instead, his look got grimmer.

"You're runnin' quite a fever there," he said.

"I feel fine," Samantha retorted. "Just need a little sleep is all."

"Then you get right to it," Hickok said gently. "We'll handle the rest."

Samantha nodded. Soon, she had buried her face in the side of her jacket and was letting out snores that could saw fir trees into planks. Charlotte carefully nudged some thicker pieces of brush into the fire, which continued to burn the damp wood under protest. When she was satisfied that the flames wouldn't be snuffed out from the wind and wet, she sat next to Hickok as the man brooded silently as he finished the last of his dinner.

"Are we setting watch tonight?" she asked quietly.

"Can't afford not to. Quantrill's Raiders did have some trackers in their ranks. And Clark's got enough warm bodies to spread out a fair amount. Get a better chance of spotting us."

"Sam needs rest in a proper bed. We all do. Y'all reckon we can make it into North Platte tomorrow morning?"

Hickok looked thoughtful for a moment. The wind howled around them, sending a stray gust of rain between the tree branches. The droplets made a series of musical *plinks* on his empty tin plate.

"Nope. We'll be lucky to make it before nightfall, if the weather keeps up."

It was a somber note to end a rain-soaked day. Charlotte bundled herself up as best she could as Hickok took the first half of the watch. She listened to Samantha's deep breathing, the fitful movements she made in her sleep.

"I hope we're lucky, then," Charlotte said, to no one in particular.

But if the three riders had any luck, it deserted them by noon on the following day. A promising morning start became troubling as the clouds reared into angry, anvil-shaped thunderheads. Rain mixed with sleet pelted them as they continued east. By the time they crossed one of the main routes into North Platte, the constant downpour had turned the road into a muddy quagmire.

Even dismounted, three hours spent struggling through the sticky mud completely exhausted their horses. An abandoned lean-to provided them with a scrap of shelter on the next night, and it wasn't until the middle of the following day that they got their first glimpse of their destination. The cheerless sight of shacks and sod-caked houses greeted them as they staggered, shivering and coughing, along the main street.

They finally got the horses in out of the rain at a nearby stable. Followed up by a visit to the town's general store. The stare from the store's owner at their bedraggled appearance vanished as Charlotte produced coins to purchase what food and drink they had.

Hickok and Samantha pulled together a makeshift table out of a flour barrel and a few boxes. Though hot food wasn't available, they wolfed down what Charlotte bought: ham and cheese sandwiches, a wrinkly quartet of apples, and a steaming kettle of hot tea.

Samantha coughed into her hand. She restrained herself from letting loose a whole barrage of coughs with some difficulty, and then spoke in a voice tinged with a rasp. "Mister Hickok…we can't stay here. Maybe we're ahead of Quantrill, but Pinkerton's got to be watching this place."

"Frying pan or fire, it seems much the same lately," Charlotte added, with a shake of her head. "But here's some good news, for a change. I overheard a couple other travellers talkin' about the trains at the counter. The one we want, the Union Pacific, is comin' through North Platte in a couple more hours."

"Then we need to be on that train," Samantha said firmly. She turned to Hickok. "Any ideas?"

"Not really," he replied. "Don't got time for a disguise that's worth a damn. Figure that if Charlotte and I buy the tickets, at least we don't match the profile they have out on you."

"What if Pinkerton's got men at the train station?"

Hickok looked troubled. "What do you mean?"

"What I mean, Mister Hickok, is that I need to know." Samantha's eyes burned, fever-bright. "Are you willing to draw down on one of Pinkerton's men if they try a snatch n' grab at the train station?"

She crossed her arms, waiting for his reply.

CHAPTER FIFTY-FIVE

Hickok took the last sip of his tea. Before answering, he swirled the unfamiliar liquid around his mouth, and then swallowed. His words were soft in tone, but direct in meaning.

"Miss Samantha, I wasn't exactly raised on prunes and proverbs. I'm no stranger to killin', and I'll stretch the Lord's truth 'til it squeaks. But I'm not goin' to draw down on one of the Pinks. Mind you, I've got no love for Pinkerton's boys. But they're close enough to the law, an' that puts them on the side of the angels, so far as I'm concerned."

Samantha started to reply. But a spasm of coughing cut her voice off. Instead, she nodded her head in acceptance.

"Well, let's get going, then," Hickok said, setting down his cup.

The train station squatted amongst the other low-slung wood-frame buildings on the next block over. Samantha and Hickok flanked Charlotte protectively as they entered. The two women's eyes darted everywhere, alert for a hundred dirty tricks. Samantha felt her pulse begin to pound. If Hickok wouldn't draw on a Pinkerton man…would she? *Could she?*

But no threat materialized. The waiting area, which had obviously been converted from a freight barn, stretched like a dark cavern over the ticket counters. Long wooden benches stretched across the open area, practically deserted. A young woman bearing a parasol on one arm and a child on the other sat some ways off. So did a couple of other nondescript travelers, all either too old or young to be working for the Pinkerton Detective Agency.

Samantha let out a breath. She sank onto one of the smoothly polished benches, grateful for the respite. She wiped her brow clean of beaded sweat.

"Maybe we are due for a run of luck," she remarked. "I'll wait here. Think I need to."

Hickok nodded, and took Charlotte's arm in his. Together, they approached the ticket counter. The clerk's eyes flicked over them, his expression one of profound disinterest.

"Three tickets for San Francisco," Charlotte said, putting on a sweet expression. "And passage for three horses, if you please."

"Ma'am," the clerk replied, "horses cost extra."

"Well, I suppose I should've expected that. How much?"

"They just changed the cost. One moment, let me check the rate sheet." The clerk stooped for a moment. The sound of a drawer being pulled open. The rustle of paper.

From behind Hickok and Charlotte came a series of terrible, chest-wracking coughs. The clerk frowned, straightened up, and peered around the two customers. A woman sat on the nearby bench, holding a sticky, wet handkerchief to her mouth.

"You okay?" he called out. When he received no reply, he spoke to Charlotte directly. "She with you?"

"And how is that any of your business?"

The agent shrugged. But inside, memory began tugging at his brain. He kept his expression tightly controlled as he said, "Horses are an extra six a head."

Charlotte dug out the money and slid it across the slab of a counter. In a moment, the clerk handed her a set of tickets. A quick 'thank-you', and the transaction concluded.

The clerk watched as the tall man and the two women left the station together. He turned, scribbled a message on a piece of scrap paper, and called out to his co-worker in the back room.

"Hey, Sweeney! You still back there? I need you at the telegraph key."

The answer was muffled, but clear enough to hear. "Sure enough. What d'you need?"

"Got something for you here. Need to send it to Chicago. Pinkerton business."

※ ※ ※

Matthew Slade slapped his badge down on the dusty red table with a *clink*. He leaned forward and got eye-to-eye. The smith was a big, hard-looking man, but Slade read him as one who'd bend, once the right pressure had been applied.

"Maybe I did see the two girls you're looking for," the smith said, raising his voice to be heard over the blowing wind and rain outside his shop. "But why do you think they came to my place, eh?"

Slade pulled out the crumpled sheet of paper he'd found inside the vardo in Des Moines. Placed it next to his badge. "This is a receipt. Tells me that ten days ago, the two women I'm looking for came to you, got their horses shoed and a wagon axle mended. And look at the bottom…I'd say that looks like your signature. So would any judge."

The man's voice quavered. "So maybe they did come in…"

"And maybe you better tell me all that you know about 'em, then." Slade pushed once more, putting all of his chips on a final bluff. "The Chicago branch still has this listed as a possible kidnapping case. I figure that I could go grab the sheriff, have you brought in as an accessory to the crime. Bet they'd have to keep you locked up out here a long, long time…"

"They weren't kidnapped!" The blacksmith's face turned ashen, and he spoke pleadingly to Slade. "Don't tell 'em to lock me up, I'm an innocent man!"

"Then take those beans of yours and spill them, friend."

"Those girls…they came in with two other men. One of 'em was the showman…he came into town a few days before. He was lookin' for real-life Injuns for his Wild West show."

"Buffalo Bill," Slade said, understanding. "And the other?"

"He came in lookin' for people to help the two girls…and he left with 'em, too. So help me God, it was Wild Bill Hickok himself."

The news rocked Slade like a punch to his gut, like a slug of redeye whiskey. He kept his face impassive, but his mind raced on ahead.

Hickok? What in blazes was a top-rate gun hand doin' traveling with them?

But Slade's mouth only growled a series of terse words.

"Hickok? How? And why?"

"I dunno how he ended up with them, I don't! But it had something to do with Quantrill's Raiders, the ones that burned up that town in Kansas!"

Slade made a disgusted sound. "That's ridiculous. The war's been over for more than ten years, and Quantrill's boys are tales they tell kids to scare them straight!"

"I don't know, Mister Slade, I heard say from my brother that he saw the Raider's Captain, Quantrill himself. Right in O'Dell's saloon, as real as you or I."

Matthew Slade considered. Right or wrong, the smith believed the tale. And no less than lawman Wyatt Earp had claimed that Quantrill was back. Perhaps there was no harm in checking to see if this O'Dell could back up the story.

A hammering at the smith's door. Without waiting for an answer, a man in a patch-covered rain slicker and a high-crowned hat pushed his way in. He made his way over to where Slade had been questioning the smith, dripping water with every step.

"Evening, Deputy MacInnis," Slade said. Earlier, when he'd arrived on the stagecoach, the local sheriff's office had been the first place he'd paid a visit. "What can I do for you?"

"Nothin, 'less you got a better slicker on you," the man grumped, holding up one tattered sleeve. But he dug into an inner pocket and handed over a small bundle of paper that he'd managed to keep dry. "This just came in over the telegraph. Someone paid a pretty penny to send these to you, and it looked urgent."

"I am in your debt," Slade said courteously, as he took the telegrams.

From Pinkerton's Chicago office, dated three days ago: "GIRLS MATCHING DESCRIPTION SIGHTED TRAVELING WITH MALE COMPANION AT NORTH PLATTE DEPOT -(STOP)- LEFT BY PURCHASING TICKETS FOR THREE TO SAN FRANCISCO - (STOP)- ADVISE PLEASE"

Slade's eyes widened. He'd arrived at the North Platte station two days ago, in order to catch the stage to Rock Creek. If he'd arrived only a day sooner, he'd have caught them right at the depot!

Next was a telegram from the Des Moines office, bearing a date and time from last evening: "MATTHEW THE CHICAGO OFFICE TRYING TO FIND YOU -(STOP)- BASED ON THE RAIL TIME TABLES THIS SHOULD REACH YOU IN NORTH PLATTE"

Finally, a terse message from North Platte's station itself, dated earlier today: "RECOMMEND FORWARD MSG TO ROCK CREEK -(STOP)- STATION MGR NORTH PLATTE"

Slade didn't hesitate. He flipped the last telegram over and jotted down a reply: "RECD MESSAGE IN ROCK CREEK -(STOP)- SEND MY HORSE ON EARLIEST TRAIN TO NORTH PLATTE -(STOP)- WILL PURSUE QUARRY TO END DESTINATION"

"Deputy," he said, "can I ask you a favor? Would you get that out on the wire to Chicago, as soon as you can? Address and charge it to Pinkerton. I have to leave immediately."

"Sure," MacInnis replied, as he glanced at the note. "But where are you goin'?"

"To convince the stage driver to leave for North Platte right now. Have to, if I'm going to pick up my horse and meet the next outbound train to San Francisco."

"It's a real toad-strangler of a storm out there. With all the mud, it'll take you a full day just to get there, if you're lucky. Why the rush? Can't your Pinkerton folks just grab the girls when they step off the train?"

"Maybe, if we *had* an office in San Francisco," Slade replied. He went to the door and threw it open. A blast of rain hit him with a wet slap. But it brought a grin to his face. "Besides, you don't know these girls. I won't be under-estimating them again."

CHAPTER FIFTY-SIX

Charlotte listened to the *click-clack* of the train's wheels, felt the reassuring sway of the car beneath her feet as she ran a currycomb along Patches' side. Her little riding horse sighed contentedly. The sway had picked up slightly, meaning that the engineer had thrown open the steam valves to take advantage of a long straightaway.

Golden sunlight sluiced between the freight car's boards. It was a drafty mode of travel, but it had kept the horses warm enough. More importantly, it had kept them out of the weather. It had made all the difference for them. Buckshot, Patches and Jubilee had been on their last legs, stumble-footed with fatigue and hunger by the time they'd been loaded onto the Union Pacific train. But with a couple of days rest and plenty of grain, they'd come a long way back.

If only the same thing had happened with Samantha.

She'd been at Samantha's side constantly, tending to her fever as best she could in the cramped confines of their sleeper compartment. Kept her to a diet of water, fruit juice, and the rich beef broths or creamy chowders available from the dining car. Helped her to the water closet when she needed it. Hickok had gently nudged her to get out for some air, for something to do other than fuss over someone who needed, more than anything else, a great deal of sleep.

But her stomach still felt clenched, in a tight knot. Because of that, both of the women had lost weight. Samantha from illness, Charlotte from worry. She tucked the comb away, promised the horses that she'd return, and pushed her way through the compartment's end door.

Charlotte wended her way through the swaying cars towards the front of the train. Each transition between the cars blasted her with the smell of coal smoke. She finally made it to the sleeper car and pulled the door shut behind her with a rattle.

Hickok looked up from across the small room, from where he sat, back against the wall and with a small folding table in front. Not coincidentally, he'd remained where he could block any access to where Samantha slept.

She came to sit by him. The light, heady smell of gun oil permeated the space, and she watched as Hickok finished cleaning his guns. She rested her chin in the palm of her hand and watched the endless expanse of high desert plains roll by the window, with only the occasional farm to break the monotony.

The landscape had been like this since the rain had finally broken. Two days ago, the train had skirted the border of a shiny expanse of water, crusted at the edge with salt. But that sight hadn't excited her nearly as much as the conductor's announcement that everyone was to adjust their watch back by one hour.

All the way to Pacific Time. The very idea tugged at her heart.

As if the click-clack of the train wheels were whispering: *Almost there, almost there.*

The emotions must have shown on her face. Hickok asked, "How're you holding up?"

"Ain't quite right as rain, but well enough," she said. "Just nerves, I guess. Like you."

"Me?" Hickok raised an eyebrow as he began sliding bullets home, reloading his guns.

"Well...I don't meant anything, but that's the third time today I've seen you clean those pistols of yours. You're expectin' trouble."

"Yeah," he sighed, "you got that right. I didn't think that anyone would try an' nab us at North Platte. But you can be sure that the Pinks got people watching for you on the trains. From what I recall, Pinkerton's stretched pretty thin out West. But the right telegram could mean that they'd board at any station down the line, pick us up."

"Or any town sheriff?"

"Naw, I don't think so. From what Samantha's told me, her father wants her back for marriage to some high n' mighty fellow in a pinstripe suit. Ain't going to help if it gets into the papers that she went skedaddlin' before the wedding. That's why he went to Pinkerton, not to the law. He wants to keep this nice and quiet."

She watched him a moment longer, as he finished re-loading his guns. "Bill, I don't see why you're still packin' iron. I mean, didn't you tell Sam that you weren't goin' to draw down on a Pinkerton man?"

"That's right." He grinned as he slid his guns back in their leather holsters. "Didn't say that I'd let them take either of you without a fight, did I?"

She smiled at Hickok's sentiment. But the warm feeling vanished as if a tub of ice water had been tossed on her as she heard a sound. Samantha cried out, a sound of fear that she'd never made, not even during the gunfight with Quantrill's men. Followed by a heavy thud.

Charlotte scrambled to her feet, just in time to catch Samantha as she half-ran, half stumbled into the sleeping car's corridor. Her face flushed red with the bright ruddy mask of fever, and her eyes shone like newly minted coins. Her voice husked out, wild and confused.

"We've got to get out of here!" she cried, "Char, I'm burning up...the sun...the mountains...my father's coming...Quantrill's coming...can't find my guns..."

She struggled, threatening for one terrible moment to overwhelm Charlotte, but then collapsed, moaning, on the floor. Charlotte let out a cry, then cradled Samantha's head in her arms. Her voice keened with sorrow and desperation.

"Sam! Oh, my beloved Sam...I'm here, I'm here..."

Hickok grabbed Charlotte's wrist and roughly pulled her up. Startled, she fought for a moment, before the man spoke to her. Not unkindly, but in a direct, flat tone.

"Get to the dining car! Ask 'em for smellin' salts and a bottle of brandy!"

"No, I need to stay!"

"She needs help, not sentiment! I'm the one who needs to stay with her. Trust me on this."

"But—"

"*Now!*"

Blindly, Charlotte pushed away from Hickok's grasp and ran for the railroad car's door. Doing her best to keep her tears in check, she burst into the dining car, startling the waiters who were tending to the passengers eating lunch.

"Emergency," she gasped, "I need smelling salts. And brandy. A bottle of it!"

The items were rounded up quickly, though to Charlotte, it felt like it took hours. As soon as the salt and alcohol had been placed in her hands, she dashed back through the cars. Skidded to a stop as she yanked the sleeping compartment's door open.

Hickok hadn't moved Samantha, but he'd draped a blanket over her and propped her head on a pillow. Samantha's eyes remained closed, but she tossed and turned, flicking droplets of sweat into the air. Hickok's eyes weren't on her. He stood protectively over her, one hand resting menacingly on his guns.

Three burly railroad conductors faced him. Their faces varied between scared and enraged. Hickok spotted Charlotte, motioned her to come around them. She did, and knelt by Samantha's side.

"Smellin' salts first," he said quietly. "Then get her to bed, an' get some brandy into her."

"You will do nothing of the kind," the senior conductor said. His salt-and pepper beard waggled as he stated, "It's the policy of the Union Pacific that any passenger that comes down with scarlet fever be put off the train at the next stop. *No exceptions!*"

CHAPTER FIFTY-SEVEN

"You don't know if she's got scarlet fever," Hickok declared.

The gunfighter's voice had gone dead, flat in tone. The nearest man blanched, swallowed hard, and looked to the senior conductor for backup.

"You can't tell if she doesn't, neither," retorted the older conductor. "She's got to get off, and her companions with her. Or I'll have you thrown off."

Charlotte froze. She paused as she was about to place the smelling salts under Samantha's nose. Looked out the window at the landscape rushing by. Again, nothing except the expanse of flat desert and dirty-white salt wastes.

"We can't get off here," she gritted. "I won't let you do that to my Samantha. Bill, you know what to do."

In a flash, Hickok drew his gun. Trained it on the old man.

"Try throwing us off," Hickok said. "See how long you live, scarlet fever or no."

The two younger men fell a step back, gibbering in fear. Charlotte watched, riveted. But the older conductor sighed resignedly.

He stepped forward and slowly raised his hand. Charlotte stared, amazed, as he rested his palm along the top of Hickok's outstretched gun, and then gently nudged it towards the floor.

"That's enough of that," he said quietly. "You ain't going to shoot me, and you ain't going to bluff your way past, neither."

Hickok holstered his weapon and looked at the old man with grudging respect.

"You got guts, I'll give you that," Hickok said approvingly. "What's your name, and how did you know?"

"The name's Jeffries, and I recognized you from all the dime novels I read," the old man said. "You're a lot of things, Wild Bill, but you're a law-abiding man at heart. Not a cold-blooded murderer."

Hickok nodded, and mumbled something under his breath about 'shootin' the damned publisher'.

"Well, then, Mister Jeffries," Charlotte said, with a firmness in her voice that would've taken Samantha aback, "You can't just put Samantha off out here, at some desert watering hole. That'll be plain murder."

"She could sicken the whole train, and the longer she stays on, the better the chance," Jeffries said. But his words lacked conviction this time. He ran his fingers through his beard and turned to his men. "Boys, let me handle this."

The two murmured assent, not taking their eyes off Hickok's face, and backed down the corridor. Jeffries pulled a map out of his back pocket, squinted at it, and tapped a spot with his finger. When he spoke, his voice carried a trace of compassion.

"I can't lose my job over this," he said, "But I won't be able to sleep if I follow my directions to the letter. So I'm goin' to fix my logs a bit. The stop after the next is the last one we make before we hit the Sierras. Y'all get off there, at a place called Stillwater. Mining town and railroad work-station. It ain't much, but it's got a doctor and a hospital of sorts there."

"Thank you," Charlotte said gratefully.

Hickok smiled, and offered his hand.

"Nope, can't do that, if'n case you do got the fever," Jeffries said, demurring. "Just you get ready, and don't make any fuss when y'all get off. I got papers to scribble over, now."

With that, the conductor stepped out of the compartment and slid the door shut.

"What a strange man," Charlotte remarked.

"Maybe, but a good one," Hickok said. "Come on, we've got to get Samantha ready."

Over the next hour and a half, Hickok and Charlotte got their gear together, and then rigged up a stretcher to take Samantha off the train without unduly jostling her. For her part, Samantha woke up without the need of the smelling salts. She remained feverish, but this time, she hadn't succumbed to delirium.

"Char," she said weakly, as they moved her to the stretcher, "what's going on? Why are you moving me?"

"Just gettin' you to the doctor," Charlotte said, tousling Samantha's hair. "You just relax."

Charlotte had moved her hand to get the brandy, but Samantha had already drifted off. The train slowed, then jolted to a stop. The rattling of multiple doors sounded throughout the train as passengers and cargo prepared to be unloaded.

Samantha opened her eyes as she sensed the changes around her, but everything became a dim blur in her mind under the sweltering heat of her fever. The hot, still scent of desert air, fresh horse manure, and the tinny smell of locomotive steam. Then the warm, smooth taste of brandy.

Things went dark for a while. Tar and sweat on her brow. Pierced with painful white light, people in white coats. Conversations took place around her.

The soft sound of someone doffing his hat, rubbing the brim. Followed by Hickok's deep growl of a voice.

"This doctor's sure that it ain't scarlet fever, then."

Charlotte, sounding halfway relieved: "That's right. Worst case of influenza he'd seen in ages, but that's all. Made worse by exposure, stress, and exhaustion."

The welcome feel of Charlotte's hand curled around hers. Then Hickok again.

"So. Medicine, taken twice a day?"

"Yes. He's sure that the fever will break any time now. Then she'll be on her feet and kickin' in no time."

Hickok let out a slow, measured breath. "Not sure that's all good news."

"What? Why on earth would y'all say that, Bill?"

"There's someone downstairs. Come on, we got to talk."

Samantha slipped back into a feverish sleep. She swam through a hot, sticky darkness. A flash of lightning. Resolved itself into some demon from the blackness. It stalked forward, spurs jingling as it approached. More lightning. With each flash, it changed faces. The man who'd forced himself on her when she was fifteen. Percy Hanover. Then Quantrill, his jagged cheekbones turning into feral wolf jaws...

Samantha sat up, gasped for air. She brought one shaky hand to her forehead, felt the film of sweat there. But her forehead was cool to her touch. She felt weak, empty and hollow like a bell jar, but she was herself again.

She looked around, trying to focus her bleary eyes. She lay in a lumpy, but comfortable feather bed. The room was well furnished, but in a style she'd never seen before. Throw rugs and quilts done up with the geometric patterns of Navajo horse blankets lay across expanses of heavy wood furniture. The sun was out, but the shutters had been left closed, leaving most of the room in deep shadow.

A pitcher lay on the nightstand next to the bed. In an instant, her throat felt scratchy. She groped for the handle, but someone else picked it up for her.

"Hold on, there. You're still very weak," said a man's voice. "Allow me get it for you."

The man fetched a clean mason jar for her, filled it with water, and brought it over. She gulped the contents down as she saw him clearly for the first time. A long, bony face with a neatly trimmed mustache. Tall, lean, wearing riding clothes that looked like they'd seen a lot of use. A low-slung holster with a Colt at his side. She stared at his vest, trying to make out any patterns of shapes on his silver concho'd garments.

"No badge," she remarked, and the hoarseness of her speech sounded strange to her ear. "You're not the law. This isn't as hospital…so where am I? What about Charlotte? Hickok?"

"So full of questions." The man pulled out a chair and reclined in it, facing her. "One thing at a time. No, you're not at the hospital. You're in the best suite at the Harvey House hotel, probably the nicest place you can find in the town of Stillwater, Nevada."

"Nevada?"

"That would be correct. Nice little place, tucked in right at the base of the Sierras. The final mountain range before California. I must admit, I'm quite impressed that you both got this far."

"I…we must've gotten off the train."

"So that's all there is for question one. Moving on, your paramour and Mister Hickok are downstairs. She agreed to let me visit you, but only after some discussion that I'd call 'spirited'. I must say, you have chosen a hellion for a companion, Miss Williams."

The man's words were calm, even kind, but they made Samantha's veins run cold. She sank back into the pillows, exhaustion tugging at her. She knew the answer already, but she forced herself to speak one more time.

"You seem to know a lot about me. And who would you would be?"

A rueful shake of the head. "Me? I'm the man you led on a merry chase these last thousand miles. My name's Matthew Slade, and both I and the Pinkerton Agency are very, very happy to finally have you as our guest."

CHAPTER FIFTY-EIGHT

Samantha stared dully out one of the open windows. Her forehead remained blessedly cool, but every joint in her body ached. Ached, as if she'd been driving a plow all day.

She gazed as if transfixed by the steep mountain peaks and ridges that reared up from the plains just outside of town. So close to her dream, and yet so far. California might've been on the other side of the moon, for all it was worth now.

Slade had left. The man had sensed her hostility, and he'd withdrawn shortly after identifying himself. For that, at least, she was grateful. Company was the last thing on her mind at the moment.

Until someone opened her bedroom door with a creak.

The two shadows in the doorway resolved themselves into Charlotte and Hickok. Charlotte let out a whoop of delight, and in an instant, she knelt by the bed at Samantha's side.

"You're awake!" she cried, and she pressed a palm to Samantha's forehead. "Fever's broken, just like Doc Kincaid said. Oh, I am ever so relieved."

"Thanks for that," Samantha said, her voice oddly flat and devoid of emotion.

"Welcome back to the living," Hickok said, and then he gave her a curious look. "Strange. Someone who's passed by death's door normally looks a mite more pleased."

"I suppose," Samantha said, as Charlotte kissed her forehead. She gave a brief peck to Charlotte in return, and then tried to straighten up in bed. "I owe you both for getting me here, I guess. But why did you even bother?"

"Sam!" Charlotte said, shocked. "You're still weak; you don't know what y'all are sayin'."

"Stop it. I do." She touched Charlotte's face, caressed it weakly. "I love you…but why did you go and betray me?"

"What?" Charlotte rocked back on her heels, as if Samantha had struck her. "I didn't...I would never, ever..."

"Then why are we in Nevada? Why didn't you keep us going? Why did you...why did you let Pinkerton catch us?"

Tears welled in Charlotte's eyes. "I didn't have a choice in any of that! Sam, you'd have died of the flu if we didn't get off here!"

"Then you should have let me die!"

Her statement struck like a thunderclap.

The room remained silent for a moment, until a dry cough rattled up from Samantha's lungs, almost doubling her over in bed. Charlotte stepped forward to help, but Samantha waved her off irritably. With a shaky hand, Samantha grabbed the pitcher by her bedside and slopped some water into her glass. She finished her drink, and then finally found her voice.

"Get out. Of my room."

"But..." Charlotte looked at her, eyes pleading.

An almost stealthy shudder ran through the room. The timbers that made up the hotel's foundation swayed, and the water in Samantha's pitcher sloshed around, as if some invisible hand had given the nightstand a push.

A gut-churning *rumble* rolled through the air. The golden sunlight that sluiced through the room wavered as dust, disturbed from its resting place, drifted down from the rafters. Hickok and Charlotte threw the shutters back on the adjoining window to get a better view. Samantha watched with horror as a white veil of snow and mist slid and twisted down the nearby mountainside, carrying dark green and brown masses of what had to be trees, shaped timber supports, and men.

"What in Heaven's name..." Hickok said with astonishment. Next to him, Charlotte bit her lip, staring. A man wearing the uniform of the Union Pacific railroad and riding a bedraggled looking horse came galloping down the street.

"Avalanche!" he cried. "We got men buried!"

Instantly, the people of Stillwater dropped what they were doing and began hustling up towards the slide area. Hickok nodded, as if he'd seen something similar before.

"This really is a mining town," he remarked. "Anything goes ass-over-teakettle, everyone jumps in to help."

"The Doc's surely goin' to need help, too!" Charlotte exclaimed. She looked to Samantha, who turned resolutely away. Charlotte shot a pleading glance at Hickok. "But…maybe I can't go to the hospital. Sam needs her tonic."

"Not until later. You go on and help out. I will too." He carefully pulled the shutters back into place, and then raised his voice a small amount. Just enough to ensure that Samantha heard him. "And I'll make sure no one disturbs our patient."

He walked to the bedroom door, held it open. Charlotte hesitated. She went to Samantha's side and gave the silent, brooding woman one more kiss. With a sob, she dashed from the room. To Samantha, the sound of the door closing echoed in her head like the slam of a jail cell.

She turned her face into the pillow.

Tried to block out the dim sounds of the chaos on the street below.

Tried to block out the world.

Sometime later, Samantha heard the sounds of boots on wooden stairs. She opened her eyes, saw that the sun's golden rays had been replaced by the ruddy flickers of lanterns that Stillwater used for street lighting. A man's silhouette appeared at the door, carrying an oil lamp.

"Slade?" she asked.

Hickok's deep voice rolled out into the room. "Pinkerton may have us here, but Slade ain't comin' in this hotel again. Not while Charlotte has any say in the matter."

Samantha clearly made out his long nose and bushy mustache as the man turned up the fuel on his lamp. He crossed the room and sank into the same chair that Slade had used earlier. His face appeared drawn and haggard.

"What happened out there?" she asked.

"Too much bad, an' not enough of God's mercy." Hickok took off his broad-brimmed hat and ran his fingers through his long hair. "Blasting cap accident at the silver mine. Brought a mess of snow down on the tracks to California. They'll be buried for at least a couple of days. Along with the four miners and two railroad workers we couldn't get to in time."

"God save us, that's awful!"

"An' that turkey-shed they call a hospital's full up with injured men. One doctor, and no nurses. Charlotte's still down there helpin' him set bones, sew up cuts, or hold someone down if he's got to take a limb off."

Samantha shivered. "Guess I can't complain about having flu, then."

"It does seem small potatoes in an over-sized sack right now. So since she's busy, I figured that I better give you your medicine." Hickok held up a small black bottle labeled *Doctor Owlbridge's Lung Tonic*. He took her glass, poured a double-shot of the viscous blue liquid into it, and then handed it over. "Bottom's up."

Samantha gagged as she downed the tonic. The sweet, sticky essence of raspberry mixed with turpentine ran down her throat. She coughed and wiped water from the corners of her eyes.

"Glad that's over with."

"Nope. I said, I came here to give you your *medicine*," Hickok said, and his voice took on a stern quality she'd not heard since they'd gone to meet Quantrill. "You've been a right snake-belly to Charlotte, and over nothin'. For a smart woman, Miss Samantha, I swear there are times you couldn't see through a bob-wire fence!"

"But Mister Hickok—"

"Oh, 'But Mister Hickok' nothin'! I normally stay out of you two's problems, but this time, I'm goin' to have my say, whether you like it or not!"

CHAPTER FIFTY-NINE

Samantha shrank a little inside at Hickok's tone. But she'd been through enough with the tall man that she innately respected his thoughts, angry or otherwise. So chastened, she listened.

"You've been out of your mind for almost a week, and it's about time someone set the record straight," Hickok said firmly. He set the oil lamp down on a nearby dresser and continued. "First off, Charlotte didn't just up an' decide to get us off that train. We were gettin' the toe end of the boot from the Union Pacific!"

"But...why?"

"'Cause the railroad treats anyone suspected of havin' scarlet fever like excess luggage, dumps 'em off at the next station. When they came to put you off, it was Charlotte who had me draw my guns on the conductors before they could touch you!"

Samantha felt her face start to burn. Not with fever this time. Shame.

"It was Charlotte who made sure that if we had to leave the train, at least you got to a hospital," Hickok continued. "She's been by your side for days, even when we moved you into this hotel. And as for Pinkerton...that Matthew Slade's one of the best man-hunters I've seen. Carries himself like a fellow who knows the range, knows how to shoot. He wanted to pack you off, even if he had to tie you to the bed and take it along too. Charlotte convinced him that you were too sick to move. That he'd hear no end of it if you showed up in Chicago as a corpse."

A single tear ran down Samantha's face. More followed. Her voice shook as she said, "Are you about done? I...don't know if I can take any more medicine."

"Just about. Slade sent word back to Illinois that he found you both. Couple of days ago, he brought Charlotte one of the telegrams he got back in reply. She gave it to me to read. I haven't gotten around to givin' it back yet."

Hickok reached inside his jacket, and pulled out a single crumpled sheet. Samantha took it. The message was short, to the point. But it left no doubt in the reader's mind as to what was offered: "CHARLOTTE YOUR MOTHER AND I ARE RELIEVED TO FIND YOU ARE SAFE -(STOP)- WE FORGIVE YOU ALL THINGS -(STOP)- WE LOVE YOU AND WANT YOU TO BE HAPPY -(STOP)- WE WANT YOU TO COME HOME TO US LOVE MOTHER AND FATHER"

"She got what I thought she wanted, at least at the start," Samantha husked out, as she fought back another round of tears. "She got the chance to leave me and go back home."

"And she didn't," Hickok said, in as quiet a tone as her. "She's one hell of a woman."

Samantha looked up at Hickok. "I had better go tell her...how sorry I am."

A noise from the open doorway. Charlotte's voice sounded in the hall, tired and sleepy.

"Tell me what, exactly? Bill, is Sam talkin' in her sleep again?"

"I'm not asleep!" Samantha cried out, before Hickok could say a word. "I need you Char, please come on in!"

Charlotte half-walked, half-stumbled in and came to the side of the bed. Samantha pushed herself up to a full sitting position and swept Charlotte into her arms as best she could. The younger woman half-fell on the bed with a squeal.

"What in—" Charlotte began to say, "Bill, how much of that damn tonic did you give her?"

"Hell with the tonic!" Samantha replied. "Let me show you how sorry I am, how grateful I am, how much in love with you I am, Char."

With that, she drew Charlotte to her. For her part, Charlotte shifted her weight so that she could lie atop the covers as the two embraced. The shared kisses and tears ran from warm to hot, delicate to insistent and full of desire.

"A-hem…" Hickok said. He rocked back and forth on his heels as his face turned the same color as a ripe sugar beet. The women took no notice of him as he put his hat back on and headed for the door. "I'll…just leave you two be for the evenin'."

Hickok closed the bedroom door behind him, wiped his brow, and headed down the hotel's stairway to the ground floor. He ambled through the lobby and out onto the broad front porch. The bustle from the emergency earlier in the day had faded, and the street was almost empty at this late hour.

Almost, that is, but for the tall, lantern-jawed figure of Matthew Slade.

The Pinkerton man leaned against the porch's corner rail, looking for all intents and purposes as if he had nothing better to do for the evening. Hickok frowned. He knew better.

"Right nice evening, isn't it, Wild Bill?" Slade remarked. The guttering light from the street lanterns threw up harsh shadows, shading his eyes into coal black sockets.

"Right nice indeed, Slade." Hickok tipped his hat brim, and then stepped over to speak to the man face-to-face. "Y'all can just call me 'Hickok', or plain old 'Bill'. That other name's just what writers and other unmentionable types like to use, likely to fill up space on the page."

"Hickok, then. My apologies, sir."

"The way I see it, I ain't the one you ought to apologize to."

Slade frowned, but it was only for a moment. "I can understand why you would say that. You've gotten close to the two girls."

"I'd call 'em older than 'girls'. Women. Maybe not at the start, but they are now." Hickok nodded up towards the second story window, where his oil lamp continued to emit a faint glow. "One's still flat on her back from influenza. You gave the other one a chance to cut out, and she didn't. Together…the two of 'em held their own in a shoot-out with Quantrill's Raiders."

Slade chuckled. "So I hear. Pardon me if I don't believe that."

"Believe what you want. Those two have plenty of grit. Charlotte just came from helpin' the doc after the avalanche today. Closed off the western route for a couple days, but the one back east is still open. I guess that's not such bad news for you there, Slade."

"You have that right. Just as soon as Miss Williams can travel, I'm taking her and Miss Harte with me. Back to Chicago."

"What if they don't want to go?"

"As I recollect, they *don't*. But I've been on a lot of jobs like this one. Somehow, I've always managed to convince my quarry to come back home with me." He smiled grimly, without showing teeth. "Maybe it's my magnetic personality."

"Let's have it plain, then, Matthew. You would take two young women against their wills. Take 'em back to a life they don't want. Back to a life that they just spent months of deprivation and danger tryin' to escape?"

Slade watched Hickok carefully before answering.

"Look, I don't like what I have to do sometimes. But I have a contract. I gave my word. I would think that's something a 'hero gunfighter' from the books would be familiar with, at least. That the job's got to get done."

Hickok shook his head as he turned and walked off into the darkness.

"You sure have a lousy job there, Slade."

CHAPTER SIXTY

The saloons in North Platte, Nebraska weren't particularly choosy about who patronized their establishments. But to a man, they were strict about enforcing limits on one's tab. Which made one particular Union Pacific telegraph clerk extremely unhappy.

"Aw, I told you that my payday's next Friday!" the man protested, in a slightly nasal whine. "The stationmaster's just been a little slow, what with my debts an' all."

"Dammit, Sweeney," the bartender shot back, "Cough up the twenty, or you're cut off, and that's final."

"Hey now," said an older, heavy-set man in suspenders, as he sidled up to the bar, "I believe I can help out a fellow railway man in need of a drink."

With that, he pushed a small pile of coins across the bar top. The bartender brightened, scooped up the money, and slid a beer into Sweeney's waiting hands.

"Well, I ain't seen you 'round these parts in near forever, Lem!" Sweeney said, awkwardly trying to shake his friend's hand while downing his beer. "Where you been, anyway? Thought you resigned from the ol' U of Pete a couple weeks ago."

"I've been around," Lem said. "Got called back by an old friend, you might say. Come on around back, I want you to meet him."

Hesitantly, the telegraph clerk followed Lem to where the saloon's tables were cast in heavy shadow. They took a seat in one particularly dark corner. The lamps on the tables guttered, having been turned down to the lowest level. Three men sat across from them. The one in the center had a face that looked like a crag of sandstone, from what he could see under the brim of the man's shabby hat.

"Cap, this here's Sweeney. We used to work together," Lem said. He turned to the telegraph clerk, adding, "I'd like you to meet...Clark. He's got a couple of questions for you."

Sweeney nodded mutely. Something about Lem's friend chilled him, as if the man threw off rays of cold. Like sitting next to an open ice box.

"Mister Sweeney," the man named Clark said, "I've been lookin' for two girls, accompanied by a tall man who looks...why, I do suppose that he looks like that fellow that gets in all the magazines. Wild Bill Hickok. The other day, one of my boys overheard the ticket agent talking about sellin' a ticket to just such a trio. You know anything about that?"

"I suppose I do," Sweeney said, after gulping down the rest of his beer. "I don't know what it's all about, I swear, but there's been lots of telegraph traffic comin' through about those folks."

Clark and Lem traded a look. "Go on."

"When they came through, I sent a telegram to Chicago. Notifying the Pinkerton Detective Agency. A couple of days later, one of 'em shows up at the station, a real tough lookin' cowpoke, picks up a horse and then heads out after 'em on the next Western Special."

"Never mind the Pink. Where'd the two girls get off to?"

"It was supposed to be all the way to San Francisco. But they didn't make it."

"No?" A stir of activity around the table, as if the clerk had jostled a hornet's nest.

"That Pinkerton fellow, he caught 'em in Stillwater, all the way out in Nevada. Relayed the news back and forth from there and Chicago since yesterday. They can't come east yet 'cause someone's ill. And they can't go west yet 'cause the tracks were blocked with an avalanche."

"Well, now..." Clark's mouth creased into a grin, one that made Sweeney think of timber wolves and nightmare monsters. "Y'all are goin' to get my men on the next train to Stillwater. All twenty of 'em, and horses to boot."

Sweeney blanched. "That's a tall order there, Mister! Even if you got the money, there's usually never more than a dozen spots for the horses on the Special."

"Then you best be off-loadin' some of those passengers here, hadn't you?"

"But that's only in case of emergencies, an' that takes the station master's approval!"

"Come off it," Lem said, nudging the clerk with his elbow. "You still got the same ol' fool in charge out here. Drunk half the time, sick the other half. He'll never know if you go swipe his books, write his name in."

Sweeney began to sweat. "But…but…it's my job, if I do it an' get caught!"

"Put it this way," Clark said reasonably, though his eyes were hard and blank, like black marbles. "Lem here tells me you owe gamblin' money 'round town too. I can make that all go away…or make sure it comes crashin' down. 'Less you want to end up in some back alley with your head broke, you better think careful-like what you do next."

Sweeney's tongue stumbled over itself in his willingness to betray his employer.

"I…I'll do it! I'll change the books…get your men on the next train."

"That's my boy, followin' orders like a good soldier." Clark pushed back from the table to address Lem and his two other men. "Saddle 'em up boys, we're headin' out west!

※ ※ ※

Doc Kincaid was a balding beanpole of a man, with a lean face that properly belonged on a greyhound. But the man knew his trade, and he'd agreed to keep secrets when asked. He had Samantha open the neck of her nightshirt, and then pressed the cold circlet of his stethoscope to her chest.

"Okay, Miss Williams, *breathe*."

She inhaled and exhaled for him a few times. Felt the tiniest flutter still down in the bottom of her lungs, but that was all. The doctor turned away as she re-adjusted her nightshirt. Inside, Samantha felt her stomach flutter as she awaited the pronouncement.

"Looks like you're well on the mend, Miss Williams," Kincaid said. "Remarkable recovery. I'd still take it easy for a day or two so you don't exhaust yourself, but all I can say is that I'm downright impressed."

"I'd appreciate it if you didn't say anything at all," Samantha reminded him.

"No worries about that," Kincaid chuckled, as he showed himself out.

Samantha finished changing into her street clothes, and then came out into the hotel's second-floor hallway. Charlotte and Hickok looked up from where they had been chatting. She joined them, a smile gracing her face for the first time since they'd left Scott's Bluff.

"Doc Kincaid says I'm bouncing back pretty well," she announced. "And I owe a lot of that to you, Mister Hickok."

"Considerin' how many daggers you shot at me with those eyes of yours over the last two days? I'm just lucky to be alive," Hickok replied, obviously pleased.

"I've been missing somethin', haven't I?" Charlotte said, puzzled.

"That's because you've been workin' all day at the hospital," Samantha clarified. "My personal physician here has been running me up and down the stairs. Doin' push-ups. Anything to whip me back into some kind of shape."

"Then it's a right fine thing that I put the fear of God into Matthew Slade about comin' back into this hotel, Sam."

Samantha hugged Charlotte close. "Right fine indeed."

"I figure that too much bed rest is bad for anyone," Hickok said. "Wish we could've gotten in some practice shootin', but that was a bit much to ask. Slade's a lot of things, but deaf, he ain't."

"Just because I can't fire my Colts, doesn't mean I haven't been working on my draw, Samantha pointed out. "My guns are oiled, cleaned, and they still fit my hands fine."

"Good. You're goin' to need to decide what you're ready for, and soon."

The finality in Hickok's voice brought the two women up short. Charlotte spoke first.

"What do you mean, Bill?"

"Slade's been runnin' a fine line by humoring Charlotte." Hickok said, tweaking an end of his mustache in thought. "He's been lettin' Samantha slide on the 'illness' excuse for a while now. Why? Because the pass to the west is blocked. He knows you ain't about to hop on a train back east on your own. And if you saddled up Patches and Jubilee, struck out in another direction? I've been checkin', and off the rail line, there's nothing but desert and bandits all 'round here for sixty miles. Easy country to track someone down."

"So we're still trapped in this town, like a ship in a bottle," Charlotte said sadly.

Samantha addressed Hickok directly. "How long do you think we have?"

Hickok stared out the nearest window, looking up at the mountains. "The work crews are just about done clearing the snow and rocks from the avalanche. Slade's bettin' on you two trying to fly the coop as soon as the first train can go through. I reckon he'll make a move tomorrow morning, maybe even at dawn."

Charlotte made a sound of dismay. "That's not a lot of time, practically none at all!"

Samantha smacked her fist into her palm. She paced up and down the hall, stifling a small cough as she did so. She looked at both Hickok and Charlotte, a determined look on her face.

"I'll think of something. *Something.*"

Samantha went back into the bedroom and slammed the door shut, ending the discussion.

CHAPTER SIXTY-ONE

Sheriff Sims wasn't a small man. But his slumped posture and glum face made him look positively puny as he sat in the Stillwater station master's office, watching the woman and the Pinkerton man trade off demands and threats. Hickok leaned casually against a nearby wall, letting the two do all the hard work of yelling at each other.

"I have been more than patient with you," Slade said. "I know that you've been stalling me."

"Stalling? Is that what a Pink calls savin' a woman's life?" Charlotte shot back. With a firmness that would have taken her mother and father aback, she got right in Slade's face and used her index finger to poke his broad chest. "Y'all ought to be ashamed of yourself, takin' a pair of delicate ladies, includin' one that's been at death's door, to get on some drafty old train!"

"Pardon, Miss Harte, but what exactly do you mean by 'delicate ladies'? Mister Hickok here claims you've killed at least a half-dozen men apiece. I'm skeptical. But if he's right…well, if you two are 'delicate', then I'll eat my hat and wash it down with a side of Kentucky bourbon."

That last bit brought out a snort from Hickok. Charlotte glared at him, then swung back to focus on Slade.

"Then if you think you're goin' to man-handle us…"

"Again, I beg your pardon, if that's what you thought I would do. I respect you both enough not to 'man-handle' either of you." Slade paused, and then said, in a completely serious tone, "Truth be told, I'm thinking more along the lines of leg irons and three-quarter-inch steel chain."

"You wouldn't dare!"

"Look, both of you," Sheriff Sims pleaded, "It's too damn early for this kind of bickerin'. What do y'all want from me?"

"I'm demanding that you arrest this man for kidnappin'!" Charlotte said primly.

"For the last time, I can't do that! He's got all the proper paperwork, so there's no crime here! If there ain't no crime, then this is a private matter! My hands are tied."

"So that settles it," Slade said, with an air of finality. "You have run a fine race, Miss Harte, but it's time to settle up. Or is there anything else you would like to complain about?"

Off to one side, the office door opened with a *creak*. Slade heard the step of a boot. He turned, gasped as he saw Samantha Williams enter.

Samantha strode confidently into the office. The early morning sun bathed the brim of her cowboy hat in s golden glow. Her buckskin-colored man's shirt contrasted with the dark brown set of trousers and leather vest. A pair of freshly polished Colts gleamed from her slim hips like a pair of silver stars at twilight.

Sims' jaw dropped. He closed it again, swallowed hard.

"The time for complaining is over," Samantha said directly to Slade. "And you're right. It's time to settle up. You still planning on taking us back?"

"That's what I have to do, Miss Williams," Slade said, though his eyes narrowed suspiciously. "And may I congratulate you on a most…speedy recovery."

"Do you have any idea what you're doing, Mister Slade?"

"I'm afraid I do. Your father, pardon my directness, is a monster. I don't believe for a moment that you want to be married. Not to the man he wants. Not to a man at all."

"You know a little, then. But you need to understand one more thing. I swore I'd die before I let anyone take me back. So if you're all fired to take me, then you have to earn that right."

Slade stared at the young woman. He felt disoriented, as if he'd been bucked off a bronco. Not fear, exactly. But whatever Samantha Williams was, he hadn't encountered it before. It fascinated and chilled him in equal measure.

"Earn it? How?"

"Out here in the street. Twenty paces. Hickok calls the draw. Winner takes all."

Even Hickok looked stunned. He straightened up, eyeing Samantha for a sign that she was playing a bluff. He didn't see any.

"You can't be serious." Slade looked to Hickok. "Tell me she that she's not serious!"

"Oh, I reckon she is," Hickok drawled. "I taught her everything she knows about shootin', and she's an ornery one, when you get right down to it."

"You're goin' to lose this either way, Mister Slade." Charlotte added, "It'll be hard to spend your reward from Samantha's father if you're in a pine box. But if you kill her, then you ain't collecting no reward either. Y'all will get a fine reputation, as a man who shot down a woman."

Slade looked down for a moment. Blew air through his mustache. Kicked at a speck of dirt on the floor. But was only a moment. He raised his head, and a confident grin spread from ear to ear. He let out a laugh and shook his head.

"You just about had me there. Knocked me back a half-step. But now, I get to fill you in about me." Slade pulled one side of his jacket back, exposed a little red bulls-eye patch that had been stitched to his heavy denim shirt. "Every three years, Pinkerton holds a sharp-shooting contest for the agents that ride the range. And as it happens, I won it."

Now it was Samantha's turn to stare.

"So here's what we're going to do," Slade went on. "We'll have our little duel, just the way they do it in the pages of the dime-store slicks they sell at the drugstores. And I'm afraid that I'll have to put a hole in you, Miss Williams. You won't come away from this walking straight, or able to hold up an arm. But at the very least, I won't kill you."

Charlotte's resolve crumpled. Her complexion went ashen, and she opened her mouth to speak. Hickok shook his head, almost imperceptibly, and she froze, silent, as Samantha and Slade went outside, followed by the curious sheriff.

"Bill, what're we goin' to do?" Charlotte whispered.

"Nothing," he said, a cast of sadness creeping into his voice. "Miss Samantha's made her play. Only thing we can do is back her up, the best we can."

She nodded, shivering, and then followed the gunfighter out the door in turn. Samantha took up her position on the street, counting off her ten paces to Hickok's right. Slade turned to face her, stepping back his ten paces on the left. Sims and Charlotte huddled in the shade of the station's overhang, just behind where Hickok stood, an inscrutable expression on his face.

"All right then," Hickok announced, raising his voice to full volume. "Y'all know what to do. You draw on the count of three. Understand?"

Samantha nodded, her jaw set, sweat beading at her brow.

Slade flexed his hands, slowly rotated his wrists, and nodded in turn.

Hickok's voice boomed out into the space between them.

"*One!*"

Charlotte could hear nothing but the beating of her heart in her chest.

"*Two!*"

She let out a tiny gasp.

Hickok took a deep breath. He pursed his lips, opened his mouth to call out the final, deadly number.

CHAPTER SIXTY-TWO

"Sheriff Sims! Sheriff Sims! We got trouble!" A high-pitched voice rang out from inside the train station. A short, skinny man dressed in the blue and white stripes of the Union Pacific bolted out the office door. He skidded to a halt as he saw what was going on.

"Stand down!" Hickok called.

Samantha and Slade hadn't moved. They eyed each other, hands not moving from a deadly hover over their gun handles. Hickok swore, and then barked out his next words.

"I said, stand down! Damn your eyes, if either one of you so much as pulls an iron, they're gettin' a gut full of lead from me!"

That got through to each of them. Scowling, they lowered their hands, slowly, and turned their attention to Hickok and Sims. Charlotte groped for the nearest wooden bench and half-collapsed into it.

"Bobby, what the blazes are you doing?" Sims demanded. "Git back to the telegraph, there's serious business going on out here."

"But this is serious too!" The young clerk goggled at the sight of the two duelists. "Is this...are you lettin' people have a gunfight in the street? Sheriff, ain't that against the law?"

"Look, I got a crazy woman on one side, a Pinkerton sharpshooter on the other, and Wild Bill Hickok backing them up! How in hell do you expect me to stop them?"

"Well, if you want a gunfight, there's something goin' on in Lovelock, just six miles up the railway. Got a telegram from the station just now."

Hickok, Slade, and the two women gathered around as Bobby read off the message.

"*Urgent, bandits attacking Lovelock station. Stop. Arrived on seven a.m. Western Special, men on track setting explosives. Stop. Send help bandits number at least one dozen…"* The clerk looked up, breathless. "That's…that's all there is."

"That don't make a lick of sense!" Sims exclaimed. "How could the bandits arrive *on* the train if they're trying to *rob* it? And why mess with the tracks?"

Hickok traded a look with the two women. Samantha spoke up.

"It's not bandits. It's Captain Clark Quantrill, and he's brought his Raiders out here, on that very train. They must know we're here, and they're trying to cut us off."

"Really?" Slade snorted. "Even if I allow that Quantrill's still around, how would he be able to ship his whole crew out here? I suppose that General Lee and the Virginia cavalry are arriving on the next Western Special too? With Stonewall Jackson and Jefferson Davis in the sleeper car?"

"I don't care if they're bringin' along Napoleon and Queen Victoria in the caboose!" Sims retorted. "Hickok, you and your protégé have got to know how to shoot. Saddle up with me, we're riding for Lovelock."

Hickok traded a glance with Samantha. "We're up for it, Sims."

"If they're going, then I'm coming along," Slade stated. "If these really are Quantrill's boys, I want to see it for myself."

In the space of a few minutes, Samantha and Hickok had saddled up Patches and Buckshot, and then ridden back to the station. Sheriff Sims waited for them, astride a black-and-white pinto. Slade came trotting up on a muscular blue roan mustang. A skeptical look remained on his face, but he'd kept his guns where he could get at them.

"Be careful," Charlotte said, as she reached up, giving Samantha a pat on the thigh.

"Count on it," Samantha replied.

Sims called on the small party to move out. They did, spurring their horses to a canter, following the railroad tracks east to the razor-sharp horizon. The desert changed from the color of a ripe peach to a sandy golden hue as they covered the miles. Each of the riders tilted the brims of their hats down so they wouldn't be blinded by the rising sun.

The tracks shifted to climb a steep rise. The shape of a train appeared as a gray shadow, one that was low-slung and in the shape of a shallow 'C'. Behind it lay the Lovelock station, silhouetted as a shadow against the morning glare. Still further off, a cloud of dust rose as a large group of riders moved off to the south. Cracks of gunfire sounded, sparks of light against the shadow.

Sims hesitated. His mouth worked, soundlessly, as he tried to figure out what to say.

"What's the problem, sheriff?" Slade asked.

"It's just that...I was elected sheriff by the people of Stillwater," he said. "I've never actually been in a real fight before. And these bandits...I ain't ever seen so many in one place!"

Hickok let out a curse. "Fine. Then let's get ourselves on down there, see if we can't stop 'em from messin' with the rails."

"I'm all for that," Samantha said.

With a *whoop*, Hickok led the charge down towards Lovelock. The four horses galloped across the desert plain, eating up the distance with ease. Slade's mustang put up a burst of speed, pulled out in front of the party. He approached the train from the front, where steam still hissed from the engine.

Suddenly, two men, clad in Confederate gray, swung out from the engine's cab. Guns in hand, they aimed at Slade as he galloped into range.

"Ambush!" Samantha shouted.

The Pinkerton man drew his weapon, fired it from astride his horse. A *crack*, and one of the gunmen dropped. He slumped over the locomotive's steam valve. The blast from the valve startled the second man. His shot glanced off one of Slade's saddlebags, nicking the mustang's hindquarters. The great roan horse squealed in pain, rearing. Slade held on, doing everything he could to calm the animal.

Quantrill's man leveled his pistol. The Pinkerton man made an easy target at such close range.

"Watch it, Slade!" Hickok cried.

Another *crack*. This time, from a rifle.

The Confederate tumbled out of the cab and to the ground in a motionless heap.

Hickok, Samantha, and Sims reined in their horses, alert for any more tricks. But the fading sound of hoof beats was a sure sign that the fight for Lovelock station was over. They dismounted as Slade managed to calm his horse down. The Pinkerton man slid out of the saddle and inspected his mount's wound.

"Blue, old buddy," he said, "That's just a scratch. Bear with me; we'll get that fixed up back at the stable in Stillwater." Slade turned to the others. "It looks like I owe one of you for that sharp bit of shooting."

"It wasn't any of us," Samantha said tightly.

One of the doors on a nearby passenger car slid open. A man with a single gray stripe of beard and a folded-brim Stetson emerged, rifle in hand.

"Perhaps I can shed some illumination," the man announced, in a cultured voice. "Buffalo Bill Cody, at your service."

"Aw, I should've known," Hickok said, striding forward to shake his friend's hand.

"It is fine that I've not lost my talent for making the grandest of entrances," Cody said, with a distinct lack of modesty.

"Well, I'm just flabbergasted!" Samantha blurted, as she shook hands with Buffalo Bill in turn. "I thought you'd headed back east to try and raise some money."

"Try? My dear, I do not 'try', I just 'do'. I was on my way to San Francisco, hoping to see whether you and the lovely Miss Charlotte would consider being part of my show." Cody paused a moment to consider. "Come to think of it, an awful lot of people must've been on board this train because of you two."

"Why do you say that?"

"A bunch of rather seedy types got on in North Platte, including a hard-bitten gent wearing the uniform of a Confederate cavalry officer. Some of the other passengers with horses were thrown off the train. The railroad people said it was some emergency out in Nevada, but they didn't care to elucidate."

Slade gaped at the news. "Well, I'm off the fence about Quantrill now, at least. And someone's gotten hold of my telegrams."

"That would stand to reason. I heard a couple of these ruffians talking about how the tracks west of Nevada were out. And how they were going to 'bring hell to Stillwater'."

Sims blanched as he heard that last piece of information.

"From their talk, it was obvious that they'd be taking over the train," Cody continued. "Twenty to one aren't good odds in my playbook. So when we approached the station prior, I secreted myself in one of the luggage cars. Waited for an opportunity to get past them. When I heard them riding off and saw you arriving, I felt it was a good a time as any to pitch in."

"Well, you did just fine, partner," Hickok said warmly. "What did they do with the train crew? The passengers?"

"Quantrill robbed 'em, trussed them up like turkeys for Thanksgiving, and tossed them in the station house," Buffalo Bill said, pointing at the nearby building. "At least, that's what most of Quantrill's boys were doing. I saw a bunch of others carrying spades back down the track."

Samantha traded a look with the sheriff. "The telegram said they were setting explosives. Come on! Let's go find–"

With a *whump!* an explosion rocked the rear of the train, sending a fountain of sand and rock flying. Samantha ran over to where a plume of dust and smoke curled skyward in a dark pillar. She slid to a stop at the edge of a six-foot crater in the sandy soil.

Ten feet of railroad track lay bent and twisted, like the roots of a gnarled oak tree. She wobbled on her feet as the realization sank in.

Clark Quantrill had cut them completely off from the outside world.

CHAPTER SIXTY-THREE

Charlotte let out a cry of delight as the party rode back into Stillwater late in the afternoon, none the worse for wear. She embraced Samantha as soon as everyone had dismounted, and then quickly turned her high-wattage smile on Buffalo Bill. As before, the veteran stage performer greeted her with a bow and a graceful sweep of his hat.

"Buffalo Bill Cody!" Charlotte smiled, "Did you just blow in from offstage, like one of them tumbleweeds?"

"Not so much a tumbleweed as a stowaway, my good lady," Cody replied, as he got down off the thin gray horse they'd taken from one of the dead men they'd left back at Lovelock.

"Quantrill and his men are here," Samantha said bluntly. "They took over the train Cody was on, so he stowed himself in the luggage car. Helped us bushwhack a couple of ambushers."

"I know that Quantrill's here," Charlotte said, a worried look on her face. "Ain't y'all wonderin' where everyone in this town's got to?"

Each person in the party stopped and listened. Even in the early morning, even in the dead of night, there were some background noises in Stillwater. The crackle of the street lanterns. A distant slamming of a door. The barking of someone's dog. The neigh of a horse from the stables.

But only the sound of the wind echoed in the streets.

"It *is* a mite quiet for this time of day," Hickok admitted.

"That's because Quantrill's men got here ahead of you, left a message!" Charlotte cried. "Before I saw it, I'd figured that they'd killed you all and were throwin' it in our faces!"

"They were heading out as we rode up to the train," Samantha said. "We couldn't head right on back…Quantrill had tied up the crew and the passengers, stuck them in the station house."

"If we hadn't taken the time to cut them loose, they might have died of thirst," added Slade. "But this is pretty damned odd."

"That message," Hickok said grimly. "Where is it?"

"It's in the station house," Charlotte replied, with a shiver.

They followed her to the station house's porch, right where Samantha and Slade had come within a single second of dueling. Their expressions went from curious to downright apprehensive as they began to see bullet holes in all the surrounding buildings.

A splash of dried blood coated the ground near the front door. Lines and drips of iron red-brown lay streaked in the direction of the office. As if someone had dragged a dead weight through the dust.

"Let me go first. I need to see." Sheriff Sims said, with a nervous swallow. He pushed the door open and the others followed. Sims let out a shuddering sigh. "Damn that Quantrill to hell! Why'd he have to go and kill Bobby?"

The telegraph clerk's spindly frame lay half-sprawled across the station master's desk. His eyes lay open, in an expression of terror. Twin holes in his chest still drizzled red down one side of his blue-and-white shirt. Pinned to his lapel was a scrap of leftover telegraph paper. With a jolt, Samantha recognized Clark Quantrill's handwriting on it.

To the Sheriff of Stillwater -
The Pinkerton man has two whores I want. I am coming for them at dawn.
Hand them over when I ride in and my boys might not burn the town and kill everyone.
- Cpt. Clark Quantrill, CSA Cavalry

"A bunch of Quantrill's Raiders rode in here, shot part of the town up, killed poor Bobby," Charlotte said. "They dragged him in here, pinned the note on him. Then they cut the telegraph lines an' rode out of town, laughin' like they'd lost their minds. Most everyone in town saw it, or heard about it."

"Then where in tarnation are they?" Hickok demanded.

She shrugged. "They ran. No one knew where the sheriff went off to. No one knew where the 'Pinkerton man' that Quantrill mentioned got to. And I wasn't about to tell anyone that the note referred to me an' Samantha."

"Ran off to where? It's all desert around here!" Slade exclaimed.

"Not completely," Hickok pointed out. "There's a few watering holes here and there, probably enough to supply the Raiders for a day or two, which is all they'll need. As for the townspeople, my guess is that they're holed up in the mountains above the town."

"Think anyone is left in all of Stillwater?"

Charlotte shook her head. "Only Doc Kincaid, he's got at least five or six wounded men in his care who can't get out of bed on their own. He won't leave 'em. Oh, and Sheriff Sims here."

The sheriff backed away from Bobby's corpse, shaking his head as if to deny its existence. His face had taken on a waxy, ashen look. When he spoke, the words fell from his lips in a dull monotone.

"I thought that...I mean...look, everyone's heard of Quantrill's Raiders. I don't know a man who actually wants to tangle with 'em. And that includes me."

Samantha watched in disbelief as Sims pulled his badge from his vest. The man stared at it as if it was some hateful, cursed talisman. She leaned forward on the station master's desk, her voice insistent.

"You can't back out now, Sheriff! Men like Clark Quantrill...if someone doesn't stop him now, then he'll go on stealing, go on killing. He'll never, ever have enough to fill the hole inside of him. He's a mad dog, and he needs to be put down!"

As if in a daze, Sims focused on the angry woman in front of him. He reached out, took her hand. Her eyes went wide as he turned her hand palm up.

"You feel that strongly about it? Then I hereby appoint you as acting Sheriff of Stillwater. Legally, it's *your* problem now. For as long as you live, anyway."

With that, he laid his silver star in Samantha's hand.

Ignoring the amazed and contemptuous looks that the other men gave him, he strolled outside and mounted his pinto. He spurred his horse in the direction of the mountains, without once looking back.

CHAPTER SIXTY-FOUR

The setting sun burned red like a dying ember. Samantha had to force herself not to stare out the window, to watch as it sank towards the mountain tops. Besides reminding her that the available time was quickly dwindling, she also couldn't help but feel that it was the last sunset she'd ever see.

Slade, Hickok, and Charlotte watched her spread out a pair of maps on the main dining table of the now-deserted Harvey House. One detailed the surrounding areas out to sixty miles, encompassing Lovelock, a handful of isolated dwellings just outside of Stillwater, and a lot of desert waste. The other was a detailed schematic of the town itself.

Neither provided her with a lot of hope.

"Cody said he wanted to check those outlying buildings," Hickok said. "Hope he finds something that we can turn to our advantage. 'Cause if we ride out of town in most any direction, it's thirty miles of flat desert. Heading back towards Lovelock ain't much better. Only six miles there, but then it's more than forty miles to the next town. And all open range along the way."

"What about the mountains?" This from Charlotte.

"Better, but a lot slower." Hickok cursed under his breath in frustration. "Face it, there's just no good place to hole up anywhere 'round Stillwater. Clark's too good a cavalry man not to have sentries out there. Even if we're able to slip past them, he knows that he can track us, and then ride us to ground."

"If there's no good place to hole up around Stillwater..." Samantha ventured, "Then we're going to hole up *in* Stillwater. We've got good cover inside this town. A lot of uninhabited buildings, no bystanders to get in the way."

"I like it," Hickok said, after chewing on the idea for a moment. "Better odds to fight it out, get the whole mess over with."

Charlotte swallowed hard. "I'm in agreement too. We all stay and fight."

"Hold on just a minute," Slade said, and his long jaw flexed as if he were trying to swallow something bitter, "I never wanted to be part of this little crusade!"

"Then let me welcome you," Hickok said, "To the land of 'you ain't got a choice'."

Matthew Slade stared daggers at Hickok. The gunfighter didn't flinch.

"Maybe he's right," Samantha said. "Maybe it's better if Slade sits this one out."

"Sorry, Miss Samantha," Hickok said, as he shook his head in the negative. "But that would mean you're not following the third rule of how to win a gunfight. *Rule one: bring a gun. Rule two: if you have more than one gun, you bring it.*"

"And the final rule?"

Hickok grinned. "*Rule three: Bring all of your friends who have guns.*"

Samantha locked gazes with him for a single, long moment. Then she grinned back at him in understanding. She let out a breath and spoke again, respectfully.

"Mister Slade," she said, "he's right. I know that we haven't met under the best circumstances. Actually, they've been pretty rotten ones. But I don't dislike you. You're a capable man. You had the guts to follow me and Charlotte halfway across the country. And…to be perfectly frank…I could really use someone like you on my side right now."

Slade doffed his hat. Ruffled his hair. He looked at Samantha, and for the first time, both respect and kindness shone in his eyes.

"You had to go and humble me," Slade said. "All right, I'm game. You two girls – that is, you two *women* – know how to follow a toss of the dice through. Even when the odds are slim to bad. I need you to deputize me to make it legal. But just to be clear: I'm not doing this because of your badge. I'm doing this because my gut tells me that it's *right*."

Charlotte beamed and let out a delighted sound.

"Mister Matthew Slade," Samantha said proudly, "I hereby deputize you in the defense of the town of Stillwater."

"Thank you kindly," Slade said, and then he let out a laugh. "Now, this is truly funny…just this morning, I was fully prepared to shoot you. And come evening, you've got me working for you as a gun hand."

"It is a little strange. But these times are anything but normal."

"I guess." Slade eyed Samantha soberly as he added, "There's a good chance that we'll end up dead by the end of tomorrow. Even if we don't…you have to realize that I'm still under contract. To bring you to your father."

"I'll cross that bridge when we come to it," Samantha said. "But don't count us out yet. If we were playin' poker, then we've got ourselves a full house."

"How do you figure that?"

"Well, isn't that what you have when you pull three kings and two queens?" Samantha smiled wickedly as Slade shook his head. "But we still got a problem: how are we going kill as many of Quantrill's men as we possibly can, as quickly as possible?"

"How close are they goin' to get?" Charlotte asked. "Close enough for pistols, or rifles?"

"Good question. Mister Hickok, you know Quantrill's methods better than the rest of us. What do you think?"

"Well, Clark said in his note that he'd ride into town tomorrow mornin'. If you're not out there, I reckon he'll do what he did in Lawrence – have his men ride up to the houses in town, set 'em on fire with tossed oil lanterns. An' that's bad. Looks like every place in this town is made of wood."

"Except this hotel," Samantha pointed out. "The walls are brick. Probably why it's the only two-story building in Stillwater."

"That makes it the safest place in town," Charlotte declared. "An' that includes Kincaid's hospital. Sam, if we're goin' to shoot it out in town, then we've got to move the doc and his patients in here. Gives them a chance, at least."

"I agree. And Char, I want you to stay in here as well." Samantha looked over the town map again, tapped it with her forefinger. "Still doesn't solve the main problem."

The sound of a footstep on the doorway announced the arrival of Buffalo Bill Cody. A coil of dark wire hung around one shoulder, and he carried a toolbox in each hand.

"If you please," Cody said, "I may have a solution to that."

"I'm all ears, Buffalo Bill."

"Well, Stillwater's a mining town, like many I've been in. So I figured that they set aside these outlying buildings for the most dangerous equipment they need." He shrugged off the coil of wire and placed the toolboxes on the table. One of the boxes contained a number of little black spools. The other, red-brown sticks like oversized cigars. Cody pointed to each in turn. "We've got fuse cord, blasting caps, and a fair amount of dynamite."

Charlotte paled and made as if to step away from the table.

"No worries, now," he reassured them. "I've spent years using pyrotechnics on my Wild West shows. Dynamite's safe enough, so long as nobody here takes a smoke. It's nitroglycerine, the stuff they make dynamite out of, that you have to worry about. And as it happens, we've got several jars of that as well. From what I can tell, they were manufacturing fresh explosives out there, at least on a small scale."

"But...storing jars of liquid nitro?" Slade shook his head. "No wonder they put it in the outermost sheds."

"Probably 'cause they needed to work the mine and open a railroad cut through the mountains," Hickok speculated. "Makes sense to mix up the raw chemicals here, rather than transporting them on a bumpy rail car."

"Nitroglycerine will go off if you shoot it. Or drop a jarful of it down a shaft," Cody added. "I'd wager that we could do a lot of damage to these bastards, if you don't mind blowing up most of this town."

"Mind?" Samantha snorted. "The yellow-bellies living here already wrote their own town off to the Raiders! If we don't destroy it, Quantrill sure as hell will."

"Well, then. What say that we all go place some dynamite and cord around town?"

"I'm all for that. But I don't like relying on cords and caps, not when Quantrill's men will be rampaging all over town."

"Neither do I," Hickok said. Now it was his turn to lean over the map. He jabbed his fingers at specific buildings along the two main roads leading into Stillwater. "Miss Samantha, I think you and Cody have given me an idea."

The group gathered around as Wild Bill explained his plan. A troubled look etched itself on Samantha's face. Slade grinned and rubbed his chin in thought.

"Risky as hell, but I like it," he said. "I'm game."

"I don't know…" Samantha hedged. "I don't like the idea of Quantrill's men getting closer to where Charlotte's going to be holed up."

"It's the best chance we got, Sam," Charlotte said. "So long as we got the doors and windows barricaded, then it'll work."

Samantha sighed. She leaned on the table for a moment, as if to steady herself in a choppy sea. Her jaw set, and she nodded to Hickok.

"Looks like we're going to use your plan." She turned to address the rest of her companions. "All right, then. Let's go pick up some of those things that go 'boom'."

CHAPTER SIXTY-FIVE

Dawn came, turning the sky pink with the promise of a new day. Samantha stood next to where she'd propped a wooden ladder next to the town's dry-goods store and checked her weapons for what must have been the twelfth time. She looked back over her shoulder at the Sierras. The big mountains shimmered and danced in the dry air like a fantastic vision. No clouds marred the open blue bowl of the sky overhead. She rubbed her eyes, stretched to get the last of her sleep-kinks out, and prepared to climb.

"Sam," came a soft voice.

Charlotte stepped out of the shadows. Her face was tired, worn, but it had an inexplicable peacefulness about it. She stepped up to Samantha, took her calloused hands in her own.

"Thought you were still asleep," Samantha said. "After all the work last night..."

"Hardly. Though given a choice, I'd have rather stuck with helping Doc Kincaid move his patients than those canisters of nitro. The doc's stuff don't blow up if you drop it."

Samantha didn't smile at Charlotte's attempt at light-heartedness. "Given a choice, I'd rather that I didn't have to put us through this. Through today. Maybe you were right after all. Maybe we should never have left Chicago."

"Don't be like that." The women embraced. Shared a kiss that blocked out the coolness of the early morning. "I was thinking about that last night. A lot. You know what occurred to me?"

Samantha shook her head.

"Sam, think where we'd be if we'd turned back on that first day or two," Charlotte said. "You'd be married now. Spending the nights in Percy Hanover's bed. And me? I'd be miserable. Lonesome. And I probably wouldn't ever have figured out why. If things go belly-up today...I'd rather have my life end this way.

Do you understand? Rather than live for the rest of it feelin' like I'm broken and can't be fixed, no matter how I try."

Samantha's eyes brimmed up. "Char…I don't have words for that right now…"

"That's okay," Charlotte touched Samantha's chin, tipped her head up so she could see her eyes. "Maybe later, then. You've got something you need to do now. Do it for us."

A final hug.

Charlotte turned and walked towards the relative safety of the Harvey House. The hotel had been prepped for battle: the first-story windows had all been boarded up, and all the entryways save the front door had been blocked with piles of furniture. And even that was remedied as soon as Charlotte had disappeared inside.

Samantha listened to the sound of furniture being moved to barricade the last entry point. She closed her eyes, sighed, and then turned to the business at hand. What she had to see though. She put one hand on the sun-warmed rung of the ladder and began to climb.

It took only a moment to reach the rooftop. She crouched, made sure that she had her targets in sight, and then looked across the rooftops the next street over for Buffalo Bill. The showman, his face hidden by his dapper hat brim, nodded to her. He squatted deeper into his crouch, doing his best to stay hidden, when he pointed off to the southeast. Out to where the two main town roads emptied out onto the desert plain.

She squinted. Dust rose from galloping horses.

Quantrill's Raiders were on their way.

Samantha waited for them to close the distance. One by one, the figures emerged from the cloud of dust thrown up by their horses' hooves. Her ears echoed with the rhythmic pounding of their steeds, drawing closer, like an approaching storm.

Though their gear was often ragged and in need of repair, each man had a hard, trail-bitten look. An evil light glinted from any exposed metal as they drew near.

Spurs. Bits. The blue-gray metal of their weapons.

She counted eighteen of them. She spotted the rotund second-in-command, the man called Lem, riding towards the front. And in the middle of the swirling mass of men and horses rode a man with a leathery face, blond mustache, and a gray Confederate cavalry duster. Samantha frowned. Too far for pistol work to be a sure shot. But a tempting target.

A jingling sound as the Raiders slowed, and then came to a halt as they entered Stillwater's outermost buildings on the eastern edge of town. She watched Quantrill signal to Lem with a gesture indicating *forward*. The man urged his horse forward to where she and Hickok had nailed a message to the town's welcome sign.

Lem tore the message down and brought it back to his leader. It was a simple message. Two sentences, six words. Unsigned.

NO DEAL. LEAVE NOW OR DIE.

Samantha could just barely make out the Confederate's frown. Quantrill crumpled the paper, tossed it aside. She pulled one Colt from her holster. The handle felt warm, welcoming for her touch. Eager for action.

Not long now.

"So it's come to this!" Quantrill's voice bellowed out from below. "Such a waste, and all over a couple of whores who've never felt the touch of a real man!"

Samantha's hand and fingers itched. She flexed her fingers. Her eyes gleamed with a coldness as her mind worked.

I don't see men standing in front of me. Just mangy, low down, dirty, dogs.

"Fine, then!" Quantrill shouted. "Y'all can burn in hell, with your town!"

Quantrill made a new signal, a wind-up gesture that sent a ripple through his gray duster. Two pairs of men spurred their mounts away from the main group. Each man carried an oil lantern, which they lit with ease. At a quick trot, each pair rode up to one of the outlying houses. A heave, and the lanterns went flying, shattering on the stoop or on the dry wooden slats that made up the roof.

She saw Cody watching her. Waiting for her move.

She saw Quantrill, head thrown back against the sudden bloom of orange flames, as if he were laughing, reveling in the destruction.

And she saw one of Quantrill's men pause, lean forward over his saddle to peer at something in the window of the house he'd just set afire.

It was a large, beer-brown glass jar. The size of the jars that she'd seen around her house as she'd grown up. Her mother had collected and stored buttons in one. The servants had kept pickled onions in another. Served lemonade in a third.

The contents of this jar had a bit more kick.

The man continued to squint.

She didn't think the man could read the jar's stained paper label: *NITROGLYCERIN*.

She figured she could help him out.

Samantha rose up. Saw Cody mimic her move from across the way. She raised her Colt. Eyes locked on her target.

She squeezed the trigger.

CHAPTER SIXTY-SIX

The house turned to kindling in a chest-sucking *WHOOMP!*

A brilliant yellow-white fireball rose from the wreckage. Eclipsing the orange flames of the lantern fire. The shadowed figures of the two men in front of the house had vanished as if erased from the earth.

A second tooth-rattling explosion as Cody's bullet found its mark. Two more of Quantrill's men vaporized. The smell of burning wood filled the air now. Mixed with the noxious smell of nitro. Mixed with something darker, fleshy.

Smell of the charnel house.

Her ears rung. Her nose felt clotted with wood ash. But it was her eyes that continued to plague her the most.

She blinked, stubbornly trying to will away the blue-white flashes that played havoc with her vision.

No one told me to look away from a nitro explosion.

A bullet made a *POCK!* sound as it buried itself into the wood slat next to her knee. Another whistled by her ear. Samantha flattened herself back against the roof. More shots. Shouts. She edged backwards. She couldn't stay there, not when Quantrill's men had spotted her. Had to keep the plan in motion.

Her sight began to return in fits and starts. Cursing, she wiped away tears, groped and found the ladder. Shimmied down more by memory than by sight.

Movement off to her right. She pivoted, saw Cody running full-tilt back towards the inner circle of buildings that made up the town. Just according to plan.

She had to keep moving, drawing the Raiders in towards the center of town while she could. Samantha staggered forward, launched into a run just as a bunch of Quantrill's horsemen appeared, a half-dozen houses down.

She ran. Breath pounding in her ears. More shouts.

Turned a corner. Saw her next objective: the town dry-goods store. Her legs pounded, taking her past the store. Perched in one window was another jaw full of yellow-white flashing death.

She clenched her gun in one fist. Knuckles white. Pain in her torso, a terrific stitch up one side of her ribs. Forced herself to ignore it. Sound of hooves heavy in her ears now, an avalanche of noise.

She kept running. Passed two more houses. Half-turned, fired to one side, blindly. Heard a man scream. A man wearing a hunting jacket the color of rancid butter tumbled out of his saddle and lay still.

The riderless horse ran ahead of the group in a panic. It reared with a whinny. Cursing, the Raiders fired wildly. Bullets meant for Samantha dropped the horse in a red spray of gore.

More bullets tore her sleeve. Exploded under the heel of her boot, sent her sprawling headlong forward onto the ground. Her empty Colt skidded away across the street. Dirt in her mouth, horrible and smoky. Blood streaming from one nostril.

She heaved herself up on one elbow. Shaking, got to a crouch. Groped for her other gun. Saw two more horsemen bearing down on her. Behind them, four more. Flash of cavalry grey. Quantrill's face among them.

She struggled to get her second Colt free of its holster. Had twisted it in her fall.

Blood pounding.

Heart whamming in the chest.

Smell of powder in the air, tingling like little electric shocks.

The deep, calm voice of a gunfighter in her ear.

"Get down."

Samantha didn't hesitate. She dropped.

Hickok stepped out from the shadows behind her. His dark coat swirled behind him in a gust of wind like an avenging angel. Effortlessly, his ivory handled pistols leaped from his sash and into his hands. A pair of shots erupted from his guns.

The closest pair of Raiders had just drawn even with the dry-goods store. They screamed as the storefront vanished in wall of flame. The blast wave caught Samantha, hurled her sideways into the hitching post of the house behind her. Pain flared in the small of her back as she took the impact.

The dry-goods store had been made of sturdier timber than the first couple of houses. Instead of turning into splinters, the upper floor's support beams collapsed forward into the street. A burning wall of wreckage blocked the street, though behind it, she could hear Quantrill cursing, shouting, and threatening his men to keep moving.

Hickok had kept his feet during the blast, though his hat brim and eyebrows had been singed black with ash. He pivoted on his heel at the sound of more shots. Rifle first, the earth-cracking *BOOM* of nitro, and then a volley of gunfire.

"Watched from a rooftop," Hickok said in a rush, "Raiders split into two groups. Sounds like Cody and Slade need help."

Samantha wobbled to her feet. Got her one remaining pistol out. Her back let out another twinge, making her wince.

"I'll come–" she began.

"No. Remember our plan! Get ready to box 'em in at the front of the hotel."

And with that, he vanished. Samantha cursed, knowing Hickok was right. She swung her attention back to the burning wreckage of the dry-goods store. She heard the breaking of glass, the clatter of hooves on wooden floors.

A chill ran down her spine.

What are you up to, Clark Quantrill?

She stepped up on the hitching post, leaned one hand on a porch column. Eyes still watering, she peered over the flames and smoke.

She watched in amazement as Quantrill and his men forced their mounts in through the back of a saloon further up the street. Samantha got down, ran around the side of the nearest house to the adjoining street. She heard a gunshot, then a second, louder tinkle of breaking glass as one of the men shot out the establishment's front window.

The Raiders spurred and whipped their horses through the opening. They galloped down the street towards the center of town, pulling far ahead of Samantha. She made one shot, but the bullet went wide. She stopped, gasping.

Quantrill was heading where they wanted him. But that was the only part of the plan still at work. The Raiders weren't supposed to be ahead of her. Samantha wasn't supposed to be without Hickok to back her up.

And Quantrill wasn't supposed to be getting this close to Charlotte.

Cursing, she ignored the pains in her side and back. She followed as quickly as she could, favoring one side, turning a fast run into a desperate, pathetic limp.

CHAPTER SIXTY-SEVEN

Matthew Slade sat on the roof of Stillwater's hardware store, rifle in hand, tracking Buffalo Bill's run. He gave the showman grudging credit – even with seven mounted horsemen after him, Cody didn't bat an eyelid. Instead, the man dodged and weaved, keeping well ahead of his pursuers.

He tracked along as Cody passed the blacksmith's shop. One, two houses further down. The horsemen closed in. Shots tore up the dirt at Cody's heels. The distance between him and the nitro was tight, but it would have to do.

Slade sighted on the jar of nitro in the window of the blacksmith's shop and squeezed the Winchester's trigger. One more of Quantrill's Raiders vanished in a white-gray cloud of explosive and wood fragments. Hot coals from the smith's fire rained down among the remaining outlaws.

One horse, already wounded by a shard of wooden shrapnel, threw its rider in a panic. The man fell to one side, twisting as he fell. His heel hung up in the stirrup and he screamed in panic and pain as the horse galloped back out of town, dragging him as it went.

The heavy-set leader of the remaining five men – the one Samantha had called 'Lem', by her description - stood up in his saddle. He shouted, and pointed up towards Slade. He'd seen the rifle flash. In the twinkling of an eye, the Raiders opened fire.

Slade's rifle shattered in his hand, sending splinters into his arm and wrist. He tumbled, caught a momentary grip on one of the eaves. Then he half-slid, half-fell, arm around one of the store's drain posts.

He landed on his feet, hard. A soft, wet *snap*. Searing pain shot up his leg as he stood to run toward the former sheriff's office. Three loping steps was all he could handle before he hobbled to a stop by an empty lot across from the front of the office. Face ashen, he slid down next to one of the street's water troughs.

The group of outlaws appeared at the opposite end of the lot, all on foot. Lem carried a shotgun, while other others had pistols at the ready. They moved at a cautious pace, eyes darting to and fro, expecting another ambush.

Slade tried to draw his gun. But his fingers refused to work. Blood ran freely down his forearm, making the handle slippery. He cursed under his breath and switched to his off-hand. His ankle throbbed like a red-hot leg iron. But he maneuvered himself to crouch on one knee. Waited until the group drew close enough.

He opened up, emptying his pistol into the group. In his off hand, the bullets sprayed wildly, ruffling the cuff of one outlaw, shattering the window next to another. But one of Slade's shots went true. A man wearing Confederate gray took a bullet in his throat. The hapless brigand fell to his knees, coughed up a red spatter of blood, and then collapsed.

Lem shouldered the shotgun and let off a blast. The side of the water trough exploded in a gout of dirty foam. Slade coughed as he was doused with stale water. He tried to roll out of the line of fire, but he knew it was of little use. The trough wouldn't stop a second shot. No cover anywhere else, either.

Quantrill's henchman brought his weapon to bear. Aimed for the dark shape huddled behind the remains of the trough. He sighted. Squeezed the trigger.

Two bullets caught him, one from each side. Spun him around so that the blast of his gun went straight into the air. The heavyset man dropped and sprawled on the ground, eyes staring lifelessly into the sun.

More shots came from Slade's side of the empty lot. Quantrill's men returned fire, but the remaining three broke and ran back towards the center of town. Slade blinked, amazed, as Cody and Hickok stepped out into the open, their guns hot and smoking in their hands.

"You goin' to be okay, partner?" Hickok said, as he crouched, checking Slade's wounds.

"I'm not shot," Slade coughed, "But I can't stand. Can't move my leg. Son of a bitch this hurts!"

"Just wait there, then. We'll send the doc as soon as we can."

"Then you better hurry up and go kill the rest of those Confederate low-lifes!"

Cody gave Hickok an amused look. "You heard the man. And it sounds like they're all headed the right way, at least."

Hickok nodded. "Let's go see if we can finish this."

Together, the two men made their way back towards the Harvey House at a dead run. Hickok slid to a stop and Cody practically collapsed in exhaustion as they heard the report of Charlotte's rifle. They split up, one on either side of the street, as they approached the hotel.

Clark Quantrill and his seven remaining men were all on foot now, all within the open square just outside the hotel. The Captain barked orders, moving his men to cover. They focused on approaching the hotel's barricaded doors and windows, their progress hampered by Charlotte's intermittent sniping from a bedroom window on the second floor. Her shots hadn't hit anyone yet, but it kept the outlaws' heads down.

Hickok's face broke out into a smile as, on the far side of the square, Samantha emerged from one of the side alleys. Her face was flush, and she looked as exhausted as Cody; but she took in what was happening and slid into place behind an abandoned hay wagon.

They were short one man, but the plan had worked: to whittle down Quantrill's numbers, get them off their horses, and funnel them into a killing zone.

Hickok opened up the Raiders' baptism of fire with his twin Dragoons. Cody and Samantha followed suit with their own guns. A look of horror crossed the face of the Confederates as they realized that they'd been lured into a cross-fire.

Guns exploded like fireworks, flashing flame and swirling smoke. Now the Raiders were the ones in a tight spot, and they knew it. But they were the core of Quantrill's men, and they weren't going to quit. They kept up a murderous fire of their own, driving Cody to fall back to better cover, blowing one of the wheels off of Samantha's wagon, and shattering windows in the hotel, keeping Charlotte's fire wild and inaccurate.

One of Hickok's shots took out Quantrill's remaining rifleman. The grizzled outlaw squeezed off a final shot as he fell. Hickok let out a cry as a bloody crease appeared in his calf. Cody dashed over to him, laying down cover fire as Hickok bandaged the wound.

"Goddamn that makes me mad!" Hickok roared. He reloaded, and let loose a volley of shots, rapid-fire, that caught another Raider in the chest.

Quantrill hurled himself with a bang against one of the hotel's side doors. The heavily barricaded entrance didn't budge. Then, with an evil gleam in his eye, he reached out and grabbed the man that Hickok had just shot.

The big Confederate hefted the corpse in front of him as he stepped up on a wooden crate, then a flour barrel, and then within reach of one of the building's large second story windows. Bullets hit the dead body with wet *slaps*. Blood poured from the body in scarlet jets.

Quantrill dropped the corpse of his former Raider. In a flash, he hurled himself towards the window.

The glass shattered around him as he tumbled through and into the hotel.

CHAPTER SIXTY-EIGHT

"*No!*" Samantha cried, as she saw Clark Quantrill breach the hotel's defenses.

Screaming like a banshee, she ran towards the Harvey House, firing her pistol as she did so.

From across the open space, Hickok and Cody watched, dumbstruck.

"What in our Maker's name..." Cody gasped.

"Quiet!" Hickok snapped. "She needs cover!"

Together, the two men did their best, even stepping out of their own cover to draw fire. Quantrill's men were too eager to eliminate an open target. Two more fell back as Samantha ran up, wounded by the lethal crossfire.

Samantha felt the pluck of bullets at her jacket, the whistle of lead through the air. Yet she remained unscathed as she dashed up to the hotel's front porch. One of Quantrill's men, his pistol's magazine empty, leapt at her. He grabbed for the gun in her hand. Together they rolled, cursing and snarling at each other, wrestling for control.

A *bang!* echoed in the confines of the porch as the Colt went off.

Charlotte heard the gun's report. But it was no louder than any of the other gunfire from outside the hotel. She was more concerned about the crash she'd heard from down the corridor outside her room. She got up from where she'd been shooting at Clark's men.

The hotel's bedroom had been devastated. Bullet holes pockmarked the interior like the field headquarters of a major battle. She hefted her Winchester. Her nimble fingers went for the umpteenth time to her pocket, where she'd been pulling cartridge after cartridge.

Out in the corridor, a tall beanpole of a man with a balding pate of gray hair and an ill-fitting white jacket stood at the top of the stairwell.

"Doc!" Charlotte shouted, "Get back downstairs!"

"I heard the sound of breaking glass!" the doctor retorted, "I thought you might be hurt—"

The report of a pistol shot echoed down the corridor. A bullet shattered the picture frame on the wall next to the doctor's head. He gave out a yelp and fell backwards down the stairs.

Charlotte gasped as she saw a dark figure silhouetted against the broken window at the end of the corridor. Captain Clark Quantrill looked more like a demon from hell than the leader of an outlaw gang. Gunpowder and nitro burns had charred his fingers, singed his hat to a crisp blackness about the rim.

His gray coat fell in tattered, red-soaked ribbons about him. Cuts on his hands and cheeks dripped blood. A chunk of glass protruded from one sunburned blond eyebrow. It glittered, pulsing obscenely with the beat of the man's black heart.

She squeezed her rifle's trigger. The report was deafening. The acrid smell of the gunpowder surrounded her in a choking fog.

A bloody crater erupted from Quantrill's bicep. He howled as he spun against the wall, dropping his gun. With a snarl, he continued to approach her, a murderous look plastered on his face.

"You got some fight in you, girl," he cackled. "You'll be even *better* than my Caroline was in my bed…"

Charlotte didn't answer. She backed away slowly, horrified, as she dug in her pocket for another bullet.

Horror turned to terror as she came up empty.

"Oh, too bad," he said, cocking an insane grin at her. "Your rifle's no good. Not if it's as empty as your pretty little head!"

"I can still figure a use for it," Charlotte snapped back.

Quick as lightning, she reversed her grip on the rifle. Held it by the barrel. Ignored the heat from the metal that burned her palms.

With a cry, she swung the butt end as hard as she could at Quantrill's head. The man pulled back, but not quickly enough. The gun connected with his chin and lower jaw. A single tooth leapt into the air like a broken piano key.

Quantrill staggered. But only for a moment. Then he lunged for her. His good hand closed around Charlotte's throat. She beat at him, but her efforts were futile. She heard a scuffling sound from back by the broken window as he bore her back against the wall.

He brought his horribly maimed face close to hers. His cracked, split lips dribbled blood on her chin as he leaned in. His sour breath on hers. His body on hers, obscenely close.

He spattered her with tendrils of blood as he spoke.

"That was a mighty nice try. But a man like me, there ain't no woman who can take him down."

From off to one side, Charlotte heard Samantha's voice.

"Maybe not one alone, Quantrill. But *two* can."

A *bang!* and a neat, circular hole appeared in the man's temple.

Quantrill stiffened. His lips formed in an unspoken *how?*

With a last, convulsive shudder, Clark Quantrill fell dead at Charlotte's feet. She looked to one side and saw Samantha standing in the hotel's corridor, gasping from the effort involved in climbing through the entry Clark had made.

Charlotte let out a cry of joy and ran to her. Samantha pulled Charlotte in close.

Holding her.

Protecting her against the world.

CHAPTER SIXTY-NINE

It had been a difficult task to drag Clark Quantrill back towards the broken window, but the two women got the job done.

"A messy job, I know," Samantha said to Charlotte. "On three?"

"It'd be a right pleasure," Charlotte responded, "To toss out this refuse."

With that, Samantha grabbed hold of Quantrill's body by the wrists. Charlotte did the same with the corpse's ankles. She didn't flinch as her hands curled around the dead flesh. On a three-count, they hefted the corpse and heaved it through the opening. Quantrill's body tumbled and bounced with a fleshy-sounding *splat* as it hit the ground.

The sound of gunfire ceased as everyone outside the hotel saw the remains of the outlaw leader, tossed out like so much offal behind the butcher's shop.

Samantha cupped her hands to her mouth and shouted at the top of her lungs.

"You there! Quantrill's boys! Take a look at your boss. There are only a few of you left. I'm giving you ten seconds to drop your guns and come on out, hands high. You do that, we'll let you get your horses and ride out. If you want to follow your Captain…then we'll damn well oblige you!"

She began her count, shouting each digit in turn, every few seconds. The street outside stayed quiet as the shooting stopped. Sounds of murmuring. Samantha got down to the number five, and then she heard one of the men from below call back up to her.

"Don't shoot! We surrender!" One of Quantrill's men, a homely looking outlaw with a pockmarked face, stepped out into the open and dropped his gun. Two others followed suit. Their former companions lay dead and dying around them in the square.

Samantha stuck her head out the window, got a good look at them. Hickok and Cody stepped out as well, watching from a distance.

"Mount up and get out," she said flatly. "If you come back, I'll kill you."

The men hurried over to where the surviving horses had been tied. They mounted up, dug their spurs in, and threw dust as the horses leaped into a full gallop out of town. Samantha waited until the three outlaws had disappeared over the horizon before she turned her attention to other matters.

A groan came from the base of the stairwell. Charlotte let out a gasp and hurried down the stairs. Samantha joined her as she helped the doctor to his feet. The man had a purple-red bruise the size of a goose egg at the crown of his head, but otherwise seemed unhurt.

"Sam, help me get Doc Kincaid to one of the stretchers," Charlotte said. But the man waved them both off.

"That's enough, that's enough," the doctor said irritably. "My own damn fault. We've got to have people hurt worse than me."

A banging came from the hotel's bullet-pocked front door. Cody's voice sounded muffled through the heavy wood.

"Hello in there! I got a customer for you, if you're open for business!"

Samantha, Charlotte, and Kincaid quickly shoved the barricade of broken furniture out of the way. Cody helped support Hickok as the gunfighter limped through the door. Both men were stained with smoke and singed from the explosions. Hickok's left leg was wrapped in a blood-stained bandage below the knee.

"Oh, Bill!" Charlotte cried, as she came around to support the gunfighter on his other side.

"How badly are you hurt?" Samantha asked, concern in her eyes.

"I ain't dyin'," Hickok replied tartly, "But it's not like I'm ready to head out dancing."

"Lay him over here, on the cot." The doctor instructed, and together, Cody and Charlotte got him halfway comfortable.

Doc Kincaid removed the bandage, glanced approvingly at the wound.

"That's more of a graze. Let me sterilize my tools, and I can stitch that right up. Then we'll give it a couple days of rest so that it doesn't tear open." The doctor looked at Hickok questioningly. "The stitching's going to sting a bit. You want some laudanum for that?"

Hickok snorted. "Please. Figure this ain't the worst hole that someone's put in me over the years. 'Sides, this place has got to have some firewater in it that can dull the pain."

"That's a safe bet," Samantha said, as she rummaged in one of the room's thick wooden cabinets and came up with a bottle of gin. She poured Hickok a glass. He downed it, though not without a scowl.

"That's got a fair kick," he said, shaking his head. "Doc, I've got what you need to sterilize your stuff. Figure you could use it on the Pinkerton man as well."

"Slade!" Charlotte exclaimed. "What happened to him?"

Matthew Slade's casual drawl echoed from the opened front door. "I decided that I'd make it here under my own power, that's what happened."

The Pinkerton agent hobbled inside, using his rifle as a cane. His ankle had swollen to twice the normal size, and he moved even more slowly than Hickok had. Samantha and Charlotte took his arms, guided him over to the cot adjoining Hickok's. The doctor came over and began examining the man's wounds. Blood oozed from Slade's forearm, where a pencil-sized splinter protruded from his flesh.

"Good thing you left that wood where it was," Kincaid said. "Looks like it nicked a major blood vessel. I'll have to operate to get it out and patch you up."

Slade took the news with a shrug. But he let out a yell when the doctor lifted his foot and tried to tug the boot off the swollen foot.

"Dammit!" he cried. "Take it easy, Doc."

Kincaid shook his head. "That boot's got to be cut off."

"These boots cost me fifty dollars," Slade protested.

"Your choice. But you got a broken ankle, at the very least. Gangrene might set in, force me to cut off your boot and the foot inside of it."

Slade paled. "Fine. Cut the boot off."

The doctor unstoppered a little green bottle and handed it over. "This is going to need more than a glass of gin. Drink this. It's laudanum. Should dull the pain, and fast."

"Naw, I don't need it."

"It's your call, cowpoke." The doctor pulled out a set of scissors and started to cut into the boot. Beads of sweat formed on Matthew Slade's brow.

"Damnation!" Slade shrieked. "Hellfire!"

The doctor paused just long enough to hand Slade the bottle of laudanum. The Pinkerton man grabbed it and took a long swig. He grimaced, shuddering at the taste, and then looked over to Hickok's glass.

"Forget it," the doctor said, catching the glance. "You don't go mixing alcohol with that."

Slade muttered a curse. He blinked owlishly. Shook his head. He looked up at Charlotte and Samantha. His voice began to slur as he spoke to them.

"Well, I guess that congratulations are in order. You both made it through alive. But don't cash in all of your chips yet…I'm still sworn to bring you to McKin…McKinley Williams."

The Pinkerton man's voice cut off. His head slumped forward with a loud snore. The doctor shook his head and left the room to fetch his surgical gear.

"Well, that's all and done with," Hickok remarked. "Our friend Slade should be out for a few hours. Enough to get you two saddled up and out of town."

Samantha shook her head. "We can't just leave you. And I'm not sure that we could get through the Sierras on our own."

"That's where you're in error," Cody said, as he pulled out one of the hotel's less shot-up chairs and reclined in it. "The doc and I can look after Wild Bill well enough. As for the Sierras…remember, I've been this way more than a few times. Just make it past the slide, follow the railroad tracks up into the mountains for two, three days. You'll end up at Colfax, the first station on the California side of the Sierras. From there, hop any local train and you'll be in San Francisco in a day."

Charlotte sat straight up, electrified at the news. "We're…we're that close?"

"Yep," Hickok said. "You're that close. And don't you worry about Mr. Pinkerton for a while yet. Between me, Cody, and a little extra laudanum slipped in the whiskey, our friend Matthew Slade won't be a thorn in your side for a while yet."

"But…y'all will come out to see us afterwards?"

"It'll be a while," Cody said. "I'm going to be rather behind schedule in recruiting people for my next show. I might have to schedule a visit next year."

"And what about you, Mister Hickok?" Samantha asked.

Wild Bill Hickok looked away for a moment, lost in thought. When he spoke, it was in a surprisingly quiet tone of voice.

"If there's one thing you two have taught me," he said, "Is that if you love someone, y'all stick to 'em like a rider on a buckin' bronco. I suppose I need to start doin' the same. I got a woman who wants to take my hand, take up my last name. Figure I ought to give that a chance."

Nothing more could be said. The two women came up, gave both Hickok and Cody a final embrace. Cody looked embarrassed at the affection shown, and Hickok shrugged the gesture off.

"Go on," he said, though a twinkle danced in his eye. "Get your horses saddled up 'fore someone gets the wrong idea."

Arm in arm, the two women left the Harvey House. They looked up at the mass of the Sierras. The railroad cut gleamed like a sharp-edged brown knife.

"Just one more set of mountains," Charlotte mused.

"True," Samantha replied. "But somehow, these don't look quite so difficult anymore."

EPILOGUE

Normally, the winter months in San Francisco were marked with little else but rain, wind, and fog that could put a bowl of pea soup to shame. But not tonight. The last day in the year 1876 had been unseasonably warm and dry. Stars twinkled over the bustling little city. The swarm of gold prospectors had slowed to a trickle these days, but they'd been replaced by railroad barons, merchants, and sailors fresh off the clipper ships from China, Java, and Japan.

The refined air of prosperity extended to the newly cobblestoned streets, the all-night gas lamps that threw off warm yellow light, and the blue-and-white Victorian mansion that graced the corner of a steep, cobblestoned street. Perched high on the slope, within sight of the newly built Grace Cathedral and the mansions that dotted Nob Hill, it wasn't hard to miss the brightly colored, friendly sign: *Two Queens Social Club: Welcome to Our Grand Opening!*

The woman in the green satin gown who came out to greet the courier at the late hour had an air about her. Stylish. Graceful. Confident. And though she looked young, those who knew what to look for would see a great deal of experience in her eyes. Experiences that weren't all pleasant, but ones that had toughened her the way a forge's heat tempers steel.

She received both a letter and a telegram, and then pressed a dollar coin into the man's palm as a tip. One delicately manicured hand flew to her mouth as she opened one message, then the other. Pausing only to greet a group of newly arriving guests, she went through the club's leaded glass doors and into an elegantly appointed dining room. The room was packed with people that made up San Francisco's high society; as per the club's dress code, the men wore tailored frock coats with ivory-colored ties, while the ladies were garbed in their best evening gowns.

Mrs. Pleasance had not exaggerated about her connections. With the capital that they received, the Two Queens Social Club had been constructed from the start to be more than a simple bawdy house. It was a casino, night club, and supper club, all in one building. And judging by the reception on their opening night – a champagne-popping bash to ring in 1877 – the new business venture promised to be very flush indeed.

Samantha, resplendent in her own red and blue satin gown, stood on a dais before the crowd. Behind her, the club's musicians paused in their playing to allow her to finish her speech.

"...And in conclusion, Ladies and Gentlemen," she said proudly, "This city has shown us its generous side, its welcoming side, for which we're both grateful. Welcome to the Two Queens, and thank you for choosing to ring in the New Year with us!"

A wave of polite applause swept through the tables like a welcome breeze. The band struck up a tune as Samantha stepped down. She headed for the manager's office in the adjoining room, greeting and thanking guests at each table along the way.

Charlotte awaited her, letters in hand. Samantha's eyes drank in Charlotte's beauty. Beauty that had filled out and blossomed, once away from the stress and strain of their travels across the West. And her lover's cheeks appeared flushed, excited and dismayed all at the same time. Samantha gave her a questioning look as the two settled into twin plush seats behind the massive teakwood desk.

"Sam, I'm all tangled up inside, I could just come apart!" Charlotte said.

"What's bothering my fair damsel?" Samantha teased her, but Charlotte shook her head.

"Oh, I got a telegram that's put my dander up...but you've got to read this letter first. First time we've gotten a message from Bill Hickok."

Samantha perked up at hearing the name of their companion on many of the long, weary miles between Missouri and Nevada.

She opened up the letter, which bore the traces of the gunfighter's strong, masculine hand.

To My Two Queens:
I hope this letter finds you both well. Thank you for the invite to the Grand Opening at your club. You may not know it but news of your place travels even to the backwoods areas I like best.
Matthew Slade was sure mad when he found out that you two had been gone for a week before that ole doc finally let him sober up. Our Pinkerton friend got even hotter under his collar when it turned out that he'd broke his foot bone as well as his ankle bone. On top of that Cody and I beat him at poker so bad over the next weeks that we pretty much had him skinned down to his bare britches. Ha! Ha!
At any rate like I said news travels all places. Plus he knew you lit out for San Francisco so if I was you I would expect him to show up pretty soon. That is if he has not already done so.
Buffalo Bill is planning on buying some property and getting everything ready for his next Wild West Show. He seems to think they would like to see the 'Wild West' in Europe. I think he has done lost his mind.
As for me, I met my wife Agnes Lake out here in the Dakota territories and have decided to face up to being a married man. Agnes can get loud but I love her and she cooks good. Figure I will be with her the rest of my life. You both taught me as well or better than I taught you.
I hope to see you sometime next year if everything works out. I reckon I don't have to worry about you taking care of yourselves. Tell the truth I kind of feel sorry for anyone that wants to go up against you.
Wild Bill
Town of Deadwood, Dakota Territory

Try as she might, Samantha couldn't keep from grinning.

"Our friend Wild Bill," she said, "he sounds…happy!"

"Well, that was the letter," Charlotte said, "Here's the telegram that just arrived, for me."

Samantha alternately smiled and frowned as she took in the words. Just outside the office's open door, waiters bustled with silver trays and buckets of ice, ready to deliver bottles of champagne to each of the tables.

But she ignored them, focusing on the telegram's contents: "CHARLOTTE THE PINKERTON AGENCY JUST NOTIFIED US OF YOUR CLUB'S LOCATION IN SAN FRANCISCO -STOP- MCKINLEY WILLIAMS TO ARRIVE TONIGHT WE ARE ON THE NEXT TRAIN FOR ARRIVAL JANUARY 1 -STOP- WE LOVE YOU AND ACCEPT ALL THINGS IF YOU ARE HAPPY -STOP- LOVE YOU MOTHER AND FATHER."

Samantha looked wistfully into the distance. "Char, this is wonderful. That is…if you're happy. Being out here with me."

"There's no need to ask such a thing," Charlotte demurred. "I'd settled all that in my mind, a long time and a lot of miles ago. It's just that…you know who's going to be here tonight!"

On cue, the sound of an argument from the front lobby filtered into the main dining room.

The two women walked out to the dining area, where the guests closest to the doors looked on curiously, wondering what the commotion was all about. The mountain-sized doorman that Samantha had hired turned and made a signal that meant: *What do you want to do?*

Charlotte watched, fascinated, as Samantha waved back with a resigned flip of her hand: *Come ahead.* Nodding, the doorman allowed two figures to enter. One was tall, refined, and wore a natty bowler's hat atop a brand new tweed suit. He limped slightly, and the flare of one pants leg indicated that he still wore a cast. The other slunk along, barrel-chested and gimlet eyed, giving his expensively tailored clothes an unkempt, slovenly appearance.

Samantha beckoned the two men into the office, and then closed the door.

She strolled around to the rear of the desk and settled back into her seat. Charlotte followed suit, eyes darting between the two generations of the Williams family.

"It's good to see you, Mister Slade," Samantha began. "I take it that you've finally collected your bounty?"

Slade coughed apologetically. "At long last, yes. Much as I enjoyed the company of your two friends back in Stillwater, I still had my word to keep."

"I suppose that I should be glad that you can still raise your head up high, then."

The Pinkerton man looked away at that last jibe. McKinley Williams took advantage of the silence to puff himself up like some kind of strange, exotic bird.

"Enough with this tomfoolery!" he stated firmly. "Young lady, I've come at long last to take you home with me!"

Samantha placed her hands together on the desk top. Her cheeks flushed, but she gave no other sign of her checked anger or frustration.

"Well, Mister Williams, we seem to have a problem, then. But I suppose you would like me to address you as father. Very well, we have a problem, father."

McKinley grunted in agreement. He started to take a seat in one of the large leather chairs set just in front of Samantha's desk. She frowned at his move.

"I don't recall asking you to sit."

"Now you see here! Don't you talk to me like that, I'm your father! You owe me some respect. I'm ordering you, forget all this nonsense and come home at once!"

"Father dear, once again, you're not paying attention," Samantha's voice dropped only slightly, but Slade saw the danger inherent in the woman's tone, her expression. Her hand dropped low, right to where she'd once hung a pair of blue-steel Colts. "*This* is my home. *This* is my place. Not yours. *I* make the rules here."

Somehow, something penetrated McKinley's shell of arrogance. Made him take a step back. He sensed something had changed, irrevocably changed inside his offspring. That she'd taken on something tough, something tougher than her father. Something that cut through his bluster in a way that polite Chicago society hadn't prepared him for.

"You...you insolent..." McKinley appealed to his companion. "Slade, do something! What have I paid you for?"

The Pinkerton man let out his first real laugh in months.

"Since you brought that up, Mister Williams, I'll gladly tell you. Our contract was for me to bring the girls to you. I've done that. But you never paid me to haul them back to Chicago for you. Not when you're standing right in front of them."

"Fine, then! I'll pay you double to throw them in irons, put them in a steamer trunk, whatever it takes! You say you're a man of your word, so hop to it!"

"Ah, but now we've got ourselves a problem," Slade sighed, in mock sorrow. "My word is indeed my bond, but only if I *accept* the contract. And frankly, your requests have never set too well with me. If ever a pair of women have earned their freedom to do what they want, it's these two."

"Damn you, you traitorous, cow-punching moron! Wait till I..." McKinley raged, until he began to sputter incoherently.

"Mister Slade," Charlotte interjected, "am I to understand that y'all are free an' without a contract at the present time?"

"That would be correct," Slade said, "Since I just rejected Mister William's offer."

"I figure, maybe we could use the services of a real-life Pinkerton agent," Charlotte said to Samantha. The two women grinned at each other, a wicked gleam in their eyes.

"Mister Slade," Samantha said, "I'd like to hire Pinkerton to perform a task for me. I'll pay top dollar for it, too."

"Ask away."

"I want you to make sure that McKinley Williams makes it back to Chicago. On the first train tomorrow morning. Safely, if possible, but in handcuffs and leg irons if you deem it necessary. And I'd ask that you pass on what's happened here to the rest of your organization, as well."

"Well now, that would be a pleasure," Slade said, with a little bow. "I accept."

Samantha turned her attention back to where McKinley continued to sputter.

"Tonight is the last time I will address you as father," she said plainly. "I have everything that I need and want with me, right here. My wish is for you to leave me now, and forget that you ever had a daughter."

"Why...you!" McKinley began, but the Pinkerton man's heavy hand came down on his shoulder like a fleshy vise.

"Enough," Slade said. "You had your say, McKinley. Don't force me to 'persuade' you."

"Father," Samantha concluded, "you have gone against my wishes for the last time. You need to leave now. Oh! And please, do try not to embarrass me...or my family."

Slade steered McKinley around to exit the room. At the last moment, he put his put his hand up to the brim of his hat. He touched it with his thumb and forefinger, giving Samantha a hidden little salute.

Samantha and Charlotte followed the men at a discrete distance, through the dining area and into the marble-lined foyer. The doorman propped the leaded glass doors open. Slade and McKinley went through and into the cool night, disappearing as quickly as they'd arrived.

The two women stepped outside as a wave of sound washed through the club. The sound of a score of popping corks, the spicy smell of champagne. A raucous cheer went up from the guests, and the musicians switched over to a bright, care-free number.

"We made it, Sam," Charlotte said, her face aglow with joy. "We made it! And now...all we have left is to pass the rest of our lives, together."

"No," Samantha replied, and tears glittered in the corner of her eyes, "we won't pass the rest of our lives together. We'll *live* them."

She brought Charlotte in for a deep, warm kiss. Along San Francisco's long, winding avenues, the street clocks chimed midnight in a brassy chorus. Answering toots, whistles, and bells echoed back from the multitude of ships docked down by the wharves that surrounded the city.

And from far above came the heavenly peals of Grace Cathedral, ringing in promise of the New Year.

AFTERWORD

Mark Twain once quoted the Greek historian Herodotus when he said: "Very few things happen at the right time, and the rest do not happen at all: The conscientious historian will correct these defects."

The same could be said for the events described in the book you've just read. *Sagebrush & Lace* was intended as entertainment with a historical flavor from the get-go. It makes little to no claim on accuracy when it comes to personalities, happenings, or even the attitudes towards homosexual relationships in the American West.

That said, part of the fun of writing *Sagebrush* was in the possibility that some of the events and meetings described could have indeed taken place. After all, many of the people and places were in existence in the book's time frame of April to December, 1876.

Pleasance, Illinois – the location of Mrs. Pleasance's Social Club – is completely fictional. However, even though they're hard to find on a map today, both Palmetto and Stillwater were towns that did exist back in the 19th Century. Stillwater, for example, is a readily visited ghost town near Fallon, Nevada.

Samuel Clemens, better known to the world as Mark Twain, was just launching his trajectory towards literary superstardom in 1876. That year, *The Adventures of Tom Sawyer* debuted in the United Kingdom. It would soon prove to be a bestseller in the U.S. as well.

The James-Younger Gang was a famous group of American outlaws, most of whom started their careers as Confederate guerillas during the Civil War. In the summer of 1876, their gang performed a daring train robbery near Otterville, Missouri. But their time of glory was short, as in September, the gang's members were killed or captured following an ill-fated attempt to rob a bank in Minnesota.

'Bandit Queen' Belle Starr had been married to Jim Reed, member of the Younger gang, until his death at the hands of a local sheriff in 1874. Afterwards, Belle decided to immerse herself in outlawry. She usually employed bribery to free her cohorts when they were caught; but when she was unable to buy off a lawman, she was known to seduce him into looking the other way. She escaped the fate of the James-Younger gang but was ambushed and killed by unknown assailants in 1889.

Wyatt Earp's best known days as a lawman actually took place in 1879, the year of the Gunfight at the O.K. Corral in Tombstone, Arizona. Back in 1876, he was busy protecting the citizens of Dodge City, Kansas as their deputy marshal.

Chief Sitting Bull served as a Hunkpapa Lakota Sioux holy man. In early 1876, he had a premonition that his people would defeat the U.S. Cavalry. In June that year, they did indeed score a major victory at the Battle of the Little Bighorn against Lt. Col. George Armstrong Custer and the 7th Cavalry. He lived until 1890, when he was killed during a struggle between his followers and the U.S. Indian Service.

One of the most colorful figures of the American Old West, William Frederick 'Buffalo Bill' Cody made his name from his cowboy themed Wild West Shows. Cody's show proved to be as big a hit in Europe as in the United States; at the close of its successful London run in 1887, over 300 performances and more than two and a half million tickets had been sold.

Captain Clark Quantrill was loosely based on the real-life historical figure of William Clarke Quantrill. Quantrill was a Confederate guerrilla leader whose raiders operated along the Missouri-Kansas border. Their actions included the infamous raid and sacking of Lawrence, Kansas in 1863. Quantrill was mortally wounded in a Union ambush in May 1865, aged 27.

The Pinkerton National Detective Agency, pejoratively called 'the Pinks' by outlaws and opponents, was founded in 1850. The company still exists today. The character of Matthew Slade was based on actor Richard Boone's portrayal of Paladin, the gunslinger from the 1957-63 television series *Have Gun Will Travel*.

James Butler 'Wild Bill' Hickok was a man who, like Wyatt Earp, became a Western folk hero. Considered the pre-eminent gunfighter and scout of the Old West, in March 1876 he married Agnes Thatcher Lake, though he left her to seek his fortune in the Dakota gold fields.

On August 2, Hickok was playing poker in the mining town of Deadwood. He supposedly held a pair of aces and a pair of eights, all black, when he was assassinated by a man who claimed that Hickok had killed his brother.

Shortly before Hickok's death, he wrote a letter to his wife, which read in part:

"Agnes Darling, if such should be we never meet again, while firing my last shot, I will gently breathe the name of my wife — Agnes — and with wishes even for my enemies I will make the plunge and try to swim to the other shore."

Enter the World of Sugar Lee Ryder

Cowgirl Up

Sugar Lee Ryder brings us into the modern world of the western with a hot romance!

Young, independent ranch woman Honey Durbin meets her match in this novella about bulls, rodeo cowboys and the difference between sex and love making.

The pages that follow provide a glimpse into the world of *Cowgirl Up*.

Print and eBook Editions available at all major eBook retailers.

COWGIRL UP:

SUGAR LEE RYDER

CHAPTER 1

I pulled my red Dodge Ram 2500 pickup in alongside the stock transport, kicking up a cloud of Oklahoma, to the sound of the radio blaring out Tammy Wynette, singing 'Stand By Your Man'. I snickered to myself. Tammy had been married at least five times.

The Double D's big rig had been parked in back of the rodeo holding pens, and Billy Bob the driver waited in the cab for further instructions. Toby, his shotgun rider sat next to him. Mr. Pickett, the rodeo grounds manager, came out of the rodeo admin office, clipboard in hand.

I slid down out of the cool AC of the cab of the Dodge; I didn't bother to look behind me as I closed the door on Tammy. She wouldn't mind, she's been dead for some time. Her music and a few husbands live on, though.

Pickett approached me with a smile and the tell-tale limp. The limp was a sign of a man that had been in the rodeo business a long time. Lucky if their brains hadn't been scrambled by a bull or alcohol. My Daddy didn't drink much, said it was liquid courage and the bull rider that drank before the ride just might as well put a gun to his head. It would be quicker and less painful.

Mr. Pickett used to ride with my Daddy in the old days. That is until a bull named Cracker Jack, decided to wipe his feet on him, and left him with a bum leg.

"Howdy! Miss Honey."

"A big double howdy to you Mr. Pickett. That second howdy is from Daddy."

"I ain't seen 'im around lately, how's that ole man of yourn doin' anyways?"

"Well if he heard you call him an old man he'd show ya just how he's doin'. But just twixt you and me, his back has been giving him fits lately. That surgery a while back left him with some chronic pain. That's why he has me doin' his leg work."

I pulled the contract out of my vest pocket and unfolded it. "It says here that I was to deliver twenty prime Brahman and Brahman mix bucking bulls." I pointed to the big eighteen wheeler. The trailer rocked as the twenty restless bulls it held shifted their weight, anxious to be let out.

"There they be." I motioned with my left hand. "Oh! As a special treat for the fans we included ole Nero."

"No extra charge?"

"Nope. Daddy Buck wants to retire him to stud soon. He has a chance to win PRCA, Bucking Bull of the Year again. If he does, it will be the 5th straight year for him. Up his stud fee an extra thousand dollars."

We walked toward the holding pen chutes. Mr. Pickett let out a shrill loud whistle to a couple of cowboys that were forking some hay into the pens. He waved at them to come join us. Billy Bob and Toby jumped down out of the rig's cab.

Mr. Pickett addressed Billy Bob. "Son, I want you to back the trailer up over ta the holding pen gate. Ma boys'll guide ya in."

Toby trotted over to help the two cowboys open the wide steel gates and guide the trailer. Billy Bob jumped back up into the cab and backed that sucker up and parked it just inside the open gate. Billy Bob was a cocky, good lookin' son of a bitch, but he sure could handle a big rig.

When the brakes were set and the wheels chocked, the three cowboys pulled the loading ramp out and down. Billy Bob joined when they opened the doors. They had to get out of the way fast. Twenty 2,000-pound living freight trains exploded out and into the bull pen where they would spend the next three days.

The cowboys replaced the ramp, buttoned up the trailer and closed the sturdy steel gate.

"Billy Bob!"

"Yo! Miss Honey." He grinned ear to ear as he strutted over to where Mr. Pickett and I had watched the whole operation. Toby joined us, while I gave Billy Bob his instruction.

"As soon as Mr. Pickett here is finished with his inspection of the delivery I want you to get back to the ranch and hand over the paperwork to Daddy Buck. He'll be frettin' until he knows everything has been taken care of. I'll give him a call on my cell and let him know the details, but you know until he has the paperwork in his hand he won't rest easy."

"Yes'um I do." With that Toby, Billy Bob and Mr. Pickett went to the holding pen to inspect the stock.

I called Daddy Buck and gave him a report and told him I was stayin' in town at the Cactus Inn and hanging out at the rodeo grounds for a few days. Because while Mr. Pickett and the boys were inspectin' the stock, I was busy doin' some inspectin' of my own.

From where I leaned against my truck, I could see the back stage of the bucking chutes. I put my phone away and crossed my arms across my chest as I watched a swaggering young man loaded down with a backpack and an armful of equipment. A bull rider, I guessed. Mainly from the tell-tale rattle of a metal bell that hung from the flat plaited rig the cowboys used to ride with. I watched with interest as he approached a bale of straw. He threw his bull rider's rig down onto the bale and from the backpack pulled out spurs and laid them next to the plaited rope pile.

My eyes swept over him. I took in the sight of his slender, well-built frame of about 5'9". The tight jeans and chap combination accentuated his tight ass and a prominent bulge in front. Since he wasn't wearing any of the protective gear required during the actual ride, I made the assumption that the bulge was for real. My interest ranged over the rest of him from the ground up. Cowboy boots with worn bull-hide heels run down on the outside edge gave him a slight bowlegged swagger when he walked. His chaps, black leather batwings trimmed in red with large initials, *JDC*, on them.

The shirt he wore was a black, bib front with a big red rose embroidered on the front of it. His sleeves were held back with red lace garters, and a red kerchief was loosely tied around his neck.

I couldn't see his face clear. The black Stetson hat with silver conchoed hat-band he wore hid it, and I was too far away to see much below it. But if the face and eyes matched the rest of him, I sure was a goner for the weekend.

When Billy Bob pulled out of the lot to head back to the ranch, I barely noticed until the dust swirled up around me and Mr. Pickett called for my attention.

"Everythin's fine. But then usually is when I deal with Buck Durbin and the Double D ranch." The smile on Mr. Pickett's face lit up his blue eyes and crinkled the laugh lines around them. My thoughts went to just how long had Mr. Pickett done business with the Double D.

Daddy Buck had done business with him ever since Daddy retired from the circuit. Momma never liked the idea of Daddy traipsin' off to the rodeos. But she couldn't deny the money he won. He was a world class champion bull rider. One of the smart and lucky ones, he sent his money home and Momma banked it. When they had enough to invest in some good breeding stock he quit the circuit and went into breeding the finest rodeo bucking bulls in the country. Old Nero, a prime example, was a product of the selective breeding program. When Momma died a few years back I was old enough to help out by taking over most of her duties in the running of the ranch.

"Why thank you Mr. Pickett, I'll be sure and tell Daddy Buck that when I get home."

"You gonna hang out for the weekend." His eyes twinkled when he noticed where my gaze was at.

"Why, yes, I'm plannin' on it."

He chuckled. "You just leave some strength in that boy, Miss Honey."

"Who is he?"

Pickett's hand that held the clipboard dropped down to his side. "That cowboy there is none other than JD Colby. He is one of the fast track, upcoming champion bull riders."

"You don't say." I rubbed my arms in thought as I admired what I was a lookin' at.

"Now Miss Honey, don't you go and take his mind offin' his business now."

"Now Mr. Pickett I ain't gonna hurt him none. I promise."

With that Mr. Pickett waved a hand at me and started for the rodeo admin office.

I looked into the truck mirror and took my hat off, ran my fingers through my hair, and swept it up into my hat, careful to leave a few blond tendrils hanging out around my face. Wet my finger and brushed up my mascara, and opened the top of my shirt one more button. Pushed down on my waist and straightened up, threw my shoulders back and proceeded to the bull-pen.

The Brahman cattle have always been beautiful to me. A full grown bull weighed in at around two thousand pounds. Nero was magnificent. He was the common, gray dun color with the black points around his face, over his neck and onto the large hump atop his shoulders, and down along his knees. He had the long floppy ears and soft brown eyes typical of the Brahman. His horns were over six foot tip to tip before they were sawed off for his rodeo career. But that was where anything common about him ended.

While I stood at the pen with one foot up on the bottom rail of the metal fence, my chin leaned on my hands as I looked at the product of the Double D. I could feel someone had approached. From the corner of my eye I could tell it was JD. Just as I had hoped.

"Say, little lady, you may want to step back away from the fence there. Those bulls are mighty mean."

I turned to face him. His eyes were brown and his hair black as Oklahoma crude. He had pushed his Stetson back away from his face, leaving an unruly bit of his mane to fall onto his forehead. His tanned, handsome twenty-something face was exposed. His eyes sparkled and danced with the spirit of an untamed mustang.

"Oh! But they look so, so gentle. I mean look at that one there." I pointed to Nero. "He looks so sweet."

"Especially that one. That there is Nero. He has won bucking bull of the year for the last four years runnin'."

"My, you know a bunch about bulls. I didn't catch your name."

"I'm JD Colby." The way he said it, you could tell he was expectin' me to have heard of him.

"Well, I am pleased to meet you, Mr. Colby. My name is Honey Durbin." I held out my hand to him. He hurried to pull off his glove to take it.

His hands were callused and his grip firm, but he did not try to crush my hand like so many macho guys do. I liked that. It meant that he could be gentle when needed.

"Well, Mr. Colby, I think you're wrong about that bull," I turned back to the fence and stuck my hand out.

JD moved quick and stepped up behind me and grabbed my hand and pulled it back. The closeness of his body made me goose-pimpled all over.

"Miss Durbin! What are you doin'?"

"I just don't believe that bull with those sweet brown eyes is as mean as you say." With that said, I watched JD's eye grow wide with genuine concern as I stuck my hand back into the pen and called. "Nero!"

The big Brahman raised his head and looked over at me. "Nero! Come here, Nero!"

JD sounded real nervous. "Miss Durbin, I don't think you should be doing that!"

I waved my hand back and forth at the big bull whose attention I had. He started to come over to the fence where my hand was. I could tell JD was torn between backing away from the fence or trying to save poor little stupid me.

"Nero! Come." The bull snorted as he continued to amble over to the fence. When he got there he put his huge head down low and waited for the scratch between the horns of the enormous head. JD's jaw dropped when I obliged.

"How's my baby doin' today." I continued to rub and pet the brute that appeared to be gentle as a kitten.

"What the hell?"

"The hell is, I all but hand raised this big beautiful baby. I am Honey Durbin, daughter and business partner of Buck Durbin of the Double D ranch. We provide the stock for the rodeo."

JD looked down at his boots, and kicked the dust. "I must seem pretty stupid to you."

"No, you don't. May I call you JD. You can please call me Honey."

"Miss Durbin, I got to go. I got stuff to do. Nice to have met you." He turned on his heel and left me standing there. The flush on my face matched the burning sensation in my chest.

"Well, Nero, I guess I got thrown first go-round." Nero looked at me and bellowed in agreement.

CHAPTER TWO

I checked into the Cactus Inn, home for the next few days, took a shower and laid out on the bed to air dry. The AC hummed as it pumped out cooling air that tickled as it blew across my bare body, and caused chill bumps to form all over.

As I lay there, the cold air caused my nipples to pucker into little hard knobs. Idly I let my hands caress my breasts as I thought about JD. Before I knew it, my right hand had begun to stroke my inner thigh while the other kneaded my left breast.

The more I thought of JD the more turned on I became. I moved my hand further up my thigh until it came to rest at a very wet pussy. Moaning, I began fingering myself, taking myself to full climax so quickly that it amazed me. I rolled over and curled up, hands between my knees and fell asleep.

Next morning I went out to the rodeo grounds and checked on the stock. The back lot was all abuzz with activity from the arrival of the cowboy and girl competitors from all over the United States. This was the National Circuit Finals, previously held every March in Pocatello, Idaho, but after 2011 the event would continue to be held at Oklahoma City. Lucky for business, we don't have to ship our stock across the country.

Ever since I was a little girl I could recite the qualification rules for bull riding and the other titles that came from winning the season title or winning the average title at the circuit finals rodeo. A competitor must have competed in one of the PRCA's 12 regional circuits, held all over the country. In addition they had to compete at one of the circuit finals in order to participate. That meant that JD must be a pretty damn good bull rider. As I thought about him and riding the bull it made me hot between my legs. I wondered where he was.

Morning passed quickly and the crowds started to fill the bleachers. I could smell the hotdogs cooking and the roasting of the peanuts, inter-mixed with the dust, dried manure, animal sweat, rosin, and oiled leather and it excited me. It always had, ever since I had been old enough to sit on a horse by myself.

I kept a lookout for JD. When I spotted him I knew enough not to approach him. The competition meant everything to him. I learned at the knee of my mother to never get in the way of a man's passion. To do so could crush his spirit and I knew that the more spirit the animal has, the better the ride.

From my vantage point I watched as JD climbed up above the bull called Twister. The bull was called that because of the way he bucked, reared, kicked, spun, and twisted in an effort to throw the rider off. It took several men to help JD get positioned so he could mount the snorting fury. JD settled onto the bull and gave a tug on his glove, tapped the rosin bag on it and gripped the flat braided rope. He secured a good grip on the leather reinforced handle and then nodded.

The signal.

He was ready.

The cotton flank strap was pulled up tight and tied around the bull's flank. The bucking chute gate opened with a bang! Like a clap of thunder it reverberated across the arena and the bull, like his namesake, stormed out. The bell hung from the bull rope and clanged with each jump. For all purposes it sounded like the churchyard bell that pealed out a message of death.

I held my breath and silently told JD to stay on the bull for that teeth jarring, tongue biting, eight seconds. JD's left hand waved in the air above his head while Twister sunfished. JD's rider form was perfect. He only touched the bull with his riding hand. His other hand held high and free for the duration of the ride. He was good. Damn him, with each jump I wanted him in my bed.

Each bull had a raw power and style of movement all their own. So did JD. One move particular to Twister is a belly roll or "sunfishing", in which he was completely off the ground and kicked his hind feet to the side in a twisting, rolling motion. Then he spun in a tight, quick circle and in less than a fraction of a second switched back the other way. JD matched him, each jump and twist.

This punishment continued until a loud buzzer announced the completion of an eight second ride. JD let go and jumped to the ground. The rodeo clowns rushed in to take Twister's mind off the man that had bested him. I held my breath for the score.

A 75!

I hurried back away from the fence and over to the admin office where I found out that JD took his option to take what was called a punishment chance to ride one bull per night. I went over the rules in my mind.

The total points scored by the end of the event would be recorded. After the first, or first two, go rounds, the top twenty riders are given a chance to ride one more bull. This final round is called the "Short go". After the end of the short go, the rider with the most total points wins the event. I fully expected JD to be the one to win. He would be Champion.

I thought of his odds at winning, and it made me want him all the more. We had not gotten off to such a good start. I needed to figure out how to change that. But I felt I had to wait, as I remembered Mr. Pickett's admonition when I first laid eyes on JD. I also remembered how fragile his ego seemed to be. The last thing he needed right now was to get a woman on his mind instead of the bull he was going to ride. Especially with the chance he would draw and be riding Nero come Sunday.

JD was indeed a very proud young bull. Spirited. I wanted him, pride and spirit intact. I wanted him. Hell, he was all I could think about. This whole thing was very new to me. I've been around rodeo cowboys all my life. I never took them seriously ever since I happened on an old rodeo cowboy Pappy Jack talking to eight or ten little boys in the back of the bleachers. He had the bunch of them all lined up for a pissing contest. He said he'd give a quarter to the one that could pee the furthest.

Ever since then I looked at cowboys all as a bunch of little boys with big boy hormones in a pissing contest. I enjoyed being with them. Their live-for-the-moment attitude made for an exciting time. Hells bells, I've been with so many I can't rightly give a number. Few of them were worth anything except the good ride they gave this cowgirl.

To read the rest of *Cowgirl Up*
please visit your favorite online bookseller
for the eBook or Print edition.

MEET SUGAR LEE RYDER
& J.D. CUTLER

Sugar Lee Ryder was born to a pair of sideshow performers. Her mother appeared as a mermaid and also as a half-horse, half-woman. Her father ate fire, was electrocuted nightly, and sewed buttons to his chest. Her most recent work is the contemporary western romance, *Cowgirl Up*.

J.D. Cutler is the author of multiple short stories in the western and thriller genres. His latest work is also available from Banty Hen Publishing in the collection *Crisis Points*.

Find out more about their latest works at:
www.sugarleeryder.com
~ or ~
www.jdcutler.com

CPSIA information can be obtained
at www.ICGtesting.com
Printed in the USA
LVHW112225251218
601718LV00001B/28/P

9 781475 260182